ALMOST FOREVER

KAREN HARPER

This title first published in Great Britain in 1992 by
SEVERN HOUSE PUBLISHERS LTD.

This edition licensed by Severn House Publishers Ltd., by
arrangement with the Berkley Publishing Group, produced
by Magpie Book Ltd., and published by Parragon Book
Service Ltd in 1994

A copy of the British Library CIP data is available
from the British Library.

ISBN 0 75250 082 1

Printed and bound in Great Britain

From the peaceful countryside of pre-war England and France, to the chaos and danger of wartime London, Italy and Germany, Karen Harper's thrilling new novel is a heartrending love story that will live forever in the hearts and minds of her readers . . .

Almost Forever

PRAISE
FOR THE ENTHRALLING NOVELS
OF KAREN HARPER . . .

"Exciting and colorful . . . Readers will enjoy the drama and splendor."
— *Rave Reviews*

"A memorable love story . . . grips the reader with vivid images that remain alive and vibrant throughout the book."
— *Affaire de Coeur*

"Passionate . . . intriguing . . . wonderful."
— bestselling author Janelle Taylor

"Most enjoyable—passionately romantic and tensely exciting."
— Roberta Gellis,
bestselling author of
Masques of Gold

"A stirring tale . . . I savored every page."
— Elizabeth Kary,
bestselling author of
Midnight Lace

"Karen Harper has out-romanced herself . . . Readers will be enthralled."
— *Romantic Times*

My gratitude to

—my husband Don for his advice and support these past eleven years

—my father's memory for his bravery and love under fire in 1944 and 1945

—the Lord God for his bounteous gifts and blessings to me always

Be good, sweet maid, and let who will be clever;
Do noble things, not dream them, all day long;
And so make Life, and Death, and that For Ever
One grand sweet song.

CHARLES KINGSLEY
"A Farewell"

ALMOST FOREVER

PART I

The Sports of Love

Come my Celia, let us prove,
While we can, the sports of love;
Time will not be ours forever . . .
                    BEN JONSON
                    "To Celia"

❧ ❧ *Chapter One*

May 18, 1939

BUT FOR FLOWERS, the only colors gleaming in the marble Gothic Westam family mausoleum were two iridescent puddles of ruby and emerald from the stained-glass windows and the daughter's stunning vermilion hair. Twenty-two-year-old Lady Lesley Westam shared the carved oak pew with her family as they mourned the passing of her father. Next to her sat an elderly woman, garbed in black—her beloved grandmother, Lady Sarah. Then followed her brother, Willis Trent Westam, the new earl, next to his mother, Lady Constance Quinn-Jones on the end. They all looked like theatregoers at different plays: some grief-stricken; another impatient, still another angry and nervous. But with her vibrant coloring, beauty, height, élan—and background—Lady Lesley might as well have been burying her father alone. All the standing mourners as well as the journalists and hangers-on waiting outside on the rolling, manicured cemetery lawn knew the stares and the scandal always came back to her.

Scandal, especially among the elite, in the western county of Herefordshire in England was not only duly noted but never quite forgotten or forgiven. Especially not a twenty-two-year-old scandal that concerned *the* family of the region. Certainly not even when King George and Queen Mary, former social intimates of the Westams, had withdrawn centuries of royal favor in pious disapproval. After all, Wyatt Westam, fifth Earl of Malvern, the man they buried today, had deserted his first wife, Lady Constance, and their seven-year-old son for an Italian beauty related to the internationally famous Valente Fur dynasty of Rome. She'd been pregnant out of wedlock and had the

3

temerity to actually go into labor the day the decree nisi divorce became final. And on that same day she produced a red-gold-haired beauty whom they named Lesley.

No wonder London's Fleet Street press, if not the more staid provincial *Wye Weekly Chronicle*, had promptly dubbed her "Scandal's Child." She'd never escaped that cruel sobriquet in or out of London. This "love child," the product of illicit passion, had shouldered the brunt of the family stigma. It flared again when her beautiful mother, the second Lady Westam, died of poliomyelitis when Lesley was sixteen. Everyone simply knew Lesley's half-brother and his formidable, social-lion mother were the only parties harmed. So they were stamped blameless in the rather untidy if titillating affair. And surely they had every right to fan the bitter feud these past years over the vast Westam holdings of farm and forest lands, thoroughbred horse farm, and sporting interests.

Her father, the earl, still loved his son. He had settled land and funds on the lad and tried to include him in his new family when he could wrestle him away from his mother. Holiday provided the excuse. Trent was invited to the rural Westam mansion to stay several weeks at a time. The gray Rolls arrived promptly to collect him at the London town house in Chelsea that his father had purchased for the boy and Lady Constance. Each time, she regretted losing her son even for a fortnight, because he was a weapon in her continuing war with her former husband. But after the initial sting of watching him leave, she'd soothe her feelings by indulging in her perpetual wild life of partying, buying jewels and designer fashions in Paris, and flagrant affairs with much younger men. Lady Constance had done her best to besmirch the family honor before the press, yet it was never she they mentioned as the cause of the Westam shame.

Lesley had been reared on the vast Westam estate, somewhat shielded from the family battles in her early years, except when Trent visited. Her parents and her grandmother had done what they could to cushion her from the hoopla. But when she went away to school, visited London, eventually went to work there, reporters dogged her heels. With Lesley and Trent's father gone now, the sides were even more firmly entrenched. The fragmented Westams had arrived in two spacious motorcars today for the funeral and had not spoken as far as everyone watching could determine.

"Gram," Lesley whispered to her grandmother and squeezed her gloved hand as the line of local civic speakers took turns eulogizing the dead earl as if he'd been the paragon of all English virtue. "I've got to step out just a moment. Sorry."

Lady Sarah tilted her silver head, framed in the youthful, crisp bob she'd made her trademark since the early twenties. "I do understand, my dearest, really," she whispered back and patted her hand, though a slight frown creased the still taut skin of the eighty-three-year-old face under the mourning veil. After Lesley's mother's death, Lady Sarah had been almost a second mother to the often beleaguered young woman. She fully understood Lesley's aversion to tight, closed places. The poor darling. Ever since her mother had breathed her last in that iron lung and they'd buried her here, Lesley had suffered from occasional bouts of claustrophobia.

Trent's head snapped around as Lesley rose and edged by Lady Sarah to step out. He was ruddy, blond, and stocky enough that the pew creaked every time he stretched or heaved a sigh. "Bloody hell, what is it now with her?" he hissed at his grandmother. "These toadies may be dishing out tripe and rubbish about the illustrious earl, but can't she sit still with that flighty Italian blood in her veins!"

"Trent, please! She'll be back straightaway. Wouldn't do for her to have an attack here, would it? Sh."

"I'll give her an attack," Trent muttered so low the old woman could not hear. But his mother did and her crimson lips set in a smug curve as she fingered her fat emerald bracelet through her long black antelope gloves and glanced back over the padded shoulder of her crepe Schiaparelli. Trent grunted another sigh and shifted so heavily that the pew scraped on the glossy buff Carrara floor.

Lesley turned around at the sound as she edged along the pillared aisle away from the service. The shock of Father's death has still not settled in, she thought, and she knew she was terribly skittish. The long speech by Reginald Hyatt, Lord Lieutenant of Hereford, thundered through the nave as she stood for a moment to listen. Even now, seeing Father's shiny, elaborately scrolled bronze coffin bordered by spiky clusters of red and white gladiolas on its raised platform, it didn't seem real. That is, not until her eyes locked with Lady Constance's slitted stare. The woman hated her and always had. Lesley's insides had felt for days as if she were careening endlessly out of the clouds toward earth in some shrieking nightmare; now the woman's cold contempt slapped her back to reality. Lesley spun, turning her back to her. As another speaker began his sonorous plaudits, she stepped outside.

On the portico of the magnificently columned mausoleum, she blinked wide-set green eyes in the rush of light and wind. She strode resolutely down the five weathered marble steps. As she approached the onlookers outside, some shifted forward, some nodded in her direction or whispered. Her exit before the end of the service would no doubt be included in every snatch of gossip and sensationalized journal article. Yet, as always, people fell back to give her a little leeway as if spellbound.

Tall and slender, Lesley forced her broad shoulders back and lifted her chin, trying to evoke the elegance she tapped when she dragged a sable or lynx wrap across the runway at Sackville's Fur Salon in London. The social and financial elite of England came there to purchase luxury coats and scrutinized her as closely as the people here. But in the salon she was sheltered by the layer of plush pelts. Lesley could almost forget that the perfectly coiffed, expensively attired audience might be staring for reasons other than the way she displayed the fashionably sewn imported furs. But now her long fingers nervously stroked the silky border of the moiré karakul suit jacket she had designed herself, then darted to grasp the long double strand of her mother's lustrous pearls the size of chickpeas around her graceful neck.

She strode past the whispering onlookers. From behind her French net hat veil, she scanned the familiar landscape. In every direction ornate grave monuments stood like ivory chess pieces on their slightly sloping board of lush grass. A beige stone wall near the church and along the carriageway edged the board, and random patches of wild white and blue violets made up its irregular squares. Just beyond the forested bend of road to the east lay the tiny village of Westam-on-Wye with its single main square of neat shops and narrow houses in ancient black and white Jacobean charm. To the west, pastures fringed by woody hills and banks of the river Wye merged with bluffs of raw rock before the distant horizon of the Welsh Black Mountains beckoned. And above it all, clouds like soft dollops of Hereford cream drifted across a robin's-egg-blue sky to temper a landscape of stark contrasts. The beauty and strength of well-tended yet unconquerable land mingled in aged harmony.

Lesley turned. The knot of onlookers now lined the walk to watch the mourners who streamed from the mausoleum. Cameras clicked as reporters recorded the final ritual in the day's events. The mourners pooled on the curb near the motorcars, saying their adieus. Susan Ashmont, her flatmate from the spiffy place they shared on Brook Street in Mayfair, hugged her for the tenth time today, getting blond hair and her favorite Country Roses dusting powder on the padded shoulders of Lesley's jacket. Lesley's latest beau, Roger Rigsby, a young partner in a solicitor's firm at Gray's Inn, heftily built and terribly polite, though not the sort to set one's heart aflame, kissed her cheek and patted her arm. They climbed into their autos to begin the trek back to London. But for leaving Gram at a time like this, Lesley couldn't wait to get back to the city, too. She intended to bury herself in hectic planning for the spring buyer shows to try to stave off this jagged, grinding grief. And to keep on the path toward having a furrier shop of her own someday where she could create and not just model the furs she loved.

She tossed her hair, which was curled loose to her shoulders in the new Joan Crawford look as the mid-May breeze tickled the veil against her tilted tip of nose. The three arched feathers on her black felt hat with beaver crown trembled in the next brisk gust. And then, beyond, she saw Melly Mott.

Despite the sadness that had engulfed her the five days since she'd heard of her father's death, she smiled. Her old friend and childhood confidant, Melvin Mott, leaned on a carved memorial angel that pointed skyward as though Melly and the winged creature were about to set off on a lark through the heavens. Still, he looked much the same as when he'd made a condolence call at the house with his parents. It had been Melly's father, Josiah, who had found the earl, dead of a

sudden heart attack no one had expected. He'd been chasing a
runaway foal and simply dropped over. She forced that scene
from her mind and motioned Melly over, but he only waved
feebly back and shook his head sheepishly to look even more
loose-limbed, gangly, and uncomfortable.

Since she'd gone away at age sixteen to boarding schools in
Shropshire and then in Switzerland, there had never been time
for Melly anymore. Still wind-tousled and perpetually wrinkled even in his best stiff blackcloth suit, he looked as he did
when she was a child and they'd hiked the Wye Valley forests
with his long-departed bronze Irish retrievers, Quick and Celt.
She felt fourteen again, helping Melly to select and arrange the
rabbit, musquash, or tiny mole pelts he'd gleaned from the
woods or marshes. Back then her mother's old seamstress
Annie would help her sew her dolls' fur coats from Melly's
pelts that were every bit as chic as any Mother's Italian family
had ever made. If only her childhood could begin all over again
bright and new with her beautiful, green-eyed mother and
vigorous father laughing and telling her and Melly to clean
their shoes and hands and nip in for tea with a scowling Trent
come to visit.

"Dearest girl, I say, but you've walked a good little distance."

She spun around to face Lady Sarah. "Oh, Gram. I see it's
over already. I did mean to come back in." At the top of the
knoll behind them, people continued to file out of the mausoleum. It was from sheer affection and not the need to steady
Lady Sarah that Lesley tucked her grandmother's arm in hers.
After all, the old woman looked and acted a sprightly ten or
fifteen years younger than her age with her elegant, trim form.
She was an indefatigable walker, always traipsing about, a
rabid gardener, forever young at heart with her love of current
films and modern show tunes.

"You know, my dearest," Lady Sarah said, "you and I
would be better served on such a day remembering in our own
ways, quite alone, off by ourselves in God's lovely world, not
some wretched man-made place like the hallowed Westam
Mausoleum with bronze drawers stuffed with family dust."
She rolled her pale blue eyes and looped her arm farther
through Lesley's. "Come on, then. To the motorcars straightaway and back for the buffet at the house Constance made

Trent insist on. Anything for a social do, that woman. We'll slog through together, you and I."

Nodding, shaking gloved hands, they exchanged words with people on the way to the line of autos parked on the gravel lane below. With a "mind your head now, Gram," Lesley shepherded her to the backseat of their dove-gray Rolls-Royce just ahead of her brother's sportier ruby Wraith Rolls. Ahead, Lady Constance stood like a silent sentinel guarding Trent's auto and glared. Her gray eyes gleamed black in her high-browed, exquisitely made-up, long face. Under the slant of a Talbot hat, the ebony streak in Lady Constance's prematurely silver hair so meticulously arranged in a smooth roll seemed to point invisible fingers at Lesley. The woman was smoking already, a French cigarette in yet another long jeweled holder to match her attire. Lady Constance looked most annoyed, as if Trent had told her just to shut her trap for once and stand clear of him.

Lesley strode around the auto's polished boot to the other side where the chauffeur held the door for her. She jolted to a halt as Trent stepped forward to block her path. At nearly five feet eight in her high-heeled pumps, Lesley looked straight into his narrowed blue eyes. He looked entirely proper in his dark double-breasted suit, the brim of his Homburg hat clutched in his hand. His hands were such a tight ball, the knuckles whitened. She wanted to detest him, but they were family. His hand shot out to grab her arm.

"You're hurting me, Trent. What is it?"

His voice came taut, low. "What the bloody hell do you think you're doing, stepping out like that before it was over? I had to step up to the casket alone before they sealed the vault, and you're the one who's been my father's perfect little darling all these blasted years."

"That's not true and I couldn't help it today. You know how it is for me sometimes. Father would have understood," she added and pulled back from his grasp. He jerked back, surprised he'd touched her at all.

"Oh, no doubt he would. Anything for his 'sweet little maid Lesley' at the cost of the whole bloody world going straight to hell if need be!"

"Not here, Trent, now now. Grandmum and I are going back."

His arm shot out to block the door.

"Please, can't we just discuss all this back at the house without the journal harpies hanging on?" she pleaded in a low voice.

"I'm sure we will discuss it. And on my terms now that the nightmare's over."

"What a wretched way to put it," she shot out scathingly, lifting her chin to combat his stubborn stance.

"Don't twist my words. I'm referring to not having any say over what should have been rightfully mine at Westam all these years."

"Trent dear, going to ride back with us, then?" their grandmother interrupted from inside the open car door where she waited. "That way you two won't need to stand about chatting and catch the ague or spring chill."

Again Trent's slitted eyes locked with Lesley's. "I'm sure Trent needs to escort his mother back to Westam House for the rest of her *brief visit*," Lesley said with decided emphasis on the last two words. She slid onto the broad horsehair seat while Jeffreys closed the heavy door behind her. For the first time today, tears stung her eyelids as Trent spun away to put his mother in his motorcar. Lesley yanked her black gloves off and slapped them on her knees. Gram's suede-gloved hand quickly covered Lesley's, which were clasped in her lap as the big gray Rolls purred to life.

The familiar voice always so bouncy and lilting sounded tired and scratchy now. "Lesley, my dearest," Lady Sarah began, then hesitated. "I had actually hoped this dreadful tragedy might foster some sort of new beginning for you and Trent, considering your father's will declares you two share Westam's assets now. But I know Lady Constance's presence at Westam is unsettling to you."

"It's dreadful! I know my mother's room was hers once, but Trent had no right to allow her in there at a time like this!" Lesley twisted her gloves in her hands as if they were Lady Constance's long, swanlike neck. The wretched woman had just taken over, hung her Schiaparelli and Chanel frocks she doted on in her mother's wardrobe and moved things out of bureau drawers to accommodate her array of French silk and lace lingerie. She sat at her mother's mirrored dressing table primping and forever checking her smug image in the glass and reeking cigarette smoke into simply everything! Then too, sterling- and tortoise-framed photographs of her parents together had already disappeared from several places in the house, including the Bosendorfer grand piano Constance played Rachmaninoff on at all hours whenever it suited her. She and Trent had even dared to go through some of Father's things until Lesley had discovered it and protested. And the woman had taken to giving the staff orders and talking about sacking some of them as though she had never been divorced, never been away for more than twenty years!

"Lesley, listen to me," Lady Sarah insisted as the line of motorcars slowly exited the cemetery behind the stately redbrick Georgian Westam-on-Wye church. "Whenever there's an ending to something, however harsh and cruel, there's also a new beginning. Nothing lasts forever. Believe me, I know. When your uncle, my Andrew, died in the Great War, I thought I would never survive, but I did. When your grandfather passed away in twenty-six, it was even worse. But there was always a new path somewhere through the pleached yew hedge, and it was up to me to find it."

Lesley nodded and hugged her grandmother's thin shoulders briefly. She felt soothed by her words. "I love you, Gram. Thanks awfully for always caring so much. But you're so much stronger than I."

"Rubbish! A backbone forged from Birmingham steel, you have, stronger than either of the dear ones who bred you. Whatever happens back at the manor, that strength and the love your parents and I have poured into you over the years will not let Trent or Constance hurt you!" She paused again and her other hand touched a single tear from Lesley's cheek. "Nor will you allow what happens to keep you from loving Trent. That's one of the things that's always been so fine about you, Lesley. You've become a clever, bright, talented, and beautiful young woman. But the best is, when you love someone, nothing ever changes that, so maybe at least love can be for always. That's loyalty, true nobility, finer than our Westam

forebears ever possessed under any of their kings. That's
strength over a too often nasty world, believe me it is!"

Tautness of limb and muscle unwound as a deep sigh
wracked Lesley; her shoulders slumped back against the
horsehair seat. "Sometimes I've been so very sure I've hated
Trent, hated both of them," she said shakily.

"Pity her, keep her at a distance if you can. Trent needs our
love, my dear, wants it desperately too, although he still doesn't
know it. She'd never let him know it, but that's on her head."

"But the way he treats me, I can hardly wait years for him
to change, can I? I have friends, a career, dreams for a family
of my own someday, if I ever stumble across the right person!"

"I know, dearest, I know. And you have that old Westam
wherewithal to make those dreams come true, all of them.
You'll see. That little poem your father loved about making
your dreams one grand sweet song—remember?"

Lesley nodded. She and Gram were so much alike; she'd
realized it more and more since she'd lost Mother. To keep that
memory from grabbing her again, Lesley glanced out the Rolls
window at the moving sweep of countryside as they turned up
the lane to the estate past the stone gatehouse with the ancient
proud motto *"Pro Rege Westam"*—"Westam for the King."
Her gaze blurred at last with tears as the avenue of oaks planted
almost two hundred years ago arched over the lane in weathered magnificence, and beyond, before Gram's lovingly
tended gardens began, the living wall of square-clipped yews
stretched out before the eye.

Life after loss was like finding a new path through these
pleached yews with their limbs and leaves so tightly inter-
twined, Gram had said. Lesley smoothed her twisted gloves
and sat up straighter as the line of motorcars pulled up before
the warm copper brick façade of Westam House that Father had
always teased was the perfect match for her and Mother's
red-gold hair. But now the house belonged to Trent. She
waited until Jeffreys helped her grandmother out of the Rolls,
then, slowly, she stepped out and walked with her chin lifted
as she swept by the butler over the threshold into the future.

Although Westam House was a classic H-shaped 1770
Georgian mansion built on the site of an earlier Westam family

seat, inside, the house was almost eclectic in decor. Elizabethan oak wainscoting salvaged from the earlier house mingled with Beauvais tapestries and a Wedgwood fireplace in the library; the morning room in yellow chintz boasted both nineteenth-century French handpainted wallpaper and a previous Lady Malvern's exquisite collection of blue and white Ming porcelain bowls. The funeral buffet in the formal dining room today had been set with William III silver and Limoges porcelain for the stolidly English fare, despite the fact Lady Constance told the guests repeatedly she much preferred Continental cuisine. In the main entry hall with hunter's-green flocked wallpaper above the chair rail where guests were now departing, Georgian coaching and hunting oils by Stubbs and Boultbee hung proudly while formal gilt-framed family portraits of generations past marched up the polished curved staircase wall to the long second-floor hall strewn with richly hued Kurdish carpets.

Lesley loved Westam—all of it, from the foaling barn to Gram's gardens adrift with roses and heady clematis and honeysuckle to river walks and an ornamental pond to the gabled attic of the great house itself all stuffed like a treasure trove with Victorian collections of butterflies, birds' eggs, rare stones, dolls, and innumerable dusty stuffed birds under glass. It was home and, wherever she lived over the years to come, she knew she would cherish it as such.

The heritage was rooted deep. The first Earl of Malvern had earned his peerage under George II. He served as both the king's vice chamberlain and—more importantly for those times—horse breeder and Newmarket racing compatriot. But Westams were more than intimates of the royal Hanoverians and Windsors. They were a talented clan who had earned their privileges. From racing to academic brilliance, they had left their stamp on history. Lesley had inherited her artistry from her father's side as well as her mother's, though the family fortune was strictly Westam bred.

Yet last year her father had sadly auctioned off hundreds of silver racing cups rather than cut back the tenanted lands even further during the harsh economic climate in Britain. The once vast Westam estate might have shrunk from some forty thousand acres of prime Herefordshire land to the four thousand the family owned today, but Lesley knew and adored every inch of it.

Only now, the Westam manor house's future looked dim. Trent had inherited the title and the house, and she had received a huge financial settlement. More land or horseflesh might have to be sold off if she and Trent could not come to some amiable agreement. So far this week, even now that the guests had departed, the talk had touched on everything but Westam and their need for some sort of reconciliation. Finally, although Gram had gone off to bed and Lesley had cornered Trent in the billiards room without his mother, he still acted absorbed only in the game.

Lesley leaned against a leather-backed chair, trying to control her impatience with his grunts. He chattered about flying—the true passion in his life. Trent had been Cambridge-educated at his mother's insistence, but he preferred his collection of small airplanes and his service in the peacetime Royal Air Force to keeping a hand in at the law firm of Kensley and Kirk in London. It galled Trent he hadn't opposed Lady Constance to go to Cranwell or Eton from which most of his RAF friends had graduated.

She listened and moved nearer the green felt pool table. She grasped the mahogany rim across from where he leaned over his cue stick. As so many times in their lives, she wished she could get his undivided attention.

"Trent, you said we could talk seriously," she interrupted.

"Blast it, Lesley, don't chatter when I'm ready to shoot!" He shifted his feet, readjusted his hands. "Besides, isn't air power in the coming war serious enough for your pretty little head? It's obvious fine marks in school didn't translate into common-sense brains for you." He lowered his ash-blond head, so much like Father's, and squinted down the length of his cue. "I'm telling you, that bloody Kraut bastard with the brushy mustache has chewed up both Austria and Czechoslovakia, and Poland's probably next." Deftly, Trent slid the polished cue forward and whacked the cue ball to scatter the other rainbow-colored balls. "Just like that," he clipped out, "Hitler's going to set off an explosive chain reaction, but if he comes England's way, the RAF lion will claw him to bits."

"The RAF will prevail, just like that," she mocked, instantly regretting the edge to her voice and curt snap of her fingers. He was at least talking civilly to her about something at last. Like the child he sometimes made her feel, she followed him halfway around the table again as he leaned over his next shot. "I suppose they'll summon you back straightaway to full-time service and give you your own little striped Spitfire, gooney bird, or whatever to personally knock Hitler's—what's it called?—his Luftwaffe right out of the skies," she said.

He straightened before taking the next shot and came at her around the end of the table, holding his cue stick straight up as if it were a ceremonial sword. "Exactly! Chamberlain's 'peace in our time' is pure bloody tommyrot. In the end it won't matter a tinker's damn that Hitler's linked the Jerries up to *your* fatherland of Mussolini's Fascist Italy in that so-called Pact of Steel the bastards signed this month."

"I won't lower myself on this of all days to respond to your taunts, Trent. Yes, my mother's family is Italian. I'd even like to visit them again. It's been almost fifteen years."

"Splendid. Why don't you—permanently? Just send back a little fur piece like the Valente Russian sable they sent you on your twenty-first birthday for me to give my lady, all right?"

"You mean you've found someone else you deem worthy of a Valente fur since the Duke of Walton told you to steer clear of his little Pamela?" She regretted throwing that brickbat the moment the words escaped her lips. Pamela Lindsey had been the only girl from his parade of women her twenty-nine-year-old brother had ever relished the idea of marrying. But the old duke had evidently smashed them up, hoping his daughter would align herself with someone from a less publicity-tainted background. Trent's eyes narrowed to a familiar grimace—the only look she could recall when she summoned an image of him. His mouth hardened even more, tugging down the right corner as he glared at her. Too late to be civil now, she thought, when she saw him go beet-red in fury. They were like children again.

"You think the old 'Scandal's Child' curse hangs over me like Pericles' sword when I find someone I want, sweet little Lesley? Just wait till you get serious with one of your proper

City chaps. That model's face—and body—forgive a poor bloke of a brother for noticing," he added with a phony leer, "won't buy you a brass farthing's worth of bread crumbs if you tumble for someone among the flawless upper crust of Mother England whose father never got seduced by some loose, scheming Italian tart and—" His face was livid. Now he would scream all the terrible things Constance had taught him over the years about her mother, and Gram would hear!

"Trent, shut up!" Lesley cried as she leaned into the heavy billiard table to fight the urge to lunge at him and claw his smirking face. But her voice was drowned by the sharper cry of his name from behind her. They both whirled around. Lady Constance had draped herself against the door frame to the hall, one raised arm bared of kimono sleeve, as if she were modeling the stunning jade and silver lamé hostess gown that clung to her angular form and exhibited a slash of leg to one knee. A plume of insolent smoke drifted into the room from the cigarette in her long cloisonné holder.

"Now, Trent," Lady Constance murmured, her voice laced with menace. "I don't think it's worth the effort to resurrect these old problems." She swept in past a furious Lesley to pat her son's shoulder, then turned her back to spin a single billiard ball across the table. It smacked several others, scattering them aimlessly. She snorted a quick, forced laugh. "Let's just keep everything in perspective now, Trent. Really, why not make it entirely clear to your father's daughter the way things will be from here on, just to avoid this sort of sordid little scene she evidently thrives on?"

Lesley bit her cheek. "I know the house is legally Trent's now, Lady Constance, but Father's will says I can live here anytime I wish," she said, framing her words carefully. She struggled to control her instinctive rage as she continued. "However, I believe his will says nothing of the kind about you."

"And you want me out, my dear." The voice was pure acid; the red mouth sneered contempt.

"Out of the house as soon as possible. Out of my mother's suite immediately."

Lady Constance exhaled a blue ring of smoke in her direction. "That suite was mine long before there was a

Contessa Caterina imported from Italy to decorate the house like so many other cheap foreign baubles." She turned to her son and implored, "Tell her, Trent, or I will. I don't need one of these little contretemps when the decorators arrive next week to redo *my* suite upstairs."

Trent leaned back on the billiard table next to his mother. A frown crumpled his high brow; his rounded, boyish face formed a mask of hawklike arrogance; his thin lips hardened and turned down again. "I'm contesting Father's will, Lesley. With the difficult time the estate has had this past decade, Father could not really have wanted me to sell off more stock and acreage to buy out your half. It's painfully obvious we're not meant to work together. Besides, morally, let alone legally, I can convince the court—the whole bloody country if it comes to a public trial—that it's all mine."

Her stomach cartwheeled. Her mind could only cling to his first words—he would contest Father's will. A legal battle. The press swarming once again over their family business, their family relationships. The sobriquet "Scandal's Child" resurrected and trumpeted in newspaper headlines. It would soil the reputation she'd worked so hard to build, coating her life in sticky innuendos, upsetting Leonard Stockman at Sackville's where propriety and reputation were of utmost importance. Stirring it all up again, Father's love for Mother, a peer of the realm's blatant desertion of a wife, a son warped by hatred. Lesley could picture them now, the stacks of copies of journals displaying those come-hither headlines in London bookstalls— the *Standard* and the *Daily Express*, which the British devoured with much more relish than they ever would Hitler's distant ravings.

Fury roiled in her. "No, Trent! No! You don't mean it!"

"But he does," Lady Constance cut in as Trent's taut smile and lifted chin bespoke his pleasure and triumph in Lesley's panic. Blast this woman, Lesley thought. She was the one who reared him, the one who took her family's photos, her mother's rooms, turned her brother totally against their sharing this common heritage. But he was old enough *not* to be his mother's son, especially when he should be grieving. Here he was trampling the wishes and memory of their beloved dead father in the dirt like this!

"Tomorrow first thing, the senior partners in my law firm will be filing the injunctions, sister dear," Trent gloated. He picked up the cue stick again and resumed his game. "You see, I've been busy this week while you've gadded about with the neighbors and played doting companion to Grandmother, whose care Father at least saw fit to give to whoever controlled Westam House. That's me, now and *ad perpetuam.*"

Lesley's mind raced. She would get a law firm, too. Father's will had been legal; he had been in his right mind. It was this vile woman and Trent who had gone insane with hatred and revenge.

"We'll just see about your injunction tomorrow morning." Lesley heard her bold words almost before she'd formed a complete plan. "We'll just see, Trent. And your encouragement earlier this week about staying here to comfort Grandmum seemed so sincere. Keep little Lesley out of London where she won't learn a thing until it's too late." She turned her furious gaze back to the now silent Lady Constance. The woman's gray glare gleamed stonelike in the mingled slash of billiard lamps and haze of cigarette smoke. She fingered her diamond choker with long, clawlike fingers.

"The only thing I can thank you for, ex-Lady Malvern, is that you've always greatly underestimated the fact that I'm a Westam, born to it as much as Trent. And children, unlike a self-centered ex-wife, cannot be legally divorced!"

Other words, curses, low names for them both pounded in her brain, but she turned and dashed out.

"Damn, but we don't need her running off from here to halt that injunction or something, Mother," sounded in her ears as she tore up the stairs to her room. Bloody hell, as he always said, at least Trent realized that was the best move she could make against their nefarious plans! Furiously, she began to pack. She knew the roads to London well enough, even the rural twisting Gloucester carriageways until she reached Swindon and the big eastern motorway; she trusted her little Austin Seven to get her there even if she had to motor all the way in the dark. By mid-morning, she'd have a barrister, get an injunction of her own. She had to halt any of this ever reaching the ears of the press, the BBC, her friends, her employers, anyone. She'd just leave Gram a quick note and get out of here tonight before they thought up something even more dire. She refused to stay one more instant in this house that woman was polluting, beginning with her mother's lovely suite down the hall!

It hit her then, and she jerked upright at the thought. Mother's suite had to be where that woman was keeping the photos she'd taken; she'd looked everywhere else including the dustbins. Besides, Lesley had no intention of leaving without the rest of her mother's most precious jewelry, which Father had given her long ago. She still left it all for safekeeping in the little wall safe behind the small Constable painting in Mother's dressing room. That woman might break into the safe and take all Mother's jewelry for herself!

She sat at her little oak secretary to write Gram a note, but her thoughts and eyes wandered. How she had loved this green and white flowered chintz and ruffled room with the pillowed window seat and her favorite painting, which Father had given her from downstairs. "Lady and Gentleman Driving a Phaeton, 1788, by George Stubbs," the brass label on the oak frame read. She loved the little painting not only for the proud prancing bays pulling the elegant four-wheeled canary-yellow vehicle but because the gentleman and lady were so obviously out for a fine lark—and so over the moon in love. Suddenly she wished she knew more about all the paintings at Westam, everything about the fine pieces she and Trent would never now be able to share. She should have listened more closely when her parents discussed it all. Mother especially knew a great deal about art, mostly because the Valente family owned many Italian masters, which lined the walls of their Roman town house and country villa. She finished the note to Gram in a rush. She'd take the Stubbs painting with her, too.

Quickly changing to fawn draped wool trousers and a navy reefer coat over a sky-blue silk shirt and her riding boots, Lesley slid the note under Gram's door and lugged her suitcase down to her little Austin coupe. She went back up for the painting and her Valente sable coat. She strode boldly to the door of her mother's suite. Both Trent and that woman were downstairs still; she'd clearly heard their raised voices, if not what they said, when she took her things down. Good. Let them argue. After she retained her barrister, she'd find a way to talk to Trent alone even if it was in a law office, away from his precious airplanes, away from his mother's clutches, long enough to try to make him see reason. She had to act now.

Yet at the door to her mother's suite she hesitated. No time to think, to remember, to grieve. Find a new path, Gram had said. It started here. The brass latch lifted; the familiar room bathed in soft peach light was somehow familiar no more. Wedgwood-blue had been one of Caterina Corelli Westam's favorite colors, and complemented her rich russet hair and gray-green eyes. The entire room was delicate blues with touches of elegant ivory and beige. Silk lounge chairs faced tasseled blue watered-silk-draped windows overlooking Gram's aromatic gardens thronged with roses. A silk-swagged canopied bed dominated the room, though she had most often slept in Father's big oaken bedstead in the adjoining suite. Lesley steeled herself and walked directly through on the mutely flowered Aubusson carpet to the smaller dressing room. Here too Lady Constance's half-open trunks and garments strewn on the silk empire lounge chair before a triptych looking glass indicated a long, ruinous stay.

Lesley put down her own painting and the sable coat to lift the Constable painting off the wall. Her heart pounding in her ears, she easily spun the silver dial on the recessed safe to the first of the three numbers. Then she heard their voices so much closer. Here. Already in the next room she'd just walked through!

She froze for a moment, undecided. Turn and face them down with more shouting and accusations? Then try to get past them with her booty? She would picture Trent locking her up, even striking her as he had numerous times when they were children. She couldn't just run to Gram and involve her in all this warfare, not when she had worked so very hard for peace in the house the day Father had been buried. Swiftly, she replaced the wall painting.

"You've got to find the little chit, Trent. She's not in her room, her things are gone, including that coat. I thought it would settle her down, but wherever could she have run off to this time of night?"

"How should I know since there's not a sound in Grandmum's room? It was your idea to tell her everything when we should have stonewalled it for at least another day. I'll go round to the Motts' and Heathley to see if she's there. I can't imagine she'd take a mount, but I'll go round to the stables, too. Her Austin's still in the garage, but I can handle that. If we can just keep her from involving the old woman, it will be easy enough to keep her here until the initial damage is done against Father's bloody will. No way in hell half of the estate's assets are going to Lesley Clarissa Westam—ever! I swear, Mother, if it's the last thing I do, no daughter of that seducing Italian strumpet who caused you all that shame will have a damned farthing that's rightfully ours!"

"I knew I could rely on you, whatever it takes, my dearest. I'll just change into something casual and join you."

Lesley dove for the huge wardrobe. One of the doors stood ajar. She huddled, knees to chest, jammed in behind a long line of floor-length gowns. Her hip pressed against something sharp on the floor as she clutched the bulky sable and painting in her arms. Instantly, the woman was in the room, rummaging in the other cupboard.

The silk, velvet, brocade, and crepe gowns leaned against her body, her skin. Her careful, shallow breathing brought them even closer to her flushed face. Oh, dear God in heaven, what if she closed the door on her in here and she had to wait inside for her to leave? It would be worse than that time the twelve-year-old Trent locked her in the wine cellar all day, because then she did not suffer from claustrophobia. Lesley held her breath. The dread she felt at being closed in began, then became trembling sweats as Constance closed the wardrobe door on her, and continued to bang about in the room.

Claustrophobia, pure and simple. Lesley knew that, even though she liked to keep from admitting it to herself. Ordinarily she was just fine, even inside a small room. Now, she almost screamed to be let out, to claw her way out of the clinging, pressing darkness, but her hatred for this woman kept her quiet. She tried to concentrate on the sharp corner of something against her hip, but it didn't help. She had suffered from claustrophobia ever since she'd seen Mother breathe her life away in that iron lung at the Mayley Clinic in London. It had breathed for the thirty-seven-year-old woman wasting away inside. It had kept her alive for several months, but

Lesley could not abide the big, hissing thing. It swallowed her beautiful mother's body and made it impossible to do more than see or touch her head anymore. Big and dark inside like this. She couldn't bear it. She was going to have to scream, to fly out of here where the smell of that woman's French perfume and cigarettes and the touch of her garments strangled her.

But even as she moved, she heard a door bang. She was gone! She had to escape!

Out on the thick carpet of the room, she sprawled on all fours, panting, shuddering until the panic eased. Then she was into the safe for Mother's jewelry. On her way out she realized that what had hurt her hip on the floor of the closet might have been the pilfered photos. Boldly, she went back and opened both wardrobe doors. She seized the stack of photos, heavy frames and all, and was out of there as fast as she could move.

Still her legs trembled from the effect of the events of this past week. And now leaving like this . . . but it had to be done. Gram, I love you. House and all the beautiful things that happened here before that woman returned, I love you too, her brain rattled on in childish farewell as she let herself out the side door into the blowing darkness of the welcoming May night. She peered gingerly around the side of the house.

Jeffreys, the chauffeur, lived above the six-auto garage that had been converted from the old stable block years ago when the vast new stables were built. His lights were on. In the silent garage she peered into the dimness lit by the single lamp. Either Trent had not been here yet or he'd come and gone.

She piled the coat, the photos, and the painting in the tiny front seat. She threw her purse in, then carefully slid open the garage door behind her motorcar. When the faithful engine turned over immediately, she almost cried in relief. At least Trent hadn't tampered with anything under the bonnet. She slid the clutch into reverse and backed out. It was nearly nine already, which meant she'd make London by two or three if she could find a petrol pump in Oxford open at this time of night. When she illuminated her headlamps to swing around into the long, dark lane, she saw Trent's red Rolls was gone from the garage. They'd motored out ahead of her, thinking she'd walked or taken a horse.

For a moment mingled confusion, exhaustion, grief, and anger almost swamped her under. She leaned her forehead on her hands on the top of the steering wheel. Then she lifted her head, shoved a loose curl back from her face, let out the clutch, and drove away from lighted Westam House into the vastness of the waiting dark.

❧ ❧ *Chapter Two*

LESLEY HAD BARELY motored five meters beyond the eastern edge of the clustered black and white Stuart-style buildings that comprised the tiny village of Westam-on-Wye when her resolve began to quaver. Four or five hours of darkened roads stretched before her, and there was not even a wisp of moon tonight. Perhaps she would go only as far as Ross-on-Wye or Gloucester and book a room for the night at some inn before it got too late. She could request a wake-up just before dawn and be on her way to London again by first light. But those petty concerns gave way to panic when the little Austin she'd bought just last year began to shudder. No, impossible! Not now and out here on a pitch-black carriageway with nothing about but farmsteads and strawberry fields and apple and pear orchards marked by the typical hand-lettered Hereford PYO signs— "Pick Your Own." The flopping sound reached her ears. It became instantly difficult to steer. A flat tire for certain.

She turned the car off onto a narrow lane that wound away between endless hedgerows, then got it onto a grassy shoulder near a sheepgate. Night sounds enveloped her; the breeze moaned against the windscreen as she cut the power. The headlamps died. The faint friendly glow of the instrument panel dimmed out.

"Bloody luck!" she cursed to keep from just dissolving into tears of frustration after the day she'd slogged through so far. For one moment she felt utterly done in. Then resolve coursed through her veins again. However had she managed to get a flat with the Austin just sitting in the garage? Perhaps Trent had tampered with the tire to strand her. Even now he and Constance could be combing nearby roads to bring her back. But for that possibility, she had not a bit of fear of Hereford-

25

shire rural lanes at night. She'd have to carry the sable coat. It meant everything to her, her only link to her mother's family. She'd have to cart the jewelry and painting, leave her bag and photos here for now. She'd simply walk up the road to Fownhope until she flagged someone. And she'd have to be very certain the auto that stopped was not a ruby Wraith Rolls before she accepted a lift. Nothing, absolutely nothing, would stop her from being in London to obtain a barrister's services tomorrow and stop that injunction.

The stiff breeze felt good after a few minutes as she was already warm from toting her burdens. A twenty-minute walk to the Roaring Lion's Pub where she could get help or ring up a garage. No autos on the road yet, but she'd expected that. Even the village folk of western England generally rolled up their lives with their pavements after nine. Raspy frog croaks kept her sweet company as she trudged around a sharp bend in the road. How had it ever come to this, she mused again, as her boots fell into a steady crunching rhythm that mesmerized her tired brain. It was then, just beyond another crudely lettered .PYO sign, on a slight hump of bridge over a rustling spring stream where she could hardly dart off the road, a huge auto leapt around the bend and was instantly upon her.

Headlamps slashed yellow streaks across her. Its big engine and heavy wheels on dirt and gravel drowned all sounds, even her own gasp and thundering pulsebeat. She pressed legs and hipbones tight against the rough stone rim of the bridge. The big auto roared past into the night.

Thank God! The monster had been white or yellow and hardly the bloody crimson Trent so favored. She stood where she was, shaking, unable to move, relieved she had not leapt off the bridge in her panic. Beyond, screeching brakes sliced through the roar of engine as the car ground to a stop. She clutched her things to her breasts as it backed toward her slowly. It was a make of car she'd never seen, sleekly lacquered in what could only be described as chrome-yellow. Relief at not being hit turned to fury at the stupid lout sitting in the still darkened front seat.

It was like a ghost car! The driver's side was completely unmanned! Her heart leapt to her throat before a gray man's face leaned over to the passenger's side where she stood. He rolled the window smoothly down.

"You okay?" A man's deep voice, not a British or Aussie accent.

"No thanks to you."

"Hey, I'm really sorry. There's seldom a darn thing on these roads at night."

Ah, an American, she thought. A deep, confident voice, not a bit contrite. Then this auto must be American too with the driver on the wrong side.

"You might have killed me, not to mention innocent sheep or dogs that might be out at night!" she retorted, her tone more strident with each word.

"On the other hand," the chipper voice went on, "in the black of night my trusty Buick did manage to navigate one of the world's narrowest bridges as well as miss you, and I haven't seen one of the innocent creatures you mentioned."

He sounded slightly amused, blast him. She was tempted to say something even more biting. But her feet were blistering and her burden pulling on her arm and shoulder muscles. Fownhope wasn't all that far to go with a stranger. She'd merely ask him for a short lift into the Roaring Lion's Pub.

"Here," he said and the still fairly indistinct face moved away. He got out on his side of the auto to come around. A light popped on inside. The interior looked golden and rather plush with wide, deep leather seats. The man was very tall, a bit over six feet. Bareheaded with dark hair, big shoulders. Evidently well dressed too from what she could tell. "Let me give you a ride where you're going, all right? What's all this stuff?"

"I could use a lift, just into the next village," she admitted, ignoring his last question. "My auto has a flat. I don't suppose you're as good at fixing tires as you are at night racing."

His teeth flashed very white in a half-grin. "Repair work and mechanical endeavor are just not up my alley," he said and left the sentence hanging as though she were to inquire what was "up his alley," then. He was awfully good-looking. She could tell even in this light. He emanated that typical bonhomie, that presumptuous American assurance that assumed instant friendship. It was admirable only so long as it didn't wear on one.

But tonight, right now, everything was wearing her down. She held tight to her sable in its canvas cover and the painting when he put his hands out for them. Was that just the scent of bitters or actually whiskey on his breath?

"Look, I don't usually just get collected on the road by strangers on the mere spur of the moment," she said and tossed her head.

"I didn't think you did. Is that a painting you're hugging there? What if a rain comes up? It should have been crated and wrapped to transport it, you know. And my name's Paul Kendal. I've been on a little research excursion to Wales, and I didn't plan to go much farther before stopping somewhere for the night. Now that you know my name, we're not really strangers, are we? Here, let me put that painting and your hanging stuff into the backseat and we're off. And your name?"

"Whatever were you researching in Wales?" she countered, holding the coat and painting even closer.

"The people, food, lifestyle." His big head tilted slightly to one side, but she still had to step back and lift her chin to look up comfortably into his face. "I've been touring pubs too, I have to admit. Actually I'm a writer, a journalist."

A journalist! she thought. What if he recognized her name when she gave it? What if he knew someone who would write the Westam story for the papers tomorrow? As good as that big luxury American auto called a Buick looked to her, as kind as he basically seemed, she didn't need this!

"Really, I don't think—" she began when another large auto rounded the bend behind them.

The other motorcar looked like a Rolls. Yes, crimson; the back headlamps of the American's car illuminated the blood-red hue and the arched winged-female emblem on the car's bonnet as it ground to a halt. Trent. Probably Constance too, and here she stood gadding along the road with this American just for the taking.

She thrust the painting and canvas-covered sable into the man's hands. "Please," she clipped out even as she managed the strange handle of the passenger's door herself, "the people in that car, they're chasing me. I had a bit of a tiff with my

ex-fiancé and his mother and they're both livid. Please, may
we go?"

She got in and slammed the door. She slid down on the wide
single front seat with her purse and the chamois packet of her
mother's jewels clutched in her lap even as the American
hurried her things into the back and slammed the door. He was
in beside her and had the engine on before Trent's deep-
throated Rolls horn sounded twice where he had pulled up
close behind them, waiting to get over the narrow bridge. The
dark interior of this car, redolent with the fragrant masculine
aromas of leather and some sort of rich tobacco smoke,
enveloped her. Then, to her alarm, she heard a door slam
outside. She craned her head back. Trent was coming up to
where they sat.

"Hurry!" she insisted, scooting down farther in the seat, her
voice suddenly husky. "I don't wish to see them."

Still a little distance back from looking in, Trent yelled
something she couldn't decipher. Her would-be rescuer's big
head pivoted to her as though his eyes and brain were delving
into all there was to know about her in that split second of
silence. The lights of the Rolls behind etched half of his rugged
face in stark detail. She noticed his black hair cropped fairly
short on the sides of his head framed by well-shaped ears. His
slightly pronounced chin sported a shadowy cleft. She could
almost feel his day's worth of beard stubble as if she'd reached
out to flick her fingernail gently across it. Thick brows hid his
eyes except for the slightest glint. And that flash of white teeth
again.

A single deep sound of amusement or pleasure leapt from his
throat; she saw his Adam's apple bob. Then he turned back to
shift the clutch. The big American motorcar belonging to a
man whose name she couldn't even remember roared off into
the night leaving Trent and his waiting Rolls in its dirt- and
gravel-spitting wake.

His name was Paul Kendal, she learned again, when they
were seated over a quite late supper of trout, jacket potatoes,
red cabbage salad, and strawberry gâteau at the Gloucester
Arms Inn on the A49 motorway. It was as far as they would go
for the night because the Buick needed petrol and out here no

station was open until seven the next morning. Unfortunately, there'd been only one room available here at the inn, but she'd insisted she'd sleep in the auto, so that was that. And she'd had to tell him a bit of a lie, that her name was Lesley Rigsby, and mentioned only that she lived near the village of Westam-on-Wye.

Still, they both sat sated, warmed, mutually relaxed in each other's company because he had finally accepted from her that small talk was all she would allow. No good to have a journalist knowing too much, even if he was an American one who just wrote a general column in American papers called "Europe's Good Life Today." He was, as he told her with that half-beseeching, half-provocative grin, from the little American village of New York City-on-Hudson.

"In the best British tradition of Stratford-upon-Avon, Ross-on-Wye, Henley-on-Thames," he said. He offered her a cigarette she refused, then lit one for himself of a brand named Chesterfield.

"It's the Welsh, as you probably learned on your holiday, who have the most wretchedly spelled names for places of all times. It's rather logical of us Brits to give locations as well as place names in one dose, don't you think?" she parried, leaning slightly toward him on her elbows across their table.

"Logical perhaps, but definitely the more set, boring way. Kind of like composing newspaper deadlines in a pat style rather than writing free-flowing fiction for one's own inner needs," he mused aloud. He was surprised again how this woman he barely knew brought out all his deepest thoughts and feelings. Then too, she blushed so entrancingly if he teased her, so he added, "It reminds me of the king's redcoats when Britain lost her American colonies. Your soldiers marched stubbornly in the old traditional military lines while they got picked off one by one by our freewheeling, chance-taking colonial army. Obviously, the expected way to do things is not always the best."

"Really? And you colonials are rather proud of that, I gather. Still, the mother country taught you everything you knew for starters."

He laughed again and flicked the silver ash from his

cigarette into the brass ashtray. He laughed easily, yet she noted a flash of brooding temperament sometimes flitted across his strong features as if he harbored deep thoughts. Still, being with him, she felt somehow safe—from everything else at least. His gaze was so very direct. His eyes, she'd discovered with a jolt of unspoken kinship and recognition, were green too, though a much darker, wavering green than hers. Again, that look seemed to probe deep inside her as though he could sometimes fathom what she was thinking.

She was an absolutely stunning woman, he thought. It was partly, no doubt, her rare coloring. She had hair the hue of rich cognac held up and swished in a crystal snifter before the warm, darting flames of a fireplace. Her skin was pale but luminiscent and made her startling sculpted crimson mouth and those shimmery, pale green eyes with delicate gray in their depths even more entrancing. Her body was outright seductive, and it intrigued him she seemed very at ease with that. She was rather tall and slender, tiny-waisted with strong shoulders, lean limbed but lush in all the right places, including firm, high breasts her blue silk shirt revealed as that navy blue jacket she'd left upstairs had not.

He loved to study her even if he had no idea in the world if she'd been telling him the truth or what made her tick. He only knew he'd been instantly attracted—his yardstick for a woman he'd be willing to spend his precious time on and break all kinds of vows over. Well, he and Melissa Pearson back in New York-on-Hudson weren't even formally engaged, and here he was with this exquisite creature of chameleon moods. But he knew better now than to ask again why she was really being pursued on that dark road tonight.

He loved her voice, the touch of upper-class accent, the barest blush of drawl from this area of the country. But there was some other tantalizing inflection in her pronunciation, perhaps a foreign one. Even with his knowledge of French and Italian he could not quite place it. He flattered himself he had a good ear for regional dialects, one of many skills he'd need when he finally got enough time to write his novel here. He'd spent a lot of time in England off and on for the past eight years, including two years reading literature on a Rhodes Scholarship at Oxford. He was an unabashed lover of things English. And he was all too fast becoming a lover of this particular Englishwoman, though he was convinced her story was full of holes.

The man on the road who'd been looking for her had called out to him at that last second before he'd pulled away that he was searching for his red-haired sister, and here she'd fed him a cock-and-bull story about a fight with her fiancé. Then too, she was obviously carting around an expensive Stubbs painting lifted right off someone's wall. And he'd bet money it was a fur coat in that canvas dress bag and a jewel case of some kind she wouldn't let out of her sight. But having a knockout mystery woman with him late at night who was possibly either a thief or a someone's runaway girlfriend shot a thrill up his spine. She obviously wanted a fast ride to London in the morning, if nothing else right now. That alone was a good enough reason for him not to publicly accuse her of anything illegal yet. Still, she made him so damned curious.

"I do have a couple questions about tonight when I, as you put it, collected you off the road," he said, his voice still light. Yet he saw her stiffen with wariness again.

"I'm only wondering," he told her, and leaned forward across the small table even as she leaned back. "What do those hand-printed PYO signs I've seen all over mean? There was one right where I picked you up."

"Oh," she said and he watched her lips pout slightly. He shifted his long legs under the table, careful not to accidently brush his ankle against hers again. "You see, when you say 'picked you up'—the connotation's different from 'collected you.'"

"My ignorance never ceases to amaze me." He grinned though she was certain he tried not to, and his eyes lit. "All right, I didn't pick you up. My loss, but I read you loud and clear, Lesley. And PYO? Protect your own? Pursue your objectives? Permit youthful outrages?"

"Actually," she said and smiled with an alluring tilt of her head, "PYO, however the locals letter the sign, means 'pick your own.' Didn't you even note the strawberry gâteau you devoured? This area, Mr. Colonial Kendal, along with Devon, is prime strawberries-and-cream country. There are also extensive fruit orchards here."

"So, you see, I did know what the signs meant after all, and did pick my own," he dared.

Her lovely face sobered again. "I really think it's time I borrowed a blanket to sleep in the backseat of your Buick."

They'd discussed this twice over dinner, but he hardly blamed her for holding fast to the idea they couldn't share a room. He could just sleep in a chair in the room, and she could have the bed, if she'd trust him. Besides, the man at the desk had the definite idea they were married. But her presence had him running on pure energy reserves right now. He'd been up since five to give himself time to work on both his column and a short story before breakfast, but he knew that he'd have to insist again she take the room. This was no Dashiell Hammett story where the lady fell so easily into bed with the man she'd just been rescued by. Nor was it some Hollywood movie like Clark Gable's *It Happened One Night* where Claudette Colbert as a runaway heiress let down the dividing blanket in the hotel room for the journalist she'd just run away with. Too damn bad fantasy couldn't be real life tonight, too!

"Please, take the room," he said again as they rose from the table. "Just in case your fiancé finds my car, he won't find you in it. I'll sleep in the backseat. I'll just walk you up."

She argued no further. Her sore booted feet floated up the stairs to the wide hallway with the four rooms the inn offered. Paul had left his bag and writing materials right next to her sable and the painting over which he'd cast an especially sharp eye. He'd told her his father owned an art import house back in the States.

"You know, I was thinking," he began at the door to the room on the first floor up. She stared down at the maroon-flowered carpet in a final attempt at nonchalance, but she knew she tensed when she jerked her gaze back up. It collided with his green eyes so heavily fringed with black lashes.

"I said I'll sleep in the auto, Paul."

He shook his dark head and held up both hands to stave off the too-familiar protest. "At home, near New York City-on-Hudson, there are signs that advertise Burma Shave—though they're not quite as cryptic as your PYO signs. There's one outside the city toward Passaic that reads, 'To get away . . . From hairy apes . . . Ladies jump . . . From fire escapes.

Burma Shave.' You wouldn't tonight, would you, Lesley? I'll
bunk in the car and have you in London by noon tomorrow."

Relief flooded through her. "And I promise I'll be up and
out by six for the hairy ape to get in to use his Burma Shave,
so we can be on our way. I can't thank you enough for all your
kindness and aid, Paul."

He unlocked the door for her and slowly handed her the key.
"Someday, when we're both wiser and more trusting of each
other, we'll find a way." One big warm hand squeezed her left
arm above her elbow. Then his long legs took him across the
blatant maroon roses on the carpet and back down the stairs.
She closed the door and leaned wearily against it. It disturbed
her how strongly his innate warmth drew her and his clever
cheekiness lightened her heart. How easily he'd just assured
her when she'd been certain there was a final confrontation
coming at the door of the room he'd insisted on paying for.
And how sad that her adventure with him would soon be over.
She'd have to find a way to give him the slip before he dropped
her at her Mayfair flat. She threw her purse on the wide bed so
hard it bounced. If the Fleet Street rags were running stories on
the Westams tomorrow, she didn't want Paul Kendal to have a
glimmer where to find her.

The man was maddeningly glib and charming the next
morning at seven when they set out at the Buick's usual fast
clip for London again. They breakfasted briefly on toast and
jam, coffee downed starkly black for him, and Earl Grey tea
for her. Then too, Paul looked terribly natty, which made her
wrinkled single set of togs appear that much drearier as she'd
surveyed her image in the looking glass before turning the
room over to him. He'd emerged all shaved and spiffy and
smiling in beige flannel slacks, open-necked wine-hued shirt,
camel's hair polo jacket with horn buttons, tan suede shoes,
and a jaunty brown slouch hat. But as they neared the outskirts
of London through the Chilterns and then the stately little town
of High Wycombe, she tried desperately not to so enjoy their
time together. She had to find a way to get him to drop her
somewhere soon. The last thing she had time for in her life
right now with the spring fur shows imminent was a man who
made oneself forget everything else but being with him.

Then too, earlier, one sleeve of her sable coat had flopped free of the canvas bag when she'd put it in his auto in Gloucester. "What a gorgeous fur," he'd said. "Is it yours?"

"Yes, of course."

"It's not mink, is it?"

"It's a Barguzin sable, sometimes called Russian Crown or Imperial sable, the fur that used to belong only to the czars," she'd informed him with a proud tilt of head.

"Such a shimmering brown color and the fur appears silver-tipped," he said and his big hand stroked the fur, almost touching hers. His intense gaze locked with hers again. He did have a fine, discerning eye, but then, he'd told her that was one primary prerequisite to being a good writer. Most people would never have noted the silvery cast to the guard hairs nor how the deep smoky brown color of the pelts took on a bluish cast in the sun. For him to see the coat better, she undid the slide fastener farther. "A real work of art," she breathed, unable to halt her words. "Sable is amazingly lightweight for its depth and warmth. This coat is every bit as much a masterpiece as a fine painting—or a wonderful novel. It took highly skilled craftsmen hours of labor to make."

His long-fingered brown hand—how was it he seemed so tanned in the spring when most Englishmen looked pale?— moved to stroke the collar. "Valente di Roma" he read aloud from the handsewn label against the ecru silk lining. "It must be worth a great deal on the market."

Quickly she refastened the canvas cover to hide the coat's sleek beauty. The fur was worth at least twenty thousand pounds for its rarity and quality, but she'd never tell that to Paul Kendal, whose father's New York business sold all sorts of luxury pieces to Americans. She'd already told him much too much.

She knew it surprised him both that she asked to stop for a heartier breakfast when they reached Uxbridge just on the outskirts of London and that she insisted on carrying her bulky items into the restaurant. She'd let them out of her sight as long as they were locked up before. "London, you know, is hardly the Herefordshire or Welsh countryside where no one ever pilfers a thing," she told him. It was barely ten o'clock and the big Buick had made wonderful time, flying down the M40, but then that seemed to be the way Paul Kendal always drove—as quickly and voraciously as he seemed to do everything in life. She sighed with relief that he was leaving her on her own a moment as she watched him get up from the table to use the gent's after they finished eating. Did he realize, she mused, she had learned a great deal about him and given back almost nothing of substance about herself?

She sighed as she watched him walk away with that angular grace peculiar for such a tall man. Suddenly she wondered how that muscular yet lanky body would look careening precipitously off a Westam-bred polo pony to swing mallet at ball, or riding with her out on the gallops at Westam, or all stretched out on a chaise lounge in the sun, redolent with drowsiness. Sad, but now she'd never know. He'd told her he was booked at the Savoy for the next several weeks. But she'd never dare to contact him there after everything, including what she was about to do now. Still, she pictured a poignant reunion they could share there in the posh lobby or in Cesar Ritz's private, mirrored Mikado dining room where she liked to go with chums. There, after a candlelit meal with wonderful conversation heightened by provocative teasing of each other, they would go up together in one of the red Chinese lacquered lifts to his suite overlooking the green Thames embankment. There she'd lose herself in those green, green eyes.

She started, as if porcelain had shattered to the floor. Whatever was wrong with her, wool-gathering like this when she had to act now? There would be time later to sort things through.

The moment he disappeared, she dropped the brief note she'd written him last night on the table with enough bills to cover her meals and the room he hadn't let her pay a shilling toward. The note read simply, "Sorry. It is all rather too much to explain now. I am very grateful. Lesley." In one minute she was out the door of the café with her jewels, painting, and bulky bundle of sable. She dashed around two corners to Broadway and quickly found a cab. She was nearly home to Brook Street before the sharp pain of regret pierced her. Then it was much, much too late.

❧ ❧ Chapter Three

LIKE A SLEEK double-stranded necklace of antique but timeless gems, the forty shops linked together in the Burlington Arcade had graced the throat of London's busy Piccadilly for one hundred and twenty years. Under the lofty arched glass roof, the traditional black and gold uniformed beadles in top hats still enforced the rules of no running, whistling, or opening umbrellas in the arcade, although they no longer had to "ward off undesirables" as in earlier, rougher eras. Above the sedate bustle of cosmopolitan shoppers, great suspended lanterns still illumined polished bowed-glass windows flaunting their scalloped linens, imported tobaccos, jewelry, men's tailoring, cashmere and tweed knitware, cutlery, and the elegant, sleek fur fashions of the staid, century-old establishment of Sackville's.

This last day of May both American and British buyers as well as preferred customers by invitation only had assembled to view the 1939 autumn fur collection. An intentionally select audience; a deliberately limited number of designs to further foster Sackville's well-tended reputation for uniqueness and exclusivity. Leonard Stockman, the exacting, perfectionist manager and owner, who had literally wedded himself to the business thirty years before by marrying the Sackvilles' only child, demanded the showing be absolutely flawless. Madame Justine Faulk, Sackville's brilliant head furrier, a Parisienne by birth, was more realistic than that.

Lesley Westam had gone to work at Sackville's as a model only so she could convince Madame she had inherent talent for grading and arranging pelts. Finally admitted to the sacrosanct Sackville workrooms, she had slowly gained Madame's trust. Lately, Madame had begun to recognize Lesley's gift for what

the furrier industry termed "the eye, the hands." Still, Leonard
Stockman was far from convinced and insisted she still model.
But for Lesley, showing the plush furs was now only a favor to
Madame and a way to gain more experience for the distant day
she would be arranging such showings of her own new lines.

"Lesley, did you see those simply scrumptious raspberry
tarts and cress sandwiches old fussbudget Stockman's had set
out by the front door?" Belinda Barnes, Sackville's current
favorite blond model, whispered to Lesley in the hubbub of the
dressing room.

"Mmm. They looked lovely. Still, food's hardly what we
need right now," Lesley murmured and craned her neck around
to check her silk stocking seams in the mirror.

"But it's all so flaming wretched that fur models have to be
so bloody slender under thick coats!" Belinda's voice was
muffled as she wriggled her svelte frame into a cherry-red
crepe dress. Sackville's fur fitter, Emma Huxley, who was
helping out as a dresser today, buttoned it in back for her, then
darted off in a flurry over misplaced earrings until the
sixty-year-old, birdlike Madame Justine produced them from
somewhere.

"No one even thinks of that tea table until you mingle with
the audience after!" Madame scolded in her rapid French-
accented English and clapped her heavily ringed hands for
silence as Emma guided Lesley's gown carefully down over
her coiffure. Madame's magnified brown eyes peered owlishly
at the three models through thick tortoise-shell glasses under a
black hair fringe. The tight bun at the back of her sleek head
seemed to tug her rouged and powdered facial skin back over
sculpted cheekbones. "Thoughts of mere food at a time like
this when you are about to adorn yourselves with Sackville
furs! Mesdemoiselles, really!"

Silence suited Lesley. She moved slightly away from
Belinda and Anne, the brunette model for this showing. Mr.
Stockman always kept a blonde, a brunette, and a redheaded
model on call. Privately booked showings, even for one
customer, featured coats on models whose hair and coloring
matched that of the fur's future owners, especially if a man
were buying. At least that was the admitted rationale. Leonard
Stockman, white-haired and balding himself, refused to admit

that a good many of the lush garments went to silver-haired duchesses, industrialists' wives, or rich American matrons.

In the world of luxury furs, Lesley thought, the key was fantasy. Women of even the highest social classes and greatest wealth purchased fur coats because they felt like a princess from a fairy tale in them, not more like themselves. Fantasy, just like all her regrets and wishes that she had not ditched Paul Kendal almost two weeks ago.

"At least my Lesley is calm and ready, eh!" Madame Justine said and threw her delicate hands up in an exasperated gesture at the rest of the scene. "But I should have known you would be. You, a Valente at heart, understand, no?"

Lesley smiled down at the petite woman who brushed an invisible hair from the padded shoulder of the draped white wool dress Lesley would wear under the first several furs. Madame and Mr. Stockman had agreed during rehearsal the dress was perfection with her ivory skin and titian hair. Norman Hartnell, designer for the queen, had excelled himself. A softly shirred bosom was gathered to a narrow waist, which blossomed to accordion pleats that swayed gently when she moved. The long, swirling midnight-blue satin dinner suit with lace inserts in the skirt and amethyst trimmed lapels, which she would wear to model the last two evening furs, was by the American-born Mainbocher.

American-born, her mind clung to that thought as Madame Justine took her wrist and led her out into the brocaded hall to the doorway. The little woman slightly parted the white velvet curtains so they could glimpse the crowded room together. Lesley stared without seeing at first, just as she had so often found herself doing these last two weeks. American-born, Paul was so very different from any other man she had known, and not just because he had that brash American streak she found so enticing—unsettling in the most elemental way. He had stirred something in her she could not put a name to. Several times she had lifted the phone to ring him up at the Savoy to apologize. Once she had even found her feet had taken her nearly to the hotel entrance just off the Strand. Too often, she had been certain some tall, well-attired, dark-haired man emerging from a cab or bent into the spring winds under an umbrella must be Paul. Her insides had cartwheeled until reality descended with a crash.

"A restless crowd in a serene setting, no?" Madame's husky voice tugged her back to the present.

"Very," Lesley agreed as her eyes scanned the room through the thin crack in the drapes. Sackville's main salon was restful, at least ordinarily, with a spaciousness to it Lesley appreciated. Beige walls with white and gilt molding framing inserts of eggshell brocade. Cream velvet Louis XIV armchairs, although portable wooden chairs had been hired today and placed in horseshoe-shaped rows. Triptychs of mirrors in three corners of the room. Potted palms along the sand-hued plush carpet, and Waterford bowls of white roses on the two marble stands on either side of the entry from the private showing room where the models attired themselves today.

Lesley was about to step back to await her call when she saw Constance, Lady Malvern come in with several of her friends. However had the woman gotten her hands on an invitation? She had not bought at Sackville's nor set foot inside the two years Lesley had worked here. Lady Malvern shopped almost exclusively in Paris where her friend the designer Elsa Schiaparelli held sway in the fashion world. Surely she hadn't come here to cause trouble just because Lesley's temporary staying order against Trent's injunction had been successful!

Yet despite the woman's presence, Lesley moved effortlessly through the show. In her element, she could well have taken on Mr. Stockman's role and recited the styles and merits of each garment to the eager, murmuring crowd. No mere musquash here today like dear old Melly Mott used to send to London to be dyed to resemble mink or sheared to resemble beaver during the Depression days of the earlier thirties. Mink, sable, fox, chinchilla, fitch, and ermine held sway now at Sackville's. As the sloe-eyed Anne Donley brushed by her in golden sable she had just modeled, Lesley sauntered out front for the third time in a silver fox stroller with huge cuffs and bolero stand-up collar.

"Ah, and now our exquisite Lesley is back in exquisite silver fox. This elegant fur is ranched today in Norway and Canada for Sackville's most discerning buyers." Leonard Stockman's bland, endless voice droned on as her flowing

stride and smooth pivots took her around the room amid stares
and ahs. Although her eyes skimmed many in the crowd, she
pointedly ignored Constance and her coterie. Only the Russian
fitch coat to go, then she must make a swift change to the blue
evening suit. In one fluid movement she removed the stroller
to display its ice-blue silk lining. With the graceful floating
nimbus of fur behind her, she disappeared through the swish of
velvet draperies as the next model took her place in the center
of the room.

Paul edged his way in past a tea table attended by two maids
in black uniforms and little white aprons. The place was
packed for a style show that was all too obviously in progress.
Her grandmother had said she modeled at times for Sackville's
as well as worked here helping to select and match the furs.
But he'd pictured himself entering a sedate, nearly empty shop
to ask to see Lesley alone. He didn't intend to stand out in the
arcade under the stiff stare of the beadles now that his detective
work had finally tracked down Lady Lesley Westam, alias
Miss Lesley Rigsby. She'd put him through a week of anger,
a few days of worry, and a quick return trip to the area where
he'd picked her up. After inquiring in the little village, he'd
almost been put off by the imperious, suspicious Lady Malvern
in the Westam mansion before being finally rescued by the old
woman in the gardens who'd turned out to be Lesley's
grandmother. He'd almost jumped for joy there among the
roses and yew hedges when he heard Lesley was neither
married nor engaged. He just had to see her again, but old
Lady Sarah had not recalled the address of Lesley's flat, only
that it was on Brook Street in Mayfair.

His eyes scanned the room just to be certain Lesley was not
in the audience. She was not, though unfortunately he spotted
Lady Malvern, who had branded Lesley a thief quite believ-
ably until Lady Sarah had set him straight. To reach a single
empty seat in the back row, he excused himself and shuffled
awkwardly in front of four rapt women simultaneously craning
their necks and wielding pencils and notepads. He folded his
big frame into the chair despite its protesting creak and the
glares of several other women nearby.

He sucked in his breath when Lesley emerged through the

white velvet curtain one model later. He almost shouted at a photographer in a front row who rose to pop several bright bulbs in her face, then scooted out of the room. Despite that confusion, the impact of seeing the woman center stage like this was staggering after two weeks of thinking of little else but her. No nervous, rattled girl wandering a rural road here. No tired, grieving woman saddened by her father's funeral and her brother's nefarious plans to disinherit her. No windblown, casually attired Englishwoman sitting across the supper table from him now. Lesley Westam owned that striking fur; Lesley Westam possessed the room. It stunned the twenty-eight-year-old Paul Michael Kendal to think she was beginning to possess him, too.

Paul's quick writer's brain threw descriptions of the scene at him as though he and not the avid women around him held pencil to paper. In a three-quarter ermine cloak over a gleaming blue satin evening suit, Lesley strode sure-footed, swirling, sending off sparks of verve and energy. Even gliding sideways as though she were above ever having to place foot before foot like mere mortals, her imposing height, the imperial grace of her broad shoulders further enhanced by the padding of coat and gown—her presence was at once stately and insouciant. Her gleaming cognac hair was swept regally up from her face and gathered on top of her shapely head in a riot of tiny, cascading curls like a fountain at sunset.

Slowly, Paul Kendal drew air into his lungs again. Damn it! For the first time in his life, a woman had actually made him forget to breathe.

Again, Leonard Stockman's words washed over Lesley as she moved, turned. Of course ermine was warm and dressy, but had *she* done the commentary here today, she would have emphasized the fantasy of its past as well as the practical luxury of its present. "Ermine, the fur of royalty, the symbol of virtue and purity over the ages." She formed her own mental descriptions with the hint of a smile on her lips. And then her roving, absent gaze smashed into the tall man's stare from the back row. The impact was more blinding than those flashbulbs of the cameraman who'd just dashed away.

Paul! Paul Kendal in the flesh! Her flow of motion almost

jerked to a halt, but she recovered to sweep the cloak from her shoulders in a nonchalant pirouette. Their eyes, across the rustling sea of hatted and coiffed heads, held again before she could either blush or think. Her lips quivered with the hint of a smile. Her eyes widened, blinked. She felt almost dizzy as she made her exit to the breaking waves of audience approval. She only knew in that moment she had once again been adrift in some green, warm, shifting ocean over which her little craft had no control.

He found her quickly in the press of people after the showing, when the models mingled with the others to answer questions or fetch a garment for another look. At least the few minutes he had to stand in a little queue to get to her gave her time to calm herself. But when she looked up into his face again this close, whatever words and excuses she had planned flew instantly out of her head.

"I wonder if you could help me," he began, those brows she sometimes expected to lift in question or surprise lowering over the unwavering eyes.

"Mr. Kendal, good to see you again," she managed with a defiant lift of chin. "I'm sorry, but as you can see, I'm working now."

"Then you can help me. I've been looking for a Barguzin Imperial Russian sable coat that walked out on me in a restaurant two weeks ago." His face looked serious. The usual teasing rasp to his voice was pure challenge now.

She could hardly blame him. But neither could she allow any sort of scene here. "We have no Barguzin sable here today, Mr. Kendal."

"Or should I say I'm looking for what walked out with the coat."

"I'm sorry, really. Please understand this is not the time or place to discuss this. If you haven't come to select something—" She stopped in mid-thought as she noted the familiar glint had crept back into his eyes. Her jangled nerves quieted somewhat. She shrugged her shoulders.

He grasped her wrist gently, then let go. His hand was so warm. "I'll take the ermine you just wore so beautifully then—delivered."

Across the crowded room, Madame caught her eye, like a rescuing angel summoning her with a flick of wrist. The spell Paul Kendal exerted so effortlessly over her was broken. She relaxed her stiff backbone, but she still sounded rattled. "Oh. Well, fine. I'm sure Mr. Stockman can arrange that. He's a rather exacting employer, you see, and you'll have to excuse me. I know you understand."

She ignored his "I'll wait," and made her way to where Madame Justine stood. Lesley's pulse quickened again. She had learned to read when Madame was annoyed. Behind her in the hall to the private salon stood a perspiring, red-faced Leonard Stockman.

"Madame, that man is a former friend, and I didn't even know he was coming. He did say he's interested in the ermine," she began before the woman motioned her to silence.

"It is not that. It is something unthinkable for Sackville's— for Stockman. I must go back out. He insisted on seeing you now," she added with a helpless roll of huge eyes and an exasperated gesture in his direction.

The portly manager led her into the back room, its size shrunk by racks of furs on both sides. He closed the door behind them. In a brocaded navy suit with hip drape, daring to smoke amid all these furs, sat Constance, First Lady Malvern.

"So, Lesley, we meet again after you absconded with the Westam House artwork, contents of the safe in my suite, and who knows quite what else." The woman's fuchsia lips formed the words as she twisted the thick gold bracelet on the hand holding the filagreed cigarette holder. "I was just warning Mr. Stockman that your pilfering is entirely likely to become common knowledge as the present Earl of Malvern's accountants do a bit more inventory work."

"How dare you come here now with these misleading innuendos!" Lesley exploded before she could quiet her voice. "And if Mr. Stockman won't mention it, I will. Cigarette smoke is wretched to get out of furs." She heard Leonard Stockman gasp behind her. Lady Constance's rouged and powdered face framed by the sculpted rolls of silvered hair changed not one iota as she blew out a perfect smoke ring. Lesley spun to face her employer.

"This is a personal family matter, Mr. Stockman, and Lady Constance is distorting facts."

"But the—well, the unpleasant publicity?" The man wiped his brow with a batiste monogrammed handkerchief, his voice a near whine. "The newspaper items after the funeral, of course, I felt I could ignore. But obviously, an establishment with the reputation of Sackville's cannot allow the threat of future notoriety among its employees, however—well, talented."

"My barristers are doing their best to see there is no future notoriety, as you put it, sir. The entire situation is over two decades old and quite private—"

"Of course," Mr. Stockman interrupted, "I must hope too that such fine previous customers as Lady Malvern and her friends, including the illustrious and influential Madame Elsa Schiaparelli in Paris, will not feel the need to stay away as long as they have now because of these—well, these family unpleasantries."

"Are you implying that if there is word in the press of this, or even if Lady Constance hints she and her friends will continue to boycott Sackville's, you would rather not have me on the premises? Despite my work with Madame as well as showing your furs, Mr. Stockman?" Lesley demanded, her voice rising precipitously as her hurt and anger swelled.

"Please, Mr. Stockman," Lady Constance said and stood as if Lesley hadn't spoken, "I really must be going before this unfortunate situation for Sackville's gets entirely out of hand. And do send round the golden sable wrap if terms we discussed are suitable."

Lesley stood speechless as Mr. Stockman scrambled to fetch a crystal sweet dish for the woman to flick her silver snake of cigarette ash into. Then she paraded from the room under the same flattering attention Leonard Stockman bestowed on all the women who bought at Sackville's, especially those of the nobility.

Blatant bribery and coercion from Constance, Lesley fumed. But what a blasted toady Leonard Stockman had always been. She saw it now. Forever sucking up to anyone with a title. And for that he was willing to allow Madame's precious furs to hang here like hams in a smokehouse! And he was willing to sacrifice a loyal employee to protect his precious family establishment, which he'd only married into and for which he'd never displayed a bit of talent! She'd been a fool to work for him and Sackville's, despite the knowledge she'd acquired from Madame.

Lesley shot out the door after the unctuous Stockman even as he came bustling back into the hallway. She fought to speak slowly, quietly. "Despite what Sackville's has given me, I've invested a great deal of hard work, loyalty, and pride in this establishment, Mr. Stockman. I didn't mean for family conflicts to spill over here. Now that the 'customer' is gone, I would like to discuss this again with you, so I might explain about the things Lady Constance said."

"But I really can't allow Sackville's to be at all compromised, Lesley." He dabbed at his shiny brow again. "I don't expect you to understand, of course, about my need to protect this revered establishment's reputation, but—"

"Then if I couldn't even begin to understand about having a reputation to protect, do not bother to sack me, Mr. Stockman." Her hands went to her hips; her chin tilted defiantly. "Starting right now you'd best look for someone reputable to model, but especially to select and sort your revered pelts to Madame's exacting specifications."

"My dear, I didn't mean this to be so—well, sudden. Indeed, I do sympathize. At least a fortnight's notice will be sufficient, as I'm sure Madame will need you with all the things going on in the workroom for a few weeks or so."

"Really, Mr. Stockman. You of all people should understand a matter of pride better than that, even if you have no idea that truth and self-respect often differ from reputation. I will not be back again but will have someone return the suit I'm wearing. And someday, I promise you, Sackville's will long to sell my designs, but they will be as unavailable as your sympathy and understanding have been." She went back to scoop up her purse and nearly slammed into Paul in the hallway when she hurried back out.

"What—" she began.

"I finally figured out the charming Lady Constance had gone back here when they called you. I thought you might need a hand."

She did not break her stride. "Then about Lady Constance—you know?"

He nodded. "I've met your grandmother too and just might be convinced to side with her in all this. You aren't leaving already?"

"I am. Permanently. I'll ask my flatmate to collect my things later."

"Then you can wear the ermine cloak I just bought. Come on." She took his arm as they collected the fur and went out together. Behind them, people stared as Madame Justine publicly berated Mr. Stockman in a mirrored corner of the salon.

A satin evening suit with ermine cloak she couldn't possibly accept wrapped around her in the middle of the warm afternoon in busy, workaday Piccadilly, Lesley thought, as Paul hailed a cab. They laughed at that together even though her blood still beat a new wild cadence at Lady Constance's machinations and Paul Kendal's second rescuing intrusion into her life.

If there was a certain lack of responsibility—even lack of sanity—in the way Lesley Westam and Paul Kendal carried on the next two weeks, Lesley laid it all at the door of the world's circumstances, even if Paul seemed a gift from heaven. She was unemployed and unable to go home to Westam House. Mr. Stockman, or perhaps Lady Constance, as the extent of the woman's vindictiveness never ceased to amaze her, had evidently threatened imminent scandal if another furrier shop hired her. So, like a child gone mad in a sweetshop, or a naughty youth living up to everyone's awed expectations of her, Lesley reveled in the first ten days of being on a wild and wonderful holiday with Paul in London. Today they'd spent the afternoon at Greenwich watching the yacht races. They'd dined on the grassy banks along the Thames from a gourmet hamper of lobster salad and champagne they'd collected at Fortnum and Mason's on the way out.

"You're certain you won't come up to my rooms for a brandy?" Paul asked her as he drove the Buick back into London.

"Brandy after all that delicious brandy-soaked cake? It's been a wonderful day, but I'd think not, Paul," she said and

settled her blue silk skirt primly back over her knees from
sitting sideways on the big front seat. She felt his eyes warm
on her as she bent to put her pumps back on her stockinged
feet.

"Alas and alack," he teased in his best W. C. Fields
imitation, "then my fate is still to be tempted all day by such
pulchritude and yet to have to settle for one or two of my little
chickadee's sweet kisses and a chaste hug in the foyer of Flat
Four, Twenty-one Brook Street?" They both laughed, but he
shot her that look of intent challenge before he slowed the car
and turned his attention back to the burgeoning London traffic.

She smiled inwardly in the electric anticipation that she
would some fine day say yes to either his teasings or his more
serious persuasions. Riding in Richmond Park, cricket matches
in St. John's Wood, browsing the Petticoat Lane Market
Sunday morning or at Hackette's or W. H. Smith's bookstores
hand in hand, she had fallen more and more in love. During
Wednesday polo matches at Cowdray Park, or at the British
Museum—anywhere—Paul's deepening affections were hers
just for the merest nod and she knew it. Yet, strangely, it was
Paul's overwhelming allure for her that at times smacked her
completely stone-cold sober.

Still, she would hardly term their parting the last few nights
or this one a chaste good-night, not for what he made her think
and feel and want to do. His tongue darted, teased hers; his
mouth slanted possessively as if to drain all resistance from her
tingling body. Had none of the English or Swiss boys she'd
ever known before had the merest notion of kisses like this?
But then the faint little voice of reason piped up from
somewhere deep inside where she'd almost exiled it.

She and Paul had shared so much with such intensity these
past ten days since the debacle at Sackville's, yet how well did
she really know him? A man like this surely had someone at
home with whom he'd learned to neck this way. She knew he
must be heading back to the States soon. He must know he had
taken her far beyond poor Roger Rigsby's gentle courting,
seduced her thoughts away from any other man she had ever
known. Tomorrow, when she could think again, she'd ask him
right out about his past with other women. Then, depending on
his answer, she could decide whether to slake this pounding

need he aroused in her. But now, his hand was warm on her hip through her sliding silk dress, moving back to gently cup and mold a resilient buttock. His hard cambric shirt front flattened her breasts so deliciously. And this quaking in her very bones made her want to flow against his hands, his mouth, thighs, into those deep-sea eyes forever.

But she never quite asked him about the women in his past as planned, not right away. They spent the next day at an auction at Sotheby's, where Paul bought six mahogany Chippendale "Director" chairs and a Mortlake tapestry for his father's Kendal and Son in New York—to appease him for not coming home often enough and for his choosing to write full-time, he told Lesley. His father had expected him to go into the fourth-generation business, but had been finally convinced writing really could be a serious occupation when Paul's short stories and columns had begun to appear in such well-known American publications as *The New Yorker* and *The Boston Globe*.

It was his sister, Kaye, who really loved the business, but their parents expected only that she would make a career of marrying and giving them grandchildren. Kendal's would probably be overseen by their father's partner if neither Paul nor Kaye produced the desired next generation soon enough. Lesley had missed the chance to ask him about any women he might have chosen to produce that next generation. Instead, she'd poured out her heart to him about her relationship with her brother, Trent, and how he had not lived up to her father's expectations for him, either.

The next night Paul and some English friends from Oxford took her and two other ladies to a riotous vaudeville show at the Palladium and then a jazz hall where they drank bitters and shandies till all hours. There Paul taught them to do the lindy hop, which the American jitterbugs doted on, with its hilarious hepcat moves of the face-to-face Shag, shuffling Suzy-Q, neck-breaking Peckin', and Truckin' with the wagging fingers. It was a night hardly conducive to serious talk.

The next day for a lark, when they tired of marathon conversations about everything in English, they blithely switched to Italian. Lesley was amazed how many words she'd forgotten since she'd spoken it with Mother years ago, but it came back quickly with Paul. After a shopping binge at Harrods, they bought a quick meal of fish and chips and, giggling like ten-year-olds, sailed a hired dinghy in Hyde Park, sharing goals and dreams.

More than anything Paul wanted to write "the great American novel but set it in England," though he wasn't certain exactly what he wanted it to say quite yet. More than anything, she wanted to design and market her own furs, but she had obviously burned her bridges here and wasn't certain what to do next. When she was with Paul, all that seemed forever muted. Everything was new, wonderful, so perfect she didn't even mention she'd been thinking about a holiday to Rome to see if the Valentes would consider putting her to work for the summer.

All of bustling, rousing London seemed to match their frantic pace as rumors of distant war circulated. Wild times, fast times, good times that made far-off reality seem mere fantasy and the laughing frenzy around them seem real. Still, there were quiet moments with Paul too when it all came back: her father's death, Trent's looming lawsuit, which was held off only by the gossamer threads of her injunction. And any possible future with the dynamic, wealthy, brilliant, and very persuasive Paul Kendal.

She finally asked him about other women in his life two evenings later at the Ritz. They'd sipped champagne in the elegant Palm Court under the Baroque splendor of the pink trompe l'oeil ceiling, then dined in the sumptuous restaurant down the mauve-carpeted hall. Even a friend of Paul's who'd stopped by at their table wanting to hear Paul's opinion of the chance of war with Germany had not dimmed Lesley's resplendent, champagne-gilded, violin-embellished view of the world tonight. Each moment with Paul was as rare as the inset marble walls or the bronze garlands draping the crystal chandeliers. From their seats they could view the empty Austrian embassy table, deserted now since Hitler's Anschluss had forced the annexation of Austria with Germany last year. But still the Viennese pastries went down deliciously with more Kir Royal, a drink made with *cassis* and champagne. The day with Paul had been so beautiful that she resented even thoughts of anything unpleasant intruding as they danced together later to American music in the cabaret downstairs.

They danced smoothly, very close together. Every slight shift in the touch of his hand on the small of her back seemed instantly discernible, perfectly correct. It no longer alarmed her that her body ached to be his even if her country-bred Herefordshire ethics still whispered to beware.

"I'm thinking how happy I am, Paul," she whispered in his ear.

Somehow he pulled her even closer and yet no one suggested they leave the polished floor for public indecency. It was the Paul Kendal touch that got away with anything, the more outrageous, the better, she mused dreamily. Yet the question she had longed to ask still simmered just below her bubbling joy.

"Mm. I've really been doing some thinking as well as feeling too, Lesley."

She tipped her head back to meet his intense look. This was very serious. Funny how she'd learned to read his moods. "About what?"

"What we've had our only disagreements about."

Her voice was so breathy she could not believe it was hers. "I, too."

His thick brows lowered in speculation. "And?"

"There's no one else for you?" There, she'd asked it, rather smoothly too, she thought.

"My sweetheart, we've practically been living together, except for a few critical night and early morning hours when we take to our diverse beds in separate establishments, or haven't you noticed?"

"I have noticed, but I mean there's no one for you at home?"

"I'm a free man, Lesley. Getting freer all the time."

Somehow that sounded amusing, but she didn't laugh. "Meaning?"

They swayed, soared together so easily with the music as he swept her and her swirling jade-green satin skirts into a faster pace for the Irving Berlin tune "Puttin' on the Ritz," which the band played every half hour before they took a little intermission. "You know what they say about people who dance so rhythmically together, don't you?" he asked, his breath warm in her ear. He didn't wait for a reply. He took her hand and led her from the crowded floor. He wrapped the ermine cape around her, paid their bill, and escorted her outside.

The night was balmy and clear with a dazzler of a peach moon perched on the rooftops of Berkeley Square behind them. "Want to walk a ways, sweetheart?"

He didn't wait for an answer. She tensed instinctively, though she managed to keep their easy stride and gentle swing of their joined hands as they strolled toward Green Park. "My father's business partner, his manager in the store actually, is a man who's been his lifelong friend. He's the one I told you will probably run Kendal's someday if my sister, Kaye, doesn't make Dad see she wants more than anything to run the show there. His name's Barry Pearson. Anyway, he has a daughter, Melissa, who's twenty-four now and my sister's best friend. I know I'm chopping this up, Lesley."

He cleared his throat and his big, warm hand gripped hers even tighter. "Anyhow, of course, the families, Kaye too, would like nothing better than to see me and Melissa become engaged. She works at Kendal's sometimes too and otherwise pretty much does charity work."

"Charity work. I see." She looked straight ahead even when she knew he turned to her.

"Not if you use that tone, you don't, Lesley. Frankly, it's my parents' expectation, not mine. But I just wanted to explain to you, because if you ever asked a friend of mine from home, they'd probably tell you Melissa and I are an item."

"Sounds like something for the newspapers—an item."

"I'm not married, not even engaged, Lesley."

"And when you go home next month, not about to be?"

"No way, unless you're planning this little inquisition to be our farewell. No way now." His frown, she thought, was not meant for her but someone else. The distant, charitable Melissa who no doubt waited for the return of those fabulous Kendal kisses that had so swamped her own senses, or his father perhaps, or the sister he loved the way she could never love Trent.

"You're implying I've come between you and Melissa," she accused.

"No more than I've come between you and what's-his-name

Rigsby." He forced a small grin. "Do you think we're getting ready to have our first real spat here?"

She pulled away to face him, hands on green silken hips. "I think we are at that, and it's hardly amusing."

His intense, direct look thrilled her. "Let's try it. I've got some terrific ideas for making up since you seem inclined to hold me off when things are going well between us."

"Obviously, especially after this revelation, I need more time," she insisted with a defiant tilt of chin.

"Time won't last forever, Lesley. Grab and use it while you can. I'm expected back home soon for my job and to see my family. And you never know about the damned war."

"There is no damned war," she blurted, then stopped. He looked so earnest—his little-boy honest look—despite the formal white dinner coat over the black trousers with silk braid stripe and cummerbund. In the street lamp at the edge of the dim park with bright Piccadilly traffic streaming by, she knew for certain she loved him. The plan she'd begun to consider lately to visit the Valentes in Rome, her worries about Paul having someone at home, her hesitations about committing her body to the man's overpowering lure, all seemed suddenly unimportant. Melissa Pearson, whoever's daughter and best friend she was, could simply go to blazes. Lesley was not even surprised when he seemed to read her mind again.

"Just stop thinking so much, Lesley, and let's take a cab back to the Savoy. It's time I really show you how much I can love you. No regrets, no fears."

In the huge, dark backseat of the cab, he reached for her instantly with hot kisses, hotter caresses. Sheer lunacy in a public vehicle in the heart of London, she told herself. Wrong to want this, do this. Danger.

But his warm, insistent fingers parted the downy fur cloud of ermine cloak, dipped into the satin oval neckline of her gown to caress, then flicker a taut nub of nipple to aching fullness. She moaned against his cheek, then with total lack of sanity, nipped the hard sinew at the side of his neck as he leaned down to press a slick kiss at the arched hollow of her throat. She was tilted nearly into his lap. Her soft hip felt welded to his hard leg. Her knee pressed to his while his hand slid the sleek satin higher along her thigh above the top of her gartered silk stocking. She was so totally ready, desirous, to let all this plunge her wilder, deeper.

"The Savoy, guv'ner." The cab driver's voice slammed them to a halt.

They pulled hastily apart. A languorous glow lit Paul's eyes; his features seemed stretched tauter on his handsome face. The insides of her thighs and lower belly felt brushed by softest mink. His grip was firm on her elbow after the doorman handed her out onto the strip of crimson carpet. With great difficulty Paul kept his eyes only on where they were walking. Somehow they moved to the steps. Someone held the door. It was then her gaze snagged the stark headline on the *Daily Examiner* journal laid open on the porter's stand.

The printed letters leapt at her, jangled her numbed brain: "Noble Westam Family Scandal: England's New Civil War," the headline shrieked.

"Paul!" she cried and jerked her arm back. "Look. Oh, no, no! Blast them, oh no!"

She pulled him out to the bookstall on the corner and then wished she hadn't. "Former Intimate of King, Dead Earl's Family Revives Squabble: Millions and Horse-Racing Empire at Stake!" one journal boasted. " 'Scandal's Child' Back in London After Two Decades of Exile," the third one sneered and sported a picture of Lesley modeling the very ermine cloak now on her back at the showing at Sackville's.

"Sweetheart, I'm so sorry." Paul's words pierced her stunned brain. She leaned gratefully against him as they bent to skim the papers together.

The black nightmare all over again, her inner voices cried: the lies, slanders, obscene accusations intruding into the world Paul Kendal had so wonderfully woven around her. The first paragraphs of the articles all claimed Trent's restraining order on her father's will had frozen all Westam assets this afternoon over a counterinjunction from Lesley's barristers, Selbridge, Smith, and Tyne. They had not told her, but then she'd hardly been home to be reached in days. She'd made a serious mistake. She'd been hiding in this fantasy realm of fun and love and beauty far too long.

"These people who write such things, they'll find me in London now that this is out, wherever I go, Paul. They'll follow me the way they did when Mother was dying. We won't be able to do a thing. Questions, innuendos. I can't tell you how it was before. You're not like one of them so you don't know. I'll leave for a while, go to Rome to the Valentes."

"This will all look better in the morning, Lesley."

"No. I'm going. I can carry on the legal fight from there. I've been considering it ever so much since I left Sackville's."

His thick brows descended to obscure narrowed eyes as she pulled away to face him squarely. "So much for our deeply shared secrets then," he said, his voice bitter.

"Secrets! How about your Melissa!" she threw at him and started back down the Strand so fast even his long legs had trouble keeping up. "I had to ask about that, didn't I, Paul? Men and their secrets! No one tells me anything. I had to wheedle even, didn't I?"

"I can't let you go to Italy. Mussolini's got both feet in with Hitler."

"Italy is not at war. Not at war, but I am now with my brother and his warped mother, and I'm going. I'm sorry but it's necessary!"

He spun her around to face him near the steps of the hotel, oblivious to the doorman and elegantly attired people traipsing in and out. "And us? I don't mean tonight, of course, but us?"

She looked so beautiful, an avenging fury from some opera he'd seen once, he thought, all streaming sunset hair and eyes of candescent radiance. Hell, he'd always thought of going back to Italy to visit and a leisurely drive down through France could provide some excellent pieces for his column. He loved and wanted this woman. He meant to have her, was considering proposing even. But now she needed holding, consoling. Surely she needed that at least from him despite that awesome look of fierce determination on her face.

Before they could argue more or attract a crowd, he resolutely hurried her into a cab and had her home on Brook Street cradled in his arms before the first tear even fell.

❧ ❧ Chapter Four

LESLEY AND PAUL ferried the Buick across the Channel to Le Havre and drove to Paris. After three days there, they motored eastward along the meandering bank of the Seine into the very heart of summertime France. Both had been to Paris before and wanted to set off to new places together. The city seemed to press in on them, Lesley especially. Shops and restaurants full of chatting, whispering, fashionable people and the kiosks brimming with broadsheets on each corner reminded her of what she wished to leave behind. Paris, like London, thrummed with the frenetic pulse of a powerful runner tearing desperately along to escape whatever shadows lurked around every corner. Perhaps, she thought dreamily, as they motored through the peaceful, verdant provinces of Burgundy and Champagne, it was her deep desire to go home to Westam that made her long for the countryside so.

As the afternoon wore on, they decided not to stop at the café in Vix for wine or tea and a ramble through the shops as they had other places that caught their fancy. The quaint stone villages hemmed by the blue-green forests and pastures of this area merged one with the next. But for the perpetual pleasure of being with Paul Kendal, the warmth and lunchtime wine might almost have lulled her to sleep today. Paul had taken to driving at a much more leisurely pace in France than she'd ever seen him do in England; the big yellow motorcar purred and vibrated ever so slightly. Comfortable and content, she sat leaning lightly against him on the big seat, feet bare of her leather platform sandals and half tucked in under her. She wore a crisp lime cotton shirtwaist with short bolero sleeves. Tortoise-shell combs held her loose curls back, and she had long since tossed her wide-brimmed straw hat into the backseat.

"It's perfectly lovely here, but I suppose this sort of wandering will hardly get us to Italy in record time," she observed sleepily.

"Who said anything about record time?" He removed his arm from around her shoulders when they came to another bridge over the narrowing Seine as it flowed away from its nearby source toward Paris. He slowed the big Buick even more as they approached a cluster of blue-pinafored schoolgirls behind a nun with starched, massive wimple and starchy posture to match. "Besides, sweetheart, I thought we'd decided we'd have no set agenda or immediate destination when we left Paris."

"I know," she said and stretched languidly, "the Paul Kendal motto of life. 'The most delightful ways to do things are not the pat, set ways, but different, unknown, challenging ones.'"

He gave a quick, deep laugh that vibrated through her even as the hum of the auto did. "I can't say you're not way ahead of me even when you're half asleep on my shoulder, Lesley. After all, if we did the expected thing, we'd be back in Paris right now hitting the tourist sites instead of out here dodging little girls who barely give us room to pass and an eagle-eyed nun who glares as if this were Satan's personal chariot."

Despite the nun's steely stare, both Lesley and the gaggle of girls waved as the Buick picked its way through their wide-eyed midst and went on. "They've just never seen a car this large or bright yellow before, and they're mad keen for it," Lesley said and yawned. She thought of her little Stubbs painting, which she'd had crated to bring along, of the lady and gentleman out for a bit of a hoot in their lovely yellow phaeton. Lately, it really didn't matter to her where they went so long as she got to Rome eventually and they were together now.

As Gram had said, when some things ended, there was a new path through the tight yew hedge of life somewhere. She felt free and strong and unafraid, however close they were to the border with Germany everyone in Paris was fretting about. They'd even begun to talk marriage, if in a roundabout way. She was ready to put her uncertainties about Paul Kendal aside as she almost had that night over a week ago before she'd seen those wretched headlines in the newspapers. As upset as she was then, she'd agreed to let him drive her to Italy under the conditions they'd have separate rooms and she'd pay her own way.

"The sun's getting low." His voice broke into her reverie as his arm came back around her shoulders and she settled comfortably against him again. "The sign said only ten kilometers to the village of Chatillon. Shall we try to find a little inn there for the night?"

"Sounds lovely. Let's just choose a place that seems as perfect for this Garden of Eden in Champagne as our cushy George Cinq Hotel was for the Champs-Elysées."

"Sounds lovely to me, too." He chuckled and flexed his long legs as she lit a cigarette for him. The Buick coasted down a small hilly lane lined with elms toward a gray-stone attached farmhouse and barn with half-timbered black and white sections gone all askew with age. Lesley could just imagine a fur coat designed along those apparently haphazard, yet naturally balanced lines: select pelts of karakul and sheared beaver, perhaps, in a garment worn for frolic and fun, not only for studied elegance like the coats Sackville's produced. When this lovely holiday ended, as it must eventually, would the Valentes welcome her to work with them in their famous Roman fur salon and would they ever let her design? How one sympathized with the plight of Paul's sister, Kaye! If Kaye only had a man like Paul Kendal in her future, she could dare to dream of a career and family, too.

"Are you watching? If you blink you'll miss the whole village, sweetheart."

"Just thinking. Paul, your ideas about getting off the usual footpaths of life—is that why you've sided with your sister about a woman running the Kendal family business?"

"No, Kaye would be fantastic running Kendal's. I wouldn't be all for her at all if I didn't think she'd handle it with aplomb. She's born to it, not just into it like I am. It's her life, like writing's mine—writing and something else now," he added and stopped the auto on the grassy shoulder of road by the silver Seine as they pressed even closer together to kiss.

He had definitely decided, he told himself. He was thinking

clearly and logically, despite the way everything inside him tightened like a coiled spring when he touched her this way. Lesley Westam was the woman he wanted permanently in his life. He had never expected that reality to hit him so fast or so hard, but there was no denying how he felt. And she was right about him. He thrived on the unexpected and the adventurous, so why had he ever even considered going back to the States to live and proposing to lovely, cool, proper Melissa Pearson, however much she adored him? Though he would always owe his parents respect and love, he certainly did not owe them obedience in that. But it had been his astounding love for this woman in his arms that had finally made all that come together for him—his footpath of life, as Lesley put it. With her, loving her, the driving desire to excel spurred him on. Themes for his writing, even the very words, came pouring into his brain as if she were a sacred inspirational muse who had opened a deep spring within him he had never fathomed was even there.

He released her reluctantly from the long, searing kiss as a hay-wain pulled by two hefty horses lumbered by on the road. The driver shouted bawdy encouragement. Lesley flushed. Paul stared into her gray-green eyes. He would get her a ring and ask her to marry him soon, and not just as an enticement into his bed. She had so smoothly avoided sleeping with him up to now even though he knew she wanted him, too. Of all the things in life he'd been certain of and desired desperately before, life with Lesley for the future was the dearest. And when he got back to her this winter after a fast trip home, he knew her mere presence would inspire him to write the novel beginning to burn in his brain. He darted one more quick, hard kiss on her pouted lips. They sighed almost in unison. He put the car in gear and they drove on, the sun warm on the backs of their necks.

"I know you would understand completely about my career," she said as they drove on. He shifted uneasily in his seat. Suddenly, he preferred the expectant silence between them. "I can't help it that it means so much to me, that I'm very certain I could be good at designing furs if I just got the opportunity. Your desire to express yourself and share with others—it's the same for me."

He nodded, cleared his throat. "Agreed. The ultimate problem, though, comes if there are children."

"But surely that could be worked out, at least with the sort of understanding we're speaking of," she insisted with a belligerent tilt of chin.

Suddenly, he wanted her so badly he was tempted to steer off the road. He'd make hot love to her on the front seat of the car, nuns, schoolgirls, and shouting farmers be damned! He ground out his cigarette butt in the ashtray drawer and kept his eyes on the road ahead as he stepped harder on the accelerator. "Vague words, abstractions, Lesley, for two people who've never been in the situation where there could be children. But yes, as long as they were not deprived or hurt by it, things like that could be worked out."

"I didn't mean we were speaking of having children, Paul." She sat up ramrod straight. "But because of my own past, I've thought a great deal about the problems of rearing children. I swear I'd never do anything to them or cause a scandal, no matter what I had to sacrifice. There are enough things in this world that harm children for parents to contribute to that. My parents wanted only the best for me, but their love hurt me and others, too. No, to protect my child from scandal, I think I could do or give up just about anything."

He drove faster, watching her in the rearview mirror as the breeze from the open window whipped her cognac hair around her impassioned face. All this talk of children when they'd never even made love, he thought. All this talk of sacrifice when he intended to see to it nothing would ever go wrong for her once he got back from the States. Suddenly, for some reason he could not explain, he felt angry with her.

"You think you can control love like that, Lesley? You wish your father had never left Lady Constance so you and Trent would not have suffered over the resulting scandal?" he shot back, his voice much more strident than he'd intended.

"Yes, in a way, I do!"

"You can't stop love when it happens. Your parents certainly couldn't, even though others ended up paying the price, too. People don't sit around and map out their lives logically in the face of powerful emotions like love. Besides, if your parents hadn't pursued their love, Trent would have been born

and you wouldn't. If you really want him to have all of Westam
without the mess of this renewed scandal, just withdraw the
lawsuit and you'll get the same result."

She turned to face him, her index finger jabbing the small
space between them. "Now you're twisting things! It's too late
for that. I love Westam! My parents meant for me to have part
of it, and I intend to."

"I rest my case, sweetheart. Despite people of Hitler's and
Mussolini's ilk, this world's a place, thank God, still greatly
inhabited by people who love and desire and sometimes get."
His eyes met hers in the big rearview mirror though he didn't
turn his head again. "Don't forget that because I'm planning on
it, Lesley." He watched as her lips pouted, her eyes darted
away. He slowed the car abruptly. "Here's the outskirts of
Châtillon. You'd better get those pretty eyes peeled, as we
crude folk from the colonies say, so you can pick whatever
place suits your logical fancy in your rational little heart of
hearts."

She adored the old L-shaped Hôtel des Fleurs on the eastern
edge of Châtillon the moment she saw it from the bend in the
lane. It sat on the green ribbon bank of the Seine at the end of
a gracefully arched bridge where the river joined the bubbling
torrent of the Douix. The gray stone and patchy shingles of the
weathered inn lured and beckoned. Bluish pigeons dotted steep
gables sprouting numerous chimney pots, and narrow Norman
panes of glass set like mosaics in huge windows flashed silver
in the sinking sun. Around it, wrapped like a paisley skirt, lay
a summer garden of tall, nodding daisies, leggy crimson roses,
and a blur of blue bedding plants. A lithe nymph standing in a
mottled stone fountain poured water from her bubbling urn
over a mossy rim of pool. A honking, patrolling gander herded
its family of gray and white geese with stark orange bills and
greenish goslings about the narrow garden walk. Even had the
finest thoroughbred mares instead of brindled cows been
munching the adjoining field, Lesley could not have felt more
completely at home. It was so dear, so distant from everything
there was to worry about out there behind them. She loved it
all instantly.

But Paul strolled back out much too soon where she waited

among the flowers, watching a goose try to coax her trio of goslings to climb the lower lip of fountain. "Oh dear, way out here, they can't be out of rooms to book!" she wailed.

"I wasn't sure you'd believe this, but here it is. The Guyon family who owns this place have cousins visiting from Reims for a week, and there's only one room left. Honest, sweetheart, though I know it sounds a little like our first night I collected you near Westam."

She smiled up at him. The sun bathed his watchful expression in ruddy hues as if his skin glowed. His eyes sparkled, yet he waited solemn-faced. She spoke slowly, distinctly. "I want to stay, Paul. One room sounds rather perfect to me."

Lowered brows almost masked his surprise. "You're certain?"

"You've been trying to talk me into sharing for some weeks now, I believe, and you're not certain?"

"Hell, no, it's only that I want *you* to be. I have no intention of volunteering to use a lounge chair like that first night. Maybe all this talk of logical decisions and sacrifice and children has gotten to me."

She took a step closer, lifted her hands to link them behind his neck. "And I have no intention of volunteering to sleep in the backseat of our canary chariot the way I did that first night. I'm ready and you said—about children, now, I mean—that you could be careful for that. Decisions like this don't have to be made in the heat of passion as they almost were in the cab that night we went to the Savoy and saw those blasted newspapers, you know."

"I do know. At least I'm learning. You always surprise me, Lesley, my love. And I admire your tenacity and how you think things through. I'll be right back and then we'll finish this discussion upstairs—without any words." He kissed her once hard, turned and accidently scattered the protesting geese in his haste as he ran back into the waiting Hôtel des Fleurs.

The sprawling garret chamber Madame Jeanette Guyon showed them was perfectly in keeping with the region's ambience and Lesley's expectations. It was a wide room with slanted walls of timber and plaster ending in four recessed windows with blowing Chantilly lace curtains and two lovely

views of the Seine and surrounding meadows. Old polished
oak furniture glowed with the rich patina of years. A massive
four-poster bed with a deep blue brocade spread and long-
stemmed crimson roses in crocks on the floor and bedside table
splashed color in the room. A tiny loo converted from a
closet adjoined, but the hand-painted wash basin and huge
porcelain tub were in the room near one of the two big hearths.
Woven rugs in the soft, variegated greens of the gardens were
strewn like lily pads across the slightly slanted floorboards.

The sinking sun threw vast, solid shafts of polished golden
light where they stood gazing into each other's eyes as the
sprightly Madame Jeanette left them alone. Her footsteps faded
away down the narrow hall, down the staircase. Lesley
dropped her purse and hat on the table. They ignored the little
pile of their luggage the innkeeper, François Guyon, had
carried up and the tray of Brie, thin crisp baguettes, and wine
the pretty Mademoiselle Anne-Marie Guyon had left to tide
them over until the evening meal below at eight.

As Paul had said, they spoke with no more words between
them in the hush of their spacious chamber, while the world
chattered and sang on about its business. They kicked off their
shoes. His hands on her waist, hers around his neck, they
moved together, danced to some ardent adagio they both heard
in their heads, or perhaps to the sounds of beckoning birdcalls
or the rustle of wind caressing green, tender leaves outside.
Perfectly in step, soft flesh pressed to firm muscle, they
rotated, slightly swaying, slowly, in love.

His lips caressed her hair. He kissed her forehead, her
brows, nose, lips. Breathless despite their slow steps, she
leaned back in his arms to venture a tenuous smile up at him
while tears of aching joy sparkled on her lashes. Their bare feet
halted on the rug-strewn floor. Hands and lips grazed where
eyes had touched. They undressed each other so lingeringly.
Unwritten choreography moved muscles, quickened breathing.
Gazes linked but for the straying, dreamy perusal of each
other's flesh. Sun gilded skin to alabasters and bronzes. Feet
waded through scattered garments on the sun-splashed floor.

His perfection staggered her. Whyever had she waited for
this so long? It seemed she had known and loved Paul Kendal
almost forever. How could she have stood being so alone

without him all these years? Hadn't she desired him, known it could be so beautiful, so natural for them from the first moment she ever loved anything in this life?

Again, again, their lips tasted, beseeching, promising, giving. Gentle hands skimmed, stroked, held warm yielding flesh. She was not afraid, not of this, of Paul, of anything. They moved again into each other's embrace so slowly, as if submerged in shoulder-deep water. She savored his warm, inviting eyes, burnished sea-green-gold by the sun. When her legs turned to water too, he lifted and carried her to the deep soft bed where the feather mattress rolled them instantly together. Ordinarily, she would have giggled, but that girl was gone. It was a woman here now, naked, desirous, ready: a loving woman whose limbs she watched so easily entwine with the strong, dark hair-flecked legs and arms of the man whose powerful body stretched far beyond her bare feet.

Suddenly, Paul's mouth, his hands were everywhere, provoking, urging responses she returned instinctively. Waves of fierce anticipation and sheer delight coursed through her. This was the desire of her body, heart, and mind. It was both rational and sensual. The deliberateness of it all heightened each glance, each caress, even the masculine aroma of him so close like this.

He flickered kisses on her eyelids, her earlobes, down her arch of throat to tingling nipples. When she stumbled over words to tell him how happy she was, he only whispered, "We love each other and will forever." She nodded fiercely, silenced by his gift for perfect words. Later, moving to the hum of her own blood and their mingled, rapid breathing, he told her, "I need you, Lesley. I loved you from the first, as if it's always been for us. Tell me you believe me!"

"Yes! Always. So wonderful—"

And it was. She wasn't certain what she was seeking other than total union with him, but she had every faith he did. It had all been somehow destined. Did he know it was the first time for her? He'd never asked, but she knew he understood. She ached to have him joined with her. She almost cried out in disappointment as he rolled away for one moment to prepare himself as he had promised her he would. Then he was back

with her, over her, hovering there as if to shut out all the
world's intrusions.

"Look at me, Lesley. Into my eyes. The most wonderful
things in life are worth waiting for, even when they hurt a
little, I swear it."

He moved to her, against her, in her. A jab of pain but it was
so unimportant, so instantly drowned in the pleasure of their
lovemaking. When she tried to move with him, his tousled
head jerked up. He grinned crazily down at her and then the
music of his breathing and rocking changed again. Dancing
together, they had always done it so well. And this too, this
varied, melodic, sweeping dance of love.

They stayed on at the Hôtel des Fleurs in little Châtillon for
one day, two, then three that flowed beautifully to four and
five. Though they made love until late at night, Paul rose early
each morning to work on his column that he mailed out once
a month, on plans for a novel, and on a short story called
"Hold Back the Dawn," which he let her read. It never ceased
to amaze her that Paul could awaken all bright and chipper to
write so cleverly no matter what they had done the day—or
night—before.

They took little jaunts before lunchtime when the weather
was fine. Once to Saint-Germain-Source-Seine to visit the
grotto where the carved stone goddess Sequana guarded her
bubbling spring that was the source of the Seine. Here the
ancient Romans had practiced communal bathing in the water
they believed to be an aphrodisiac. But Lesley Westam and
Paul Kendal hardly needed that sort of bath. The large painted
porcelain tub in their room had provided quite enough aphrodisiac communal bathing.

They went to Dijon and toured the palace-museum of the
Dukes of Burgundy, then sat all afternoon at the Café du
Chapeau Rouge on Dijon's main square drinking the rich
currant liqueur, *cassis*, downed with the traditional escargots,
spice bread, and piquant mustard of the region. One day they
drove farther northwest into the province of Champagne,
where green belts of vineyards of the white Chardonnay and
black Pinot Noir grapes on the mountain slopes awaited
harvest. They brought back bottles of Moët and Chandon,

Montaudon, and Veuve Cliquot to share with the Guyon family and their cousins from Reims. Their hosts had fed them so well and adopted them so wholeheartedly, except for the seventeen-year-old daughter, the pretty chambermaid, Anne-Marie. She had remained rather brusque, even snippy the few times Lesley had spoken to her.

They spent the entire last day of June, when rain scribbled all day on the windows, making love and talking of their future. They lay in bed still drowsy from their passion, which Lesley had found paradoxically both drained and renewed her body and mind. Under the sheets and downy quilt, they cuddled face to face, languid limbs entwined, her tousled hair a bright splash on the feather pillow they shared.

"I can take you to Rome, be certain you're all settled with the Valentes, then still keep my reservation on the *Athenia* from Liverpool in early September, Lesley," he assured her, his voice suddenly alert. He propped himself up on one elbow to stare down at her, and inadvertently let in a little gust of cold air into their warm cocoon. "That way, I can settle both business and personal things at home and be back to you in Rome by Thanksgiving."

Personal, she prayed, meant not only another temporary good-bye to his parents, but a permanent one to Melissa Pearson. She tugged him back down to tuck the covers in and forced herself to ask only, "Whenever is Thanksgiving?"

"The third week in November." He snaked an arm under her shoulders to tilt her against him. "It's a holiday for lovers who reunite permanently," he said, his voice now warm and amused.

He was teasing her somehow, but it didn't matter. She snuggled closer, wrapping an arm tight about his waist. "Permanently?"

"I want you to marry me, Lesley." His lips vibrated the skin of her temple as he spoke. "I can work in Europe. If we ever decide to live in the States, we'll make certain you're well established by then and can start your own shop there." He lowered his head to kiss her throat, her shoulder. A slick tip of warm tongue traced a crazy pattern there. "Well?" came muffled to her ears. "I promise I'll ask you again later when we're both dressed and standing."

She laughed throatily. "Yes," she promised. "Yes, yes!"
But she was soon lost in his touch, swept away again by all the
infinite possibilities of love and life together forever. Then, a
rattling of the fastened latch, a rapid knocking on the door
intruded.

They both froze. "Damn," he whispered, then lifted his
head to call, "What is it?"

"Oh, *pardon*, monsieur. I did think you and Madame go out
by now." Anne-Marie's heavily accented voice sounded through
the door.

"Later, Anne-Marie!" He gazed down at Lesley as she
stared up at him from the mussed linen pillow two heads had
hollowed out. His voice came raspy now. "Where were we,
sweetheart?"

"She'll know what's going on," she whispered. "Your voice
sounded all drowsy and annoyed."

"Annoyed, not drowsy. And so what if she knows?" He
shrugged his big bare shoulders. "She's old enough—and she's
French."

"But so unhappy, Paul, you've seen the way she looks at
us."

"I didn't know you'd noticed. Those hot, dark eyes say she's
more curious than shocked, so let's not worry about it," he
murmured and bent to kiss her pouted lips.

She pushed both palms hard against his hairy chest. "Hot,
dark eyes, indeed, Paul Kendal!"

But the flowing rush of love soon spun them under. It was
only later, when Lesley tried to strike up a conversation with
the testy Anne-Marie, she found the reason to ask Paul to move
on from their lovely little trysting place at Châtillon.

"Anne-Marie, I was just wondering if there is anyone
special in your life," Lesley asked. She watched the pretty
young brunette feed the geese out behind the inn after supper
when the skies had cleared. "It's only that you seem often
alone here, and you're such a lovely girl. I don't mean to pry,
but are there no young men about in Châtillon?"

The eyes—which were dark and hot at that—darted to
Lesley and then back to her task. Her words were halting and

so quiet that Lesley had to strain to grasp them. "There was my Claude, *oui*, but now there is also the war."

"But France is not at war."

Huge fistfuls of grain rained down at the gathered geese. "There will be, they say. Madame, do you not know that north of this province is Alsace-Lorraine on the—the border with Germany, and even Alsace-Lorraine is filled with Frenchmen who are Germans at heart?" Her fist, which clutched the top of the grain sack, hit her breast for emphasis, though her voice remained small, an angry hiss almost. "Have you heard nothing of the great war the Germans fought here across the Guyon fields but twenty years ago?"

"Of course I have, Anne-Marie, and I'm sorry this area had a rough go of it. My uncle died here in France in that war. But France and Britain have given Germany an ultimatum not to go one step farther to invade Poland, let alone come here. Your Claude has gone into the army, then?"

"Claude and my brothers now, soon all of France's young men." She sniffed and turned away, but her words still barely floated to Lesley in the cooling evening breeze. "It does not help me you are sorry, for you and Monsieur Paul being so in love before my eyes. Claude is tall like him, Monsieur Paul. He laughs like Monsieur Paul, but if the Germans come here no one will be laughing again."

Lesley wanted to comfort the girl, but her back was so stiff, one fist thrust so hard into the hemp sack, that it seemed she would punch the bottom through. "Anne-Marie, if the French army is being built up, surely France will stand firm no matter what Hitler tries, and your Claude will return to you forever."

The girl sniffed again and gave the smallest shrug. "My *grandmaman*, she told me before she died, 'I have seen the fall of many things eternal.' I am young, but I know she spoke the truth. But I wish you happiness with Monsieur Paul." Clutching the empty sack tightly to her, Anne-Marie turned away, and the door of the kitchen quickly swallowed the dark slash of her streaming hair and green dress.

But Lesley could not forget, and so for the sake of Anne-Marie and her own peace of mind, she told Paul what the girl had said, and they moved on the next day.

* * *

Three weeks later, after a leisurely drive through Bordeaux
where the fiery Gascon lifestyle of being "free fighters, free
lovers, and free spenders" suited Paul and Lesley perfectly,
they drove into Italy to Venice where neither of them had ever
visited. The serene pace of Venice made Anne-Marie's words
and France's fears of fighting more muted than ever. Paul had
the Buick sent back via ship to England when Lesley talked
him into spending the rest of their time here together.

They wandered the canal-laced city endlessly by gondola or
on foot from their luxurious suite in the palatial fifteenth-
century, fancifully arcaded Gritti Hotel. Painted barges under
their second-story windows drifted by with singing musicians.
Hand in hand they strolled vast art galleries where they studied
the great Venetian masters Titian, Tintoretto, and Veronese.
Lesley recalled that the imposingly stern Cesare Valente,
brother to her aunt Rissa's husband, collected works by these
artists. Both her aunt and uncle, Franco Valente, had died, but
Franco's elder brother, Count Cesare, oversaw the fur empire
and reared the two orphaned Valente sons. It was Count Cesare
she hoped would give her at least a temporary position in
Rome.

Meanwhile, during their respite in Venice, she and Paul set
out for the Commedia dell'Arte Theatre one evening only to be
caught in a monumental jam of gondolas on the water. Once
inside, they laughed more at the noisy, elaborately attired
audience, for whom the night was dedicated less to seeing than
to being seen. The chandeliers were left lighted during the
entire performance to reveal two delightful comedies, one on
the stage and one in the seats.

On the third Sunday in July, they joined the entire city in the
Festival of the Redeemer in rather lively thanks for the city's
salvation from a sixteenth-century plague of typhus. At the
austere white Palladian church Il Redentore across the wide
Guidecca Canal, rejoicing Venetians whiled the day away. In
their own boats or in others', pressed tightly together like a
floating city, they ate, drank, made noise and music, and
shared the traditional dishes of sweet, purplish mulberries.
Then, every stranger suddenly a friend, the entire flotilla
rowed to Lido Beach to watch the sun rise.

Lesley saw the outside world now through the filmy scrim of their love. Each movement, each sensation they shared was vibrant, but all else seemed drifting and diaphanous. Memories of precious moments were like treasured jewels nestled in the soft velvet box of her mind. The light from shuttered afternoon windows spilled zebralike across their naked bodies on the silk-sheeted bed. He had turned to her just after they had set out on a gondola ride one morning and whispered, "I need you again. Right now!" and they had paid the grinning, shrug-shouldered gondolier to turn about, bumping other boats to rush them back to their hotel where they fell into the bed they had just left.

Once over breakfast when she had asked him what sweet roll he fancied, his green eyes had darkened, his mouth had tightened, and he'd said, "Only a sweet roll with you." Their pastries and morning drinks had gone stone-cold as they'd made love joyously on the couch next to the waiting table. Once, he'd pressed her into the corner of the small, mirrored red-velvet lift and held the door closed while they kissed so hotly they were oblivious to where they were until someone rang the emergency bell.

She blossomed and flourished in the warmth of his love, became more skilled and daring in the tumultuous impact of emotional and physical union. She adored the feel his caresses gave her body—slightly swollen lips from his kisses, a languorous fullness in her breasts and thighs, and a tingling all over her skin she compared to being brushed with softest mink when she merely thought of him. Devastatingly in love with Paul Kendal both in bed and out in a way she had never imagined, Lesley both floated and soared through their treasured, fleeting time together.

And so the last days of August before Paul must return to the States and she go on to Rome hurried by, merging like the reflections in the rippling canals below their windows. Colors seemed slightly smudged, shapes softer than reality. Everything real wavered in the nearly tideless motion of water. To be totally immersed in their love made everything else stand still except their plans, their future together. So easy not to hear someone occasionally shout Mussolini's motto "Believe, obey, fight!" on corners or young soldiers in the plazas singing the

Fascist anthem, "Giovinezza." So much better not to notice
Blackshirt posters about big rallies called *adunate* posted on
crumbling walls under an ageless Renaissance balcony with its
pots of innocent hanging geraniums.

Let the fog draining the colors from St. Mark's Square and
the blizzard of pigeons there obscure everything but the pink
tracery of arches on the Doge's Palace and their love. Surely
their passionate commitment to each other could make time
itself stand still. Eons hence Lesley Westam and Paul Kendal
would still be sitting here at their table in Florian's Café with
their favorite bottle of Frascati and linguine salad with golden
caviar. Here on the square Paul wrote his column, hoping, he
said, for inspiration from Henry James's ghost, as he had loved
this café in Victorian times. And Lesley would be here,
smiling, forever drawing sketches of mink and sable coats far
into their last afternoon.

But dinnertime came, and night would, too. And then
tomorrow they would take trains in separate directions away
from timeless Venice and each other.

"You look absolutely stunning tonight, my sweetheart,"
Paul told her as she joined him on the carved marble balcony
of their suite where they had decided to have their last dinner.
His gaze swept her from elegantly sculpted rolls of thick
burnished hair to the gold lamé sandals. She wore a flowing
moss-green and white silk draped gown held to her slender
body by the twist of gold belt. Her mother's pearls and
matching eardrops were the best of the jewelry she'd brought,
as she'd left most of the rest behind with her grandmum. She
pivoted slowly to reveal her back bare to the waist in the soft
frame of fluted drapery. She'd packed this dress she'd once
modeled in at Sackville's in case the Valentes ever had her to
a formal do at their Roman town house or villa, but this night
was surely far dearer than that occasion could ever be. The
huge full moon across the sweep of the Grand Canal threw a
path to their window. Paul's gaze glowed with love and
moonlight as if illumined from within. She had the distinct
feeling those intense eyes could see clear to her Parisienne
flesh-rose lingerie—and beyond.

He too looked formal and elegant tonight in a double-breasted oyster linen suit with navy blue shirt, white buckskin shoes, and matching dotted scarf and handkerchief. She plucked one dark red carnation from the centerpiece on their small round white-linen-covered table and put it in his buttonhole while his big hands gently clasped her waist. On the rippling canal waters below, the words of Lord Byron's now familiar Venetian song drifted to them accompanied by the plaintive thrumming of a mandolin: "So, we'll go no more a-roving so late into the night, though the heart be still as loving, and the moon be still as bright."

"You're the most beautiful woman I've ever known, Lesley." Paul's voice broke into the song that moved them both nearly to tears. She tilted her chin up; a hint of smile trembled on her lips. "Beautiful inside as well as out," he whispered, his voice unusually rough with emotion. "I have something for you I had intended to give you later, but I don't think I can wait."

He loosed her to take out a small green leather box filagreed in gold. He extended it to her. "I'm not sure I ever really formally proposed, and since this is our last night—for a while—I want you to have this." He cleared his throat. His eyes were as moist as hers. With trembling fingers, she lifted the lid. A ruby ring glinted up at her all set in spirals of antique gold roses and nestled in white velvet. She stared down at it for a moment as her tears blurred the box, his big hand. "I'll bring you a good old American diamond engagement ring, a wedding ring too when I come back," he rushed on. "But since you're going to be in Rome as you wanted, alone for a while, until things are settled with the Valentes, I want anyone you meet to understand you belong to me. Will you marry me, Lesley? Will you wear this ring and wait for me to come back?"

The wistful song began below again, but she paid no attention to the words now. "Yes, Paul." She threw herself into his arms. "Yes! Yes, I promise!"

The ring fit beautifully, so beautifully, just as everything with Paul did in this single, suspended moment. And together, if they loved hard and long enough, they could surely, somehow, as his little piece of fiction said, hold back the dawn.

❧ ❧ *Chapter Five*

LESLEY AND PAUL parted at Venice's Stazione Santa Lucia at seven in the morning. As her train lurched, then chugged away, he ran briefly beside her window, his face so intent, his black hair tugged back from his creased forehead. His mouth repeatedly formed the words "I love you!" but she could no longer hear over the shriek of steam and whistle. She stuck her head out to wave a lace handkerchief while he dropped farther and farther behind. His tall form grew smaller, merged with the others shifting across the long platform. He waved his hand madly, like a child. Her carriage snaked around a bend of track. Sunlight outside blinded her, and he was gone.

She dabbed tears away from her slick cheeks and took her seat, self-conscious for the first time at the stares of others. One lady flashed her a smile; a thin old woman winked as if she understood. At first she sat rigidly, staring out at the blur of countryside. But her shoulders and bravado slumped as the first hour slipped by. Separation from him stunned her. She was hardly aware of the first stop, of people exiting the carriage, of rotating views streaming by the window.

But now, hours later, she felt rather ill and so wretchedly tired. They hadn't slept a bit last night, then had risen at five to meet their trains. But in the months ahead, before they would be reunited for good, she had much to do and had to keep her mind on that. Her resolve surged back to challenge her anew. She sat up straight, lifted her chin. Today was a new beginning, she told herself, and their love would carry her on as surely as this train.

The baking August sun drenched her compartment, so she cracked the dusty window a few inches and pulled the parchment shade down farther. She'd insisted on paying for her ticket herself. She certainly had enough money to get her to Rome and then some. This part of her journey to earn her way with the Valentes must be on her own. She could cable her grandmum for other funds she'd left with her if a position did not work out in Rome.

She refused to fret about her reception by the Valentes. Her mother had lived happily with them in their Roman town house for several years after her twin sister, Rissa, married Franco Valente. And they had been kind to her and Mother during their holiday there fifteen years ago, although that was before both her aunt Rissa and uncle Franco had died. Surely, she encouraged herself, her ties to her aunt Rissa's family as well as her skills as a fur model, sorter, and matcher would make Count Cesare and his two nephews, who had become more or less his stepsons over the years, willing to take her in and give her a go at obtaining more experience.

She sighed and readjusted the window shade again. The Italian concept of *prime classe* coach accommodations, at least under Mussolini, left something to be desired. Worn leather seats, window-shade tassels frayed or missing, the carpet terribly threadbare and mottled. And nine hours to Rome with stops in Padua, Bologna, Florence, Arezzo, and Orvieto—despite the fact this was dubbed an express, *treno diretto per Roma*. At least the other passengers in the glassed-in compartment had gotten off. She stretched her tired legs up on the seat, pleased to have it to herself now.

She ate only a little of the fruit she'd purchased from a vendor in Bologna. Fascist posters plastered everywhere in the squat gray-stone station had oppressed her and made her stomach more queasy. "Nothing above the State," the printed broadsheets shouted in bold black letters with the skull and crossbone symbol of Mussolini's special *squadristi* police in sharp red. The people had looked aimless. The station in Florence had depressed her, too: wailing children, frazzled women, elderly men or scrawny boys or the Blackshirt soldiers with their rifles guarding against who knew what. Unable to hold her eyelids open any longer, she dozed sporadically as the fields of Tuscany slipped by.

"Nothing above the State," the outrageous motto danced through her brain, but she knew the words lied. Paul came first, their love, their future. And the furs, piles of them all ready to be stretched, cut, and sewn. Mounds of their luxurious softness, like the Valente sable she'd brought along and insisted on hanging here in this compartment, though her luggage and the painting of the lovers in the canary phaeton were stored in the baggage carriage. Deep-pile furs like the feather bed in Châtillon where she and Paul had made love all those nights above the gardens, before Anne-Marie knocked on the door and said that nothing lasts forever, nothing but the State.

She jerked bolt upright. A woman with raven-black hair pulled back in a neat knot, wearing a faded blue suit, grasped a huge-eyed girl about five years old firmly by the hand. They both stared at her. Quickly she twisted to put her feet on the floor.

"*Scusi*, signorina," the woman said, "but I knocked on the door first. We may join you?"

"*Si*," Lesley told her. Although the girl seemed meek, the woman yanked her sharply into the compartment. Lesley frowned, then forced a taut smile. They were an odd pair to be in first class. Lesley almost asked to see their tickets, but she'd let the conductor do that if he ever showed his face again on this ill-run train. The woman's hand cupped the child's knee; she hovered much too close to her with the heat and the wide seat, as if to be sure she behaved. But the child squirmed away and boldly rolled up the shade a few inches to press her nose to the window.

Their clothes looked shabby but clean; their skin was brown, their worn hands had broken fingernails; to have spent extra lire for a first-class compartment. The woman looked perhaps thirty. She had once been pretty, but now cobweb lines around her mouth and harsh eyes had ruined that. Her gaze roved the carriage, curiously examining Lesley's crisp blue linen suit, her hanging canvas bag in the corner hiding the Valente sable, even her ruby ring she nonchalantly slid under her other hand. Without a word the woman dominated the child and the compartment. She had the bearing of someone who was where she ought to be.

Lesley recrossed her legs the other way again. Her muscles ached. She felt closed in now. She wished the child had rolled the shade up more so the adults had somewhere to look away, too.

"My name is Lidia Comi, and this is my daughter, Daniela," the woman told Lesley finally in her rather rough Italian and continued her thorough perusal of the compartment from under sooty lashes.

"That's a lovely name, Daniela," Lesley offered, though the child hardly looked her way. "I'm Lesley Westam. Are you from Arezzo where we just stopped, then? I'm afraid I was a bit done in and nodded off."

The woman's eyes narrowed at the question; her voice was rough. "From Cortona, but the train does not stop there. I am a widow taking my only child to Rome."

They chatted more easily about the countryside, and Lesley shared fruit with Lidia and little Daniela who, unlike many Italian children Lesley had seen, had evidently been taught to be seen and not heard. Lesley had intended to ask them about the political situation in Cortona and Rome, but she hesitated when Lidia boasted of Daniela's participation in Mussolini's club for young children called Il Duce's Sons of Wolf. The girl merely nodded, and edged as far away from her mother as she could. Their stilted conversation tapered off, and eventually they all began to doze as the afternoon heat threw a pall over them.

When the train chugged into the little Orvieto station at the foot of the mountain-clinging town itself, the last stop before Rome, Lesley woke to see Lidia also peering anxiously out the window. "This is not Rome yet, you know," Lesley assured her with a smile.

"No. No, of course not, only I shall take Daniela for a walk here," she announced and grabbed the girl's hand.

"It looks rather crowded out there," Lesley protested mildly.

"Good for the legs and to make the time have wings. We will be here twenty minutes. I checked," Lidia told her and pulled Daniela to her feet. "You know, since Il Duce rules the Empire, the trains run more on time. Will you step out with us, too?"

Lesley shook her head only to realize she had a headache. "No, thanks awfully though."

"You know no one in Orvieto?" Lidia turned back at the door to inquire.

"Not a soul," Lesley admitted. "You and Daniela be careful now."

When Lidia tugged Daniela outside, Lesley lowered the shade to keep from being stared at. More posters, more people, more of Il Duce's soldiers with rifles. That woman's adoration of the dictator was all too obvious. She seemed bossy and overbearing when Lesley had expected Mussolini's followers to be meek as sheep. She wondered what the Romans, especially the Valentes, thought of Il Duce Benito Mussolini. Despite the heat, she shut out the sounds by reaching up under the shade to firmly fasten the window. She closed her eyes and leaned her head back on the seat. Her thoughts drifted again to Paul. Strange to find the love of one's life almost by accident on the day they buried Father. Poor Anne-Marie Guyon's French *grandmaman* had been wrong about nothing being eternal. Her love for Paul would be. She opened her heavy eyelids to glance dreamily down at the ring on the third finger of her left hand. Someday, on an anniversary perhaps, she and Paul would return to lovely Châtillon and she would find Anne-Marie to show her some things could last forever.

She jumped up as someone rapped hard on her window from outside. She lifted the shade a few inches and peered down. The Italian woman, Lidia Comi, with tears streaming from her coal-black eyes.

Lesley yanked up the shade, the window. "Whatever is it?"

"Daniela, my Daniela. Please, please, Signorina. She has wandered off in the crowd and she is all I have. I am searching, then I think the English Signorina Westam, she is kind to us. She too knows my Daniela's face. We have at least fifteen more minutes. Please, Signorina, or my Daniela will be lost forever."

Lesley hesitated. She should just say no. Perhaps the conductor who had not put in an appearance for hours could help. She could at least find him as she had no desire to traipse through that crowd out there. And however could that child have escaped her grasping mother? But the woman's pleas, her tears, a lost child overcame her reluctance and fluttery stomach.

"All right. Yes, one moment," Lesley promised the woman who had not budged. She gathered up her purse and her canvas bag with the sable so as not to let them out of her sight in this apparently untended carriage.

The woman had at least found others to help in the frantic search, and Lesley felt better about it as she hurried down the iron steps to the terrazzo station floor. Soon, she found herself at the head of a small search party the nearly hysterical Lidia had somehow collected.

Lesley's eyes skimmed a hundred faces as some local lad who seemed to know the area herded them toward one side of the station. Lidia, barking orders to her group, went the other way. Dust hovered in the stifling air. Lesley wiped her brow with her hand and shoved loose curls back from flushed cheeks. Walking this far, she might have to board the train in third class and walk through the swaying carriages back to first class, she thought, and her faint feeling of nausea from the long ride rose to weaken her knees again.

The others dropped away when the crowd thinned out near the end of the station. "Look, I really must go back," she told the thin lad at her elbow. "I'm sorry, I just don't see the girl."

The boy darted ahead. He turned, spun one thin arm like a windmill, then called back to her across the narrow lane where the few stone buildings surrounding the station began. "Lady, there's a little girl over here. She's crying!"

She dashed around the corner, one ear attuned for the warning whistle of their train. And there, where the boy pointed, sat the sobbing Daniela. She sighed with relief. She would pay someone to carry the child back. They would meet the crying Lidia Comi, and they could all cry with joy together. Wait until she wrote Paul about this, an adventure of sorts on her very first day away from him when she had been so certain her life would be not half so exciting now.

"Quick," she ordered the lad, "you find the mother and I'll see to Daniela." Despite the bulky bag she held, she knelt to examine the huddled girl. But instantly, Lidia appeared, coming up a flight of stairs at the other end of the alley. Lesley's head jerked up. She stood. Puzzlement creased her warm brow. The woman was no longer crying, though Daniela sniffled on pitifully.

"I am sorry, Signorina, but if you wish to catch your train, you must leave the clothes bag, your money, and the ruby ring with us," Lidia Comi rasped, her voice so cold.

Lesley's insides leapt. All this a ruse then? This woman and this sniveling child intended to rob her? Run! her brain screamed even as she heard the first, now too distant, shriek of the train's warning whistle. But when she darted a glance back, the boy had returned. Worse, he'd been joined by another—a brawny man she'd never seen. Blast them, a whole family of thieves!

She lunged over the hump of child in the narrow alley, thrust hard at the woman. She seized the canvas bag, tore it away before Lesley grabbed it back. The man and boy pulled at her, yanked the sable away. This was not happening. Nightmare only! Her eyes rolled in fear. She struck out blindly.

"No! Help me!" her scream shredded the air as the train shrieked again.

She kneed the man, flailed out at the lad. They had her now. She had to stop, but she couldn't bear to part with the ring too. Fury roared through her. At the top of the steps, she kicked the lad away as he tore at her purse. Frenzy to be free of their hands energized her. The man tried to clamp his dirty palm over her mouth. She bit down hard and tasted blood. His big fist came from nowhere at her face.

Stark surprise slammed into her. And stars, stars or rockets at home on Guy Fawkes Day. Then steps down! She hit them, rolling, falling. Pain crushed her head, her arm. She gasped for air. For release. She reached out to press herself into Paul's warm embrace, but cold night held her hard.

She swam upward from vast blackness slowly, tugged at by pain if she moved an arm or turned her head. She hurt all over. Why? Why? A long parade of endless marching dreams stretched out behind her. The days in France with Paul. Under their balcony the lapping waters of Venetian canals she drank so greedily in the heat when Gram's gentle hands held the water to her lips. That was surely Gram's touch, and she was home again at Westam. Mother had died in that big black breathing machine and Father had gone now, too. But Gram was still there in the gardens by the little inn feeding the geese and bringing Paul to her through the thick yews cut in the most fantastic shapes of ruby rings and sable coats and rushing trains.

Her eyes shot open. A white ceiling, a dimly lit small stucco room she'd never seen. She remembered and gasped.

A figure rose from a chair by the narrow bed and slowly, painfully, Lesley turned her eyes. A nun. A plump nun with a kindly smile and huge gilded crucifix swinging free from her ample bosom on a bright blue cord that matched the one around her large waist as she bent over the bed. Then she had been very sick, and the nurse had not been Gram but this woman.

"*Buon giorno.* All is well, is fine. Not to be afraid," the woman murmured. The pursed mouth smiled. The warm brown eyes did, too.

Lesley's mouth felt dry. So stiff, her tongue heavy. She tried to speak; a frown crushed her features at the exertion. Her forehead was taped, bandaged. She could feel each separate sore muscle. "I speak Italian, holy sister," she managed, her voice scratchy.

The smile in the plain face broadened. The eyes actually twinkled. "I did not know. You spoke only English in your fever. Praise the Holy Mother you are back with us now."

"But where?"

"In Orvieto, safe with the Sisters of Mary Immaculate, our little hospital here. You fell down a flight of stairs near the station below Orvieto. Poor dear lady, you were robbed."

It all spilled back over her, the woman who admired Mussolini and the sobbing child she had warped to be the pawn in the whole thing. All those dreadful Fascist posters, those Blackshirts standing about. Her stupid naïveté in helping them, the struggle, the beating, the fall. She shuddered, then with a great surge of effort lifted her bruised left arm and saw her ring was gone. "My engagement ring! I had a fur coat with me too in a canvas sack!"

The nun took her trembling hand and pressed it down gently to the cool bedsheets. "I am so sorry, but, indeed, you are blessed of God to have your life. Your ribs and arm are better, your head contusions healing. Worldly things, well . . . You were found with nothing but the clothes on your back. When Dr. Orazi, who comes to us once a week, realized you might have been on the train to Rome, he checked for your baggage. I am sorry, dear lady, but there was nothing of yours on the train but a painting they have sent back to you. See."

The sister loosed Lesley's hand and moved away to lift the crated Stubbs painting. Tears flooded Lesley's eyes as she fought to focus them at the distant figure and object. Her dazed mind fought to encompass the impact of it all: her luggage gone, her money, the Valente sable, Paul's ring—Paul. She ached all over lying here in this tiny room when she should have been with the Valentes—when? Yesterday. But bandages shrouded her throbbing head and right arm. Her pale skin looked mottled black and blue. No, she would not be going to the Valentes until she was more presentable. She hoped the nuns would let her stay a day or two.

Her eyes slipped closed. She struggled to open them and failed. "Sister, forgive me, I'm so sleepy now. Just a little nap."

"Of course, dear lady. The tag on your painting says you are Lesley Westam, a British subject, en route to Roma's Tiburtina Station. Is it so?"

The bruised lips barely moved. "Yes."

"You sleep now. I will tell everyone our English lady has regained consciousness and speaks such lovely Italian. I shall call Dr. Orazi when you awaken next time. He is back today and wishes to see you again."

Lesley's eyes slitted open. "You said he comes only once a week."

"Yes, dear lady, but you have been with us for nine days already. Rest now," she said, yet hovered near the bed.

Nine days, nine days lost. Paul would have already sailed from Liverpool on the *Athenia*. He might have tried to call or cable her at Valente's and would have heard she was not there. He would be frantic with worry. She lifted her heavy eyelids again. "Sister, is it September second yet?"

"September third and much has happened in the world, but we shall tell you later. Sleep now and I will bring the doctor. Sleep."

Sleep. Paul was out on the sea and she was here adrift in an aching, injured body without him. She tried to summon up his face, his voice to comfort her, tried even to picture the lord and lady of her little Stubbs painting out for a drive in their canary carriage. But everything moved and hummed around her as if she were riding in Paul's Buick, and so she slept.

Dr. Orazi was short and wiry, but his voice boomed big and reassuring. Absolutely nothing had happened to her that time wouldn't heal, he assured her, and behind him her guardian angel, Sister Theresa, smiled and tears filled her eyes. "I am sorry for the things you lost, but since you say you have family to go to in Rome, we shall not worry for your future, *si*?" he said. "We shall tell the *polizia* what you told us about this Lidia Comi and her little band. Meanwhile, the Sisters of Mary Immaculate will keep you here with them until you are ready to go on. Believe me, in times of future trial they can be a great source of support and strength."

Lesley leaned gratefully into the pile of pillows the nun had plumped up to support her. "But you said I am healing fast, doctor. Is there something else you haven't told me?"

The little man shifted nervously where he sat on the foot of her narrow bed. He moved closer, rustling his papers on her tests in one hand and took her wrist in the other as if to check her pulse again. "Sister Theresa tells me one of the things you said the thieves took was an engagement ring. Your young man then, he is not in Rome?"

"No," Lesley admitted, with a tilt of chin. "He's an American and sailing home from England on this very day."

"Then what I have to say you must hear alone for now. Our examination of you, a few tests when you were first brought in . . . You see, Signorina Westam," he said, lowering his deep basso voice at last, "the other injuries aside, you are with child."

Her body twitched in a painful jolt that nearly heaved her into him. She grabbed her wrist back. "I? With child. Pregnant? But it cannot be! He used—I mean we—"

"Were careful? An old story, Signorina Westam. Forgive me for speaking frankly, but diaphragms, condoms—all but abstinence—can fail," he said and shook his head.

Color flooded Lesley's face, spread down her body as if a fierce fever attacked her again. But they'd never—never without Paul's using a safe. He had told her it was safe! A child and he was sailing half a world away from her and the Valentes!

"A shock, of course, but the man is your fiancé whatever thieves dared to take your ring, *si*?" He patted her hand while, like an idiot, she gaped at him. She *was* an idiot! She had actually believed her monthly curse was disturbed by their frequent lovemaking when all the time—all the time, they had made a child together in that little room in Châtillon. And after she had told him she would sacrifice anything to protect a child of hers from scandal! She had thought her upset stomach the last weeks in Venice and on the train was pure emotion!

Despite the pain, she lifted her left hand beseechingly a few inches from the bed. "When, doctor? The baby—when?"

"Perhaps you can tell me better, *si*?"

Slowly, barely moving her fingers, she counted the months to herself, once, twice. "I am not certain. Late March or April, I suppose. I just can't believe it."

"But, praise to the Lord Jesus, your beating in the hands of those brigands and your fall did not harm the precious life you carry," he said and stood at last. "I shall see you next week then, and Sister Theresa will sit with you now if you wish."

"I'm fine. I'd like to be alone."

"*Si*, of course." He started to the door with Sister Theresa in his wake, then turned back. "Do not grieve for the gift of life from God, Signorina Westam. And, a blessing the man has promised to marry you."

She stared down at her body shrouded in the sheets. A baby growing there when she seemed so slender, so frail. She pulled her eyes back up. "Whatever I grieve for in my life, Dr. Orazi, it will never be for that man or our child, for I shall always love both."

"*Si*, a strong woman, I knew it, Sister Theresa!" he boomed out, and the portly little nun's face beamed even as tears filled her eyes again.

Two days later Lesley sat on a stone bench in the brown travertine courtyard. Around her lay the fragrant medicinal herb garden of the little hospital of the Sisters of Mary Immaculate, sometimes called the Blue Nuns for their distinctive cobalt-blue waist and crucifix cords. Among the neatly

aligned plots of blooming pinkish foxglove, nodding red and
white poppies, and aromatic feverfew, she let the afternoon sun
warm her. Her head was no longer bandaged nor her right arm
wrapped. Her bruises were finally fading, her strength slowly
returning, but her cracked ribs were tightly bound and she felt
them each time she breathed. Her hands rested almost protectively across her stomach. She wore the full, long-sleeved
black cotton dress of a postulant tied in back like a pinafore,
which the nuns had given her to wear while her blue linen suit
was cleaned and mended. Of her extensive wardrobe, including things in her stolen luggage and what she'd left with her
friend Susan Ashmont in London, it was all that remained.
When the thieves had used the claim tags in her purse to get her
luggage off the train, the Stubbs painting was evidently all they
had missed. What a triumphal entry she had planned for Rome.
Now she would arrive pregnant and destitute, at least until the
funds she had asked Sister Theresa to cable her grandmum for
in England came through.

She'd fought a pathway through so many jagged emotions
since awakening two days ago: anger, relief, longing, disbelief, joy, fear. Of all the things she longed for in her life, a
child was surely one of the most precious. Of all the things she
dreaded in her life, a child born out of wedlock as she had been
and suffered for was one of the most awful. Paul had promised
to be back to her in Rome in November, but she would be over
four months pregnant if he made it back then at all. The most
terrible things had happened in the world outside as well as in
her own. Four days ago on September first, Hitler's forces
invaded Poland. Britain and France had declared war. In
England, women and children were being evacuated from
London to the countryside in case of aerial attack, and the
cities across the country were being blacked out at night to
avoid becoming targets in the dark. The nuns had told her. She
hadn't had the heart to read the newspapers they offered her,
not with the pro-German slant to the news from Mussolini's
censorship of the press. She couldn't help it: she still mistrusted and detested all such papers and those who wrote them.

Sister Theresa came toward her across the courtyard and
Lesley stood slowly. The portly little nun glided in a slightly
rolling gait like a determined ship in a storm, her black

billowing skirts about her feet the breaking waves before her sturdy prow. Lesley's heart fell. The perpetually smiling woman had not even been cowed by news of the war, but her face was grim now. She and two other nuns had walked into town to inquire about Lesley's cable for money and to give the *polizia* her written statement about her attackers.

"Sit, dear Lesley, sit. I know your strength has not returned yet," Sister Theresa insisted and indicated the bench with her plump hand.

"But it does one good to stretch. And my father taught me to stand in the presence of someone I respect and admire, Sister Theresa. You have been such a help to me, and I'm awfully grateful."

Still no smile. Not even a hint of the smile that so often lit her soft brown eyes. "And you have been a blessing to me, my dear Lesley. Now sit, and I with you."

They sat close together, their black-draped knees almost touching. "The news about my cable for the money from England—Mussolini's alliance with Hitler has held that up as we feared?"

Sister Theresa grasped her big crucifix in her hands. She looked briefly off across the neat patchwork-quilt garden of herbs other nuns were tending, bent over hoes or on their knees in the sun. "Yes, no messages to or from England are being allowed through yet." The eyes sought Lesley's again. "The war will cause so many harsh things we must find faith to accept."

"Quite, but as you said earlier, holy sister, we must not fret for only worldly things." Lesley inclined her head and leaned forward to touch the nun's arm. "Now that I have the child to think of, I have come to accept that better. Is there something else? The Germans have not brought their blitzkrieg to France or England, too?"

"No, my dear, not exactly. But there is another disappointment I fear you must face." Her voice rushed on now, the eyes round velvet pools of agony. "You are so lovely and strong, in heart and soul as well as body. I know that will take you far in life, and yet sadly I must tell you something terribly hard to accept, but with God's help, you shall."

Lesley's insides cartwheeled. She bit her lower lip. Her

grandmother had died. A message from Paul through Lady Sarah? His family had insisted he marry that Melissa Pearson. But no, no. No messages from England were being allowed through, and Paul could barely be back to Canada, where the *Athenia* was to land, let alone to New York City yet. She gripped the edge of the tilting carved stone bench and did not let go as Sister Theresa slowly removed from the folds of her flowing gown a page from an Italian newspaper and unfolded it on her black-skirted knees.

"No. What is it?" Lesley asked, her voice catching. "Something more about Hitler or Mussolini?"

"Besides the invasion of Poland, there was another reason Britain declared war on the godless Huns on September third." Sister Theresa's voice began to quaver. "I'm afraid, you see, a German U-boat torpedoed and sank a British ship out from Liverpool, and one hundred twelve passengers including twenty-eight Americans were killed. They have printed the list of the dead here, dear Lesley, and I am so sorry that—"

"No!" Lesley screamed. "No!"

Nuns stood and stared. "Journalists always lie!" she shouted at Sister Theresa, who dropped the paper on the grass and reached out to seize Lesley's hand. Tears leapt to Lesley's eyes, coursed down her cheeks. She shook her head fiercely, and her loosened hair blinded her. She leapt to her feet, pulled away from Sister Theresa's touch. "Not the *Athenia*! Not his ship!" she shrieked, and the courtyard echoed her words.

"May heaven comfort you, I am so sorry. Yes, yes, it is here, the ship you told me, his name you told me—"

"No, no! He can't! He can't! He can't!" she repeated in a frenzied litany of stubborn defiance. She screamed at the journalists who wrote Paul's name on that paper. At the men who made this war. Father should never have died to leave her alone. Trent detested her. Paul had left her all alone with the child!

Sobbing pitifully, she collapsed in the little nun's sturdy arms. Around them, the others crossed themselves and knelt to pray amid the herbs for the poor English lady whose pain no medicine could ever cure.

❦ ❦ *Chapter Six*

ALL ROADS lead to Rome, they said, and today it was finally true for Lesley Westam. She was grateful the vegetable lorry driver from Orvieto the nuns had asked to take her to the city on his way to market was so talkative. She had spent endless days and nights grieving and praying silently for Paul in the echoing quiet of her room or the little Maria Immaculata chapel. She had tried desperately to accept her life with his child but without him.

Paul's death wracked her more deeply than even Mother's or Father's had. Paul had been not so much her past or present as her entire future. Sometimes his loss hurt so much she wasn't certain she'd been better off to know him. He'd come into her life like some bold, rescuing knight in his canary phaeton and taken her for the most wonderful ride. Then he'd let her out into a darkness of soul much vaster than that he had saved her from that night on the road near Westam.

Until her battle with Trent and this European war were settled, a life for herself and her child with the Valentes was her only option, although the Sisters of Mary Immaculate had offered to have her stay on with them until the baby was born. If the Valentes would not take her in, she really had nowhere to go since her passport and money were gone and the borders toward home closed. But whatever happened, she was done with daytime tears now except for the eternal inner ones. She sat up straighter on the blanket-covered seat of the ramshackle lorry and thrust out her chin as they jolted along the busy four-lane Via Flaminia into the pulsing core of Rome.

Yet panic momentarily froze her as it had in great chilly blasts these last twelve days, much like an attack of claustrophobia. She should have written to let the Valentes know she was coming, to tell them what had befallen her. They would want no part of her now that her mother had been dead for years and her mother's twin, Countess Rissa, had died in an automobile crash seven years ago. Especially not when they eventually found out she was illegimately pregnant. An internationally reputable firm like Valente's would have all the models and fur sorters it needed. She and the child would be homeless with the war escalating, aliens at the mercy of a vast city where she knew only the Valentes.

But Lesley firmly seized hold of her rampaging fears and emotions. She brushed back windblown hair, then clasped her hands tightly in her lap again. She was better for having shared her life with Paul. Oblivious to the driver's—Mauro Rugano's—off-key singing, she nodded from time to time to boost her morale. She had an unborn child to protect. She had a career to pursue and beautiful memories to cherish forever. And yet, as Mauro sang tune after dissonant tune, the words to the melody sung under her and Paul's window in Venice haunted her again as it had for days: "So we'll go no more a-roving so late into the night, though the heart be still as loving, and the moon be still as bright—"

"Your family here on the Via Condotti we get to soon." The man's gravelly sing-song voice jarred her back to busy Rome. "How many in the family, you say?"

She stared out the window even as she answered. "Cesare, the head of the fur business and the family, is my deceased uncle's brother. Let's see, I imagine he must be about fifty now. He has two nephews, my cousins, Guido, the eldest, probably about my age, and Carlo, four or so years younger. But I remember them only as lads from my visit in nineteen twenty-four."

"Nineteen twenty-four," Mauro crooned as he wheeled the bouncy lorry left onto the Via Condotti. "A good year, nineteen twenty-four." Lesley leaned closer to the dirty windscreen to study the fashionable shop façades as people strolled up and down the narrow pavements or zigzagged across the street in front of clogged traffic. Mauro's voice rolled over her like an aria from a warped gramophone recording. "In nineteen twenty-four, I marry my Lucia, start a family with her, right away, we did."

Lesley tried to ignore his words. Excitement coursed through her despite the fact her entry into Rome today was the final humbling experience to settle any lofty hopes she had once harbored. Even the imperturbable Romans stared at the sight of a rickety, noisy lorry piled high with bouncing cabbages and lettuce on the elegant Via Condotti. Jewelry, leather, and clothing filled shop windows, and— There was Valente's nearly at the bottom of the street with the Piazza di Spagna just beyond! How well she recalled the piazza's sweep of white marble steps all aglow in the tumble of red and white azaleas. She pointed until Mauro halted his long-winded description of his children to jerk the lumbering lorry to an abrupt stop before Valente's.

For a moment Lesley just sat and stared. It was so imposing, better than she had remembered it. But perhaps she should have gone instead to the Valente town house. Even in her blue linen suit the nuns had mended so cleverly, she wasn't attired well enough without a hat, a purse—and without courage now that Paul was no longer alive to love her.

"This is it, no? The place the holy sisters say to bring you?"

"Quite right. I can't thank you enough, Mauro. And for being such jolly good company all the way." His weathered face split into a huge grin; the massive, rounded shoulders shrugged.

"I can wait here in the street until you go in, see everyone, see if your family is there."

"No, you go on now and get your greens to the market. I'm certain I'll be fine. Thanks awfully again, and tell Sister Theresa I will write." She shook the man's hand and retrieved her crated painting from the floor under her feet. Cradling it to her, she climbed down from her lofty perch to the wide running board of the rusty black lorry and then to the brown paving stones of the street. Ignoring stares of passers-by, she did not even turn to wave as Mauro ground the gears, blared the horn, and rattled off.

She narrowed her eyes to study the façade of the fur salon—a blinding forehead of white marble with glass eyes glinting in the late afternoon sun. A boldly striped black and white awning arched over the entryway with the words "Valente di Roma" scripted in gold on the carved wooden door. Gold-veined Carrara marble from the floor inside stretched out onto the pavement like a polished doormat. Two recessed windows across the front each displayed a spectacular coat fanned out across draped white velvet. As she slowly stepped closer, she saw one was a smashing Russian broadtail with sable trim and the other a uniquely bias-cut silver ondatra with a posh blue fox collar.

Her reflected image stared at her in the glass, superimposed over the lush fur: a sad, wan face framed by soft coppery tresses that looked so plebeian on this street where sculpted heads of shorter cuts browsed. But had these blasé women lost the two men they loved most in just a few months' time? she asked herself as her eyes assessed those in the glass. Did any of them know what it meant to rush headlong into love as the world rushed headlong into war, only to have that war devastate one's life?

Resolutely, she strode over and pushed the door open to enter a quiet outer salon. Perhaps the Valente staff were still out for the midday closing, but the door had been open. She nodded in recognition of the distinctive style the salon exuded. Her sharp gaze drank it all in even as she heard someone approaching from out in back. The cool polished floor met pale celadon pillars in the room's four corners. Sedate groupings of overstuffed raw-silk-covered gold chairs and loveseats strewn with pillows of white Russian lynx were reflected in two facing walls of Baroque gilt-framed mirrors so that smaller replicas of the room seemed to go on forever. Urns on pedestals trailed ivy and flaming orange oleander plants. Only a petite white and gold desk in the back corner and two circles of white carpet elevated one step up for models to show coats suggested the graceful salon was anything but someone's elegant town-house lounge.

Lesley turned as the sound of high-heeled footsteps came closer. The slender saleswoman's face registered a flash of such surprise that Lesley almost fled. Surely, she was not that inappropriately attired! If this woman didn't believe her story and agree to summon one of the Valentes, she would feel so deflated! "May I be of help to you?" the woman inquired with a graceful sweep of hand. "We are only just opening again for the afternoon and evening."

"Yes, please. I'm a relative of the Valentes, a niece of Franco Valente, a cousin to Carlo and Guido, Lesley Westam from England. I—"

"The niece of Rissa Valente, of course. Your face, you see," the elegantly dressed woman said, and her stiff expression softened to a smile at last. "Please, do sit, one moment please. Just wait until they see you, signori Guido and Carlo. They are here upstairs, as Count Cesare has gone to Copenhagen on business. Wait here, Signorina Westam, please!" she said and scurried out.

Lesley perched on the edge of a chair. But she rose on trembling legs to smooth her skirt and brush her hair back with her hand when quick footsteps sounded from the back rooms. The brocade curtain shot open.

Two handsome young men who hardly looked like brothers rushed in. She squared her shoulders and lifted her chin. Tears filled her eyes as they each exclaimed their surprise and gave her the traditional kiss on both cheeks.

"I am Guido," the taller, thin man told her. His mussed-looking black hair was very straight, and he had a somewhat sardonic, long, patrician, handsome face. A quick hand brushed his hair back as he spoke. He was impeccably attired down to a gold watch and a stickpin in the elegant red silk scarf tied at the throat of his white silk shirt. His eyes, even when his smile flaunted perfect teeth, were austere and guarded.

"Cousin Lesley, I am Carlo," the shorter man told her in a voice that was quiet compared to Guido's assertive tones. Carlo actually flushed when he kissed her. His hair was rich with waves, his face rounded, less olive in hue, more boyish, his dark eyes a rich velvet texture and not polished obsidian like Guido's. Carlo hung back staring at her, instantly admiring for some reason; Guido held her off at arm's length to look her over again as a man would a woman who is hardly his cousin.

"So, indeed, whatever will the count say when he is surprised by you, dear Lesley?" Guido said with a smug smile. "The long-legged, giggling colt of an English girl who visited us once years ago is no more, and you, praise the saints, if Il Duce allows them anymore, are the perfect picture of—of what, brother dearest?"

While Lesley flushed, Carlo frowned at Guido but shook his

head in apparent amazement, as if he'd swallowed the canary. "She is beautiful, Guido, beautiful and welcome whatever the surprise. Uncle Cesare will surely be pleased if a bit startled, and you know it!"

"Of course, I know it, even more surprised and welcoming than we, eh!" He chuckled and flashed his quick smile.

"I've so much to tell you," Lesley began, filling the awkward little silence as the brothers exchanged tense glances she could not read. "I was robbed on the train to Rome, you see, and would be ever so grateful for a place to stay for a bit. I was en route from Venice—"

"Ah, Venice!" Guido interrupted with a dramatic flourish of one arm. He laughed again, ignoring Carlo's wary jab of his arm for him to behave. "*Madre Maria*, you know what they say about ladies from Venice, Lesley, so I am glad you are here in pious Rome where women know how to behave, eh, Carlo? You see, in Venice, virtuous women limit themselves to a husband and one lover. Those who have three or so are a little wild."

Carlo laughed a bit too heatedly, as if to cover up for something else, and Guido's ragging about beautiful Venice where she and Paul had spent their last days together only twisted her pain sharper. As two customers came into the salon, she was relieved to have the Valente brothers escort her upstairs to see the secluded workrooms and introduce her to their staff of seventeen.

Here in two large, busy chambers outside Cesare Valente's private office, wisps of fur floated like sunbeams in the air beneath the single open skylight and harsh lamps. Her eyes watered with joy, not grief, for the first time in days as she sneezed, then sneezed again.

It excited her to hear the familiar chugging hum of the treadle sewing machines that put together the muslin patterns for the coats and assembled the pelts. The faint odor of tannin and damp, stretched furs; the glare of stark workroom lights; the slice of sharp trimming knives through leather; the thump-thump of the drummer tumbling furs in sawdust to clean and fluff them; the hiss of the steamer finishing the seams; all thrilled her. For one brief moment, her burdens lightened and her facial muscles and body relaxed.

Eagerly she peered over shoulders. On one side of the room they were assembling excellent Norwegian silver fox pelts with black stripes for stylish, bulky-look coats with epaulets. On the other side, two men and a woman constructed jackets of Himalayan marten, which she recognized but had never seen worked. Her pulse quickened. She longed to stroke the furs, to ask a hundred questions.

"I've worked as a fur model and a sorter and matcher," she explained eagerly to the Valente brothers as they walked her farther around the shop introducing her to everyone from Cesare Valente's head designer, Sandro Martelletta, to trimmers, slicers, and liners. "I actually came to see if I could obtain a position with Valente's, a design apprenticeship if possible," she said fervently.

Guido took her hands and turned them palm up to study them as if he would read her future. That sharp, quick smile again. "Your mother, when she lived in Rome with the Valentes, the Count told us, always loved the furrier shop, just as much as our mother, the so beautiful Countess Rissa, loved other pursuits, eh, Carlo?"

"Guido, really, I don't think—"

"Lovely hands, furrier's hands, indeed," Guido said, interrupting his brother's quiet plea, "all soft from the oils of furs, sensitive to the feel of each nuance of touch. And beautiful gray-green eyes to discern the shading of pelts, too. If it were up to me, of course, you'd have the position in a minute, Lesley. When the count returns from the auction in Copenhagen—if he manages to get back with this stupid war Hitler's Huns are likely to drag us into—and when the count salvages the operations here at Valente's, which he entrusts to his beloved nephews only in his direst need, he will like these hands, and your eyes, and ask you to stay on, I'd bet my life on it."

Despite Guido's smooth tone, his hard, assessing gaze belied his kind words, making her uncomfortable, more for what he didn't say than did. She bit her lower lip and tugged her hands back. She wasn't certain if he was mocking her or Carlo or his uncle. He seemed to unnerve his brother too, whose boyish face hinted he was on her side in whatever subtle family battles waged among the Valente sons and their uncle, whom Guido insisted on referring to as "the count."

"Count Valente's *sanctum sanctorum* can wait for another day," Guido said abruptly, as if he'd heard her thoughts, and retrieved Lesley's hand to pull her away. "Come on, Cárlo, where are your courtly manners? Let's pile our gorgeous, long-lost cousin Lesley and her painting in my humble little Maserati, get something to drink in the Piazza del Popolo, then give her a quick jaunt through Rome to the royal palace, eh?"

"The royal palace?" she asked, as she hurried to keep up with Guido on the steps down to street level and Carlo clambered along behind them.

"I refer, of course, to the palatial Valente town house on the Piazza Foro Traiano right across from Mussolini's little thirty-room hovel, which used to belong to the poor king," Guido threw over his shoulder. "The count's not likely to be back for three days or so, and I need a little diversion from being cooped up in this place, though Carlo's got sweet little Stella right next door at Sollo's Fine Leather Goods shop for that. Right, my boy? *Madre Maria*, pile in, then. Carlo, hang on in the back and keep that damned mutt's tail out of my face if it's coming, too."

A beautifully clipped Airedale terrier nearly leapt into Carlo's arms; the dog apparently slept in the shade of the narrow alley behind the line of shops. "Come on, Caprice, good girl," Carlo cried, and his face lit as he hugged the dog, then pulled it in to sit on top of him in the narrow slit of seat in back. Behind the dog's panting face, Carlo shyly smiled encouragement at Lesley. Guido put her next to him behind the split windshield in the racy, topless cobalt-blue auto and they roared off, dodging afternoon traffic on the Via Condotti.

Even to Lesley who had been reared in a home of grand proportions amid art objects and precious antiques, the Valente town house fronting the busy Roman square called the Piazza Foro Traiano seemed awesome. As Guido had said, it faced the larger Palazzo Venezia on the adjoining square, King Victor Emmanuel III's abandoned private residence, which Mussolini now used for his offices. All the elegant edifices in the immediate area were fifteenth-century brown stone buildings, erected with materials plundered from the ruined Colosseum a short distance away. The Valente town house was three stories of exquisite rooms with a large balcony garden adjoining the top floor. The entire mansion had a refined Mediterranean feel with a touch of museum, as Cesare's extensive art collection dominated by Italian Renaissance masters graced most rooms.

All the chambers on the first two floors had high ceilings, huge windows, ornate stucco work, and marble or mosaic floors. The ground floor boasted a huge entry hall called an *androne* with black and white marble floor tiles reflecting a statue of Diana, red brocade walls, and matched settees. Cesare's private library, Guido had told her, was off limits to everyone when he was away, so she hadn't seen that yet. Beyond that, a lounge for entertaining, and at the back, a large kitchen as well as cook's and maids' quarters. The second level included both a formal dining room, which seated thirty under a gold-leaf rosette ceiling, and a more intimate family dining room served by dumbwaiters from the kitchen below. Lesley favored the lovely sitting room all in blues with ceramic-tile fireplace, Bechstein white grand piano, and family touches like photos of the boys and an extensive collection of Sèvres porcelain figurines—as well as tastefully displayed Titians and Tintorettos.

The second floor also included butler's quarters, one guest suite, and extensive storage. The third floor was the sleeping floor with its modernized marble-floored baths attached to family bedrooms, studies, and dressing rooms. Cesare's suite at the back opened directly onto the lovely rooftop balcony with dolphin-boy fountain and tiny pond. Across the hall was the suite her aunt Rissa had used the five years of her widowhood until her death, where Carlo had told her no one but the maid had been for years. Then came the boys' rooms, and toward the front overlooking the piazza, two guest bedrooms, one of which they had kindly put her in.

She looked her lovely chamber over again, as she had three days ago when she'd arrived. Now her Stubbs painting she'd finally found the courage to uncrate and lean on the top of her bureau added its touch of yellow phaeton to the muted tones of the room with its two Canaletto landscapes. Yellow, gray, and white striped wallpaper, gold satin bedspread piped in gray, white furniture, a lovely little haven she was so grateful for. It was strange to sleep alone in the big bed after sharing one with Paul all those weeks before the—the accidents.

She smoothed the layer of breathy chiffon over the white satin underskirt along her knees and blinked back tears that threatened her blue eye color. Nervously, she examined her upswept hair with tumbled curls in the looking glass and dabbed a touch of Lanvin's Rumeur behind each ear. Guido had been miffed when she'd mentioned getting her hair trimmed, so for now, she just wore it up. After all, he had also insisted on taking her shopping for clothes she so desperately needed. Gratefully, she had allowed it, although she hardly approved of several of the elegant and expensive gowns he insisted she would need to live with the Valentes. Especially this ivory chiffon and satin one with long fitted sleeves, clinging waistline, and soft, low-draped décolletage. She considered the dress slightly too old for her, but he had let it slip that his uncle would like it.

After all, if it came to having a dress a certain way to please Count Valente, she could find a place of her own as soon as she began to earn a salary at the fur salon. But Guido had been so kind, taking her about Rome and seeing to her needs, that she had tried to overlook his sardonic tone and subtle cuts about his uncle. It was evident they did not get on at all. She bent closer to the mirror to check her lipstick, then stood. Tonight, she'd see for herself how things were and would be. Tonight, in just a little while, Count Cesare Valente would be arriving home.

She took a lace-edged handkerchief and opened her door to the hall. It had become her habit now to carry a handkerchief everywhere, though she had long ago exhausted tears, except at night in the private, lonely dark. She tried to halt the perpetual thoughts about the life that grew within her, innocent of the scandal of illegitimacy he or she was doomed to because of a mother's love. It was all exactly, painfully, what she had sworn to Paul would never happen to a child of hers. She bit the inside of her cheek to stop the prickle of tears behind her eyes.

Partway down the first flight of stairs, she paused. Carlo's angry voice sounded from Guido's room, though she could not imagine him raising his voice to anyone.

"It's a blasted rotten trick and you know it, Guido. He'll

really have your head now. Can't you just accept she died that way and let it go?"

"*Madre Maria*, what the hell do you know! You were only twelve and worshiped her, worshiped her like she was some golden saint. And she was only plaster, worse than plaster—a real hollow goddess, little brother. I just want to see what he does, that's all. The great Cesare Valente rattled at last, just like all us corruptible, fallible little mortals!"

"I'll have nothing to do with it! I didn't know you'd planned it like this, you wretch!"

"Wretch, Carlo? Go ahead, say what you think! Bastard? Son of a bitch? But then the sainted madonna Clarissa becomes the bitch in heat, like your damned little dog, eh, Carlo?"

Lesley stood frozen on the top step, one hand on the carved banister, her mind racing. They sounded as if they would actually come to blows and their uncle was due home any minute. She would knock on the door, pretend she hadn't heard them, ask if they were ready. But what was the trick on their uncle they were arguing about?

As she turned to go to the door, it yanked open and Carlo exploded out of it. He slammed it hard behind him before he saw her. "Oh! Hello, Lesley. Guido and I—we didn't bother you, did we?" He tugged his shirtcuffs down from the sleeves of his midnight-blue dinner jacket and fussed with his wing collar and silk bow tie as if his elegant togs did not fit, even though they were obviously custom tailored.

"I did hear you arguing."

He forced a sheepish smile. "Brothers, you know."

She nodded. "Yes, I do know about that."

The angry look on his face when he'd run from the room crushed his pleasant, boyish features again. "I get so damned tired of having him run everything down, that's all," he told her quietly as he took her arm and escorted her down the stairs. Her heart went out to Carlo as it had from the beginning. He was a kind and gentle soul, not the sort meant for skirmishes with someone as witty and bitter as Guido. She decided then to do whatever she could in her time with the Valentes to help and protect Carlo. He was only nineteen to Guido's twenty-three and entirely too loving for his own good at times.

He jerked them to a stop in the marble-tiled entry hall by the central statue of Diana at the hunt. The graceful goddess stretched her hand back eternally to draw an arrow from the quiver between her graceful, naked shoulder blades. Puzzled, Lesley turned to face him. "Lesley, I've decided. You look so beautiful in that gown, but he's not going to do it. I didn't know until tonight the extent of it. And, I swear, he's not going to do it!"

"Do what, Carlo?" she asked as he took her hand and pulled her gently toward Cesare's private library. "Carlo, what is it?"

"The welcome home for our uncle is to take place in here with you in that gown standing under the portrait of our mother. I'm only amazed my clever brother didn't insist her old hairdresser accidently drop by tonight to fix your hair the same way!" he raved as he opened one of the double doors to the library and tugged her in after him. She stopped just inside and stared aghast, her hands clasped to her breasts.

The room glowed in umber hues reflected in the fire burning on the hearth even when he turned on two lamps. The odor of rich leather enveloped her. The walls were covered to the ceiling in hand-tooled moroccan-bound volumes, except for two Titians and the massive fireplace—and the magnificent and astonishing portrait over it.

"See? Do you see now what he's been doing, what he intends?" Carlo's cry pierced her as she gaped at the massive oil painting.

The beautiful woman was no doubt her aunt, the dead Clarissa Valente in all her glory, seated in an ornately gilded bronze Napoleonic chair with sable wrap thrown carelessly across its back. Lesley knew she resembled her aunt more than she did her mother. She recalled the old photographs instantly, the images of the lovely, vibrant woman she had met on their stay here fifteen years ago. But to see her in this stunning portrait with her reddish hair all loose to her shoulders like a cloud, and in a gown nearly identical to the one Guido had insisted she wear tonight to welcome Count Valente home! In one grinding crash it was painfully obvious that for some reason Guido had intended to shock his uncle by her resemblance to the dead woman.

"See? Do you see?" Carlo repeated at her side.

"Yes. I—it's amazing."

"Everyone who knew her and has seen you has remarked on it. Funny, that my mother and yours were twins but you look like your aunt." Carlo's voice softened almost in awe.

Lesley leaned on the edge of a leather chair arm and marveled anew. At least she had put her hair up tonight so that was different, and she wore no emeralds about her throat. But Aunt Rissa's eyes—except they looked so restless, so challenging. And her tiny wry twist of mouth suggested where Guido had gotten his mocking manner.

She swiveled to face Carlo. "But what was Count Valente's reaction to be, then?" she asked. "Does Guido hate him so or want to shock him or what—"

Behind them Guido crashed into the room, smacking the heavy door into the paneled wall, shaking the paintings. "Damn you, Carlo! He's here, but then so are we all." He looked flushed, glassy-eyed as he glanced up at the portrait and then back to Lesley, who faced him, hands on her satin hips. She had to escape this room, this little plot Guido had woven for his uncle with her as bait. She wanted so very much to please Count Valente.

"Guido, you had absolutely no right to perpetrate this—" she began, but behind the defiant, jubilant Guido appeared the silver-haired Count Cesare Valente. He was not tall, yet he seemed to fill the doorway, even shrink the room. Carlo had shown her a recent photo of his uncle. He looked now as she had expected, prematurely silver-headed but with his eyebrows still coal-black. Solid, handsome for his age. It was hard to believe he'd never married. Still, she had not reckoned on the impact of the man. Though slightly shorter than she, he commanded the room, and for once, Guido was silent. She dropped her arms to her sides and stood rooted to the floor directly under the portrait of her aunt. She had the ludicrous impulse to curtsy. Instead, when Carlo moved back as if expecting an explosion, she stepped forward with a defiant tilt of chin. She extended her hand. The man's eyes glinted metallic in the fireglow.

"Count Valente, your nephews, who have been so kind—" she said the words with an edge to her voice surely Guido could appreciate—"have offered me your hospitality until you returned. I am Lesley Westam from England, your brother's wife's niece."

As he came closer she could see the man was all muscular bulk with a broad chest and a bit of belly to him that even his elegantly cut garments could not hide. He was square-shouldered, almost stocky with a riveting gaze that demanded attention. He emanated vigor and force under the thin veneer of refinement. Her extended hand wavered as his eyes examined her face in a flash, dipped for one split second to the gown to take her all in, lingered on the low, soft folds of the white satin bosom. Only when the natural olive hue of the man's complexion rushed back did she realize he had gone pale. The jowls moved, a nervous clench of muscle.

"Lesley, how beautiful you have become since that visit so long ago. What a wonderful surprise, eh, Guido, Carlo?" His big voice boomed and, ignoring her extended hand, he pulled her into his strong arms for a hearty kiss on both cheeks.

She had been sleeping poorly since Paul's death, but now, even when she had driven herself all week trying to learn everything at the fur salon, she could not sleep. Cesare had taken over her life like a benevolent magic genie from the *Arabian Nights,* which her mother had read her as a child. At least Guido, except for smart comments under his breath, had learned to behave, but she still woke several times a night exhausted. Or she'd awaken at three or four and never get back to sleep in the big silent house, thinking, remembering. She had not told her new family she was pregnant yet. It would be weeks before she would show, and then she would have a salary that would enable her to move out if they were scandalized.

She had found that if she avoided breakfast, it kept the morning nausea down. It was something for which Gram back at Westam would have scolded her soundly, but it had to be done . . . had to be done, just as she had to go on and live her life without Paul now, she thought in the stretch of dark silence.

How thrilling it had been when Count Cesare himself had taken her to Valente's and let her spend that first day with him in the front room upstairs. There he and his head designer,

Sandro, created the lines of furs that had made Valente's famous. The drawing boards, big-shouldered canvas mannequins, huge wooden table covered with stiff, heavy paper and muslin for the patterns, the bundles of luxurious furs Cesare had shown her that were stored in the sealed vault below the first floor of the shop—she could see, feel it all again while she waited for sleep here in bed. And then, because she'd asked him for a position she could tell he didn't think at first she should have, she had flaunted her skills. Even now, lying here tossing and turning in the rumpled satin sheets, she could feel his sharp brown eyes on her again in the cool fur vault with its single ceiling light as she had lifted a pelt to demonstrate.

"Now, if I worked for Valente's as an apprentice designer, or even a matcher or a sorter, I could tell certain things about this natural brown mink pelt," she had begun and smiled straight into his eyes to hold his attention as she knew she could. He had not blamed her for Guido's attempt to surprise him as the resurrected Rissa, but she knew her looks intrigued him, and right now, for this chance, she used all her cleverness and skills.

She had run the long guard hairs through her fingers, checking for evenness of length. "Yes, this is excellent," she told him, "no uneven hairs to make the finished mink look scruffy or waxy." She snapped the skin rapidly to bring up the soft underfur and squeezed it to test the fullness. "A lovely female mink skin, though I'd need a better light to judge or match the color." When she blew on the pelt to uncover the fur nearest the leather, she had the oddest feeling he would like to pull her to him, and she stepped back. "No defects or balding spots will show up here when the coat is sewn together," she concluded with a toss of her head.

He smiled broadly. His fingers lingered over hers as he took the pelt back. "All right," he said, "you want to work for Valente's in the daytime, you can. But what I said about having a hostess in the house for my dinner parties and your going with Carlo and me to Capri this weekend and to the opera with me Wednesday still holds," he insisted, jabbing the narrow space between them with his finger. "I don't usually fraternize with my employees, but for you I make an exception, you see. Guido's a playboy Lothario and lush whose wily brain for business turns to rot on his damned dry Martinis, fast cars, and faster women. And Carlo, like his father, is too soft to be a businessman or a furrier. He's best caring for his dog and overseeing the Valente art collection and the villa. But you, bright and clever and very determined, if you want to learn with me at Valente's, that is fine, and you'll put both my nephews to shame here."

She'd wanted to stand up for Carlo at least, wanted to ask why Cesare needed her to be a hostess or attend the opera with him when Guido had told her he'd kept a wellborn mistress for years. But she was so pleased to have this chance, so excited to be able to actually learn from him and have a salary of her own to pay them back for all the clothes and the kindness.

"You know," he'd gone on, his voice quieter now, "although your beauty is reminiscent of my brother's wife, I am grateful you are more like your mother. She too asked to work at Valente's once. She too had the inherent gift to select the furs. But times were different then, you know, a wellborn woman of my family working among the others . . ." He shrugged. "I said no. It was not long after she met your father here in Rome when he was visiting the British king's ambassador. Despite his marriage and his son, they loved each other desperately, and she was lost to us after that. If I had let her fulfill her need to work at Valente's, perhaps such fierce emotion would not all have gone to loving the Earl of Malvern, eh? But best not to question and agonize about the past. At least where your mother's and your talent for working with furs came from is a question best left to God, and only treasure and enjoy, eh?" he concluded, his voice gone almost silky.

Touched and grateful, she had spontaneously kissed him on the cheek. When she'd stood back smiling, she'd seen something in his eyes that puzzled and frightened her, something lurking there she had not meant to unleash. But he had smiled back over his imposing beak of a nose and taken her arm with his strong fingers against the bare skin above her elbow and tenderly brushed a hanging pelt of sable against her cheek. For one minute, when he'd turned off the single light, she'd thought of being trapped in the tightness of the little room with hanging pelts pressing against her in the dark. But he had propelled her out into the light, his sure hand briefly touching

her, as he often did to move her about here or there when he
pointed out things or explained sometimes. It was only what
she'd seen him do with others he seemed to control—everyone, really, but Guido. After all, Cesare's touch was hardly
like Paul's caresses against her skin.

Remembering Paul, she sighed fitfully and drifted in the sea
of satin sheets as the night wore on. Paul was gone into the
waves where it was dark, but she was here in a sea of furs with
Cesare Valente. She stroked the furs again to help select them
for the posh coats she would design someday. She stroked into
the blackened water searching, calling out, for Paul on the
sea. His ship was burning, sinking. She had to find him, save
him. She struck out at the woman who tried to take her sable
coat. She saw Paul then, swimming toward her in the waves of
ebony mink and sable. She called out again, but he slipped
slowly downward into the waiting black shroud of the sea. She
grabbed for him, sinking with him. She tried to breathe; the
dark closed in, the clinging silk of sea and rolling darkness of
Mother's breathing iron lung of ocean and furs—

A woman's scream sounded in her ears, distant, then close
enough to wake her. She sat bolt upright, wrapped in clinging
sheets. The shriek still echoed in the room. A nightmare! The
baby! She had to keep calm for the baby.

Footsteps pounded in the hall. For one moment she was not
sure where she was until the door shot open and a man's form
stood there. Her heart leapt. No, she was just disoriented. Paul
was gone. She was here in Rome, in Rome at Valente's, and
Cesare stood in the doorway.

His form loomed larger against the rectangle of harsh hall
light as he approached the bed. "Lesley? What happened? Are
you all right?"

"I'm so—so sorry, ashamed. A nightmare. I guess I
screamed."

"It's all right now, sweet," he crooned, and pulled her into
his arms as if she were a child. "You're the new favorite in the
house," Carlo had teased over dinner that night, and Cesare's
commanding touch was only comforting, wasn't it? But he had
taken to calling her "sweet" since he had consoled her about
the loss of her things and her injuries and sent a large

contribution to the Blue Nuns' hospital in Orvieto last week. "It must have been bad, Lesley. Want to talk about it?"

"No, I'm fine now." A lie, she thought. She'd never be fine again without Paul. Cesare shifted her slightly closer. The side of her brow grazed his slight stubble of silver night beard. He wore red silk pajamas. His open hand touched her heated back as his embrace pressed her satin-covered breasts against his big chest. She felt the slight bulge of his belly and hip. The moment she tried to pull away, he let her. But he captured her hand and tugged her damp palm to his lips in a lingering kiss that changed all the rules between them. His big square hand stroked her cheeks to wipe away the tears she had not realized were on her face.

"Both of us need comforting in our own ways," he whispered more to himself than her. "For you, I thought it was just in the daylight hours, but maybe not, hm?"

He stood reluctantly and bent to fumble with the bedside lamp on his way out. In the glare of the light, he looked back at her briefly where she sat tousled and disheveled in the bed, holding the rumpled sheet up to her breasts now. She stared back unspeaking. Although the door closed quietly behind him, she regretted they had both done something tonight to open another door between them.

Chapter Seven

THE SIX OF THEM emerged from the opera and waited for the their chauffeured Bugatti Royale coupé to pull up in the line of hovering vehicles. The Valente family motorcar, sleek and massive, a custom-made jade and cream version roomy enough inside for all of them even with its recessed desk and teakwood bar, was the largest in the humming line of headlamp-gilded luxury limousines. Although the night was mild for late October, Cesare rested his hands on Lesley's shoulders as if to wrap her gold lamé cloak lined with golden sable more closely around her. Guido's guest tonight was his latest lady of the last few weeks. The sloe-eyed, red-gowned woman pressed her plush curves against him despite Cesare's trying to move them along. Carlo escorted the petite, lovely Stella Sollo, whose family owned the luxury leather goods shop next to Valente's. Stella's bright eyes in her appealing, heart-shaped face watched Guido's every move, however properly her arm clung to Carlo's.

Men in the crowd wore either military dress uniforms or black tailcoats as did Cesare and his nephews. Bow ties, pearl studs, and silk hats were *de rigueur* at night in the Roman social circles to which Cesare had introduced Lesley; a sporty, yet refined casual look ruled the day at such places as the Acquasanta Golf Club where he had taken her to lunch. And he had been adamant about providing her with an even larger wardrobe than Guido's initial purchases. A woman from a haute couture shop had come around for her to make selections, among them the Patou emerald lace dinner suit she wore tonight with diamond earrings he'd said were perfect for the opera or the entertaining she was helping him with at the town house.

With one hand now on the small of her back, he propelled her toward the curb. "Back to the town house for a nightcap of champagne and a little buffet—all of us, Guido." Cesare's voice rose above the hubbub of chatter, auto engines, and the sharp shouts of vendors hawking their evening papers or flowers among the well-heeled crowd.

"A brief pit stop for a little repast? Why not?" Guido agreed with a shrug as his hand swept his hair back before he replaced his top hat at a jaunty angle. "But I really must take Patrizia home before the witching hour."

Patrizia's throaty laugh entwined with Guido's as she lit the cigarette he offered her from the tip of his thin, dark cheroot. He often smoked, even though Count Valente hated the smell of tobacco.

Lesley watched Stella's face. Poor Carlo, she thought. He simply doted on her while it was evidently the acerbic, womanizing Guido whose arm Stella would have liked to adorn. True love was blind, they said. What heartbreak for Carlo if he found out; how sad for him if he did not. Someone like Guido would chew up and devour the naïve, sweet Stella Sollo like so much antipasto.

The Bugatti pulled up at the foot of the stretch of carpet, but as Lesley and Cesare approached it, he tugged her back. A bone-thin woman with an elfin, entrancing face crossed in front of them, her arms laden with newspapers. Her hair long and wild, she looked almost a gypsy. Her glittering eyes lit on Cesare and she jerked to a halt in a swirl of full skirts. She flashed him a smile, a brief nod, then tried to cover what was perhaps mistaken identity.

Quickly, she extended a copy of the small, single-page broadsheet to him. *"Vinceremo!"* the young woman declared. "We shall overcome Il Duce! Look, this paper is free, free as Italy shall be. Read here the truth."

"I think not here," Cesare told her, the slightest edge to his voice, and refused to take the extended paper. "Lesley, get in before we attract undue attention," he muttered and moved her again toward the waiting motorcar.

"Libero, eh?" Guido said and bent his head to read the title of the paper the girl held out. With a quick flash of ivory teeth, he took the paper. "I shall be brave enough to read it if the

count will not," he declared loudly in a speech all too obviously aimed at Cesare. "After all, hasn't our illustrious Duce told us it is 'better to live one day as a lion than a hundred years as a lamb'? And *Madre Maria*, so I shall, however lamblike to the slaughter my uncle goes!" He handed Patrizia in to sit on one of the two leather upholstered jump seats that pulled down, and joined her on the other, facing the four of them.

"Not a very clever speech before Il Duce's most intimate cohorts in that opera crowd, Guido," Cesare groused, punctuating each word with a jab of index finger as they drove away. "Especially considering your brother has just been inducted into Il Duce's forces despite my influence. You are no doubt next, despite your sporadic classes at the university. Nor was all that a very successful insult to the uncle to whom you owe more respect than that, but I should know to expect nothing by now. And do put out that smoke in here."

"Must I put out Patrizia's, too?" Guido countered cheekily. Lesley tensed at Guido's rudeness and marveled anew at the lid Cesare kept on his temper in public.

"Patrizia may smoke as perhaps she does it for her own pleasure and not only to annoy others."

"This newspaper is only one little broadsheet of several harmless underground papers some poor dissidents are putting out, Uncle," Guido went on as if he hadn't been scolded. He fluttered the paper in the dark. His sharp, baiting smile flashed in an oncoming auto's headlamps through the sweep of windows. "Poor fools. Communists, partisans, whatever frightened wretches sponsor things like this *Libero*. Nothing will stop Il Duce."

"Not now, Guido, not here." Cesare snuffed out the smoldering argument decisively, and Lesley breathed a sigh of relief that there would be no family shouting match with Stella and Patrizia present. But it had been odd back there. The street girl with the copy of that incendiary paper had seemed to recognize Cesare, and she'd obviously never been in the position to purchase a fur coat. She would get that paper from Guido later and read it, Lesley thought.

On the Valente balcony in the moonlight, the scent of oleander perfumed the air, leaves rustled gently, and the dolphin-boy fountain splashed silver as the six of them ate, drank Dom Pérignon, and chatted. Such a beautiful setting, Lesley thought. Yet it hardly moved her, not as it might have if she had been with Paul. Five weeks with the Valentes—as busy as she was, as kind as they all were to her in their different ways, except perhaps Guido at times—had barely dulled the pain of Paul's loss. If only they had not parted that day in Venice. If only he had taken a different ship or not gone home at all, they could have been together tonight, other nights like this. Then she would not be here on the wrought-iron bench with Cesare Valente's arm draped casually but possessively behind her shoulders as Guido and Patrizia said their good-byes and Stella Sollo's deep brown eyes resentfully narrowed at the other woman.

"I'd best drive Stella home now too, Uncle," Carlo said. "What a day! Now that I'm in the cavalry, I just hope Hitler doesn't pull our armed forces into his mess. If it wasn't for being with my family and Stella tonight, I never would have gotten through that maudlin induction ceremony." He lowered his voice even out here on the private patio. "Mussolini's bad, but I think Hitler's crazy. Did you hear about that wireless broadcast where he had Goebbels claim the war is all Churchill's fault, including that attack on the *Athenia* by the U-boats?"

Lesley stood to move away to the buffet table. She had not discussed the *Athenia* disaster with any of them. Now, Cesare would notice if she were not careful; he watched her like a hawk. She forced a smile and waved as Carlo and Stella made their exit behind Guido and Patrizia.

"I'm shocked," she told Cesare, her voice shaky, the moment they were alone. "Imagine Hitler being so ridiculous as to accuse Churchill about blowing up an English ship."

"Never ridiculous, Lesley," he said and moved to stand close behind her. "You must learn not to underestimate a man like Hitler. He's cruel, vindictive, utterly dangerous." His warm hands lifted to capture her shoulders and pull her firmly back against him. "But you're not to worry. You're here safe with us, and I swear that Valente money and influence will do everything to fight your legal battles in England, even if Italy goes to war. Trust me, you'll see."

His lips moved against her hair, newly shortened and curled to fashionable chin length, then traveled to her ear, where his warm breath lulled her for a moment. So easy to just surrender all her worries to this powerful man who obviously cared deeply for her, she thought, but she felt so little for him in that way. Gratitude and admiration were the only feelings she had for him that she could put a name to. No stirring of the blood, no tingling, no sense of soaring as she had felt with Paul. Gently, she moved a few steps away, then spun to face him.

"Cesare, I'd like to know before—before our relationship deepens, as you've mentioned—"

"As I have mentioned, hinted, implored, my sweet." He took a step to pursue her, then thought the better of it and sat back down on the bench they had shared earlier with his arm thrown casually across it again. "What would you like to know then, Lesley?"

"It isn't just because I remind you of Countess Rissa?" she asked in a rush. She was afraid for a moment she might have overstepped. Surely he had felt affection for his sister-in-law, especially after Franco's death when he had become her protector and, in deed if not fact, the boys' stepfather.

"Of course not. Besides, you don't, not from the moment you first spoke, and when I learned how kind and, well, reliable you were, though I must admit redheads with beautiful faces have always been my weakness. And is there more? Something else? Lesley, is there *someone else* between us?"

She looked frozen where she stood. She shivered. "No one on this earth," she said, then shook her head at her dramatic choice of words. Her eyes met his; he was studying her in that probing, demanding way he always did, however gentle and polite he remained. He frowned, then intentionally erased the look from his brow.

At least she must not know she is lying to me, Cesare thought and struggled further to compose his face. She must actually believe her American lover, Paul Kendal, died on that ship Carlo accidently mentioned tonight, since it clearly upset her. Cesare's investigation had revealed the man's name was originally printed among the dead from the *Athenia* disaster. A confusion with the identity of the wounded during the rescue by two British destroyers, the journalist whom he'd consulted had told him. And if it weren't for the six-week-old cable that he'd intercepted at Valente's two days ago, he would never have suspected that this beautiful woman had had a lover or that she did not know he was still alive.

Cesare had agonized over what to do for two days now, but tonight he'd decided. He wanted Lesley Westam, he needed her—and meant to have her. Besides, he could surely do more than some wounded, distant American to promote the career she ambitiously desired. He would protect her endangered heritage back in England, even her life in these tenuous times.

Then too, the closer he watched her, the more he wondered if she might be with child by this passionate American whose long-delayed cable had vowed eternal love. Eternal love! As if such a thing existed in this world of liars and deceivers like Rissa had been. Yes, Cesare Valente knew women. Actually, if Lesley did carry an illegitimate child, that could serve to bind her closer in an offer of protection. She obviously worried for her reputation, because of her past, no doubt, for which he was suddenly very grateful.

He wanted her so desperately he could barely keep his feelings for her leashed or his hands off her. She distracted him from his work at Valente's, even from his patriotic duty to get *Libero* on the streets to neutralize the poison Benito Mussolini spread through the body of his beloved Mother Italy. He would accept this Paul Kendal's child to have her if that is what it took. He must play his cards very cleverly so she would never desert him for another as Rissa had. It had taken him four years after his brother's death to convince Rissa they belonged together as husband and wife, and then she had betrayed him! Cesare Valente!

Tomorrow he would send Paul Kendal, recuperating in that Canadian hospital in Montreal, a cable simply stating that Lesley regretted his injuries but that she would be working permanently at Valente di Roma and intended to become Countess Valente. If that cable got delayed somewhere for weeks as the other had, so much the better. However long it took him to convince or coerce the stubborn Lesley, he meant for all those things he would write the American in the cable to come true.

He watched her as she stood unutterably breathtaking by the

fountain in the moonlight. She stared strangely at him. So, she tried to read him as he did her. But his secrets were his own and would remain so. He smiled.

"Despite your reluctance, dearest Lesley, I will be so bold as to press my suit. And I swear, in answer to your unasked question, there is no one else for me, my dear," he vowed and leaned forward to rest his elbows on his knees. "There was someone who filled the lonely nights upon occasion these last few years, but that is over now. And if at last you tell me no, I shall accept that, too," he lied. "But not now, not until we have had our lovely times together, eh?" He rose and moved toward her. "And now best off to bed before my halo tarnishes and I touch you again. As the sharp-tongued Valente heir to all this," he said and swept his hand in a grand arc at the lighted townhouse behind them, "reminded me tonight, 'It is better to live one day as a lion than eternity as a sheep.' "

When she only nodded, he mused, "Poor, sarcastic Guido. Would he be relieved or resentful if I produced my own heir someday, eh? Go on now, before I change my mind." He concluded his pious little speech and glanced down to study her waistline again as she moved to go inside.

She obeyed Cesare Valente, and wondered again how long his aura of refinement and control would hold with her, since he sometimes exploded at wayward, disobedient Guido and even gentle Carlo, who did not come up to his fierce expectations, either. But as she lay in bed and the church bells pealed midnight in the heart of Rome, she still thought she could hear the distant splashing fountain. Not the one on the Valente balcony off Cesare's suite, but the little French one where geese swam under the window of her and Paul's bedroom in Châtillon.

Wind yanked Lesley's scarf and hair as Cesare whipped his red Atlantique Bugatti sports car along another cliffside railing of the two-lane serpentine Amalfi Drive. Below, little hotels, villas in tiers, scenic restaurants, and beaches now bereft of bright umbrellas in the first chill winds of November looked out on the cerulean Bay of Naples glittering like an amethyst in the sun. It was the same route they'd motored along to Naples to take the ferry to the Isle of Capri for weekends at Villa

Valente, which she so loved. But Cesare was nervous and driving faster than usual; something was afoot today.

They stopped at the white terraced town of Atrani, tucked like stacked white cubes into the base of the cliff fold called Valley of the Dragon and went into the Ristorante Belevedere. Few were about in the resort restaurant in late morning at this time of the year. From their table sheltered by a glass partition overlooking the windy beach, they dined in open privacy on basil chicken stuffed with prosciutto and milky-white mozzarella. When they finished, she waited for whatever she knew must come.

She had steeled herself for it. If he asked her to be his mistress, she intended to decline gracefully and hope he would keep her on at Valente's. She would move out of the town house before her pregnancy gave her away. And if, as she feared, he would actually propose marriage to her, she must still refuse and pray he would let her remain part of the family that had given her so much warmth and acceptance these last two months.

"Lesley, I asked you down here on a weekday when we're both rather busy for a very special reason."

Her gaze collided with his brown eyes, narrowed in the slash of sun under the awning of grapevines. She took a careful breath, her slender fingers toying with the stem of her wine goblet. "Yes."

"You think you know?" he demanded.

"Sometimes I feel I know so little of you."

"I hope and pray you would like to learn more, then. Lesley, this is not the way I had meant to begin, but I must tell you that your aunt died up there on that Amalfi Drive several miles back." His hand waved in that direction. He yanked it back to thump it on the table. "Her car went over the cliff onto the rocks, into the water—"

"Cesare, I didn't know it happened like that, and—"

He shook his head and lifted a big, open hand. "No, sweet, let me finish. They didn't find her auto for three days, but when they did, she was with a lover. But what you need to know to understand me, and to cope with Guido better, is that I had previously asked her to marry me and she was actually leaving me for this man. Karen had been widowed for four years.

I thought I was her guardian, her strength. She was so beautiful. Surely, I thought, she must love me as I do her after all these years. But she was running away with him when she died, Lesley, though she so kindly left me and her sons a note." He spit out the words, his voice cutting and bitter. "Damn, this was not how I had meant to begin!"

Her hand reached out to cover his fist on the pink linen-covered table. His expression was so intent, his high brow edged with silver hair deeply furrowed. She frowned too, and tears filled her eyes. "I'm so sorry, Cesare. I didn't know all that."

"Guido blames me. For loving her, driving her off some-how, I suppose," he said and shrugged. "But neither that explanation nor your compassion is why I tell you this. I only want to make it clear to you that I had never considered marrying anyone before Rissa, and then she—let me down. So," he said, his tumbled words slowing now, "I would never take a step toward marriage lightly."

"Marriage." The word hung between them, not swept away in the freshening sea breeze. She took her hand back and rose to move a few steps away from the glass protection to the corner of the railing over the breaking foam below. He moved immediately behind her and put one big hand on either side of her on the round rail as if to close her in.

"I love you, Lesley. I need you, want you, desire you, everything you might need to know, to understand. I'm asking you to marry me, to become Countess Valente."

An inner shudder wracked her but still she stood straight, her hands just inside his on the rail. "Cesare, I'm deeply moved. Honored. But, I am sorry." She turned to face him, although the move nearly trapped her in his unyielding embrace, her lips just inches from his. "Forgive me, but for my own reasons, I cannot."

"Because I'm nearly thirty years older, or wanted to marry your aunt?"

She shook her head; her windblown tresses whipped her cheeks. "No, honestly. Please try to—"

"Because of someone you must have loved then who left you with the child you carry!"

She swayed against the railing. She leaned back as if she

could fly up and away from everything to impale herself on these surrounding sharp cliffs. He knew! Or he had guessed. The one thing, the very thing that might have made her consider marrying him he held in his hand.

"Lesley, I don't know who the man was—or is," he lied. "I only know I love you enough to cherish and rear the child as my own. No one will know but us."

She forced her teary eyes back to his face. "You would say the child was yours?"

"Yes!"

Her shoulders slumped. She heaved a deep sigh. No scandal. A firm, respectable parentage, especially if they were wed soon. But no, no. Whatever was she thinking?

"Listen to me, Lesley." His hands grasped her upper arms as if he would shake her. "You're an intelligent woman, you'll be a brilliant furrier, a clever businesswoman too when I've taught you all I know. No doubt you'll be an excellent mother for this child, for others if we should be blessed in years to come. Lesley, with me you can have all that and my admiration and devotion, too!"

All that. He looked and sounded so impassioned. With Cesare, she could have everything that she and Paul had planned so hopefully together.

Her voice wasn't her own. Some other woman's, some words on the wind from over the sea that had drowned Paul. "He's dead, Cesare." She stared at the racing pulse at the base of his throat just above the burgundy cravat. "The father of my child. I still love him, but he's dead."

He seized her hands. "Listen to me, I said. You've got to accept that it's all in your past as Rissa is in mine. As my wife you will have the career you've longed for. You can design with me until you're ready to strike out with your own line—the Countess Valente line, we'll call it. I understand you want the career as well as a family. Carlo adores you, Guido can be made to come around, and I would be desolate without you. We can all be a family. I will love your child like my own, and you will be a very wealthy, very secure woman in your efforts to win that part of your English heritage your brother and his mother are trying to take from you! I will even understand if you don't love me now, and trust that will come with time. I only ask that in return you swear never, never to betray me and the Valente name as Rissa did, not even if events change things for us in the future. My sweet, I'm offering you the world!"

He pulled her hard against him. His hands on her back pinned her to his hard, bulky body, and she was glad. Now he would not see the bitter tears of grief and pain and longing for something she could never have. Paul was gone forever. She had told him once she would sacrifice anything for a child of hers, and now, however much she gained in return, she would sacrifice herself. Valente power, the money, the reputation, or even the gift of her lifetime dream to design fantasy furs—none of that would have been worth a puff of air if she could still have Paul. But for the child's sake, she would put away her agonized love and loss and marry Cesare Valente.

He held her hard in the tangy breeze while she found the words to vow her loyalty forever. His kiss was domineering, demanding, a side of himself she had barely glimpsed. Yet when their waiter eventually wandered circumspectly back out, Cesare took her hand gently and coaxed a smile from her. And he left the man a gratuity large enough to throw a posh, grand wedding of his own.

Sitting at her marble-topped dressing table in her bedroom at the Villa Valente on the Isle of Capri, Lesley dabbed her face and neck with the huge swansdown powderpuff, then sat back to assess her coiffure and face. A few freckles had dared to pop out across the bridge of her nose in this Italian sun, freckles she hadn't seen for years since she and good old Melly Mott had roamed the forests and banks of Westam far away and forever ago. But she looked fine, she assured herself, fine enough for a pregnant bride who was marrying a man she did not love.

She sighed and tried to marshal her self-control for the long, demanding afternoon—and week of honeymoon—ahead. Rebellion roiled in her today. Nor did it help that she could hear the buzz of the assembled wedding guests like so many bees mingled with bird cries in the gardens below. The occasional clink of crystal or sterling as the servants arranged the buffet on the long tables by the pool floated to her. The restless whisper of sea breezes seemed to screech along the veranda just outside the jalousies. She rose to close them without another glance at the blue-velvet Bay of Naples.

On the ground floor, the large rooms of Villa Valente spilled together as if eager to reach the sun and sea outside. There was white everywhere, from marble-arched doorways with carved columns to linens to plump couches and ottomans and fine porcelain. Spacious, spotless white, accented with splashes of magenta, and hot and pale pinks to echo the poolside bougainvillea in pillows, plants, paintings, tiles. Some antique wooden furniture provided the only dark hues in Villa Valente besides the deep purples and reds of the Kurdistan carpets underfoot. Everything was beautiful here, just waiting, hers for the merest plucking, but memories bombarded her and she seethed inside.

She hadn't been alone all day but for the private time she'd insisted on to take her bath in the sunken marble tub in this suite that had once been her aunt Rissa's. Even then Lucia, her maid when they visited the villa, hovered in the next room. Lesley sat quietly in her silk bridal lingerie and nylon stockings with lace tops and jeweled garters under her pink quilted silk robe. Still she was wretchedly nervous. Bridal jitters, Carlo had teased her last week when she had snapped at him for the first time. Or perhaps the pregnancy she was still hiding from everyone but Cesare was changing her personality, she thought. People were likely to discover that the young Countess Valente was nearly five months pregnant soon enough anyway, and then they would all assume the father was Cesare and that's why he had married her.

She paced the azure mosaic floor back and forth before the huge Tiepolo painting with glorious sunlit skies full of cavorting gods and goddesses that dominated one wall of the bedroom. After today, her child would not be illegitimate, not a scandal, she thought, trying to buck herself up. A life with Cesare fulfilling her longtime dreams at Valente di Roma now that Paul was gone was surely no hardship. She was fortunate, blessed, and she had to forget everything that came before. There is no past now, no Paul to mourn. She would be another man's wife, rear Paul's child as that man's child among the new family and friends she had made here in Rome these last months. Still, if only she could go home to Gram, if only Trent would let her live at Westam.

She sobbed once aloud, but grabbed hold of her emotions as she'd done during these busy days while they'd planned the wedding and their life. The sprightly Lucia knocked and bustled in from the sitting room with Lesley's small silk velvet wisp of calotte hat and the attached veil that fell slightly below her shoulders. Lesley watched while she draped it carefully across the big white silk bed, a bride's bed, Lucia had gushed earlier, as she and Cesare would be spending the next week here at Villa Valente before returning to Rome.

Lucia ran to answer the knock on the door. Perhaps the others were back again—Adriana, wife of Cesare's banker friend Mauro Fracci, from Rome; Baronessa Consuelo, Cesare's elder sister from Milan; the two other maids who would help her into the stunning candlelight crepe de Chine wedding gown and princess cloak with train all adorned with pearls and trimmed with Valente's best rare ermine. She had designed the ensemble herself in the three harried weeks since Cesare's proposal.

Lucia ran back in, wringing her hands. She was forty but seemed younger. She had been her aunt's personal maid here at the villa for years. "Signorina Lesley, it is the Signor Guido," she whispered. "I told him no men can see the bride before the wedding, but he is very insistent. And he's drinking again," she hissed.

"It's only when the bridegroom sees the bride that it's bad luck, Lucia, and probably everyone's been drinking downstairs," Lesley managed calmly with a taut smile. "I've a few minutes before I need to be gowned yet. Tell Guido he may come in."

Lucia shook her head and threw up her quick hands, but hurried to obey. Guido looked marvelous in his double-breasted black cutaway, gray waistcoat, and white chamois gloves, the exact replica of what Cesare and Carlo would wear. It was only the open bottle of champagne in his right hand and two glasses in his left that ruined the effect.

"Thank you for seeing me, Countess," he declared grandly and swept her a low, mocking bow that splashed fizzing champagne onto the tiny, patterned floor tiles. She sat on the corner of the bed and wrapped her quilted dressing gown more securely about her.

"I'm not a countess quite yet, Guido. And are they handing out entire bottles of that before the ceremony downstairs?"

He put his finger to his lips. "Only to the privileged and elite. Immediate family members of the count, you know." He laughed, then shot her a sharp smile. "And the count, being the most privileged and elite here today, of course, could have the entire Bay of Naples out there filled with champagne if he decreed it, a modern-day Caesar, just like his name. You came, he saw, he conquered," he declaimed with another flourish of the bottle, sloshed champagne into both goblets, then set them down on her dressing table, rattling the crystal bottles there.

"A toast to the bride," he announced despite her disapproving stare. "We who are about to die salute you! Here, take it." He rose to thrust the glass at her, splashing more out onto the floor and his glove. His words were clipped, not slurred in the least. If anything, Lesley had noted, drinking only made Guido more acidic and witty, not all foolish as Carlo got when he on a rare occasion drank a bit too much.

"Guido, I'll have some champagne later, all right? And I thank you for the gesture if not the toast itself. Go on now and mingle with the guests, as I've still much to do."

She took both goblets from his unresisting fingers and gently shooed him toward the door. But when she reached to open it, he turned back, seized her shoulders, and thrust his face close to hers. "*Madre Maria,* all this about a modern-day Caesar, Lesley, I'm joshing, of course, but he can be so ruthless. I know it well enough, but do you?"

"Everything will be fine, Guido," she insisted with a defiant toss of her head. "And I hope that you and I will get along better now than we have since that little plot of yours when I first arrived. I know you're not pleased I'm marrying your uncle, but I hope we can both make an effort toward family peace."

"Peace in this day and age? In Count Valente's family?" He snorted a laugh. "I doubt it, but I offer this as a truce between us. Can you live with the man and not cross him? And if you do, what then? Take Tiberius Caesar, for example, that old bastard who had the villa just up above us here on Monte Tiberio that's in ruins, you know." He gestured grandly, then leaned both hands on her shoulders again. "Old Tiberius used to make those who displeased him cast themselves off the cliff into the sea. *Madre Maria*, Lesley, this Cesare did the same damn thing to my mother, so if you had a brain in that beautiful head of yours, you'd be on your way out of here alone, however much you want to get those furrier's hands on Valente's!"

"Guido, please!" she protested and pushed him away. "This is dreadful! You've no right to come in here today to insult your uncle and me! You've had too much champagne, and you're drunk!"

"No, Countess—ah, shall I dub thee aunt or pseudostepmother? Guido Valente is a lot of things but never drunk. I hold my liquor like the count holds his own counsel. But he's damned lucky to have you." He shrugged dramatically. "I wanted to say that too, despite how it's probably all doomed. Listen," he said as his voice rose and his hands returned to her shoulders, "just don't betray him, or who knows what he's capable of. Just don't!"

Lesley's mouth dropped open in surprise. This was a strange new tack for one who fought Cesare both subtly and blatantly without ceasing. "I won't, Guido. I've vowed it to him, and I'll keep my word. Go on now, see if that scamp of a brother of yours and his Stella have arrived on the ferry yet, will you? And don't drink more until later, all right?"

"Sure, sure," he promised and flashed her that swift smile again. "They ought to be here by now or Carlo will never get dressed in time. As for Stella, hell—she probably won't let him go long enough so he can get his pants on! A pretty strange one, Stella." He shook his head and went off down the hall with a hand raised in farewell.

Lesley closed the door and leaned against it. Someday soon, now that she was to be Countess Valente, she must have a little chat with Stella about exactly which brother she really cared for. She moved to the windows along the veranda, which could be opened to embrace wind, sun, and the vista of sky and sea. She had preferred the restful dimness of the room before, privacy in case guests strolled the veranda, but now she lifted one of the brass handles to pierce the room with a shaft of sunlight. She shaded her eyes to look down at the terraced gardens where guests strolled among the fourth-century Roman statuary, awaiting the wedding on the level above the two acres of Valente groves of carobs, almonds, myrtles, and grapevines. Above all that the heavens were clear but for a few graphite clouds on the distant horizon.

Despite Guido's resentment, she would become not only Countess Valente but assume her place in Roman society and the Valente business at the side of one of the most powerful, well-known men in Mussolini's Rome. The dictator had even had wedding gifts delivered by his personal chauffeur in his own black Asturia: a sumptuous set of Venetian blue enamel and gilt-edged crystal stemware by Salviati, and a signed photo of himself in full uniform of the militia, which Cesare had mumbled and frowned over. But it was Il Duce's son-in-law, Count Galeazzo Ciano, who represented him here today.

"Signorina!" Lucia's cry whirled Lesley away from staring out the window. "First il signor Guido demanding to see you, but now—now your bridegroom himself! It just cannot be done, but no one says no to Count Valente!"

The maid admitted him, though he had made it clear last night he would not see her before the wedding. He was already impeccably attired. "What's happened?" she cried. "Did Carlo and Stella arrive all right?"

"Yes, yes, almost an hour ago. They both wanted to see you, but I told them you'd need some time alone." He motioned Lucia out with a flick of wrist, then closed the door behind her.

"I appreciate that, but then what is it?"

"Sit, my sweet. Sit," he ordered and steered her over to the bed. "A bit of a surprise, I'm afraid, but one in all honesty I could not hold until after the wedding, even if it should upset you."

She did not sit, so he pushed her down gently on the bed beside her fanned-out veil and sat beside her, making the bed sag. "A cable apparently came to Valente's yesterday and Carlo and Stella brought it with them today."

"From my grandmum? Is she all right?"

"It's not from England, Lesley." His words came at her

quietly and yet with a hint of something dark and unspoken. He watched her closely as he said, "It's a cable from America, from New York City."

She gasped and wrapped her arms across her stomach, then held out her hand for it. There was no envelope, only a folded paper. "But from whom? Let me see. You—you've read it?"

His intense stare riveted her where she sat. "The cable is to me, Lesley. Brace yourself. Your Paul Kendal, it seems, is quite alive, apparently a mistake on the initial listings of survivors off that ship—"

She exploded from the bed then bounced back to it. She pressed her hands to her mouth to keep from crying out, from screaming her shock and joy. Alive! A miracle! It could not be! "Alive! Alive, are you sure? But it's been months without a word! Is he hurt, wounded?" she shrieked until his cold gaze quieted her.

"I wouldn't know, not from what's written here, although it does mention something about his health. He sounds entirely hearty enough to me, but that he just didn't get around to contacting you before now."

Despite Cesare's words, her heart soared. She was free with those flying goddesses in that painting behind Cesare's head, free to go away to find Paul, to be with him! But this was the day of her wedding and she'd pledged herself to Cesare and the honor of the Valentes forever. She jerked her head back to Cesare's watchful face. "The cable came to you for me?" she asked and again put out her hand for it as he slowly extended it to her.

He watched her shakily unfold it, read it once, probably twice. She frowned, bent over it. Damn, but it seemed to be taking her so long to digest it. He would never, never, he thought, have shared it with her today of all days except that it played so perfectly into his plans. He could not have timed or composed a better message himself to be sure she would go through with the wedding. He'd studied the cable from every possible angle this last hour. It seemed safe to him to let her see it. Evidently the cable he'd sent Paul Kendal nearly a month ago had done its work well. The return cable, which her slender hands held to so tightly her fingers turned white, read,

November 16, 1939

Count Cesare Valente:

Please inform Lady Lesley Westam that she is formally and completely released from any plans which passed once between us. Best wishes to her in all endeavors she undertakes for her career. Whatever her plans, mine must of necessity remain my health, my writing, my family, and vows to the woman who waited for me.

Regards to the House of Valente.

Paul Kendal
New York City

She stared so long at the words, especially his name, that they tilted and blurred. Paul Kendal. Her Paul of New York City-on-Hudson with the quick laugh and alluring green eyes and heavenly, warm embrace. She did not resist when Cesare put out his hand for the cable. Paul was alive but he had betrayed her, forsaken all they had planned. Worse, there was no other way to read it but that he had decided to honor a previous vow he had made to his family and to Melissa Pearson. Even now, Lesley would not have wanted to marry him if it were only a child which made him stay true to her—to their vows, the love sworn between them forever in Châtillon, in Venice, even that last morning at the train. Swept away on their romantic little lark in London and through Europe, he had lied about a former promise to that woman. Then, when he returned home after the disaster of the *Athenia*, he'd realized he loved Melissa and no other!

"Lesley, sweet, forgive me for sharing this with you now, but I thought it best. You see, the man you've been grieving for is alive and committed to someone else, and so he really isn't worth either your grief or your love. And not worthy of the child you carry. The child we shall rear together."

She couldn't bear to lift her head to look at Cesare, couldn't bear to have him say these dreadful things about Paul, but they were true, true. She felt broken, so very empty despite the precious life that grew, truly fatherless, within her. It was the first time since she'd known she was with child that she'd felt so empty. But for the child she would stand now and lift her head and go on with all of this. A dream—everything with Paul had been only a fantasy, a dream.

A great shudder wracked her body, but Cesare marveled to see her stand straight and meet his gaze. Her beautiful eyes were agonized pools of tears that did not fall.

Her voice was very tiny. "I still would like to be alone for just a few moments, Cesare. Then Lucia will help me dress. She and I alone shall manage, if you'll just send her in to me on your way out."

"Of course, my sweet. Lesley, I adore you, I love you deeply," he vowed, extending his hands toward her as if to prove each word. "I am sorry for this shock, but we stand on the threshold of a wonderful future together."

She glanced away. "Yes. I'll see you in the gardens soon."

She looked stunning as well as stunned, and he stepped back in awe. A magnificent woman with strength like stone when she needed it, even though she must be shattered. "In the gardens then, my love, soon," he repeated. As he slowly closed the door, he glimpsed her standing in the narrow patch of sun from the single opened jalousy. Her crimson hair looked ablaze. Her back was erect, chin lifted, her profile seemed carved from marble. But her hands rested protectively across her belly. Her gaze looked forever distant, as if he'd never really touch her again, never get her back. But, by all that was holy, he would!

"She wants you now, Lucia," he called to the faithful maid as he moved down the hall toward his own rooms. "See that she's ready soon and don't leave her alone until she comes downstairs." He clipped out the orders. "And I'll send some others up again, my sister, Signora Fracci, perhaps Stella Sollo, too."

In his room, he leaned his shoulder against the wall. That deceit had drained him, but it had fallen so perfectly into his lap. That angry yet controlled cable was such a far cry from the first passionate one the man had sent. He did possess a gift with words, a great writer indeed, as Lesley had said. If only they had such a man to work with them on their secret little paper, *Libero,* to rail against that destructive bourgeois Mussolini, to raise Italy to arms against their dictator, not for him.

Cesare shook his head and wiped his brow. He had thought he would revel in this victory over Lesley, this complete ruination of her love for that other man, but the power of her heart and soul had quite conquered him in a way he had never expected. She actually loved Paul Kendal still, maybe always would, he could tell. And yet, he somehow dared believe that any vow Lesley made to him or the Valentes would be kept for life, especially the vows she would make in the garden among their guests today.

He straightened his bow tie in the mirror and nervously smoothed his thick black eyebrows. He darted a look back out into the hall. Lucia had gone in. Lesley's door was closed as he hurried downstairs to await her final and permanent entry into his gardens and his life.

PART II

Voice of my Heart

Oh! hast thou forgotten this day we must part?
It may be for years, and it may be forever;
Then why are thou silent, thou voice of my heart?
                                    JULIE CRAWFORD
                                    "Kathleen Mavoureen"

❦ ❦ *Chapter Eight*

THE MULTITIERED STONE MANSION was by far the most magnificent in the fashionable Roman neighborhood of Parioli. Despite the nip of an early March wind, the noisy party spilled out onto its ornately decorated, lighted patio. Here the host, Mussolini's chief to the Supreme General Staff, Pietro Badoglio, held court with a group of cronies amid a profusion of flags, flowers, and lanterns.

Lesley excused herself from the wives, who stayed inside to cluster around the polished mahogany bar at the far end of the lounge. She sank gratefully onto the huge U-shaped couch and let the crisp night air from the open French doors clear the air of cigar smoke and her head of nearly two hours of chatter.

Next month when the baby came, she could finally escape this ungainly body that did not seem to be hers anymore. She felt as if she were held hostage by the flow of the months, yet wonderfully invaded by the tiny fluttering, then the pokes of fists or feet that had lately turned her ivory skin blue in spots. But she would also be glad to escape the social circuit of wealthy, elite Rome for a while. She had plunged into the melee of entertaining and being entertained as readily as Cesare, but for different reasons. He liked to show her off as one would a newly acquired Titian or Tintoretto. Something that suggested one's prestige and power. She was only too glad to have something else to do to help forget her loss of Paul.

"Sweet, are you certain you're all right?" Cesare's voice cut through the party buzz. Her eyes shot open. He bent over her solicitously with his martini glass halfway to his lips. "You actually looked as if you were nodding off for a moment. Here's your club soda with a twist of lime."

"Thanks, dear. Just getting off these wretched ankles for a

minute to escape those cigars host Pietro smokes one after the other. I promise I won't be asleep at our first party where Il Duce himself is to put in an appearance," she said, smiling up at him.

Although he had been headed outside with the men, he carefully tugged up each black silk trouser leg and sat beside her. "Lesley, I hadn't meant to bring this up here, but when Carlo was home last weekend, he suggested you're working entirely too hard at being both furrier and countess lately, and I suppose he's right."

That would be the day, she thought, when Cesare took advice from either of his nephews, but she said only, "I love keeping busy. I'm fine."

He put one hand on her knee and leaned closer. "But perhaps this month just resting would be wise. We can't go dashing off to your beloved Capri now in case the birth is early. You've got to remain home and relax more, as I intend for you to do for at least several months after."

She tucked her hand in his arm as if they would stroll somewhere together and took a long drink of soda. She felt warm affection for her husband of three months, especially when he was concerned for her feelings, or those of Carlo or Guido, as he seemed now. Still, his possessiveness had been wearing on her lately—as if a woman more than seven months into her first and very heavy pregnancy would go skipping off somewhere to disgrace him or the Valente name!

"We've discussed this, my dear, and I told you," she assured him, with a tilt of chin, "that if I feel too tired, I'll sleep in or go home early from the shop. And as for afterward, we can decide then together how long before I'm back at Valente's when we see how I really feel."

"Ah, my sweet, I'd give a king's ransom to know how you really feel," he began so intently, then craned his head away suddenly as if to eavesdrop on the little group just outside. In that slightly condescending schoolmaster's voice he so often used with her, he swiftly changed the subject to describe the current titles and political maneuverings of several men on the terrace.

She tried to concentrate on his words, but exhaustion assailed her again. When the dance band in the next room began another American tune, she hardly took in what he said at all.

"And to top it all off, that damned Ciano can't take his eyes off you again." Cesare ended his little recital of information. She forced her attention back. "I don't care if the man is Mussolini's vaunted son-in-law, he has the morals of a tramcar Lothario—even worse than Guido's, I might add—and I don't like it. A man that close to the ultimate source of power who lives separately from his wife, even if he does escort her to the occasional party like tonight, is a disgrace to Italy. Of course," he added more quietly and shrugged, "Il Duce sets the moral tone for the entire damned government. So Ciano cavorts with film starlets on the beach at Ostia and pursues amorous domestic affairs when he should be running his Ministry of Foreign Affairs. Needless to say, my sweet, the man is not to be trusted any more than Il Duce himself, and I don't like the way his eyes devour you."

"Really, Cesare," she remonstrated gently, trying to recall where she'd read Ciano described in those very words as a tramcar Lothario. "The man barely glanced this way, and no one could fancy a woman who rather rivals the Colosseum in size lately." She did not even look over at the thirty-four-year-old flabby Ciano with his carefully pomaded hair whom the social set of Rome snidely dubbed the "Ducellino" behind his back.

"Anyone depraved enough to pinch a bride on her wedding day in front of her new husband is not to be trusted, I say," he insisted, with a pointed finger at her. "But then anyone Il Duce approves of would have to be a moral degenerate."

Lesley's eyes widened, not only at the acidic tone but at the livid flush that stained Cesare's face. Daily, she came to more completely grasp the extent of his contempt for the Fascist regime and those who ran it. Yet he mingled with them, seemed to seek them out. He had no doubt called many of them his friends for years, and wanted to know everything about them.

"Come on now," she soothed, afraid he might actually get a coughing jag or even drink too much and tell some of these people what he really thought. She'd heard the gossip that the resistance was financed by some of Rome's best businessmen,

who detested Fascist control of Italy's economy for the war
effort. Cesare had denied any part in that, and she hoped he
was telling the truth, for she didn't need her husband in trouble
over anything else. She only wanted to get through having this
child, be a good wife, design her furs—and somehow be happy
in a country that was at peace with the world if not itself.

"Let's take a little stroll outside like the rest of the sheep
waiting for the wolf's arrival," she teased. He nodded and
managed a grim little smile. "Besides, you said you thought
the women of Mussolini's family were to be admired, so Il
Duce's brood can't be all bad," she insisted.

He helped her rise. "At least his wife," he admitted, and let
her take the martini glass. Most Italians agreed that Mussolini's
wife, Rachele, was an innocent victim of Il Duce's womanizing. He had a line of mistresses and a long-time inamorata,
Claretta Petacci. But his daughter Edda, Ciano's estranged
wife, resembled her father in personality and ambitions.
"Edda," Cesare said, with a hard glance at the auburn-haired,
laughing beauty at the other end of the room, "has finally seen
the error of her ways concerning Ciano. At least some cast-off
women eventually do."

As usual, Lesley let the subtle jab slide by. "Perhaps Il Duce
won't even come now that it's so late, Cesare. Poor Badoglio
with that dance band eternally warming up in the ballroom."
She blinked quick tears away as she recognized the lively
strains of "Puttin' on the Ritz," which she and Paul had danced
so wonderfully to that night at the Ritz Hotel in London.

"Il Duce hates dancing, so no one dares to do it until he's
come and gone, however late he is. His habit is to suddenly
appear when he's least expected, but he won't stay long,"
Cesare told her as she put their glasses on a passing silver tray
toted by a butler in black tailcoat and they went outside.

The air cleared her lungs and her head until the heavy cigar
smoke drifted her way again, as pervasive as the oppressive
atmosphere of the party. She urged Cesare away from Colonel
Eugen Dollman's little group. Not only was the man they
called *Standartenführer* an SS colonel and Hitler's representative in Rome, but she personally found the man offensive. His
manners were effeminate, his tapering hands clinging, his
looks weakly genteel, as if to lure one into some gossipy

confidence. Mussolini had met last month with the American under secretary of state, Sumner Welles, and had apparently ignored President Roosevelt's plea for neutrality and request for a meeting. The German star, under Dollman's fussy tending, was on the rise, and she wanted no part of that.

"Ah, Cesare, you've decided to share your English beauty with us vultures," the guest of honor, Mussolini's ruler of Libya, Marshal Italo Balbo, teased as the little group of men they had walked past parted as if to draw them in.

"Never to share, Cesare, eh?" their usually taciturn host, the elderly Badoglio razzed. Lesley glanced around the group. These men were all elite advisors to the dictator. Power reeked from them like the cigars she hated. Yet lately their unctuous, smug self-satisfaction had been disturbed by alarm and even hints of panic as possible war with all Europe careened closer.

"I hope we're not interrupting important secrets, then," Cesare told them almost as if urging them to continue their discussion. Several of the men shifted glances to the Valentes or each other. The breeze that sighed through the line of myrtle trees screening the lighted swimming pool and rustled the huge tricolor Italian banners over their heads suddenly shot a chill up Lesley's spine.

"Of course nothing any intelligent observer wouldn't know," Badoglio said pointedly and glanced behind him. "Just that Hitler's aspirations and Dollman's pleasant manners aside, Mother Italy is ill prepared for war. Our army divisions have hardly been supplied with fifty percent of their necessary gear, we're pitifully low on fuel, and have rusting artillery from the last war included in the tallies of our empire's so-called modern armaments, that's all."

"Damn, and we're holding on to that rat hole Libya by our fingernails with century-old cannon mounted on garbage trucks," Balbo put in. "I don't care if Il Duce did tell Roosevelt's man that the decision for Italy is as if 'The minute hand is pointing to one minute before midnight,' I think for all our sakes—"

"*You* think what, my Balbo?" A sharp, strident voice cut off the man's heated words. Everyone turned, snapped to attention. Mussolini had entered through the back gardens. Heels clicked together in a nervous staccato, hands were raised in the

Roman salute reborn under Mussolini's empire. Cesare stood unmoved while Lesley clung to his arm. From inside, peopl. streamed out to encircle the dictator and his little entourage of bodyguards. As if the musicians two rooms away had sensed Il Duce's arrival, the music stopped.

Lesley studied Mussolini while everyone was introduced and greetings exchanged. He was very short: the newsreels had lied about the size if not the impact of the man. But the blaring loudspeakers of Rome had all too often correctly reproduced the man's grandiose, bombastic tones. He looked rather flabby, with a receding hairline and snowy temples. He was fifty-six but seemed older, despite the broad shoulders, bantam rooster legs set in a wide stance, and belligerent scowl. He embraced the beaming, effusive SS Colonel Dollman like a long-lost friend but did not seem to care a bit for his own son-in-law, whom he ignored.

"You were saying, Balbo?" Il Duce prodded with a dramatic sweep of his arm when Balbo in his turn greeted him with a nod and sharp salute.

"Only quoting your words, as all of us are urged to do, Duce."

"Quite wise since you know I control events and not the other way around," Mussolini intoned, his square chin outthrust. Then his eyes lit on Lesley. "So, a lovely woman—and a beautiful example of Italian motherhood even now." He extended a perfectly gloved hand that enhanced the impact of the high tunic-necked, black commander in chief uniform respendent with gold buttons and an array of rainbow-ribboned medals.

Lesley flushed both at his words and avid scrutiny as she of necessity stepped away from Cesare to accept Il Duce's hand. He seemed suddenly the beaming father, or courtly gallant, she mused, and fought to keep from grinning. Whatever the man was, he was above all a fine actor.

"I must admit I am in the throes of rather advanced would-be motherhood at the very least, Duce," she admitted with a modest shrug.

"For which we should all be proud." His voice boomed out over the little group as if he were addressing one of his massive crowds in the Piazza Venezia. "I have urged that true Italians owe it to Italy's destined future to produce many new lives for the fatherland."

Cesare stepped to her side but did not pull her hand from the dictator's as he would have anyone else's. "Twelve children is the sacred number I believe you have decreed, Duce," Cesare put in, his voice all too obviously a taunt. Behind Mussolini, several men exchanged glances, but only Il Duce's son-in-law had the nerve to snicker.

Il Duce's black eyes went hard, cold, but still he smiled. "Then you are Count Valente's new English wife," he said as if Cesare had not spoken. "Charmed, Contessa, and pleased to have one who is so obviously a clever and lovely lady choose Italy over the land of her birth. Next time your Duce desires to purchase a fur coat he will not have to put up with only the count's sour face, perhaps." He shouted a quick laugh at his own joke while the others joined in nervously.

"And now, Balbo," he added, and loosed her hand to turn back to his marshal of Libya, "I tell you, Italy *is* ready now to fight. The olive branch of peace must spring from a forest of eight million bayonets." The arm swept away in a wide arc; the chin jutted further. "As for our ally, Germany, I meet the Führer again next week, to assure him when and where Italy's greatness will be revealed. But as for England, there are only two ways to defend oneself against an enemy, to kill him or embrace him. Beautiful English ladies who marry those loyal to us we may embrace, but England itself—well, I am sorry to be blunt, Contessa Valente," he concluded grandly with a shrug of the broad padded shoulders as if to dismiss her and England.

When SS Colonel Dollman led the others in a round of applause, Cesare pulled Lesley back away from the crowd. "I could tell you had a reply on your lips, but not now, Lesley. Someday perhaps, but not now, not this way," he warned in a low voice.

"After this, I think I've been in the man's presence enough to last a lifetime. Yes, I have a few things I'd like to tell him, but I'm starting to feel nauseous, and I'm not certain if it's him or all that blasted cigar smoke."

"I'll get you home. I've heard all I need for now."

He steered her across the vast, deserted main lounge toward

the cloakroom, while the little alfresco rally continued on the
terrace with Mussolini's voice booming out occasional comments they could no longer discern. "Then it's definitely war
for your country against mine," she murmured.

"I hear he changes his mind several times a day, and no
doubt at the meeting with Hitler he mentioned that damned
bloodthirsty German guttersnipe will decide for him. Sit here,
sweet, while I fetch your cape."

"I'll just nip in the powder room for one moment," she told
him and hurried away, hoping the roiling in her stomach would
not betray her before the two maids, or in the auto on the way
back to the town house.

Inside the small, silk-lined room, she jerked to a halt and
steadied herself with one hand on the wall. The baby moved,
punching her so distinctly under the soft lime-green ruffles of
her draped chiffon gown to make her feel all wobbly legged
while bile rose in her throat. Edda Ciano, Mussolini's daughter, was bending over to stare closely into the long gilt-framed
mirror while she repaired her lipstick, and worse, she wore
Lesley's stolen Valente sable coat!

Blast them all, she could not believe it! She knew instantly
from the nuances of color, the unique match of the pelts, that
it was the coat taken from her by force en route to Rome. But
however could this wealthy woman have come by it? Lesley
fought back her urge to be ill, controlled her impulse to tear the
coat from the back of this woman sprung from the seed of that
obscene man spouting threats out there.

"Oh, hello again, Countess," Edda said and straightened. "I
might have come with my husband, but I'm going home without him, you know. He has to stand at attention out there
listening to all that, but I don't. Married to one man, in love
with another." She rolled brown eyes framed by spiky mas-
caraed lashes. "Now don't look so shocked. I'm sure you've
heard that's how it is between me and Galeazzo, though Il
Duce hardly approves."

Married to one man, in love with another, Edda's words
taunted Lesley. She tried not to stare at the coat as if she'd
taken leave of her senses. Edda moved toward the door while
both maids ludicrously curtsied as if the woman were royalty.
The sable was definitely the same coat with its wrapped cuffs,

the perfect swaying natural scallop of French hem when it moved. Lesley longed to touch it.

"No—I understand," she managed, her voice shaky. "Excuse me, but that coat looks like one designed at Valente's."

Lesley had actually begun to tremble, and a back pain shuddered up her spine. Surely, this was only a new trick her body played; it could not be labor already so soon. No one would ever believe this child could be Cesare's if she went into labor already. But the coat—she had to know—

"Actually, an admirer bought it for me on the black market, so there's no designer label in it at all," Edda Ciano told her with a smug smile and quick upward dart of eyes. "Simply everyone's putting oodles of money into furs or jewels as a hedge against inflation in case there's a war—"

Lesley closed her eyes. Had the woman left the room and was only speaking now through the door? And where was Cesare? She had to tell him about the coat, to get it back, buy it back—anything.

"Countess Valente, are you quite all right? Sit. Here, sit down, and I'll send a maid to fetch your husband."

Lesley nodded. "He's just outside," she thought she said, and someone held her head when she became very sick in the fluted ceramic basin. She was sick, she told herself through the murmuring of Cesare's voice, of cigars, and politics, and hatred, and Edda's coat, and doing without the man she loved so she could have his child in wedlock.

"She'll be fine now, just fine. Just get my chauffeur so we can help her out." Cesare's voice drifted to her amid the waves of longing and hurting. Paul—Paul would have just lifted her to carry her, she thought, but she accepted Cesare's embrace to stand, then walked out past the wide-eyed Edda in her precious, stolen coat.

For three weeks after that night of false labor pains, Lesley rested at the Valente town house while Roman life and the sunny spring of 1940 went blithely on without her. Cesare refused to approach Edda Ciano about the sable, but had promised Lesley that she could accompany him to the fur auctions in Leningrad next January and select pelts for a Barguzinsky sable coat of her own design. So she sketched that garment and others, sat on the patio in the shade, and listened to the BBC Overseas Daily News to keep abreast of England's tense wait for German planes that never came in what they were now calling "The Phony War" at home.

She wrote a weekly letter to Gram. The post was abysmally slow if it got through at all, but trunk calls to England were nearly impossible. She'd only had one return letter from Gram in the five months she'd been in Rome, and that had grieved a great deal more for Lesley's separation from that "charming, determined young American" than it praised her marriage to Cesare Valente. Oh yes, Paul Kendal was both charming and determined, Lesley told herself bitterly when she read those words: charming at seduction and determined to select which of his whimsical vows to his women on two continents he would honor. Of all people, she had expected Gram to sympathize with her and support her fully. Lady Sarah had wished her congratulations on her marriage and the approaching birth of the child Lesley had let her assume was Cesare's. Still, Lesley couldn't help thinking Gram somehow believed she had taken the wrong turn through the thick yew hedge of life. That weighed heavily on her, as did Paul's desertion.

Trent, her grandmum had reported, was now flying dangerous reconnaissance missions full time over the Channel with his beloved Royal Air Force in a new Spitfire plane he "simply doted on." Lesley found herself often thinking of her brother—and worrying about his safety in spite of all their differences. About the source of her alienation from Trent, Gram had written that "bossy, belligerent Constance" came and went from Westam, tried to order her about, and spearheaded the continued court battle over Father's will. If there were other, later letters either from Gram or Lesley's solicitors, only Il Duce's shabbily run postal system knew. Lesley could tell this letter had been opened and read, and she decided then never to write anything but the most innocuous news home.

During the days and occasional evenings, Cesare was gone a great deal working at both Valente's and with other business ventures. But Carlo came home for a week on leave, and they enjoyed each other's company as always. Sometimes he brought Stella Sollo to visit, though Lesley had never yet had the girl alone long enough to discuss her apparent attraction to

Guido. Guido had stopped by only once since he had taken up permanent residence at a nearby *pensione*.

There had been a terrible late-night row between him and Cesare over the fact that Guido continued to bring the radical anti-Fascist paper *Libero* into the house and promote it to his friends. Guido had called Cesare a hypocrite to socialize with the dictator while he ruined Italy both economically and morally. It was an argument anyone in the house could hear, but when Lesley tried to discuss it later with Cesare, he insisted it had been private. And he'd forbidden her to ever look at *Libero* again when she'd mentioned that an issue she'd seen espoused the exact sentiments, in similar words, that he'd shared with her on the qt at Badoglio's party.

Cesare's use of his private time puzzled her. When she asked about it, he assured her he was only meeting occasionally with a coalition of Roman merchants, trying to hedge their bets in case Italy went to war. She was certain he didn't have another woman, even in the months their marital relations stopped. He was entirely too attentive and possessive for that. The months after the wedding when she and Cesare had made love seemed a distant blur now, almost as it had even while he'd touched her so assuredly, so demandingly in bed. Sex with Cesare was not like what she had experienced before with Paul, but she had not expected it and was therefore hardly disappointed. Despite Cesare's obviously well-honed erotic skills, even with her desire to please him, she never felt anything approaching that bone-shaking splendor she'd had with Paul Kendal.

Lesley sighed and stretched her legs where she sat propped up on the silk lounge chair under the canvas awning. She tossed aside the copy of *Osservatore Romano*, the Vatican paper, which was one of the few Il Duce did not control. Though she still mistrusted journalists and journals, she had taken to reading papers these last few weeks to keep abreast of the news. With both France and England facing Hitler's possible onslaught and Italy likely to be drawn in, she felt she needed to be informed on the latest developments, even though it all seemed so distant to her. Lately, her memories and her desire to have this birth over and her child or children in her arms were all that she could really focus on. After her false labor pains, the doctor had been certain he had heard two heartbeats—two! The impact of that possibility had been enough to keep her off her feet these last three weeks.

She heard the phone ring in the hall, and Lilla, the upstairs maid, answered. Soon their large staff would be swelled by a nurse, and eventually a nanny when she went back to Valente's as she hoped to—if she could convince Cesare without an argument. Lately he had been terribly on edge and his comments, both subtle or blatant, could be so hurtful. They only proved he had not truly accepted that she could love these children without loving their real father.

"Contessa, the phone." Lilla's voice interrupted her musings. "It is il signor Guido at Valente's. There has been a fire, it seems—"

Lesley swung to her feet to the floor and grabbed the receiver Lilla extended toward her. "Guido, what happened? What is it? Where's Cesare?"

"Calm down now. I'm only letting you know there's been some smoke damage, a little fire in the count's office. Do you know where he is?"

"I thought he was there." She stood and, despite her bulk, began to pace. "How ever did a fire start in his office if he's not there?"

He ignored her question. "Then he's probably at one of his little meetings with his cronies. Just tell him he'd better stop by when he gets back."

"But how bad is it? What happened?" She gripped the receiver hard to her ear. "You know if there's been smoke, all the furs and the things they touch are going to have to be aired and fumigated immediately. Smoke can ruin furs for months."

"Yes, Countess, it clings—like women."

Lesley distinctly heard a giggle in the background. What if Guido were drinking while Cesare was gone and no workers were in the shop after noon on Saturday? What if there really had been some damage he wasn't telling her? "Guido, I'm coming round."

"In your condition with the baby or a whole brace of them due any minute?" he screeched. "That's crazy, and the count would kill me if you do."

"I'm all right. I'll just have the big Bugatti drop me off. And Guido, if any of this is your fault, I just might kill you, too."

Over the servants' protests, she was dressed and at Valente's in twenty minutes. She should not have gone, no doubt, for the ponderous weight she carried had shifted so much lower, but the furs needed tending more than she did now. If Cesare came in, she would go back home. Besides, her doctor was just a call away and the coupé could deliver her to the Santa Clara hospital in minutes if she began to feel any worse. Being back at Valente's even if for a few minutes might be just the thing she needed to lift her out of her three-week malaise.

It was the climb up the narrow stairs she had not reckoned on, but Guido helped her, protesting and scolding all the way. She sank wearily onto the cutter's bench at the top before venturing farther. The work area of the room looked blessedly untouched though smoke hung heavy in the air. "That smell is dreadful, Guido!" She lifted her head and met his nervous eyes. "Exactly what burned? Tell me, as I intend to find out anyway."

"Of course you will. Nothing stops the Countess Valente when she has a cause," he groused, and brushed stray locks of hair back from his high forehead.

"I'm weary to death of your innuendos and accusations, Guido!"

"And have you wearied of *his* yet?"

"My relationship with my husband is my business! And I obviously need to look for myself at what has happened!" She heaved herself up and pushed his arm away as he stepped forward to help.

"I'm sorry, really, Lesley. Things just get out of hand between the count and me." He dared to flash her that winning smile. "I don't mean for you to get pulled in, really."

"I'm a Valente now, Guido. I'm already pulled in." She shrugged his hand off again, then turned back to face him squarely. "At least the fact you can admit you're sorry and not call me 'countess' or 'auntie' or 'stepmother dear' in that wretchedly snide tone of yours means a great deal to me."

Slowly, she shoved open the door to Cesare's office. It seemed so heavy, her arms heavy, her upper body pressing down on her pelvis and legs. "Oh, Guido, blast it all!" she cried as her watering eyes surveyed the room.

Paper patterns had evidently flamed on the design table and

been shoved to a burned heap on the floor to be doused and stamped out. Two of the four stuffed muslin mannequins had burned. The drapes had been torn down to be sloshed with water, which still stood in puddles on the blackened floor. The impact of the heavy, acrid odor low in her belly made her almost double over with pain where she stood, and she grasped wildly at the door knob, then at the frightened Guido.

"*Madre Maria*, Lesley! You shouldn't have come! I knew it!"

"I think it's only the smell. Let me sit down back out there." He helped her to a bench in the outer office. Despite the open skylight pouring in April sun and breezes, the room—everything—seemed so oppressive, bearing down on her. "Guido, please ring the hospital and tell them I'm coming in. Then get on the phone to the insurance people," she gasped, "get as many of the staff up here as possible to air the place. At least the pelts locked up downstairs will be untouched and—Oh!" Her agonized cry and the look of shock and pain on her face shot Guido to action. But by the time he was back to her, her water had broken and the pains were coming hard and so very fast she would not let him or the chauffeur move her. Guido rang desperately around to locate her doctor and finally left a message. At her instruction, the two men made a bed for her on the floor of the work area—soft pelts covered with fresh rolls of muslin from downstairs. Then, soon, she lost track of time as the full force of contractions hit her in great crashing waves of pain and fear.

"Guido, please don't leave me until the doctor or Cesare comes." She clawed at his arm, grabbed it. "Did you get the doctor?"

"A doctor's coming. And see, I've brought Stella from next door. It might help to have a woman, I thought—"

"Yes, yes. Guido—" She crunched his fingers together in her hand. His eyes watered, darted. He looked very frightened for the first time, more like the boy Carlo always was. Perhaps Guido really needed her too; that thought calmed her. "Guido, you accidently started the fire, didn't you—your cheroot? But why were you here?"

"I still oversee things when he's away. Just rest now, please, Lesley!"

Stella Sollo's face appeared near Guido's where they knelt by the makeshift pallet, and they exchanged guilty glances. The woman's giggle on the phone. Oh, blast it, he'd been up here alone with Carlo's beloved little Stella and somehow caught his uncle's private room on fire. Lesley closed her eyes as another crunching pain swept all that away. One doctor came, then eventually her own. Later Cesare appeared to hold her hand before the doctors shooed everyone downstairs. She could hear him yelling at Guido through her hard breathing and the moans she could no longer suppress.

"Tell them not to fight," she gasped out to whomever was holding her hand and wiping her wet brow now.

"All right, we'll tell them, Contessa. Bear down now. I believe we are going to have double duty here today, and we've sent for some other help and some portable baby cribs."

Two babies, she thought, in her exhaustion as she bore down hard again as they said. One for Paul and one for me to hold, but that would never happen now. If they looked like Paul, she would never, never be able to bear it, bear it—

She drifted in and out of pain with something they gave her. "A girl and one more yet to come, I'm certain of it now!" a man's voice boasted. "Tell the count there will be two, Signorina Sollo. Twins and a first birth, no wonder they are premature."

Had Cesare convinced them or paid them for that? Lesley wondered. Cesare Valente could have, could buy anything he wanted except peace with his nephews, the honor of his country, and his wife's love. Twins, a girl first. A girl, but Stella Sollo was the girl using Carlo and now Guido might be using her. Using, what were they using on her now?

Later, before she slept again, they told her, "A beautiful girl and a slightly smaller boy, Contessa, and we're going to have you all at Santa Clara when you wake again. Rest now, everything's fine, just fine . . ."

She sighed somewhere deep inside and her muscles unwound, floated. She hadn't told them they could put her to sleep, but where was she now? Not at home. There had been a phone call, a fire. With the furs, that was it. She was with all the furs her young friend Melly Mott had tanned for her and she and Mother would make fur coats for her two little dolls in the sunny sitting room at Westam.

"You've done so well today, sweet, so well, and I'm very proud of you," Mother assured her in a man's voice and held her hand. She tried to answer Mother, but she was already deep asleep.

Lesley was in awe of her beautiful twins. She had never believed, except for the love she had once felt for Paul, that she could ever cherish anyone so much. She just looked at them for hours if she could not be tending or rocking them. They fit so perfectly into her arms against her shoulders. The twins would never desert her. They needed her love. Their ever-curious eyes lit up to see her; their downy heads turned at the mere sound of her voice. When she suckled them it was if just the three of them existed, not Cesare, no one else!

Their velvety hair was soft black and their eyes bluish tending to green, but they could well enough pass as her and Cesare's children. He had been adamant about naming them after Lesley's mother, Caterina, and his own father, Paolo.

"But you are certain about the name Paolo, Cesare?" she had asked him, still light-hearted from the births and the massive array of flowers, the emerald jewelry, and new teal-blue Alfa Romeo convertible he had showered her with all at once. Paolo was Paul in Italian, the last name she'd expected him to suggest. "It's just that we could name him for you if you wish," she prodded.

"I prefer the tradition of using grandparents' names, sweet. And since that other one by that name is forever gone from your life, what's the harm? Unless it will be too painful for you to give our son that name for some reason, of course," he'd added and studied her face intently, his dark eyebrows poised in expectation.

"Of course not, if it's what you want," she'd agreed. She was grateful once again that he seemed to care sincerely for the two precious mites with whom God had blessed her—blessed them.

But today when Cati and Paolo slept, Lesley hurried to the front of the house, to her old guest bedroom, which overlooked the Piazza Venezia. Rumors were rampant that Il Duce would actually declare war today from his elevated balcony. Since early morning when Cesare had gone out, droves of lorries had brought in people and spilled them out into the square. After all, how long would Italy stand by and not throw in with Hitler's victorious, ravenous panzer forces, which had invaded France five days ago and were already overrunning the low countries and Scandinavia? Outside, a crescendo of humming droned on like a swarm of hornets threatening the sunny June day. But the twins would sleep on undisturbed. She only prayed that it would be so throughout their childhood if Il Duce did indeed declare war on their mother's homeland, making her a marked person here despite her marriage to Cesare Valente.

She was surprised to find Guido, nattily attired as always, standing at the open window to the bedroom. Since the fire at Valente's over two months ago, she and Guido had kept a mutual truce, because she had never mentioned to Cesare she had discovered its cause. "I didn't know you were coming, Guido."

He bestowed a flash of smile before turning back to the scene below. "I never miss free tragic theater, especially not Il Duce's imitation of Juliet ranting from a balcony," he told her and exhaled a plume of cheroot smoke out the window.

She joined him and they stared out at Il Duce's balcony with its huge, carved fasces symbol on both sides and loudspeakers sprouting under it like ugly black mushrooms. "You know, Guido, I truly wish you and Cesare could cease your own battles over his not taking a public stance against all this," she urged gently. "Cesare hates Fascism as much as you do."

"All the worse, then, that he's such a coward and cuddles up to Mussolini and his bastards—especially at the expense of cuddling up to you."

"We're fine, Guido, and hardly likely to take advice from someone who can't keep the same girl for more than one month straight. You haven't seen Stella anymore now that Carlo's been at camp, have you? You know—"

"Sh!" He cut her off, evidently relieved Mussolini would speak now. He shoved his mussed hair back from his face. "He's come out, look!"

Feeling utterly helpless, Lesley wrapped her arms about herself. "I can't believe the size of this crowd."

Guido snorted a laugh. "This is just a small, intimate gathering for the man who spent millions of lire blazing 'Heil Hitler!' in lights across the hills of Rome when *der Führer* visited. And for his perverted dreams of glory, he'd just as easily spend a million lives," he growled and flipped his cheroot butt out the window.

Her hands on the marble ledge, she leaned out over the vast sweep of square. It was a shifting sea of heads dotted with occasional tricolors or Fascist flags clear to the Palazzo Venezia, where Il Duce stood, and beyond to the huge, ornate monument to King Victor Emmanuel. Although she had been watching the crowd swell all morning, the impact of such great numbers awed her to silence as the truculent tones of Benito Mussolini boomed over a dozen loudspeakers.

"Fighting men of the land, the sea, and the air," his high-pitched voice blasted out. "Blackshirts of the revolution, men and women of Italy, of the empire and of the kingdom of Albania, hearken! An hour marked by destiny is striking in the sky of our country, the hour of irrevocable decisions."

"I can't believe this tripe," Guido hissed in a low voice as if Il Duce could hear them. "The bastard's insane, and he'll pull us all down with him, Germany or not."

"Why can't he see it?"

Cesare's voice came from behind them as he put his arms around Lesley and nodded to Guido. "He sees it, sweet, and he's not insane, only corrupted by power. And Guido's right. Even Mussolini's closest advisors know Italy's future is doomed either with Hitler or by Hitler."

They stood, three tiny insignificant people at the window, above the ocean of heads, and listened to the rantings of the winds of the times: "The democracies of the West have always hindered the advance and often plotted against the very existence of the Italian people. We have done this and will do this with Germany, with her people, with her victorious armed forces."

"Because we'll have none of our own," Cesare put in, uselessly jabbing the air toward Mussolini with his index finger. The voice crackled on. Lesley felt chilled. It was almost as if in this vast open-air arena the clutches of claustrophobia, which had not bothered her for so long, threatened again. She turned away, only to be enclosed in Cesare's firm embrace.

She went stiff in his arms. "I need to look in on the children, Cesare. This isn't real. This isn't our war!"

"Not yours or the innocents', anyway, my sweet. And don't worry. Dictators come and go but Rome, the Eternal City, somehow endures forever. Go on then. Guido and I will watch together."

She walked away. Ordinarily, that tiny sign of reconciliation between feuding family members would have warmed her. How much she had longed for such a gesture from Trent all those years; but he hated her. They were as much at war as the nations. Paul had deserted her and was lost to her forever. She vowed it would never be so for her beloved twins, and perhaps here, as a Valente, there was new hope for family unity and love. She looked back at Cesare and Guido standing shoulder to shoulder, then hurried to the nursery with the droning words of the man the government called the Divine Duce ringing in her ears: "People of Italy, to arms! Show your courage, your tenacity and your worth."

She cuddled her babies in her arms and feverishly prayed this war would never touch the house of Valente, nor the precious little lives that were all she would ever have of Paul.

❧ ❧ Chapter Nine

A WEEK LATER Lesley invited Stella Sollo for tea. Together they awaited Carlo's arrival from his camp in Foggia for his last weekend leave before he would be sent somewhere on secret orders in Mussolini's declared but not yet genuine war. Guido had received his induction papers this week and was in a perfectly wretched mood when he'd roared off in his Maserati to fetch Carlo.

On the warm balcony of the town house, while the twins slept nearby in their net-draped prams, the two women chatted over Twinings tea, raspberry crumble, and scones with cream—all of which, including the prams, Lesley was proud to have found herself on her short rambles around Rome in her new Alfa Romeo. She adored motoring about, buying what she fancied without the servants, designing furs, and spending time out in the open air on the top-floor balcony with its wonderful view over the rooftops of Rome. They were the few things she could do lately to make herself feel free in Rome's brooding atmosphere of looming war. Though Cesare preferred she not come back to Valente's for more than an hour or two each morning yet, she kept very busy.

"Mm, these are *so* delicious," Stella rhapsodized and accepted another scone piled high with crimson jam and clotted cream. "We Italians have got it all wrong, I'd say. Why just have pasta and wine and a nap midday when we could import these wonderful English teas?" She glanced down again to be certain Carlo's Airedale, Caprice, still snoozed at her feet—as if the dog, at least, knew Stella was supposed to be Carlo's girl.

Lesley sat back in a pillowed wicker chair, one of a new set she had bought to replace the uncomfortable wrought-iron

149

furniture. She smiled at Stella's exuberance. Both women wore
flowered print silk dresses today, Lesley's in moss-green and
Stella's an endearing pink that made her honey complexion
seem to glow in the mellow light of a Roman afternoon. She
was twenty but seemed younger somehow with those big,
appealing eyes set in a heart-shaped face and her habit of
drawing out key words in her sentences when most Italians
talked at a quicker, sing-song pace. The petite woman was
entirely capable of responsibility, something Lesley had seen
her display both in helping her widowed mother run the posh
Sollo leather goods shop and in assisting the doctor deliver the
twins before additional medical help arrived. Still, at times she
seemed so naïve and trusting that Lesley had begun to actually
fear for her as much as Carlo in this evolving romantic triangle.

After all, Stella was only three years younger than she and
could almost have been the sister Lesley had so longed for,
especially with Trent the way he was. And the two young
women held in common their concern for Cesare's nephews,
who were all too often at odds with each other as well as their
uncle. Lesley had partly invited Stella to join her for tea
to keep her from accompanying Guido on the two-hundred-
mile round-trip to Foggia. Now it was up to Lesley to see if she
could get Stella, of whom she had become so fond, to decide
which of the Valente nephews she really cared for.

"You know, Stella," Lesley began, choosing her words
carefully, "since Cati and Paolo were born I've often wanted to
thank you in person for all you did that day."

Stella's head jerked up, causing the natural ringlets she
could not tame in her fashionably rolled coiffure to bounce.
"But you did thank me, you and the count both. Carlo, too,"
she said, her tone wary for the first time.

"But not Guido?" Lesley went on, her hands clasping the
wicker arms of her chair. "Fortunate he knew you were next
door to fetch you so quickly when it all began. I won't breathe
a word to anyone, but, frankly," she went on, leaning forward,
"I was rather wondering if perhaps you had helped Guido put
out the fire before he rang me up."

The young woman's teacup actually began to rattle in its
saucer as she put it back on the linen tablecloth. "Stella, I'm
only asking because I want to understand about you and

Carlo—and Guido," she assured her and took a deep breath. She forced herself to sit back more casually in the deep chair. "I'm not accusing you about the fire, as that's all in the past."

Stella's wide eyes dropped to her linen and lace napkin across her knees. "Honestly, I—I'd say, in a way, the problem still is a fire of sorts, and I don't know if it's in the past or not," she admitted with a little shrug. "I've wanted someone to talk to about it, not Mama, of course, certainly not Carlo. Oh, Countess Valente," she cried, her eyes bright with unshed tears, "I hope you won't hate me for this, but I was with Guido upstairs at Valente's just before the fire started, but I didn't see how it happened, really!" Her voice rolled faster and faster, and she stood to whirl behind her chair with both hands gripping the woven wicker.

"Stella, I said I wasn't accusing you. I merely wondered because, to tell the truth, when Guido rang me up about the fire, I heard a woman's laugh in the background and then he fetched you so soon after I arrived."

"But I wouldn't laugh after a fire—not ever."

"Then you weren't there with Guido? But I thought—actually, it's only that I thought perhaps with Carlo away, Guido had overstepped, and I wondered—I had noticed that perhaps you cared for Guido—as well as Carlo." She sounded like an adolescent country girl about to make some dire confession, Lesley scolded herself, as she rose, too. They stared at each other across the tall back of Stella's chair while the little dolphin-boy fountain splashed on. Stella's face had gone white and she nodded slowly, her front teeth biting her lower lip.

"I apologize for prying, Stella. Please, let's just sit back down and speak as friends," she urged and indicated their chairs with a quick sweep of hand. "I only wanted to help and didn't know how. I didn't mean to vex you, Stella, really."

"It's all right. I've really been vexed for a long, long time over this—Carlo and Guido." They sat down; Stella's voice was quiet now, as if the babies would care what she said.

"You see, Countess, I've been Carlo's girl for so long. Everybody knew it. But when I was with Carlo, Guido was about now and then. Guido was older, worldlier, I suppose

Karen Harper

d say, so intense and volatile. He was obviously very
happy over his mother's death and all. In my heart, it's as if
Carlo and I have always been friends, but I suppose I couldn't
help but see Guido as something unreachable, something
more." She shook her head, then shrugged again. "Of course,
he's had lady after lady friend and never looks at me that
way—until recently anyhow. Then everything got so mixed up
with Carlo I just couldn't stand it."

"Because Carlo has told you he loves you?" Lesley asked.
But she thought to herself, It's because Stella's love for Guido
has been so obvious lately that Guido the wolf could not resist
a little taste of the entranced lamb.

Stella retrieved her napkin and smoothed it over her knees
repeatedly. "Yes. Carlo loves me in a way beyond friendship
that I just can't return. Everyone thinks I'm more or less
promised to him, but I can't help thinking about Guido, even
though he's obviously flying high over someone else all the
time."

Suddenly the girl's words seemed to accuse her. Everyone
knew she was Cesare's now, but she could not rid her heart of
Paul, who was obviously flying high over someone else—

"Countess, I didn't mean for this to upset you so!"

Lesley forced her narrowed eyes back to the girl's impassioned face. "No, it's only that I want to help, Stella." She
blinked back tears. "You said you were with Guido at
Valente's earlier the day of the fire?" she prompted.

"He asked me to come over for some wine and I went. I
knew everyone else had gone home and that he drinks too
much and still I went. But we were there only a few minutes
upstairs—he only kissed me once. It scared me how much I
wanted him to, how I didn't even think of Carlo. And then this
woman, a blonde, came to see him and rang the bell. I looked
out the front window. When he went down to talk to her and
stayed a while, I just went to our shop by the alley. I was
shocked to hear there'd been a fire and even more shocked
when he dared come back to get me again after that other
woman left. Then he said you were in labor. But don't worry!
That other woman's taught me not to get burned by ever
trusting Guido Valente again!"

Lesley sighed and nodded. "I knew it couldn't have been

your giggle on the other end of that phone when he rang me," she soothed her, and leaned forward to pat her hand. "Perhaps it was a good lesson, but the problem of Carlo still remains. He cares for you so very much. Perhaps it would be best, Guido aside, to make it very clear to Carlo that you look on him only as a dear friend."

"He'd be so hurt. He's such a gentle person, but I can't help it—I'd feel all closed in if I ever married him and had to see Guido as a brother-in-law the rest of my life. Still, Carlo needs me, more than ever now that Il Duce's going to ship his division away somewhere. I know Guido's not for me. With his string of women, he'd only hurt me, worse than he has already. I know that at least, so I feel I can handle it all now."

"But knowing and feeling are two such different things, dear Stella." Lesley stood quickly as Paolo, the more easily wakened of the two babies, began to fuss. Stella rose too to bend over his pram as Lesley comforted and lifted him.

"I do know that thinking and feeling are different things, Countess, really," Stella insisted intently.

Lesley smiled over Paolo's head as she bounced him slightly to lull him to silence. "I rather think after today you must call me Lesley, Stella."

"Thank you. It's helped me so much to just talk, to have someone really understand and not fret and judge the way Mama would," Stella admitted gratefully.

How could she ever judge Stella for that? Lesley thought. She loved the one man who had hurt her and was bound to another she would not hurt for the world—and to these babies who somehow belonged to both those men.

Stella and Lesley whiled away the rest of the afternoon playing with the twins, walking Caprice around the square, trading gossip, even memories of childhood. It was the first time Lesley had enjoyed a real friend almost her own age since she'd left her flatmate Susan Ashmont back in London. She knew Cesare would hardly approve of her being so open with the girl who was Carlo's girlfriend, but he was in Milan for two days on Valente business. Without him, Lesley thought the four of them had a better chance to get through a civilized dinner tonight. And perhaps it would be "out of sight, out of mind" for Carlo and Stella when his division was posted. Lesley knew only too well the bitter truth of that, but it was Guido who had come lately to take on a decided kinship with Paul Kendal in her mind. She'd come to resent both Paul and Guido more than ever, though she worked very hard to bridle those feelings.

But when Carlo and Guido walked in two hours late nearly at six and Stella's eyes still went to Guido even while Carlo hugged her, Lesley soon found the day swept out of her control again. "Welcome home to Italy's most dashing soldier!" she said to Carlo when he hugged her in turn. "That is, of course, until Guido is in uniform too, and then you'll have to share that honor, won't they, Stella? Carlo," she said and tilted his chin up with her hand, "whatever are they doing to you in training? You have a dreadful bruise rising here."

She could always tell when Carlo was holding something back. His arm around Stella again, he glanced at his older brother. "All right, Guido, what is it?" Lesley demanded, turning to him.

"I can only say I'm grateful the count's in Milan for whatever business is more important than a few days with his nephews, who are about to be shipped out to God-and-Mussolini-knows-where," he told her and took his time lighting a cheroot. "All right, I just wrecked the Maserati on the Via del Corso. Hell, who needs a fast car when one's heading for some mud trenches soon enough anyway, right, Carlo?"

Stella gasped. "Thank God neither of you were really hurt," Lesley began calmly before the impact of Guido's continued carelessness drowned relief with fury. "But you wrecked the Maserati? And now I guess we're supposed to be grateful to see that you're not both dead. We're to pass it off and go on with the welcome-home party." She faced Guido squarely, her hands on her hips. "Your uncle will be furious just when things were getting better between you. I'm sure you were speeding again! Guido, you cannot just continue to run amok like this, and motorcars should not be an outlet for your childish emotions any more than your parade of—" She bit off her last words, appalled at her rising voice. Cesare was right about Guido. This latest trick could have killed Carlo and himself— killed others!

"That's right, Countess, I take my feelings out by driving fast, maybe living fast too, but at least I don't marry just to get the power and position to yell at someone who's only one damned year younger!" He blew smoke in her face; she saw red, remembering how Constance had done just that when she'd stood up to her.

"Guido, blast you! I won't allow—" she began.

"Hell, Lesley," Guido screamed at her, "can't you get this straight! I don't want you for a cousin, aunt, or stepmother any more than I want the vaunted count for my so-called stepfather!"

He stalked away with Lesley after him. "Guido, I certainly never intended to replace your mother! And, I'm not finished yet!"

"*Madre Maria*, I wish you were finished around here, for good! You're close enough to Carlo to be his stepmother, damn it, and you're always worming your way in with everybody, isn't she, Stella?"

"Guido, that's not fair," Stella put in, her voice so quiet compared to the others'. His wild eyes raked her; she leaned harder against Carlo's side.

"So what's fair in life, little girl?" Guido demanded, his handsome face flushed. Only now did Lesley notice his mussed hair and dusty clothes. He flashed a sharp, wolflike smile at Stella, then Lesley. "There's your precious little Carlo, delivered with no more than one tiny bruise to both of you waiting ladies, so enjoy him. Sorry I couldn't save you this little scene, Countess, by just killing myself in the auto like my mother did once. I've already fixed it up with the police, all right? Just forget I exist, would you—all of you!"

"Guido, you come back here!" Lesley raged, but he tore inside and down the hall.

Carlo shot by her to give chase. "Guido, Guido, she didn't mean it like that! You can't talk to her like that!" The two women could hear him yelling as their voices faded. Stella and Lesley stared helplessly at each other with tears in their eyes, then looked away.

Lesley flopped into a wicker chair, her head in her hands. "I'm so very sorry, Stella, so dreadfully sorry," she murmured.

"Guido was wrong." Stella's words caught in her throat and she sobbed once. "But I've been wrong, too. Poor Carlo."

They waited, then held their breath when quick footsteps sounded back down the hall. Carlo hurried out onto the balcony with Caprice cavorting at his heels as if nothing were amiss. "He's gone. He just needs to be alone right now. It's more having to serve Mussolini than you, Lesley, really. Oh, this message came for you. It was just dropped at the door by a man from across the square—from Il Duce's office at the Palazzo Venezia," he explained and extended the letter to her.

"Il Duce's office?" She stared at the plain white vellum as if it were red-hot, then stood before she took it.

"I'm sure it's fine, Lesley," Carlo's gentle voice prodded. "I think the man who delivered it was just one of Mussolini's secretaries. I mean, you and Uncle Cesare do socialize with the man and his friends. Open it."

She shredded the envelope, skimmed the note. Tonight at eight, it requested—no, it demanded—the Countess Valente should come to the Palazzo Venezia with a collection of mink and fox stoles for Il Duce to make a selection for a woman in his family. She was to come alone and model the garments herself. He wished continued sound health to her; to her husband who was in Milan on business; to Cesare's nephews, both of whom owed full loyalty to the grand armed forces of the empire now; and to her two-and-a-half-month-old twins he regretted he had not been asked to godfather.

"Lesley? What is it? We can get hold of Uncle Cesare in Milan if it's an emergency," Carlo said and touched her arm.

"No, everything's fine. We'll simply eat a bit early, the three of us, and then I have to see Il Duce about a fur stole. It's just business, you see, no problem. I'm glad to be able to cover things for Cesare while he's away. Come on, you two, let's have a little aperitif, then I'll leave you two to get caught up on everything."

Exactly at eight, Carlo drove Lesley and sixteen mink and fox stoles across the busy Piazza Venezia where people strolled and autos and tramcars rolled by. The wheels of Carlo's Lancia crunched the gravel courtyard, which was hemmed by clipped oleanders and dotted with ludicrously out-of-place statues of

Cupid, before the guards stopped them the second time, then passed them on.

"Carlo, I appreciate your coming, but I think I'll have to go it alone from here," she told him, hoping her voice sounded light.

He shook his head. "I can't allow that. Besides, I'll help you carry the stoles." His soft smile calmed her. "Stella understands we'll be back shortly, and if it weren't for Il Duce's reputation, I might even have let her come along. Very few citizens are summoned inside this medieval palace, so if Il Duce asks, we'll just say I wanted to see it before I get shipped off to fight for his empire's glory!"

She returned his smile in the glimmering reflection from the sweep of lighted windows of the vast palace. "I'm glad you're along, and I think you're right about both of us going in. I swear, if one of these furs is going to his daughter, Edda, I'll simply demand my sable back in return first."

"I was only teasing about that earlier!" Carlo protested with a little shake of his head as they got out to gather the garments protected by linen sheaths.

"I know. He probably really wants a new stole for Claretta Petacci," she whispered. She ordinarily hated gossip because of her own cruel childhood experiences in England. But here when it dealt with Il Duce in this land of censored newspapers, gossip somehow seemed not malicious but almost necessary for sanity and survival. Perhaps, she thought, a capital city with scandal sheets on every corner was preferable to one where the dictator's party lines decreed every word printed. Mussolini touted himself as a devoted family man. His four-year affair with a much younger mistress whom he showered with gifts, including her three-room suite on the top floor of this government palace, had never once been mentioned in the papers. Instead, they were full of what Cesare called "the cult of *ducismo*": news of the dedication of the tombs of Mussolini's parents as a national shrine, photos of peasants kneeling in the fields when he passed by, his name in capital letters every time it appeared, in contrast to the lower-case print Guido's favorite underground *Libero* used each time it mockingly quoted Il Duce.

Two soldiers helped them with the stoles and led the way up

the sweep of marble stairs past Fascist pennants and black-coated footmen standing rigidly at attention. As Carlo had said, this medieval palace of past popes and kings was magnificent. In the vastness their feet echoed across inlaid marble floors, to stone-mullioned windows, huge oaken cross-beams, and high gilded and painted ceilings.

"One moment please, and I shall announce you to Il Duce in the Sala del Mappamondo," the soldier announced with a crisp bow, and went in through the tall guarded doors.

They stood waiting while two other soldiers hung the stoles on a rolling rack and removed their covers. "The room of the world map," Lesley whispered to Carlo. "Maybe it's a war map and we can study it to guess where you're going to be sent."

Their guide returned quickly. "Il Duce is correct in recalling that he wishes only to see Countess Valente alone to model the stoles," the man said, his loud voice echoing in the chamber. Both door guards seemed carved from stone, as if they did not hear or see a thing.

"But this is Count Valente's nephew; he will assist me," Lesley insisted, her eyes meeting his unflinchingly. "I am certain *I* am correct in recalling that Il Duce wishes to be shown these coats by my family for his family."

She stood facing the tall soldier as an awkward silence stretched out through the lofty hall. The man looked surprised, then confused. "But of course," he said finally, his forehead crumpling to a frown. "The count's nephew and I shall just wait at the back of the Sala while you show Il Duce these lovely furs."

Lesley's victory was short-lived. She and Carlo both gasped when they stepped inside. The room was mammoth, so long that Mussolini's desk at the far end under a massive fireplace with the carved fasces symbol of the government seemed kilometers away. The furs were quickly rolled in by their guide, who motioned Lesley across the ocean of shiny, patterned marble floor toward Mussolini while Carlo and two other soldiers waited farther and farther behind.

This end of the chamber was better lighted at least. On Il Duce's large wooden desk a fringed umbrella lampshade illuminated his bent head like a spotlight. Behind his desk like a backdrop stood a massive beflagged wall map of Europe too distant to read. The rack clattered in the quiet. Their footsteps echoed in the room, in her brain. Someone had opened her letters from her grandmum. She was an Englishwoman, and he had sent for her at night. He knew all about her family, that Cesare was in Milan, about her new twins. Despite domestic grumbling and resentment for his declaration of war at Hitler's side, this man held Italy in the very palm of his hand. She remembered how he had reeked of power the one other time she had met him, how he had staged his entrance to that party, written the script. And this vast room where one was forced to walk like a tiny bit player up to a gigantic center stage with that heroic chair behind the desk was certainly calculated to impress and terrorize.

"The Countess Valente here to show you some furs, Duce."

The look of pleasure and surprise on the man's face almost made her laugh, and her apprehensions subsided somewhat. Did he actually expect them to believe he had not heard them coming because he was so engrossed in his work? An actor indeed, but she had no intention of suspending her belief that the man was dangerous.

"So pleased you could come on short notice, Contessa. Valente furs are Roma's best, and therefore deserving to grace my wife's birthday celebration, yes." He rose and rounded the desk to take her hand. The guard walked away. The closing of a door echoed distantly across the room. Mussolini kissed her on each cheek; his hands firmly grasped her upper arms.

"Duce," she said with a formal nod and pulled quickly away. "I know how busy you are, so let me begin immediately. What is your wife's coloring, skin, hair, eyes? I brought mostly furs for tawny skin, dark hair, is that right?" she plunged on. She slipped on a silver fox bolero fur to protect herself from the way his black gaze assessed her, openly running up and down her fitted, knee-length navy blue crepe dress.

"Incipient motherhood is desirable, but you look even more attractive to me now," he replied, the square chin jutted at her. He sat back against the edge of his desk, crossed his arms and booted feet, then changed his mind and got up to approach the rack of stoles. He skimmed his hands over the garments so they

swung slightly, then reached out to grasp her arms again, so
strongly he crushed the deep pile of the pelts she wore.

"You may select the fur for me without modeling another,
though I like the idea of you putting them on, taking them off
while I watch," he said, his voice an intimidating rasp.

"Please, Duce, I—"

His black eyes bored into hers. "Please what, my most
lovely Englishwoman? If you were Churchill's secret weapon,
even Il Duce would have to surrender, yes." He grinned at his
lame joke, then sobered instantly.

She thought to call for Carlo. But there were guards with
him, and she and Mussolini stood now on the far side of the
rack with all that distance between. Despite Duce's heeled
black boots, she too lifted her chin to look straight into his
eyes.

"I will choose the fur for your wife proudly, Duce. She is a
fortunate woman to have a husband who loves her so."

"So, shall we duel? I used to be a fine dueler, yes. 'Live
dangerously' is my motto, but it is seldom I find a woman
willing to match that."

"Please release me. My husband's nephew waits with your
guards and—"

"Which one? Guido? Carlo? You see, I know so many
things about the Valentes, Contessa. Did you think I desire you
only to have you refuse me? No one refuses the new Caesar of
the Empire anything."

"But my Caesar is my husband, Cesare Valente, and I am
grateful you understand that," she said, faltering.

"Yes, yes, of course, and I never meant otherwise," he said,
his voice no longer that skin-prickling, insinuating whisper. He
hugged her hard, then released her. "That stole you wear will
do. It is as lovely as you are. But I must tell you, Contessa
Valente, there will come a time when you will wish for me to
have more than a fur from you."

The man's manic ego staggered her. He was not acting now;
he believed his words. Her stomach churned. "The Valentes
have already given two soldiers to your service, Duce, and one
of them awaits me. He is home on his last weekend before
he goes—somewhere." Even though she stepped away to

remove the stole, he came quickly forward to seize her left wrist in an iron grip.

"Listen to me, daughter of England, and listen well. If you want that husband of yours to be your protector, tell him to stay home more—all the time if he must! Tell him I was once an editor of two great newspapers, tell him! *Avanti!* and *Il Popolo d'Italia* were both for war, for the greatness of the Italian nation at whatever cost. My writing swept Italians off their feet! Even today I am paid thousands of American dollars to write for their Hearst publications. Tell him not everyone should run a paper!"

She knew she gaped at him, her mind racing. Why was he ranting on about newspapers? He was the one censoring what the people should know. He was the one daring to control lives, rule by threat and innuendo, push people around—to grasp an unwilling married woman's breast under the stole like this! "No!" she shouted and yanked back before she knew she would move.

She was appalled to hear her cry echo so loudly in the chamber, then quick footsteps came faster, closer. His hooded eyes narrowed. He released her, then moved several steps away, his implacable profile to her, his arms crossed, legs astride in the theatrical stance of his newsreels. But this was real. Carlo hurried up with a guard right behind him. The guard skidded to a stop on the slick marble. Both men saluted Il Duce.

"Carlo, no one cannot say Il Duce is not a man of decision," she said, her voice still shaky. She quickly divested herself of the fox stole and placed it on the vast desk. Her words came as fast as her pulsebeat. "This is the fur he has chosen and we shall leave it with him. I could barely convince him not to take the entire rack for gifts for friends, but since that would have depleted Valente's of stoles, he was kind enough to understand."

She held her breath until Mussolini gave a curt nod. "Good evening then and thank you for your thoughtful words to the Valentes, Duce," she added, not daring to glance at him again. What else could she have done, she thought, her stomach twisted in knots. The man was an enigma: he had actually made a sexual proposition to her, but she was not certain what his angry warnings had meant. She needed Cesare to figure that out. She had no intention of falling into another man's arms, especially Il Duce's! She barely gave Carlo time to salute the stonelike, silent dictator again before she took his arm and hurried them out.

Cesare was livid when she told him, and it took him over an hour of his own ravings to finally calm himself. "But whatever could he have meant about 'not everyone can run a newspaper'?" she asked him again. She sat on their bed while he still paced back and forth just beyond it. "I just can't bear the thought he knows so much about us in intimate detail. He can't be watching every influential family in Rome that closely!"

Cesare finally stopped his rapid pacing and got into bed, then patted the sheet beside him so she would come closer. Grateful for the change in his temper, she came into his arms. He leaned back against his pile of pillows where he slept nearly in a sitting position as if to be ready to vault up in the middle of the night. She noted for the first time how his crimson silk pajamas clashed horribly with the pink of her negligee.

"About his ranting over newspapers, Lesley, who knows? I admit I have donated anonymously to an anti-Fascist broadsheet or two in my time, as have many good businessmen who've seen what Fascism does to the economy, people's hearts, and minds—and souls."

"How it would warm Guido's heart and mind and soul to know that, Cesare. He needs that from you, something!" she urged. "How can you abide hearing him call you a hypocrite when you could at least share that with him?"

"Guido's not to be told." His finger jabbed the small space between them, but he caught himself and merely touched her tip of nose, then flopped his hand down on the sheet. "I didn't even want you to know, sweet, and you'll ask no more questions."

She lifted her head from his shoulder. "Cesare, there isn't more, is there?"

"No more, I said!" he warned brusquely, though his voice was smoother now. His eyes slid down her body while his free hand lifted to pull at the ribbon ties of her satin and lace negligee. "And especially no more of anything ever between you and Il Duce, I swear it. I'll abbreviate my travels. The man's insatiable in every way, but I will live to see him stopped. You're mine, mine alone, Lesley, always. Swear it!" he added harshly as his hand plunged into the low-cut gown to grasp a naked breast.

"Of course. I was terrified, sickened, but I didn't dare not go, I told you," she managed to say before he rolled them down onto the cool silk sheets and yanked the drawstring loose at the waist of his pajamas. He would be especially forceful tonight. Anytime another man so much as looked at her, it was like this.

He tugged her gown above her hips, not bothering to remove his pajama top. She held to him, her husband, kissed him back, willed herself to respond warmly. She wanted to love him very much, to never hurt him, although she still longed for that betrayer Paul Kendal in her innermost dreams. She would be loyal to the vows she had made to Cesare and the Valentes always.

His large stomach pressed her down, the buttons across his big chest imprinting themselves in her soft flesh even as he entered her, then plunged to a rapid pace of full possession. But why was it she never felt a part of him, never experienced that full, deep flowing with him, into him even as he filled her? Her hands stroked the back of his bull neck but her thighs quivered. He was touching her as the brutal Mussolini would have, if she had been spread across his desk on the precious Valente furs in that vast room at the palace across the square. And even there, no, here in Cesare's big bed, the knowledge, the fear that the great freedom of deep, fulfilling love for a man in her life was gone forever came closing in on her, grasping her tight in the dark places of her heart until it was ended.

❧ ❧ *Chapter Ten*

SNOW, THE FIRST deep snow Lesley had seen since her last winter in England, covered Rome with a six-inch plush mantle of purest ermine. Despite the dull, pervasive ache of homesickness as her second Christmas in Italy approached, she smiled and laughed with the rest of the milling crowd. The Valentes strolled along shop windows in the Piazza di Spagna, gazing in at somewhat meager displays of goods marked *"Saldo"* or *"Vendita Promozionale."* The traditional December sales were on despite inflation and the dominance of black-market goods from Germany. Burdened by depressing war news, food rationing, and a foreboding of perhaps worse yet to come, Roman revelers were nevertheless out in force. The Valentes stopped to watch squealing daredevils sliding down the snow-slick Spanish Steps or others skidding on their rumps on *ristorante* trays across the impromptu skating rink in the piazza.

Cesare and Lesley headed the Valente expedition and the chauffeur, Antonio, who was too old to be conscripted, brought up the rear. Stella carried Paolo while the Valentes' portly fifty-year-old nursemaid, Eleana, toted the heftier Cati. They had left the Bugatti at the shop just a half block away after a drive through a fairy-tale Rome that reminded Lesley more of a sleigh ride through the grounds of her dear, distant Westam's fields and gallops. But things were different in England now. War had shaken the country this autumn as the devastating German blitzkrieg rained bombs on London and other major cities. Gram had written that Westam House had been requisitioned by the government as a training base for what she called special soldiers.

"Oh, look at that crazy old man skating in Bernini's

fountain," Stella shrilled, her cheeks pink with laughter and the nip of wind. "Skates in Rome! Guido always said the Roman motto SPQR really meant *'Sono Pazzi Questi Romani'*—'these Romans are crazy!' "

Cesare shook his head, his lips pressed together in a hint of smile. "Guido's said a lot of things in his time I wouldn't listen to if I were you, Stella," he warned, as he steered them all onward.

Everyone but Stella laughed again, Cesare the loudest of all. Stella and Lesley exchanged a brief glance. Carlo had been gone for nearly six months in Mussolini's disastrous attempt to conquer Greece, which Hitler would probably have to bail him out of with German forces and arms. Guido had been posted to Ethiopia, which the Italians were likely to lose too without Hitler's intervention. Both of Cesare's nephews had been made officers under Il Duce's *figlio di papa* policy that helped upper-class soldiers to be quickly promoted. As far as the family knew, they were safe, but the burden of worry weighed on them all.

War had invaded Italian territory too last month when England had bombed Mussolini's "cardboard" navy at Taranto. The word was Mussolini was terribly shaken. His mistress Claretta had become pregnant and almost lost her life by a miscarriage in September, and the disaster in Greece had devastated him. Cesare said that the dictator's powers of judgment and decision were becoming more erratic. Lesley didn't even want to think about that as long at Il Duce left her and her family alone.

"A heavy little mite, aren't you, *bambino*?" Stella's words to Paolo interrupted her thoughts. Lesley put out her arms for her squirming, eager son.

"My turn to carry him for a bit, Stella. I know the little demons are getting to be lumps to tote about," she admitted and snuggled Paolo to her. Lesley was togged up against the chill in a gray woolen coat with beaver trim and beret, gray wool slacks, white flannel shirt and red suede waistcoat with fur-lined gloves that Sollo's leather shop made from Valente's mink scraps. Both twins were outfitted in bright blue wool suits with new slide fasteners, the same sort Lesley had wanted to utilize in an informal design for some saucy raccoon coats.

Cesare had told her the idea was ridiculous, so she'd let it pass for now.

"Come on, everyone," he announced grandly, and urged them along. "I'll get us all some roasted chestnuts and chocolate truffles at Marcello's down here." Everyone applauded in exaggerated joy, then stood about as he purchased and distributed handfuls of the treats. Lesley and Stella wandered off a bit to peek into the various pushcarts called *bancarelle* with their sparse gifts under suspended lanterns. The Romans were breaking both curfew and blackout rules tonight, but after all, it was less than two weeks before Christmas.

Cesare propelled his little entourage back into the square to survey the lively revelry. Lesley and Cesare each held up one of the twins so they could see. They were both avid crawlers, and Lesley wondered what they would do loosed in this melee of snowy merriment. Cati was still larger, more outgoing, even demanding if she did not get her way; Paolo was solemn and more easily contented, with an amazing self-discipline he had inherited from who knew where. Even now their avid little eyes under their hoods took it all in, yet occasionally they would check to be sure the other was near, as if they passed secret, unspoken thoughts between them.

Lesley sighed. Cati and Paolo would, blessedly, be dear to each other over the years, something she and her brother had never shared. But the twins would grow up without their real father, and she had never had to face that. Tears stung her eyes. It was only this wretched grasp of homesickness for Gram and Westam and English Christmas scenes snatching at her again, she told herself fiercely.

"Are you all right, sweet?" Cesare interrupted at her elbow, his eyes watchful.

"Quite," she assured him with a toss of her head. "Just thinking of home a bit, I guess. All that's a far cry from these palms drooped with snow."

They gazed together at the burdened trees struggling upward to the lofty bell towers of the Convent of the Trinity with its dark Nativity scene on the white brow of the frowning Pincian Hill. In the unearthly dim light of street lamps painted blue, the entire town seemed to cavort in fluorescent purple and black silhouettes against the pall of stark snow. Even the distinctive bagpipe and flute music of the seasonal strolling *zampognari*, with their sheepskin leggings to commemorate the Nativity shepherds, added to the surrealistic scene. It all looked so unreal, she thought, as if even now she dreamed it all: that she had come to live here, married Cesare, had these children because of a love that was so distant, so unreal now, too.

"Nothing else you're missing?" Cesare probed, his gloved hand briefly stroking her cold cheek.

"I'm fine, my dear, really," she told him with a sure nod. "Let's go home."

"All right," he called to the others, "let's head back."

The sounds of shrieks and laughter faded, muffled by the snow until only their own crunching footsteps echoed in the night.

The bell of the telephone jolted them both awake the next morning. Cesare snaked an arm out for it, and Lesley cuddled back into the warmth of the bed. He often had early-morning calls, but seldom took them here. She sighed and tried to shut out his voice as she snuggled deeper into the depths of the big bed.

"A trunk call, Lilla?" His sleepy voice instantly sharpened. He bounced the bed when he sat up. "No, I'll take it here."

She sat up too at that, wrapping the downy blanket closer. A foreign call. Oh, dear God, surely that wasn't the way they informed one if something happened to a family member serving in Greece or Ethiopia! Her heart pounded as she tried to read Cesare's face in the dim room, tried to discern what the call was about from his terse, brief responses. At least it didn't seem to be something dire about Carlo or Guido. Finally, he said, "Yes, I'm certain I can arrange it somehow. No, I'll convey all that to her. Good-bye."

Fear chilled her. "To me? Cesare, what is it?"

"Your brother—and the battle over your father's estate. Brace yourself, my sweet," he warned as he turned slowly to her, one leg bent on the edge of the bed.

"The Westam estate! The court's ruled and he got the estate?" she shrilled and threw the blankets off to jump to her feet. "Blast him! Damn him and his conniving mother!"

He rose and came around the bed but she pulled back from his hands. "Lesley, that's not it. Listen, my sweet, the estate may be easier to get now than ever. That was your London solicitor's office. Trent's plane crashed two days ago trying to intercept Nazi Stukas approaching London over some place called Tilbury. He's dead, Lesley, and they think you should come home for the memorial service and to renew your claims so that—"

His words went on. He was saying something else to her. But all she knew was she had just hated and cursed a brother who was dead, who had died for the England she missed so, and somehow, somehow she was going home.

She weakened against Cesare, sank down onto the bed. Trent dead after all the terrible things they'd said, all the cruel things he'd done. He'd hated her for being her mother's child, hated her for having Father those years at Westam. Now he was gone. Cesare held her while she shuddered and sobbed as a flood of memories crashed over her in brutal waves. Trent locking her in the wine cellar, Trent lying to their grandmum about things she'd done. Trent looking for her that night she fled the house and found Paul Kendal. Trent dead in a plane crash because he loved flying and he loved England but he could not love his own sister.

"Lesley, my sweet, the man deserted you, turned on you," Cesare was saying. "You're shocked and grieved, of course, for all he could have been to you, but he chose otherwise—" The words pierced her when the rushing thoughts in her brain began to ebb at last. But was he speaking of Trent or Paul? she asked herself, and the grasp of grief smothered her again.

One week later she sat next to her grandmother, Lady Sarah, in the great north-south transept of London's Westminster Abbey at the memorial service for Trent and three other downed RAF pilots. She held Gram's hand tightly. She was reminded of that day when they'd buried Father and the walls of the Westam Mausoleum had closed in on her and Trent had been furious with her for leaving. But never again would Trent glare at her or scold or hate her. And the lofty, vast, vaulted interior of cool stone here was surely too spacious to ever close in on one or cause the slightest panic.

Her eyes wandered the crowd again as the Archbishop of Canterbury's lengthy exhortations rolled on. King George, Queen Elizabeth, and the two princesses were in attendance as well as Prime Minister Winston Churchill and most of his war cabinet. Numerous members of Parliament, families of the four fallen airmen chosen to represent the many who had died in the cause so far, even many strangers who had just come to express their gratitude. For, as Churchill had just said in his part of the service, "never had so few done so much for so many in what was assuredly their finest hour."

She'd seen the crowd of journalists clustered at the back, but it didn't faze her. Surely, for once, they were here only to report this inspiring service honoring the "British knights of the air" to bolster the nation's dedication even more. Lesley had seen the proud, defiant words of unity painted all over the city in bold graffiti or crudely printed signs: "London can take it!" If so, she must learn to take it, too.

England stood strong in the struggle against the punishing nightly onslaught of Hitler's bombs. Even the royal family had suffered hits at Buckingham Palace, and that had bonded them to the lower classes, whose homes in the East End by the docks had been devastated for months. Even now, as the organ vibrated the venerable old stones of the church and swelled everyone's heart as they rose to sing the patriotic words of "I Vow to Thee, My Country," Lesley could feel the fervor and purpose for England's cause. She was ashamed to live in Mussolini's Italy where a pact with that Satan Hitler had been forged and was still honored.

"I vow to thee, my country, all earthly things above, entire and whole and perfect, the service of my love." The song rolled throughout the Abbey. Her teary gaze snagged with that of Trent's mother in the seat just across the aisle. Cold slits of steel-gray eyes behind a black net veil, molded silver coiffure with the pointing ebony streak, hard jaw, the perfectly elegant black mourning suit trimmed in sable. The dark look of hatred jarred Lesley like a slap across the face even as the melodious song encompassed them all: "The love that asks no question, the love that stands the test, that lays upon the altar the dearest and the best."

Lesley had not yet had the opportunity to speak with

Constance, but that single glance told her exactly what she could expect. There would be no unity of shared grief, however brief, no moment's respite from hatred or revenge or Constance's greedy desire for the Westam estate and assets, which the woman thought were her due. Lesley's solicitors had warned her that Trent's mother would carry on the fight with tooth and claw, and she didn't doubt it for one moment. "The love that never falters, the love that pays the price, the love that makes undaunted the final sacrifice." The deep organ chords and hundreds of voices reverberated in her heart and soul.

After the service the RAF families were presented briefly to the gracious, comforting royal family, then made their way slowly through the crowds, outside to the line of waiting autos. Lesley and Lady Sarah were staying at the Connaught for two days until the reading of Trent's will. Then for Christmas they would go back to Westam where Gram was stubbornly residing in the chauffeur's quarters over the garage with special permission from Churchill's SOE division posted there. On December twenty-ninth Lesley would return to London for the homebound flight to Italy via neutral Spain on a supply carrier DC-3 as Cesare had arranged for her. He'd allowed her to come for the sake of the estate, but he'd berated her for being so soft as to grieve for a man—and he had implied men—who only deceived and disliked her.

Lady Sarah took her arm and squeezed it. They blinked in the bright, cold December sunlight outside while the breeze rustled their hat veils. Gram wore a black mink coat, Lesley curly ebony Bukhara over a wool mourning suit. The barest dusting of snow powdered the ground here. Lesley's sharp ears again caught the whispers that had greeted her arrival inside for the service, and she was glad Gram's hearing was not all it could be anymore. "Countess . . . Mussolini's Italy . . . Valente's Furs . . . Westam dispute." The sibilant sounds of the *s* words floated to her as people evidently pointed her out.

Ah well, she had known to expect some of this, especially since she lived in enemy Italy now. As they crossed the Dean's Yard to the street, she lifted her chin and squared her shoulders to face the Fleet Street reporters waiting for the airmen's families near the line of motorcars. She saw pencils poised, a photographer or two among the clump of journalists.

They surrounded her and Lady Sarah before they could get anywhere near the Rolls with the crowd of onlookers still pressing in from behind.

"Countess Valente, is it true your Italian husband is an intimate friend of Benito Mussolini's?" one man asked and leaned very close. Other voices, sharp questions slashed at them. "You realize this will be a point of honor with the British, don't you, Countess?" someone demanded. "You know, Italian interests trying to take an English estate away from a Brit RAF hero who died for the homeland while you've gone off to the enemy. A new scandal really—"

"That's an extremely slanted version of the entire story and frightfully unfair," she replied and propelled Gram toward the auto even as the old woman surprised Lesley by speaking up.

"All of you had best write down that Willis Trent Westam was defying his father's will. That makes him an enemy of his own father's memory however much a war hero he's been." Lady Sarah's sharp voice carried in the chill air. The old lady wagged a gloved finger at the men. Pencils scratched away; flashbulbs popped in their faces.

Lesley turned to shield Gram from the crush. "Actually, my grandmum and I don't think this private family matter should be of concern to the public. But you may print that I love England as my homeland every bit as much as my brother, Trent, did!" Her firm voice drowned out Gram's sputtering anger and even quieted the crowd somewhat.

And then, beyond the cluster of journalists, as a dozen harsh questions and rejoinders clawed at them at once, in a splash of winter sun, she saw Paul Kendal.

Her knees nearly buckled and she leaned hard on Gram, her hands clutching the old woman's thin arm through the mink. Lesley's bravado crumbled to dust. He was staring at her, his face—concerned, no, crushed to anger as he strode quickly closer. Their eyes locked as the blur and buzz of the crowd drifted, faded. He looked thinner but still very strong and determined. She stood rooted to her little spot of pavement while Gram said something up at her and the hard line of Paul's mouth opened to speak. She stared dumbfounded at a small white slash of new scar that dipped from the left side of his forehead to make one eyebrow seem to pucker in fury. When he spoke, it wasn't to her at all.

"All right, gentlemen, enough questions for now. It's been a memorial service, and the ladies are in mourning." He actually shouldered several men away, clapped one on the back. "You understand, don't you, Tony?"

"A story's a story, you know that, Kendal, so you can forgo that inherent Yank charm. If I tell the chief you whisked these two away without a good quote for us, he'll hardly let you use our morgues for your flaming novel research next time, old chap."

Morgues, a novel. Lesley's mind tried to grasp the words, but the fact Paul Kendal dared to stand here in the flesh so close made everything else rattle by as the merest nonsense.

"Come on now, gentlemen of the press," Paul's deep voice cajoled, "if Their Royal Highnesses inside can overlook Countess Valente's personal Italian alliances, surely you can too at least for today, okay?"

Inside. Paul had been inside the Abbey for the service, but worse, his voice, memories of the way he looked and moved and spoke had been inside her all this time, and that terrified her. He was taking Gram's arm. Lady Sarah trotted readily at his side with a smile and pert nod up at him while Lesley pulled back until he turned to her.

"Get in the car now, Lesley." Those words registered. But his help was the last thing in the world she needed or wanted. She hated him for being here, for even rescuing her in the first place from that dark Herefordshire road the night they'd met nearly two years ago. She hated him for the fact both twins had his clear sea-green eyes and Cati actually had inherited a softer, feminine version of that disarming cleft from his chin.

"Come on," he insisted, his voice harsh now, and seized Lesley's elbow to propel her forward. "Take good care of Lady Sarah, at least," he commanded, with deadly emphasis on those last two words. He half helped, half pushed her into the backseat of the Rolls behind her grandmum. Lesley could tell Melly Mott, who'd motored Gram from Westam since their chauffeur was posted to Gibraltar, had started the engine by the smooth purr of its vibrations through her body. Paul leaned in, his hard eyes going over her once where she sat as silent as if she'd lost her voice and her sanity. "Keep out of their sight, Lesley, so maybe they'll just forget about you," he threw at her and slammed the heavy door.

Gram bent down to wave her gloves to Paul and called through the side window, "Thanks for all your help, thanks awfully!" When Melly Mott gunned the motor and jerked them quickly away from the curb, Lesley craned her head to look back at him standing so tall in the midst of the milling, noisy crowd.

But Paul Kendal's words to the Fleet Street journalists had not stopped them from printing their usual flagrant stories, Lesley and Lady Sarah learned the next morning on their way to Trent's law firm for the reading of Trent's last will and testament. "Another War: Il Duce's Favorite Countess Still Doing Battle with Dead RAF Hero," one headline screamed. Another broadsheet stacked on the corner bookstall by their hotel snidely remarked, "And from the other Italian-British Front, death has hardly halted the bitter Westam family feud."

But all that, she thought, was nothing next to facing Constance or the final words from Trent—or the life-wrenching shock of seeing Paul Kendal at the Abbey yesterday. She'd hardly slept all night, exhausted from the plane flight, emotionally drained from Trent's death, her return to an England under siege, the reunion with Gram, the memorial service itself—and then Paul.

She took her place between her solicitor, Charles Selbridge, and her grandmum for the reading of the will in the wood-paneled conference chamber. Across a little space Constance sat alone, twisting her ropes of pearls around one crimson-tipped finger. Smoke from her jade cigarette holder curled around her like some living thing while her stony profile stared straight ahead. Twice the woman had rudely shrugged Lesley and Lady Sarah off without so much as speaking when they'd offered condolences.

"So, all assembled, all ready to begin?" Myron Kirk, one of the senior partners of Trent's firm, asked and cleared his throat. "Copies of the last will and testament of Willis Trent Westam, Sixth Earl of Malvern, will be distributed to all parties in attendance. But let me summarize for you all by simply saying that the late, admired war hero, being without spouse or issue"—he coughed behind a tight fist—"has bestowed and bequeathed his entire estate to his mother, Constance Quinn-Jones, First Lady Malvern."

She jerked her head to stare at Constance, who never moved but continued to toy with her pearls. "The will," Myron Kirk continued after another brief coughing jag, "contains the Earl of Malvern's wishes that Lady Constance—oh, here it is exactly, 'continue the deceased's right and judicious efforts to retrieve the entirety of his parents' estate, which is his legal birthright, from his half-sister, who'—I am still employing the deceased's precise words here—'has through her most recent actions, as well as her lifelong attempts to take over the estate, proven her loyalty to her Italian mother's heritage over any possible loyalty to Westam or England.'"

Papers rustled; Myron Kirk hacked; people shifted in their chair; Lesley saw Gram dab at a tear. Had they all known but her this is what Trent would dare to say even from the grave? He who hoped to be forgiven in heaven could not offer the slightest glimmer of forgiveness to his own sister?

At last Constance turned gloatingly to her, crossed a silk-stockinged leg, and exhaled a perfect circle of smoke. "I am so *awfully* relieved," she drawled, her ruby mouth a slash of smirk. "My son's clearly legal battle for Westam will perhaps not be so terribly encumbered now."

"The only thing that ever encumbered Trent was your teaching him to hate, Lady Malvern," Lesley shot back. They were not going to do this! Trent was a dead hero, but that didn't make him right! She felt strength suffuse her tired body. This woman was not, *was not* going to do her in!

"How dare you speak to me like that!" Constance's voice shrilled at such a pitch that Lesley knew instantly she had taken her by surprise. "You're a worse Italian strumpet than your mother, going off like that to the enemy and marrying your uncle's brother, of all people, to get your hands on that fur empire—"

"That's enough!" Lesley countered, jumping to her feet, even as Charles Kingsley plucked at her sleeve and Gram too grabbed for her. "Unlike you, madam, I do not thrive on public notoriety and filthy innuendo in this dispute, so I will only tell you that you will be hearing from Mr. Selbridge here about my further suits in this matter." Lesley stepped forward to tower over the livid Constance. "However, since we are not likely to meet again, I will tell you before these witnesses I do not believe English justice, even in an atmosphere of war fever and patriotism, will be blind. My father's will is valid, despite the fact he once chose to love an Italian woman in place of a bitter, self-centered Englishwoman who never cared one whit for anything but herself! No true court of English law will be swayed by the vendetta of a woman who was legally divorced years before and has only lived to warp her son and turn him against his father—until now, of course, when Trent's escaped you the only way he really could."

"You vicious little bitch, this is unthinkable!" the woman screeched. She leapt up to face Lesley, shook her cigarette holder in her face. "You hated my son!"

"No, I loved him, always wanted to love him, but you wouldn't allow that! And now, my grandmum and I are not going to be bullied or coerced by your hatred anymore, the way Trent was. I am only grateful that Mr. Churchill's war effort has temporarily put Westam House itself out of your reach, or we'd be likely to find it more ruined than when you moved in immediately after my father's death.

"Mr. Kirk," Lesley said, her voice lower now, "I'd appreciate your giving my copy of the will to my solicitor here, as Lady Sarah and I really can't afford to waste our limited and precious family time in the presence of a woman to whom neither of us is related." She seized the jade holder with the stub of cigarette Constance still flourished in her face. She jabbed it out hard in the large glass ashtray on the table, once, twice, then dropped it while Constance gasped and sputtered. "Good day, everyone."

She escorted Lady Sarah out and they were in the lift before Lesley could even breathe normally. Her grandmother's ice-blue eyes still watered, but her wrinkled mouth lifted in a grimace of a smile. "Bravo, my dearest girl! You've a backbone forged from Birmingham steel, but I've told you that before."

"I just couldn't let her do it again, Gram, trample all over us. I couldn't stomach another minute with that poisonous woman."

"Nor I, dearest. Sometimes I just can't remember who I've said what to, but did I tell you what she did to the decor of the house before Churchill's SOE men claimed it to train those agents or whatever they are? Mauve and pink in your mother's suite and Danish modern and Bauhaus pieces all about, indeed! And she loved to torment me about little things. Tossed out all my Frears Almond Biscuits I'm mad keen on for tea, insisted on Cook serving those imported French coconut things, she did. I'd gladly live over the garage for the duration to have that witch, or whatever they call a woman like that these days, out of there." The impassioned old face softened. "But Lesley, is it only Constance and those wretched Fleet Street people you don't wish to face again?"

Their eyes met under the single ceiling light of the oak-paneled lift. Lesley suddenly felt as if the narrow walls might close in around her. "Paul Kendal belongs to my past, Gram, not my present or future," she insisted, and looked down at her hands gripping her purse strap. "Our meeting yesterday was an accident, and I'm sure I won't see him again. Besides, I assume he's married his American sweetheart by now."

"Sweetheart," that word hovered in her thoughts; he had always called her sweetheart those last weeks in Venice. She took a deep breath and pushed open the door of the lift. In the little carpeted ground-floor lobby several newsmen waited. Obviously Constance was tipping them off to their where-abouts, hoping it would cause them further embarrassment and pain.

"That was fast," one of the men observed to the photographer with him. "The other blokes aren't even here yet, so we'll scoop this one, Michael. Excuse me, Countess Valente," he said, planting himself firmly between them and the door. "Would you mind giving us a brief statement, now that the memorial service is a thing of the past and we respected your wishes on that yesterday?"

Only because a certain brazen American hustled us into our motorcar and slammed the door on us, she thought. She lifted her chin and took a deep breath. "Yes, of course, if you'll get out of our path," she told them and borrowed Lady Sarah's

handkerchief from her hand to quickly wipe her own eyes
rather than bending over to fish for hers in her alligator bag.
Gram stared up at her in astonishment as Lesley escorted her
through the door the obviously surprised man held for them.

She turned to face them in a little patch of sunlight. "First,
you must realize, for those of us who knew and cared for him,
the mourning for my brother is not over even if formal
memorial services are. But about this private family business
over the Westam estate you seem so avid to learn about, you
may tell your readers that if a father cannot leave half his
worldly goods legally to his daughter who was born a British
subject, then England's not really England anymore. And they
should be rather concerned for that in these trying times for our
country."

"Oh, sure, Countess," one man said and began to write
despite the annoyed look on his face.

"And tell them that Constance, First Lady Malvern, would
love to see me and my grandmum reduced to having to share
a handkerchief like this"—the photographer popped bulbs at
them both when she waved it at them—"in order to grieve for
the grandson and brother whom we both loved dearly despite
our differences. The Westams wave no white surrender flag to
her mercenary obsessions." She headed Gram toward the
parked Rolls again and motioned for Melly to get back in.
"And hereafter, sirs, I would appreciate it if you would dog
Lady Malvern about the streets instead of us, as it is she who
revels in the sort of sordid notoriety you people peddle. Excuse
us, please."

She felt good to have said all that, no matter what slanted
lies it bred. She hurried Gram to the Rolls, ignoring their
babble of questions. She was fully in control of her life again,
without gaping like a fool while that betrayer Paul Kendal
rescued them from these vultures. She slammed the Rolls door
on the demands, the flashbulbs, and the faces as Melly put the
big motorcar in gear and they dro e off.

"Whew," she breathed. "I didn't mean to talk to those
cheeky blokes at all, but that woman infuriates me. I'm
convinced she sicced them on us."

"You've never fought back quite like that before, only tried
to avoid the pain, tried to always patch things over, my dear.

Your time away, perhaps being a mother yourself with lives in your keeping now—something has strengthened you even more, and I'm awfully, awfully proud of you," Lady Sarah told her with a pat on her knee.

"And I'm so proud to be your granddaughter and to be heading home with you, Gram," Lesley said and hugged her. It cheered Lesley immensely to be leaving London. Seeing Paul after all this time had made it clear to her how deeply she resented his desertion of her and two helpless babies. And she guessed he would probably not care a fig for the twins if he knew they existed. She and the children would survive, and happily; she would see to that. She would flourish as Countess Valente, designing her furs. She would prosper even if the rest of the world went to flaming destruction about her!

The Rolls veered around a fenced-off bomb crater still unrepaired on the Strand as they turned westward out of the city. As Gram pointed out places that had been bombed, she found herself wondering if Paul had brought his wife, Melissa, back with him. She dabbed a tear from the corner of her eye before she saw she still had Gram's handkerchief.

They held hands, not speaking now, while Melly, who was an outdoorsman and horseman at heart and not a driver, tried to negotiate the big Rolls through Notting Hill Gate traffic. Here and there, even in this far West End of town, stood the random, gaping ruins of dismembered houses, or blocks of flats displaying their inner muscle of brickwork, veined wallpaper, the exposed bones of stacked fireplaces, so anyone could gape at the interior upheaval. But she would not allow the newspapers or Constance or anyone else to strip off her outsides with some sort of cruel, unfair assault and peer into her heart. Not even dear Gram, with whom she would never share the truth about Paul's fathering the twins, about the way he had deserted her for another woman. She would be just like London weathering the bombs. She would take the brave poster slogan "Make do and mend" to heart. And for Father's memory, as well as her own pride and integrity, she would defeat Constance, no matter what it took.

She sighed and patted Gram's fragile hand and leaned back against the old familiar horsehair seat as the rolling rural suburbs of London beckoned to lead her home to Westam.

❧ ❧ *Chapter Eleven*

AT FIRST Churchill's secret service Special Operations Executive branch, called the SOE, had given Lady Sarah Westam permission to occupy the small flat above the large garage with access only to the small herb garden. But soon, her unflagging petitions to be allowed to work her precious flower beds wore down even men being trained to handle evasive action, covert escapes, inquisition, and torture. At last she had been permitted entry to the extensive gardens where Lesley walked with her this mild Christmas morning.

"Quite lovely of the Motts to invite us to dinner," Lesley remarked in a moment's lull from Lady Sarah's patter of pointing out various plants and shrubs. "I wouldn't have minded doing up a saddle of mutton for us in that sparse kitchen you've got, but your food supply is dreadful."

"Don't need a thing but my almond biscuits and tea in the flat as Samantha sends all my meals over with Melly. You know, the boy's still wretchedly ashamed the army wouldn't take him with that collapsed lung the doctors never quite got right when he was a lad. Over here in this octagonal bed, Lesley, I'm hoping to use a yellow and blue scheme, you know, golden wings, May gold, lobelia, iris, and the like. Did I tell you, by the way, Constance absolutely forbade me to have my Frears Almond Biscuits in the house when she was continually flitting back and forth to London after you left? She only did it to be nasty."

"Quite. I think you told me." The old woman lectured her way along on their little stroll through the patterned beds near the old gazebo. From here generations of earls had watched their thoroughbred race horses, polo ponies, or hunting mounts working out on the distant gallops past the tracery of trees now just bare bones against the pale December sky.

Lesley breathed in deeply of the peace and grandeur of Westam. The earth lay damp and expectant where robins hopped about for food. The smell of wood smoke tinged the air. The land evoked the rich sense of generations of Westams who had loved and tended it. It still echoed the muted history of warlike Celts, the Romans, Saxons, and William the Conqueror's great marcher lords. All cherished their English border lands despite their own wars. And now, as always, overhead the blue-gray sky was alive with birds: the red kites of Wales soared majestically, and woodpigeons clattered aloft en masse. It all seemed so untouched, so unchanged here, no matter what happened in the world outside. But when Lady Sarah and Lesley emerged from the clipped ash hedgerows by the garage, Lesley knew her sanctuary here could be invaded, too.

Across the gravel drive, under the windows with lace-trimmed starched curtains of Gram's little upstairs flat, sprawled a large canary American automobile.

"Oh, my," Gram said, one hand darting to Lesley's arm. "I've seen that big, bright thing before, I think, but can't recall who owns it."

Lesley let her breath out slowly. "It's Paul Kendal's."

"Indeed? How lovely he'd come calling way out here. We'd best nip in to see him then, perhaps ask him to tea before we go over to the Motts'. Just think," Gram said, "he's come clear out here from London when petrol rationing is what it is, and you're going to have to even take that slow, wretched motorcoach back because the Rolls has eaten up all our coupons for a fortnight." Her feet turned to lead, dragging her back, as Gram's sprightly steps took her immediately up the inside stairs without another look.

Lesley's gaze scanned the grounds where she and Gram had just walked. The twins and Cesare and her life in Rome had blocked any path back to Paul, as surely as he himself had barricaded her way. Blast it, blast him! She jumped at the squeak of a window cranked open over her head. Gram stuck her sleek silver head out between the fluttering curtains.

"Lesley, our visitor is up here. Melly Mott let him in when he came to tell us the goose would be done a bit early!"

When Gram disappeared, Lesley ambled slowly into the garage, empty now but for Father's old Rolls and her dear little Austin covered with a tarp. She put one booted foot on the first stair and halted. It was so wrong for Paul to come here after all that had passed between them, all he'd done to her. But she was Countess Valente now. And she had to protect the children whom this man had created and then deserted when he betrayed their mother! She climbed the steps faster, smoothing her tweed jacket over the hips of the jodhpurs she'd worn for her morning ride. She yanked off her tweed hunter's cap, then patted back stray tendrils flown wild from her chignon. At least Paul would not be staying long, as she'd have to change her attire and get them over to the Motts' earlier than ever if the goose was nearly done. She could handle this, handle whatever she had to.

His big frame overwhelmed one of Gram's Georgian brocade chairs she'd imported from the big house when the furniture was stored. He slowly shifted to his feet. He dwarfed these oak-paneled rooms and the feminine, ornate, and frilly things Lady Sarah had surrounded herself with in her exile. He seemed rather spiffily attired for a country jaunt: gray wool suit with a waistcoat, white shirt, bright red tie and matching pocket handkerchief, perhaps a concession to the holiday. He did not smile. His green eyes narrowed at her. What right had he to invade Westam and stare at her like that?

"Lesley, you're looking well."

"A bit windblown from a ride, but I am well, thanks," she said with a toss of her head. She put hands to hips, then clasped them before her around her crumpled cap. "And thanks for the help the other day at the Abbey."

She tore her eyes away and stared at Gram, though she hardly saw her. She hadn't meant to sound too grateful or friendly. There was a tiny silence in the room; she looked back at Paul. "You look well, too."

"I'm off to Wales for three days and thought I'd stop to say hello to you and Lady Sarah. That was so rushed the other day."

"Another trip to Wales," she ventured breezily.

"For my novel, *Lions Roar*. I needed a main character, an outsider, to observe London during the blitz. I didn't want to use an American—too close to home, so I made him Welsh," he said and shrugged.

She took three steps farther in and sailed her hat on the flowered sofa. "I see." Another pause.

"The book's about how the Brits struggle to resist the pounding of the Nazi war machine."

"And do they still manage in the end?" she countered, not yet approaching where he stood so awkwardly at the edge of the mauve Aubusson flowered carpet. Gram's head pivoted from one side to the other as if she watched a tennis match.

"The ending of the novel's not done yet, but yes, I'd say so." His guarded voice sharpened now. "I've seen at close range how well some English can take care of their own hides no matter the cost to others."

"Speaking of standing up, you don't have to, you know," Gram piped up. "Lesley, sit over here by Mr. Kendal straight-away while I just fetch us a few biscuits and a pot of tea. I do hope you like Frears Almond Biscuits, Mr. Kendal. Sit down, please. So lovely to have visitors, especially a gentleman caller, as they're rare enough in England these days."

Lesley stalked over and sat, poised stiffly on the edge of her seat across the small table from him as Gram bustled off to the tiny kitchen. "I resent your implication about some English taking care of their own hides, as you crudely put it, and I really don't know why you came after—after everything that's happened," she said pointedly.

Paul leaned toward her over the arm of his chair. "Let's just say, to see a real live Italian countess up close in the flesh, or maybe I'm still doing research for my novel. I'd be fascinated by a chameleon character who was so beautiful and convincing on the outside but really quite different inside."

"I?" Her voice squeaked before she grabbed control again. "Your cable vowing you intended to marry Melissa Pearson came the day of my wedding. I had no idea you were even alive at first!" she shot back and folded her arms over her breasts.

"The cable didn't say I intended to marry her, but I see the Italians have been working on your temper," he told her. His rugged face looked smugly pleased by something now. "Will Lady Sarah mind if I smoke?"

"No, and don't bother asking what I think, because really I don't care what you do."

"Likewise, Countess," he shot back as he produced the familiar pack of Chesterfields and lit one while she grudgingly scooted a small Meissen dish he could use for an ashtray partway toward him. "So, let's just declare a temporary truce and say I'm here today to congratulate you on how well you now handle the journalists you used to run from," he needled, as the flame from his gold lighter engulfed the tip of cigarette. "There's a copy of this morning's Christmas tidings from London's bookstalls in the backseat of the Buick if you'd like to see how badly they've misquoted you on that clever little attack you made on the charming Lady Constance the other day." He leaned back while she glared at him, but his long legs and arms seemed to eat up the space between their chairs.

"Lesley, I'm sorry if you thought I was dead when I wasn't." His voice was serious now. "It was hell when the *Athenia* was torpedoed, and the rescue boats simply mixed up one poor bastard's bloody corpse with me—and I was enough of a mess among strangers in Canada that no one identified me for days, either."

"But couldn't *you* tell *them*?" she asked, her hands gripping the arms of her chair. Tears stung her eyelids, and she desperately blinked them back. He'd been cut up—that scar on his forehead, another one across the hand that held his cigarette.

"I was unconscious for three days and just as well," he told her, his eyes steady on her. "When the ship listed, I slid down over the hull to get into a rescue boat. The only trouble was the barnacles along the hull sliced flesh like a cheese grater. My 'red badges of courage' my father said, but the truth is, I was as scared as I was angry when it all happened."

"Oh, Paul, I didn't know!"

He thrilled at that heartfelt, pained look that belonged to the old, sensitive, concerned Lesley. He'd vowed not to kid himself over anything she might say. Still, the need to see her again had been eating at him for months, even when he knew she had betrayed her promise to wait for him. She'd married

Cesare Valente for his power and position in the fur industry—
maybe for his fortune too. Perhaps he should have made it
clearer to her that his grandfather had settled a large trust fund
on him whether or not he ever went into the family business,
but he had never had any intentions of buying her loyalty. At
least she'd never tried to hide her ambition to design furs at any
cost. He reminded himself again she'd lied to him that first
night he'd picked her up on the road near here. And she'd run
out on him in the restaurant when he'd driven her to London.
Hell, if he'd had a brain in his head, he'd have learned not to
look for her. Yet, today, almost two years later, here he sat,
chasing after her across the width of wartime England when he
could easily have gone to Wales next week, next month for that
matter, and not have showed up in the middle of Christmas
Day.

He cleared his throat in the awkward silence. "I appreciate
your concern," he said, hoping his voice hid his need to know
if she still really cared, however long they'd been apart,
whatever man she'd married for whatever reasons. "If you
thought I was dead, for a while I might as well have been, but
I heal quickly once I put my mind to it."

His intense gaze riveted her where she sat. "You have some
scars," she observed foolishly.

"Yes, and a few of the kind you can't see."

"Yes, well, I suppose," she rushed on, afraid she'd blurt out
her inward pain. "I'm glad you've started your novel. Things
are hardly the same in Italy with the Fascists trampling
everyone down. I'm very busy, very happy. Did Melissa come
back to England with you, then?"

"Melissa's in the States." He carefully knocked ashes in the
delicate dish, then looked up again to meet her eyes. "I didn't
marry her, Lesley."

"You mean not yet? But your cable said—"

"I know what it said. And it wasn't that I don't appreciate
her for being faithful and waiting for me. So you did know I
was alive before you married him, didn't you, Lesley, and
married him anyway?" His voice rose before he could stop
himself. He had to know. He had to hear it from her before he
walked out of her life forever.

"Yes, but that's not fair!"

"What is fair, then? And I don't mean to imply I'm not going to marry Melissa, because it just so happens I do want a wife I can believe and trust, a family of my own, children—"

"Just a spot of tea here," Lady Sarah's voice interrupted as Lesley darted up gratefully to relieve her of the heavy silver tray. "Speaking of children, were you? Lesley, did you show him pictures of your twins? Green eyes just like their mother, who is a daughter of a twin too, you know." Lady Sarah chattered on while Lesley fought to keep from screaming and dashing out. She tried and failed to keep her hands from trembling as she sloshed tea into the cups and the saucers.

But Lady Sarah did not leave them alone again, and by the time they sat down to Christmas dinner at the Motts' rambling stone house farther back on the estate near the river Wye, Lesley had calmed down enough to accept two dire facts. When Melly Mott had come over to inform them dinner was ready, Melly and Gram had actually invited Paul to stay for the meal and he had accepted. And Gram had wangled an offer from him to stop by for Lesley on the twenty-ninth on his way back from Wales and see her safely to her plane in London.

To be anywhere near Paul Kendal any longer than necessary was the last thing she wanted. Yet the familiar, mellow Mott hospitality flowed over them all. It was something she'd cherished since her happy childhood, long before she knew of such things as family scandal and brotherly hatred. Josiah Mott had been her grandfather and father's fowler and trapper in the old days before the Motts became grooms to tend the horses. She saw joy and gratitude on each face at the table before they bent themselves over the holiday repast. She looked at Paul and was secretly glad it was not only hatred between them. In four days she would be back to her life as a Valente in Rome, and they might never meet again. Silently, she gave thanks that his life had been spared, and also, with a twinge of guilt, that he had not married yet. Despite herself, she began to enjoy this strange meal in the England she had missed so much.

Paul, at least, had not inquired about the twins' ages. If he asked her alone, perhaps she should simply subtract a few months from their ages to protect the children and herself. If

Gram told him, she'd simply have to weather his questions. Now, blessedly, the conversation ranged from Paul's novel and work as a war correspondent to rationing to the warm weather. The six of them devoured roast goose with apple and rum stuffing, jacket potatoes, red cabbage and quail salad with hazelnut and honey-vinegar dressing, and the traditional holly-sprigged plum pudding trailing its rich, dark aroma. Ever since the First European War when Gram's eldest son, Andrew, had died in France, she'd refused to drink French wine and stuck to her sherry. But today she'd asked the "SOE blokes," as Melly called them, to bring up a case of wine from the Westam House cellar and keep most of the bottles for themselves. Perhaps it was the wine, Lesley told herself, that made her feel so relaxed after the meal despite the fact Paul Kendal sat directly beside her. Their hands almost touched on the damask tablecloth if she wasn't very careful.

"So you and Mel were childhood playmates here on the estate?" Paul asked—a harmless enough question with everything at stake between them.

"Yes, we rode and hiked, and I used to help him select and arrange the pelts he trapped. With Trent the way he was, Melly was the closest thing I ever had to a brother I could admire," she admitted while the portly, rosy-cheeked Samantha beamed and tall, thin Josiah Mott nodded at the memory.

Melly cleared his throat and stared down at his plate, flushed with pride. He was dressed in his best tweed suit for the day, his unruly hair slicked down with brilliantine. "Lady Lesley was quite the kindest, most trustworthy friend I ever knew," he said, his eyes warm on Lesley. His scratchy voice broke. "The blokes at school used to rag me and call me Smelly Melly, they did, and all 'cause I used to work with tannin' the hides. But she always stuck up for me and did the right thing by me, Lady Lesley did. Only now, I can't help but wish I could go fight for England, be like one of those brave men in your book, you see, Mr. Kendal."

Lesley could tell Paul was as deeply moved by those words as she. It was the longest speech she could recall Melly making. "Listen, Mel," Paul assured him, "there's a fine English poem that says, 'They also serve who only stand and wait.' Not everyone can fight for England the same way. By being here and helping these folks around Westam, keeping the horse barns going with your father and tending the grounds for Churchill's men who are using the mansion, you're making an important contribution too, don't you think so, Lesley?" His eyes narrowed at her in challenge. "Mel's honest and trustworthy and that goes a long way in my book."

She pressed her lips together and nodded. Paul Kendal had lured her in again, then found a subtle, clever way to slap her down, to accuse her so no one else would know.

"What a wonderful meal," Paul told Samantha Mott in an obvious attempt to lighten the mood. "And here I've been told all these stories about stewed squirrel, cormorant eggs, vegetable cutlets, and turnip and boiled beef tea with all this war rationing."

"But for game Melly bags and our veggie garden, can't say we'd be far off that, eh, son? But we're delighted you could share our home's hospitality, sir," Josiah put in as they all stood to stretch. "And sorry you're nipping off to Wales after the meal, as we could put you up here the night, Mr. Kendal. Haven't heard more int'resting stories of the blitz told by anybody, I haven't."

He's fine with fiction, even believes it perhaps, Lesley was tempted to put in, but she held her tongue. No, she wasn't going to play Paul Kendal's journalist innuendo games with him. It hit her then, and she clenched both fists hard at her side in the soft folds of her plaid wool skirt. What if Paul had actually sought her out to get some sort of inside story on Mussolini's Italy? After all, he knew those newspaper men he'd so easily discouraged from bothering her the other day. Maybe he'd even agreed to get another Westam article for them so they'd let him use their so-called morgues for his precious novel. Whatever had been wrong with her that she'd almost acquiesced to a walk outside with him after dinner even if she'd insisted Melly go along? At the very least, when Paul got her off alone he'd ask her all about the twins.

"You know," she told them, "if you don't mind, I'd like to be alone for a little while. This meal has been wonderful, but I miss my family very much and I'm still frazzled from the shock of Trent's death. You wouldn't mind would you, Gram, and you'd take good care of Paul until he leaves shortly?"

"I'm sure Lady Sarah wouldn't mind as she's always been very kind and gracious to me," Paul put in, without so much as a flicker of expression except for that tiny clench of his jaw muscle that gave him away. "And Lesley," he said, much lower now, as he took a step toward the hearth where she could feel its heat on the back of her legs, "I will be through Westam about noon on the twenty-ninth to—collect you. Wouldn't want to offend by saying 'pick you up.' You will be waiting for me as agreed, won't you?"

"Yes," she whispered. She realized everyone in the room had dropped their voices, too. She had no intention of making a scene. Louder she said, "And I quite appreciate your offer of the ride as I can't wait to get back home. As you've been telling us, London's rather a frightening place with the nightly raids. Fortunately, the two nights Lady Sarah and I were there, the attacks were very light."

His eyes burned into hers as though there were no one else in the big, bright room. "There's fear and danger, yes, but excitement and awe too to experience all that explosive power over which you have no control. Good-bye until Sunday then, Countess Valente."

They kept the truce not to discuss their past on their way into London Sunday. Blessedly, Paul must have thought that meant the twins as he did not bring them up. She actually began to enjoy his company, to relax as the countryside sped by on the M40 motorway, which was uncrowded but for rare private autos, supply lorries, army vehicles, and the occasional rambling motorcoach. Only, he drove as fast as ever, and memories bombarded her: their first ride into London together; their journey to what she had mistakenly thought was mutual love through the green, green countryside of France, which Hitler's panzers stalked now in their goose-stepping boots. Had the dreaded Nazis captured or harmed the charming Guyon family, or had Anne-Marie's young man, Claude, died in the war, even as she and Gram had lost forever the hope to ever reclaim Trent's love?

"By the way, did you hear Churchill's broadcast to the Italian people on the BBC the other night?" Paul said, interrupting her musings as they entered the outskirts of London.

She sat up straighter on the seat. Now that they were back, would he begin to ignore their tentative cease-fire?

"No, I didn't, and I doubt if most Italians did unless they listen to the forbidden stations on the wireless. Did he lambaste the entire nation, then?"

"Not at all. He blamed Mussolini entirely for leading Italy astray, him and the man Churchill calls 'that Attila over the Brenner Pass with his hoards of ravenous Germans and gangs of Gestapo police.'" He turned his big head to her. "Lesley, whatever differences we've had between us, I hate to put you on a plane back to Rome."

Her insides leapt. She made the mistake of looking into his deep green eyes and saw real concern there beneath the smothered anger. It came back to her how well she used to read him. That was something she had not managed to master yet with Cesare. She longed to reach out to touch his hand, to actually throw herself into his arms and sob for all they had once had and for all they had lost. But then, she was terrified she would tell him about the twins, so she looked away. "Rome's my home now, Paul, however much I'll always love England, and Cesare Valente, my husband—"

"And father of your children," he added, the intonation of his voice more question than statement.

"That's right," she said and turned her head away so he would not see the tears crowding her eyes. She stared at the distant camouflaged government buildings along the Mall and the women sweeping up broken glass from last night's raid into glittering piles in the cold sun. Oddly shaped silver barrage balloons bobbed over St. James's Park to stop low-flying aircraft. They did not speak the rest of the way.

She waited with her luggage in the Buick outside the Savoy Hotel while Paul went in to see if there were any messages and to catch up on the news from the foreign correspondents who gathered there. Because the "Fleet Street boys" sometimes dropped in too, he had her wait outside. He'd told her an orchestra played and a great cabaret went on every night in the Savoy's underground River Room with its attached bomb shelters. Without sharing the thought, they had remembered their happy days dining and dancing through nighttime London before the war. She couldn't bear to leave London under siege like this, afraid she would never see it again, and yet she couldn't wait to get away. Paul and London: best get the separation over with and never look back again.

He opened the door and got in, tossing a sheaf of papers into the backseat. "It's wild in there," he told her. "Some Royal Navy Wrens are their guests tonight and a couple of drunken bastards have started that awful song about 'up with a lark, to bed with a Wren.' The ladies are joining right in. Maybe it's the sign down in the cabaret that claims 'no intercourse' that makes the women think they're safe with mere journalists!"

She laughed despite her previous somber thoughts. Quite amazing how he could still sweep her from mood to mood with him. "I'm duly impressed that a Yank like yourself knows 'no intercourse' in this country means 'no main course served' at a meal! Rather lighthearted, aren't they in there, considering how things are?"

He swiveled his big body to her with one knee bent between them, his arm stretched along the back of the seat to almost touch her hair. "There's only so much people can take, Lesley. If they don't want to crack under the strain after a certain point, they get a little crazy. But we'd better get you to the airfield before it gets dark, because that's when the good old Heinies usually come calling. I detest driving in the damn blackouts."

"I am grateful for how kind you've been to my grandmum and me, especially considering everything. I—I am very grateful we can at least part friends," she told him as he pulled out into traffic. He didn't speak until they passed Nelson's tall sand-bagged column cluttered with pigeons in Trafalgar Square.

"Can we part friends? But for Lady Sarah, at least, I'll say 'you're welcome.'" His hands gripped the wheel hard. "Lesley, I might as well tell you she told me when I asked that the twins were born in early April."

Her heart plummeted. She tried to sit very still, concentrate on controlling her voice. She could not admit they were his. Who knew what he would do, would demand, or what she herself would accuse him of then? She could not bear to shatter this calm wall of pretense between them that protected them all. And then there was her vow of utter loyalty to Cesare. She needed no wars between the Valentes and Paul Kendal over her and her children. She shrugged her shoulders carefully, her eyes staring straight ahead. "They were a bit premature. First pregnancy and twins, you know."

"But April? You had only married Cesare five months before."

"I know when I married him, Paul."

He wheeled the car over to the curb on the Millbank at the Victorian Tower Gardens just past Westminster and dared to turn off the motor. "Well, no problem, then!" he exploded, his face frozen in fury. "Even if they were a month early, that only means you went from my arms in September with vows of eternal love and marriage—with an engagement ring, even—to Rome where you hopped into bed with Cesare Valente to snag him and his fur empire the very next month, while I nearly bled to death in a Canadian hospital!"

She flushed crimson. Her hands lifted as if to ward off his anger. "That's not true and not fair!"

"Explain it to me, then!" He snatched her closest wrist in a hard grip, scooting her toward him on the smooth leather seat. "Hell, I can count, Lesley, even if I can't read you the way I thought I could. Oh, that's right. You thought I was dead. Maybe spreading those beautiful legs for the count was just your way of mourning for me then, right?"

She yanked her arm away and scrambled back. "Just stop it, Paul! Get out of my life! I never wanted you in it in the first place! Just open the boot of this auto, and I'll get my bag and find a cab somewhere!" she shouted. She jerked open the door and darted out onto the pavement. He slid over and came after her as she stood at the back of the auto, her crossed arms clutching her purse across her breasts.

"Get back in the damned car, Lesley. You and I aren't done with this, and you'll never get a cab now just before the blitz usually starts, you little fool— Damn it, wait!" he yelled as she turned and ran along the nearly deserted gardens back toward Whitehall.

She had money in her purse, she thought, and her special permission for the carrier plane to Spain and Rome, too. She couldn't bear one more moment with this man. It had been a horrible mistake to let him near her. He would find out about the twins, try to take them away. He'd call her all the dreadful names Trent and Constance used to call her mother. He might even print stories about her life in Italy in his columns, get her in trouble back at home with Mussolini again. Cesare would find out she'd seen him, spent civil time with the wretch! He would make her tell him everything, even that she still loved him, still loved him more than she had ever loved another man or ever would!

As he caught up to her again and whirled her around to face him, they heard the wailing rise and fall of the air raid sirens. Dogs began to howl; a low, uneven, throbbing buzz came louder, louder. The approaching *crump*, *crump* of bombs sounded somewhere in the city to the northeast.

"Damn it all to hell, I knew they'd gone lighter on us the last few weeks for some demonic reason. It's not even dark and they're starting already. This will be one bitch of a raid!"

"Just give me my bag, don't worry about me!"

He yanked her nearly off her feet against him, held her with an iron grip on her upper arms. "The few days you spent in London earlier were nothing compared to most bombings, Lesley! Don't be as stupid over this as you have been over other things. I'll get you to your plane later if I can, but we've got to find a shelter, maybe something back by Westminster. Now come on and no arguing!"

He pulled her back down the street at a run, not even stopping to close the open door of the Buick. Her heels slowed her, but a screaming sound like a tearing sheet and dull thud of collapsing walls close by terrified her enough to tear along at his side. No one was on the streets in this area on a Sunday evening as they ran to shelter near the government offices. Burglar alarms were triggered off a few blocks away. At the last minute, he hurried them across Millbank toward a squat stone building at the corner of Great Peter Street. Just before he dragged her into a stone arch of doorway, she saw the first bombers come screaming overhead, line after line, dropping little black sticks falling, drifting toward the earth, just falling—

Paul's hard body pressed her into the harder stone as the first bomb blasts shook them. Somewhere nearby an ack-ack gun answered in the din, throwing shell fragments clattering against buildings and onto pavement. She clung to Paul, her face buried against the warm green sweater he wore under his jacket. His hands clamped them together. Her arms were wrapped hard around his waist. She molded herself to him in abject fear as the world exploded around them. She trembled with the ground under their feet, terrified the building would crumble on them. And yet, it bonded them closer, not only their quaking flesh where her softness pressed to his hard, angular lines, but all they had shared and struggled for and fought over. After an eternity of noise, in the tiny lull, she lifted her head to breathe.

"Are they gone?"

"I don't know. Maybe another pass. They got something big down the street, I think."

"I'm sorry I ran."

"You've run before and I should have known—" he got out before his voice was drowned out again by a blast so violent it threw them both to the ground. Stunned to silence, huddled there against each other on the brutal pavement, they looked up awed into a sky of fantastic, fiery display. A dozen hot Italian suns over London. Sweeping arcs of blackout searchlights along the Thames probing the smoke-laced sky for bombers as night fell. Ocher and apricot and magenta hues like Christmas baubles dotted with amber and greenish parachute flares from the next approaching squadron of German planes. Dust in the air seared their lungs; the sickly sweet smell of a blitzed chemist shop mingled with the stench of ruptured sewer lines. Rescue sirens stabbed through the cacophony of noises. But this time, the planes came like roaring lorries, line after throbbing line of them, passing over to drop their devastation farther west while Lesley and Paul could only stare helplessly up at them.

He pulled her to her feet, steadied her. "We're going if the car's intact. If they come around again, who knows what they'll hit. The streets may be blocked or barricaded, but I'll try to get you to the airport."

She found her purse in the eerie light of flaming buildings, but hobbled along beside him without bothering to look for a shoe that last blast had somehow twitched off her foot. At the car he grabbed her and pulled her hard against him to kiss her once, his mouth slanting hungrily, possessively across hers.

Her feet dangled clear of the ground. The impact of his touch was as fierce and devastating as all this around them had been, and she responded mindlessly. Then he pushed her into the Buick, which waited ghostly white with plaster dust both outside and in from a shattered back window and open door. He drove them in, out, and around a rabbit-warren maze of streets to get her to the little military supply airfield outside Mitcham as Cesare had arranged. Their lungs burned with the stench, the dust, the smoke. They said nothing on the entire harrowing ride while London from the Tower to Westminster seemed ablaze in cavorting, grinning flames behind them.

The runway was totally blacked out, and they could barely see each other. At the steps to her plane, he turned her to him once again and she braced for another kiss. He felt her stiffen, released her and stepped back. He was only tormenting himself and evidently her, too. Hell, he'd lost her just as surely as Britain was losing its war. He leaned very close to memorize her pale face streaked with dust and smoke and tears; her body quaked as if the bombs still hit.

"Don't be afraid," he comforted. "The first time it really happens to you—they call it shell shock."

"It's only I can't believe it all happened so fast."

"And then ended. Just like us."

"Yes. Nothing's forever, maybe not even England."

"Don't think that. Like the song says, 'There will always be an England,' Lesley. Go on now, back to those babies who need you. Lady Sarah told me their names, too."

"For my mother and for Cesare's father, who was named Paolo."

"Of course. I didn't think it was anything else."

The single green winking light from the wing of the DC-3 etched Paul's stern profile as he turned away. She tried desperately to imprint it in her mind so she would have at least that, but it kept flickering, merging instantly with the night.

His voice was more distant now. "Go on then, Lesley."

"Thanks, Paul, for my safety." She started to cry again and blessed the dark for hiding it. She hated her feet for refusing to run up the metal steps and her own weakness for wishing he would kiss her again. But she'd made vows to Cesare to uphold the Valente name and never be the sort of deceitful woman her aunt Rissa had been. She lifted one hand to Paul Kendal in farewell. She saw a flicker of flame and the red glowing pinpoint of his cigarette as he walked away. Then, despite the fact she hobbled on one shoe, she turned and marched straight up the steps into the waiting plane.

❧ ❧ *Chapter Twelve*

VIBRANT WITH EXCITEMENT, Lesley held tightly to Cesare's arm as they stepped from the chauffeured limousine on Leningrad's cold, windy Moscow Prospect. Before them stretched the massive Fur Palace where they had come to select and purchase pelts at the world-famous fur auction. It was the one aspect of the industry that was so far as foreign to Lesley as this Russian city, which had once been Peter the Great's capital of Saint Petersburg. The deep snows of late January cloaked Leningrad's impressive tree-lined boulevards, parks, town houses, and palaces. The knife-edged wind froze the river Neva to glass under its hundreds of little bridges. Their breath vaporized to crystalline clouds before their faces. Still, the entire experience heated her blood. It was precisely this bitter-cold climate from the Urals to the Siberian pine forests that produced the magnificent furs they sought here at this vast, snow-etched temple, the mecca of wealthy furriers the world over.

It had only been a little over a month since Lesley had left Paul behind in burning London. Since then, she'd dedicated herself wholly to being Cesare's wife and assistant and tried to forget that distant devastation. Only the twins came before her efforts to please her husband and to learn all she could at his side, however short he was with her at times. At least, besides asking how the lawsuit to obtain her parents' estate had gone, his total lack of interest in what she'd done in England had saved her from a terrible scene. She had decided on the long, lonely return flight to Rome she would tell Cesare the truth. She owed that to her husband if not to Paul. In the end, she kept as silent as Cesare. Yet she would almost have preferred his jealous anger to his disinterest. It had set her to wondering again what really went on inside this man she'd married.

Had it been this way for her aunt Rissa too, so that she'd tried to run away with someone else after Cesare Valente wanted to marry her? Had Cesare's preoccupation and moodiness shut her out so she'd turned to that other man she'd died with? Rissa's husband, Franco Valente, had been more quiet and gentle, more like Carlo while Cesare was more like Guido. Perhaps that was why Guido and Cesare were always sparks and tinder together, Lesley had decided—too much alike.

"Watch your step on this ice, sweet," Cesare told her as they bent briefly together against the wind. The huge bronze doors of the Fur Palace swept open. Lesley gazed about the foyer in awe. The place looked even vaster inside with its buff stone floors, muted lighting—surely not enough for anyone to successfully mark and select furs—beige stone walls, and young women in tan smocks. She and Cesare soon exchanged their winter coats for smocks similar to those the young women wore. Everyone seemed to recognize Cesare. He introduced her to other buyers, brokers, and wholesalers in the wings of the auction hall. A sprawling war encompassed Europe, but it seemed quite a league of nations here: the Swedes; the French, no doubt with permission from their conquerors; a few Germans; several Americans; and one or two from British furriers.

But for the faint, pervasive odor of the tanned skins, it was somewhat cozier here in the wings of the open hall where buyers sat at individual tables under glaring lights. Lesley followed Cesare's lead and accepted a cap with a bill their guide offered to help protect their eyes. All around them, men in these strange hats that hid their faces bent over piles of pelts, studiously marking down in notebooks the grade, use, and top prices they would bid for each lot.

"I feel quite outnumbered here, Cesare. I see only one other woman down the way," she observed as she scanned the area.

"You'll outshine them all, Valente's little secret weapon with the marker's hands and eyes," he whispered and hugged her shoulders. "Let them all think you're just a stunning fur model, as I did at first, and then we'll take them by surprise."

He turned to the serious-faced young woman who still

waited at their side. "First bring my wife your top sables—all wild, no farm lots—while I look at some white fitch," he instructed her. "Later we'll be marking ondatra, lynx, mink, and all the foxes you're showing." The girl nodded, clicked her heels, and disappeared. They sat side by side on the polished wooden bench at their designated table.

"These benches get as damned hard on the rear as the sharp lights on the eyes," Cesare groused and shook his head. "But it can't be helped. No one ever said the Russians were good at providing creature comforts. Remember that brown bath water back at the Astoria that surprised you? But they've got the premier *grand luxe* furs of the world and that's that." He bent toward her as if they shared some grand conspiracy. "Now, listen, Lesley, we'll be buying especially heavy to get us through two years or so of this hellish war if need be. It's a financial gamble but so's life lately."

"I wish you wouldn't say things like that all the time," she protested gently. She tilted her head to look earnestly into his guarded eyes. "And I just hope the war's over in two years."

"If not," he said, his voice husky, "it will be the death of Italy and perhaps the rest of Europe the way things are going for everyone but Herr Hitler. All right, here come the furs." He fell back into his old schoolmaster voice, as if he were lecturing a novice. "Now we've only got three days to examine over fifteen thousand pelts. After you've selected the prime skins you want for your own coat to replace the one Edda Mussolini 'borrowed,' keep in mind we'll need enough for ten or fifteen other sable coats for the duration, somewhere between thirty to eighty skins per coat depending on how you think they match. This afternoon we'll do lynx together as we can't afford any mistake with them. It takes at least one hundred sixty pelts to get sixty to match well."

She pressed her lips together and nodded stiffly. She knew all that and was actually more adept at grading and matching than he was. She said only, "Yes, fine, dear," and bent to her work.

The morning raced by. Her eyes burned, her neck and arms ached, but the thrill of handling pelt after glorious pelt kept all her senses at fever pitch. Instinctively, she weeded out the lesser pelts and kept a careful, prioritized record of all lot numbers in her little notebook. She could envision each piece she touched as part of the whole. Sometimes she pictured specific sketches she had made months ago, a completed garment to grace and enhance some fortunate woman's life.

She ranked the sable lots by preference, judging the Bargunzinsky and Yakutsky pelts for full coats by the sheen of their dense, silky fur against her soft hands. The smaller, flatter pelts of Amursky sable she chose for jackets and capes that would bear the proud label of Countess Valente in her first solo line this spring. The fullness of the Kamchatsky sable they would use only for collars and cuffs. And she fully intended to utilize unusual furs for garments in her collection. It was an idea Cesare ridiculed, but she hoped to win him over. She felt confident and very proud. Cesare fully trusted her judgment in selecting sable, at least.

At one o'clock they mingled with the other buyers as they assembled for the full meal laid out on buffet tables in the next room: caviar, smoked salmon, sturgeon, hot and cold meats, excellent borschts. They drank only a glass of wine apiece and strong tea from the polished brass samovar. Cesare had warned her off the vodka their hosts proffered with big grins. Not only was it potent but the Russians always insisted anyone opening a bottle finish it.

Word soon spread among the buyers of the expertise of the young red-haired woman Count Valente had married. She had the gift of "the hands, the eye," they said. She felt so grateful and fortunate. In the late afternoon, when her entire back ached so badly she was beginning to fear she would remain forever hunched over, someone tapped her on the shoulder. She squinted up from under the brim of her cap. Before her stood Madame Justine Faulk, the petite French designer from Sackville's in London.

"Madame Justine, I had no idea you were here!" She slid off the bench to hug her. "I saw one woman earlier across the room, but not at luncheon, and I never thought it would be you!"

"Ah, that Leonard Stockman, he wanted me to work through the meal. I didn't mind, but I would mind not seeing you!" They released each other's shoulders, then Madame darted kisses on both Lesley's cheeks. She looked as animated as ever, Lesley thought. A quick, clever sparrow, the models at Sackville's used to whisper. "Like every furrier with any funding at all," Madame bubbled on with a pat on her arm, "Sackville's is here to obtain furs for the duration of this mess the Germans make, no? My beloved France, well, none of that today, as I am so honored to see you. Just wait until Mr. Stockman hears you are here. We knew of your good fortune to marry the admired Count Valente from the London papers, but to see you here again after the sad way we parted, *c'est formidable!*" She threw her hands up in pleasure, and her big rings glinted in the cold ceiling lights.

"If Leonard Stockman's here, and he's been reading the London papers, it won't be *formidable*, madame!" Lesley protested with a grim smile and shook her head. "He'll avoid me even if I do have a foreign title now."

"Ah, still angry, but then I do not blame you. Time and again I say to myself that after the war, I will leave that man who knows nothing of furs himself or of loyalty or kindness to other people, no. But I cannot now go home to France with the vile Nazis sitting there like spiders making webs, and so I stay at Sackville's until better times."

Lesley introduced Cesare to Madame Faulk and spoke in glowing terms of how Madame had taught her much of what she knew when she first came to Valente's. Cesare was gracious and charming. Again Lesley assured herself how fortunate she was to have a husband of such reputation and kindness. Her nimble mind began to hatch a little plan she would speak to Cesare about later.

Lesley understood now why Cesare insisted on a masseur coming to their suite the first three evenings after their preliminary work at the Fur Palace before the auction, which took place on the last day. Restored by a massage and a hot meal each night, they took in *Swan Lake* at the Kirov Ballet, or went to hear a balalaika concert, or enjoyed the private evening tour of the Hermitage Museum in Peter the Great's vast, impressive Winter Palace. They dined with other furriers, and from their subtle warnings, Lesley became certain Leonard Stockman was not only avoiding her but perhaps spreading rumors about her, too. She detested revenge, petty or otherwise. She'd had her fill of it with Constance and Trent, but from someone of Leonard Stockman's caliber, it was inexcusable.

Since Stockman left Madame Faulk on her own when she was not selecting pelts for him, Lesley and Cesare dined with her their last night. At the dinner, they formally asked her to come back to Rome with them to work at Valente's. Cesare had readily acquiesced to Lesley's plan because he admitted many things could keep him busy in days to come. In addition, several of their best mechanics in the shop had been conscripted into Il Duce's forces. Then too, he wanted Lesley to have a block of midday time free for the children and him. But despite the fact they promised Madame a large salary increment and an apartment and wardrobe until her things could be sent by a friend, Madame sadly shook her head.

"I assure you, I am thrilled at the offer, and I feel very little loyalty to Leonard Stockman, you know that, my Lesley." She rolled her huge eyes behind the thick tortoise-shell glasses. "But you see, since Italy is on Hitler's side at war with England and my France, I must be loyal to that part of it."

"But, believe me, Madame, many Italians are neither Fascists nor Nazi sympathizers," Cesare told her passionately. "My wife still has ties to England too, though it is best not to speak of that—" He paused and swallowed hard. Lesley's pulse quickened. Had he not asked her details about her trip home because he was afraid to know in case someone asked him of his wife's loyalties, political or otherwise? "And I, I assure you, have a fidelity to Italy that is far deeper than any forced, superficial support of Il Duce!" Cesare concluded vehemently.

How Lesley wished he could speak that fervently and honestly to Guido, for he needed to hear just that. At least the three of them here had parted friends. Lesley hardly blamed Madame for refusing to flee England even under siege, considering all her earthly goods were back in her flat in London. She only hoped that fool Leonard Stockman, who kept pointedly ignoring her and even Cesare, was kinder to the talented, clever Madame.

* * *

The fur auction overseen by the Soviet fur committee, Sojuzpushnina, droned on for hours, and the Valentes had been clever and fortunate so far. They had just outbid the large, prestigious Berlin furrier Herpich for prime lots of white Russian lynx. There had even been applause for that small victory, led boldly by the Swedes and the French, for reasons no doubt more political than professional. But Leonard Stockman's scowl from across the aisle only reminded Lesley of Lady Constance's acrimony at Trent's memorial service. It was obvious that Stockman was bitter that things had gone so well for her—or was he afraid she had told Cesare and others about the cruel way he had dismissed her? Lesley merely glared back and whispered to Cesare how she'd like to wipe that look off the portly Englishman's face. But except for one batch of golden sable Stockman had not seemed to want anything the Valentes bought up.

The natural silver muskrat called Russian ondatra, a very versatile fur for which Lesley had great plans, was added to the Valente tally. "We're really cutting my budget close, but the way the wind's blowing," Cesare whispered, "we may not be allowed to leave Italy to come back here next year or to go to future auctions, either."

Her clear brow furrowed in concern. "Why not?" she whispered back.

"I only mean travel may be more and more restricted as gasoline is rationed further," he hastened to explain. He looked obviously regretful he'd upset her. He patted her knee. "We've got everything we need now, I'd say, so nothing more, or we won't have lire for the thread and silk to put together these pelts for your new line."

She knew—or thought she did—that Cesare was only teasing, and she sat back to relax through the rest of the auction. That is, until Leonard Stockman began bobbing out of his seat to bid on some lots of silver fox.

"I remember those lots, Cesare." She flipped through her notebook. "Here, I've got written down that they were powder soft, fluffy, supple, and true silver with perfectly lovely black stripes. But they were ranched and you said to stay with the wild lots."

His black eyebrows puckered; he stared straight ahead. "So I did," he muttered. "Then let's pass on them."

"Up!" Leonard Stockman screeched in his high-pitched voice across the aisle, raising the bid by hundreds for these lots instead of increments of ten. No, she told herself, she didn't believe in revenge and yet teaching someone a good lesson was hardly the same thing. The man was perched on the edge of his chair, his face and shiny bald head red and perspiring. How utterly wretched he was at this after all these years, Lesley thought. If he wanted the lots so badly, he should at least adopt a calmer, steelier demeanor. On the other side of the man, Madame rolled her eyes at Lesley, then whispered something to Stockman.

"No!" Lesley distinctly heard him scold the petite French-woman in a momentary hush in the bidding. "You don't know one flaming thing about this part, and are likely to ruin things for me here just as your cowardly countrymen have for Britain!"

Several people close to Stockman and Madame gasped. Cesare's hand covered Lesley's. "She chose to stay with him though he treats her like that," he warned with a shrug. "Women are foolish about men that way, and I will never understand why even you—" he began.

Lesley pulled her hand back from him, shot it into the air to get the auctioneer's attention, and called out, "Up!"

"Lesley, the man has pushed the price a little high, and I told you how things stand," Cesare hissed, his lips barely moving.

"I'll sell my auto, some jewelry. He's abused Madame and me too long, insulted the Valentes. He has no right to act like—like an abusive schoolmaster to her! And besides, I have a wonderful idea for those pelts even if they are ranched. Up!" she called to top the sputtering Stockman's latest offer while all the other bidders dropped away.

The disgruntled line of Cesare's mouth curved into a reluctant little smile. When he patted her hand again, she held to his in silent thanks for his support despite what he'd been about to say. All her life would be like this now, she vowed silently as she matched Stockman bid for bid while the crowd buzzed and gasped. She could take control, win Cesare over to trust her, exorcise the past with hard work and determination.

Applause exploded. Someone clapped her on the back when the auctioneer called out, "Silver fox lots four hundred nineteen through four hundred thirty-six to Countess Valente!"

Cesare hugged her stiffly. Madame flew across the aisle, her hair fringe waving. "I told that vile man, no more insults to me, to France, to anyone! This time I told him *I* will follow behind the lady with the title, my countess! I hope you and the count will still have me because I have just told Leonard Stockman to go to perdition!"

And so it was that the airplane with the crates of Russian pelts carried three fine furriers instead of two back to Rome through winter snow, until the warm hills and plateaus of Tuscany lay below them and the chill January sun of Italy welcomed them all.

The Roman sun steeped the vast Piazza della Republica in light, heat, and humidity where Paul Kendal waited in the July afternoon. In a sliver of shade, he leaned nonchalantly against the stone wall of the Church of Santa Maria della Vittoria. It was one of those days when you could supposedly fry an egg on the paving stones, he thought. If eggs had been easier to get—the damned rationing was much worse here than in England.

Paul Kendal had decided to fight this war his own way as an undercover war correspondent in enemy Italy. Until America actually declared war, it was the most he could do. At least President Roosevelt had vowed to help the Brits economically with the Lend-Lease Act. Meanwhile, Hitler had attacked Greece and the previous German ally, Russia. The war had shifted somewhat away from England with the cessation of saturation bombings in May; things were heating up further in North Africa and the Mediterranean. So Paul had volunteered to put himself where Hitler would be focusing much more of his attention in the future. Besides, it would be good fodder for his next book. An American publishing house had bought his novel *Lions Roar*, about the bravery of England under the Blitz, and were rushing it to print. Now, he'd write about Il Duce's Italy.

Nervously, he stroked the thick black mustache he'd grown to look more Italian for his elaborate charade. He'd taken to letting the stubble of his thick beard show lately, too. His meager wardrobe had been purchased in Milan, where he'd gone to establish his identity as a Milanese book salesman. And for months he'd been working doggedly to improve his Italian.

He dropped his cigarette butt underfoot and ground it out with the others he'd smoked while he waited for the man he sought. His eyes stung from squinting across the square as no Italians wore sunglasses even in this glare. He sighed. Yes, at last. His information had been correct. The stocky, silver-haired Count Cesare Valente emerged from a large, chauffeur-driven Bugatti across the way and strode off. Paul let him get a head start. He lifted his heavy leather briefcase full of books, then pursued him at a distance.

Gian Donato was the name Paul would go by in Rome while he researched and wrote whatever columns he could get out of the country through his contacts to the south. He knew them only by their codenames, Cervo, Stag, and Coniglio, or Rabbit. A friend from the States would continue to write his columns for him from London so that no one would miss him there. He knew it was a damned dangerous game. But the most wrenching part of being in Rome was knowing he was so close to Lesley and having to swear to himself he would never seek her out again.

Now she might be in terrible danger because of her husband's secret, traitorous activities, he thought, as he strode quickly across the broiling piazza. A frown wrinkled his forehead and tugged down the corners of his mouth. The first good lead he'd had for an article about Rome's anti-Fascist underground presses had led right to Count Valente. Paul couldn't believe that Lesley, feeling as she did about any kind of vituperative press, could know about her husband's inflammatory *Libero*, but with her, he was never sure anymore.

He stalked the man southeast toward the train station. Cesare Valente turned the corner and disappeared into a squalid tufa building with peeling brown paint in a little cul-de-sac off a street called Amendola. The shrieks of train whistles at the central station just a block away mingled with the shouts of children and stray dogs. The shrill voices of women coming from iron balconies draped with laundry and reeking of stale cooking smells pierced his ears. If the count were indeed involved with *Libero*, it made sense that he would choose a poor, out-of-the-way neighborhood to print it in.

Paul leaned his shoulder against a building across the street and lit one more cigarette. He watched the door to see if anyone else went in or out. He hated the bitter Spanish tobacco he had to smoke here; he didn't dare be seen with an American brand. His pulse quickened at the thought of facing Count Valente. He not only admired the dangerous work the man was doing for a noble cause but hoped he would be able to help him by writing about it anonymously. This was the man Lesley had fled to, slept with, damn her, borne the twins he had once hoped, briefly, might be his. He shook his head to clear it of fantasy and yearnings. What the hell was the matter with him? Cesare Valente could hate his guts when he found out who he really was, and that hatred would not be in the slightest tempered by the admiration Paul felt for him. This whole thing could easily blow right up in his face like one of Hitler's demonic incendiary bombs. He threw the half-smoked cigarette down and ground it out under his heel, shooing away a hovering skinny black cat who thought it might be food.

He sighed as his eyes locked with the wide yellow gaze of the cat, which had retreated only a few yards away in the alley. His sister, Kaye, loved cats, had a soft heart for all animals. He'd always shared that with her, though he was more partial to dogs. When they were kids they'd taken in any stray they could find. Once their parents had protested and they'd hidden their little menagerie behind the big coal furnace in the Kendal mansion's basement. Those carefree days and Kaye and Long Island seemed so far away from all this, he mused. The swift stab of homesickness surprised him. He unclasped his briefcase and rummaged for the package of cheese and pastry he'd bought at a shop this morning. He crumbled the entire chunk of gorgonzola on the alley stones and watched the cat attack it before he turned away feeling immensely better.

He crossed the deserted street and knocked quietly on the door. It was opened a crack by a thin, almost ragged girl with a pert, elfin face, lovely cheekbones, and flashing brown eyes. She looked like a hungry cat herself, a bohemian. Behind her he could see nothing but a dark curtain. *"Si? Cosa vuole?"* she asked with a saucy toss of her wild black hair.

"I'm a salesman from Milan come to see Cesare," he told her in Italian, with a little smile she did not return. Then he repeated, exactly as he'd been told, "To sell him important books."

Her wide eyes openly assessed him now. "There is no Cesare here," she'd begun when Count Valente's wary face replaced hers in the slit of open door.

"It's all right, Carla," Cesare told her with a stiff nod. "Take your goods and be off now." Paul breathed easier. His contact had told him the right passwords to get this far.

While the girl evidently went out a back way, Cesare opened the door for Paul, and he stepped in. Cesare leaned out to survey the street, then closed the door and motioned Paul behind the curtain. No one else was in the dingy room. Bingo! Paul thought. Cesare had taken him right in. Two typewriters, trays of type, printing plates, an old-fashioned press, a hand-cranked mimeograph machine, and stacks of paper cluttered the single large work table made of boards set on wooden carpenters' horses. They faced each other across the jumbled, sprawling table.

"You have a story for me from Milan? We're grateful for it as I never dare to go there myself anymore," Cesare said with a shrug. His eyes remained hooded, mistrusting.

Paul braced himself. The man looked tense, tired, jumpy, Paul thought. He had quite a paunch on him and must not be much taller than Lesley, but he had not meant to think at all about that. "Count Valente, I'm really an American, but I live here now and go by the name Gian Donato. I'm telling you this so you'll trust me. I'm a journalist and I want to help promote your cause."

Surprise and panic flushed Cesare's olive complexion ruddy. Coal-black brows crushed the narrowed eyes. "An American journalist? Am I really to believe that?" Cesare demanded with a sharp jab of index finger. "Here in these dangerous times? And what is your real name, then?"

Paul had hoped this part of the truth would not be required, but he knew better. The man was hardly a fool. "First, let me tell you that if you're the brain behind *Libero*, as a trusted associate of mine has said, you are to be congratulated. The paper is bold and daring, the writing clever. I have in my briefcase your last issue mocking Mussolini's maniac propaganda attacks on Churchill and President Roosevelt," he said, in an attempt to assure Cesare. He put his briefcase down on the stone floor and leaned toward Cesare with his open hands on the big table as if that would steady them both.

"Ah yes, I admire whoever writes and prints that paper too, I must admit," Cesare returned smoothly, stalling for time. "Imagine Il Duce claiming you Americans and the British would force the Italians into slavery, confiscate our art treasures, sterilize our young men, slaughter our citizens, and deport our children en masse if you ever conquered the Axis powers," he said, his voice laced with sarcasm. "That is, however, what the Führer might do."

Paul's tense neck and shoulder muscles relaxed slightly. The man was obviously proud of his work, though careful not to admit to it. But desperation glittered in his eyes. His obvious exhaustion and the brittle tone suggested someone right on the verge of disaster. Poor Lesley.

"But you have not answered my question, Gian from Milano. Your real name?" Cesare insisted and actually quivered inside. Their eyes locked in the split second before the American answered. Cesare cursed silently; he knew what he would say.

"All right. My name's Paul Kendal, Count Valente." The American straightened to his full height. "I trust you, you see, and need your help to write about your part of the resistance movement, of course without any names being used."

"Oh, of course," Cesare repeated, his tone pure acid. "You trust me and I am to trust you, Paul Kendal, is that it?"

"I find professional admiration for you easy to come by because of all you've done," Paul told him as his long arm swept the makeshift printing office. "I had hoped, since we're both journalists striving for what is true and just, you might put aside personal matters to be willing to help."

"What is true and just about putting personal matters aside?" Cesare exploded, then lowered his voice. "Am I to believe you are here in Rome only for this noble purpose, then?"

"I'm here as a journalist and nothing else."

"Not to see my wife?" Cesare cried and drew himself up to his full height.

"No! I haven't seen her and don't intend to. That's all in the past; the real need is here in Rome, so—"

"You may be assured my real need is here in Rome," Cesare roared at him. He'd never been so afraid before. The fear of Mussolini discovering *Libero* and the traitor's death that could mean for him was nothing compared to his fear of the love and power this man must once have exerted over his Lesley. The twins—Cati had his chin, they both had the man's hair and eyes, damn him! He knew Lesley still loved this man, though she had hidden it quite well this last year, had tried very hard. But now his arrival in Rome had ruined everything. Cesare Valente would gladly die for Italy's cause if need be, but he would also die before he would ever let this man she loved come back into her life!

He came around the table toward Paul, one hand on its edge for support, one fist raised. He was terrified the nightmare would come true! Lesley would flee from him along the Amalfi Drive with the twins and this man, her lover, who had been until now faceless.

"Mr. Kendal, Signor Donato, or whatever your name really is," he told the intense, frowning American, his voice controlled now, "I cannot help you." He hunched his shoulders helplessly, shook his head. He prayed he was convincing. "I have donated money to certain anti-Fascist papers, this I admit, I have visited them with funding like my visit here today. If any of what you say is true, I ask you to keep away from this place, others like it. They print mostly advertising brochures here, believe me. Do your own writing, but do not endanger the innocent people who work here." Cesare paused, cleared his throat. He remembered well Paul Kendal's dynamic and bold style from the two cables he'd seen, his ability to capture emotion in a few well-chosen words. Truly, if things were different, and if they could work together for Italy, for America too— But no! "I myself shall just leave my donation here and go, and I insist you be on your way, too."

Paul felt floored, so disappointed. He knew Count Valente's claims were lies, but that was hardly the point. His first opportunity at getting a story for the American public about the brave spirit of the Italians under Mussolini and he'd lost it because of who he was. He'd been stupid to believe otherwise, of course.

"I will go then," he said resignedly and extended his hand. The man met his intense gaze unflinchingly now; his arms remained riveted to his sides. "I trust you not to expose my cover, not to tell the authorities I'm here in Rome. But even journalist to journalist you don't trust me, and I regret that." He bent to pick up his briefcase and turned away.

"Are you crazy, man? I'm a furrier, not a journalist! And how could I ever trust the one who used my bride the way you did? But she was mine, only mine, in bed and out, from the beginning. Mine!"

Paul spun around. Fury drowned disappointment. "She was seduced from the first, in bed and out, by your wealth and power and the furs, you mean!" he shouted.

Cesare pursued him, shaking his fist. "Mine in the love we shared from the first!"

"The twins were born rather early, weren't they?" Paul accused before he could grab the words back.

The man's face contorted to a livid mask. "Twins? You know of my twins?"

So Lesley had not told him they had been together in London seven months ago, Paul thought. He could tell him now, but who knew what that would mean for her? "I know Lesley's grandmother, Lady Sarah. She told me," he clipped out.

"Meddler! Both of you! But what of my twins? Is it the first time a man and woman have produced children from their passionate love affair as Lesley and I did? And I married her!"

"So you did, and you're welcome to her!" Paul beat down his raging desire to strike the man. Lesley was to blame; it was she who betrayed him for a title and career and life she wanted at any cost. He stalked to the door, then spun back again. "Whatever we've said here, I won't betray you, Count Valente. Better look to your wife for that."

Cesare watched the door slam, then scurried over to lock it. He leaned his palms and forehead against the wood, hearing again those dreaded words about betrayal. Women were never to be trusted, not Rissa even when he'd offered her everything, not his Lesley whom he adored as he never had anyone else.

He braced himself, panting as if he'd just run kilometers. He could actually feel his heart thudding in his chest, a vein throbbing in his forehead. He was so exhausted but there was no time to waste. *Libero*'s offices would have to be moved again immediately, all the carriers told. And then he had to get Lesley and the twins away, maybe to Capri for a while. If she would go now that her big Countess Valente line was debuting this autumn. Yes, she would go if he insisted.

How prophetic and strange, he thought as he shuffled back to the table, his shoulders slumped. He'd been certain all these months Lesley had been his that Paul Kendal would barge into their lives someday. Cesare cursed her anew for how much he loved her, how desperately he wanted to keep her entirely for himself. He had no intention of surrendering her to anyone else any more than he had of surrendering to Mussolini's personal *carabinieri*, who'd been breathing down his neck more and more lately. And somehow, if it was the last thing he ever did on this earth, he would find a way to make Lesley's hatred for Paul Kendal prevent that man from ever touching her again.

❊ ❊ *Chapter Thirteen*

THE SUN was a warm kiss, the breeze a cool caress in the hillside gardens of the Villa Valente on the heights of Capri. Lesley and Lilla, the young upstairs maid she'd brought with her from Rome, watched the twins play on the grass. Cati's sturdy legs took her back and forth, her dolls peering unconcernedly from her wicker doll pram, while Paolo crawled behind his little metal model of a bi-wing airplane, running it through the grass with sound effects as if it were an auto. Beyond the twins in a splash of July afternoon sun, Carlo's beloved Airedale, Caprice, sat alertly with cocked head as if she'd been given the specific task of guarding the twins. Lesley bent over to tie her blue felt cork-soled sandals back on her feet, her chin-length permanent-waved hair pulled back by a silk band blowing free in the wind. How perfectly marvelous, she mused, to escape the bustle of Rome on holiday and savor the little unhurried pleasures of life.

It had been a lovely nine days here despite the fact Cesare had not joined her on the weekend as he'd promised. He'd sent a note over on the ferry with their chauffeur, Antonio, that he had further important business. She'd had rather mixed feelings about Cesare's coming this time anyway. She knew he needed to escape Rome for a while because he drove himself mercilessly. Lately, she and Madame had assumed most of the responsibility for running the shop both upstairs and down. He'd told her he was involved in raising money to protect private businesses in Rome in case the increasingly desperate Mussolini tried to take over more than just armament factories and big industry.

Both Cesare's health and his temper were obviously suffering for it. He'd come home one day distraught from a meeting and insisted she take the twins to Capri for a few weeks. Their last night together he'd been so dominating and forceful in bed that she'd nearly found herself beyond responding. She cared for Cesare deeply and was grateful to him but, war or not, she was coming to the point where she had to stand up to him when he treated her like a possession and tried to control her.

Her robin's-egg-blue pleated cotton sundress blew against her bare legs as she rose from the marble bench and paced to the brow of the hill beyond the statues of centaurs and nymphs. She gazed out over the terraced green acres of trees and grape-vines below, and then farther down at the toylike town and glittering azure sea. So beautiful and restful here, but it did not calm her thoughts. She was going back to Rome tomorrow, whatever Cesare commanded. She had a great deal to do at the shop even though the Countess Valente line was finished. Guido, who'd been wounded and hospitalized briefly in Sicily, would be home soon for a week before he was returned to duty. She needed to be there to ensure family peace and to see if she could help Cesare and Guido settle their differences before something more dire happened to Guido.

"Countess Lesley!" The voice startled her. She turned to face Lucia Belli, her maid from the villa. "That girl, she is letting the twins get all dirty in the grass," Lucia complained, shifting from one foot to the other. "They are both off the blanket I brought out!" Lucia's usually pleasant face looked like a thundercloud again, as it had far too often since Lesley had brought the charming young Lilla along from Rome to give the girl a little respite from the big town house.

Lilla was more patient with the twins than the nursemaid Eleana, whom Lesley had given the week off to decide if she really wanted to retain her further. The twins laughed and chattered their nonsense back to Lilla when she played peek-aboo, patty-cake or other little games with them. But since they'd arrived on Capri, Lucia Belli had been picking on the girl. Lesley heaved an inward sigh. With the war taking the men away, she felt like an Amazon queen reigning over a warrior kingdom of nervous, fretful women.

"We can hardly expect the twins to stay on a blanket, however dirty they get, Lucia. We'll just let them splash about in the pool again later. They're bundles of energy, and it's good for them to explore," Lesley said and touched the maid's arm comfortingly.

"Yes, of course, but if they are not watched enough, with all the hills and cliffs on Capri—well," she said, sniffing. "That girl is just not used to Capri, that's all. Up on the cliffs above Tiberius's Villa, my parents used to actually harness me to a line at times when I was that age," Lucia protested.

The Belli family, whom island tradition claimed were actually descended from a Roman official in the service of the Emperor Tiberius centuries ago, were sheepherders and farmers on the highest part of the mountain. Lesley had met and admired her elderly parents when they came down to work the Valente vineyards for the estate. Salt-of-the-earth people, she recalled, with their leathery, sun-browned faces and strong bodies, their joy. And they were proud that Lucia and her husband worked for the Valentes, but also proud of their own land and rich heritage. She thought again as she had before: if it weren't for Cesare and Valente's, she would not hesitate to flee here with the twins to the villa and live as the Bellis did until the war was over.

"I'm sure you're right about keeping a good eye on the twins," Lesley told her with a nod. "Let's go back straightaway and help Lilla watch them. She's been content being just an upstairs maid, Lucia, but she's good with the babies too, just as you've always been more to me than a lady's maid."

That ended it temporarily, Lesley noted with relief as she and Lucia strolled companionably back toward the raucous scene of twins and cavorting dog. "Whatever's the matter with Caprice all of a sudden?" Lesley asked the auburn-haired, blue-eyed Lilla, but then she heard a voice. A man back by the pool or on the veranda calling her name. Caprice tore off like a shot. Perhaps Cesare had come after all. What if Carlo had come home unexpectedly and Caprice recognized his voice? "Someone's calling me. You two stay here together with the twins," she ordered over her shoulder. She broke into a run up the twisting path toward the villa.

She emerged from the screen of cypresses onto the white gleaming marble blocks that surrounded the oval swimming pool. Across the turquoise water stood Guido and Stella arm in arm. They jumped apart as if their touch were suddenly white-hot. "Guido, you're home!" Lesley shouted, feeling suddenly foolish at that observation as she hurried around the lip of pool to hug him while the dog jumped and barked in circles.

Guido looked gaunt, sunburned. Bandages on his left arm and shoulder made his Fascist lieutenant's uniform look terribly misshapen, but he seemed to be all in one piece. The shrapnel wounds on his neck did not appear to be too bad. His flared ecru breeches looked sharp and crisp. His polished high boots and medals of rank and valor glinted in the sun. She accidently knocked his visored cap awry as she hugged him and dared to kiss his cheek. However much Guido claimed he hated to wear his uniform, he looked handsome in it. But his face was wary and grim; even Stella looked distraught. Lesley let go of Guido's good arm and hugged Stella.

"Stella, good of you to come along," she said, and forced her shoulders back to face whatever they would tell her. "What's happened, Guido? Didn't Cesare come with you?"

"He couldn't—" he began, his voice rough with emotion.

"You haven't heard anything bad about Carlo?"

"No, Countess. You'd be the first to hear that."

"Guido," Stella said, her voice quiet, "I'll just wait inside for a few minutes." As if some cue passed between them, she put out her hand and Guido gave her his hat, which she cradled to her breasts as she walked slowly away. Running his hand nervously through his hair, Guido watched her, and Lesley sensed again that something had shifted between the two young people, no doubt at poor Carlo's expense.

"Guido, what is it?" she demanded, her heart pounding. "I assume you didn't traipse clear down to Naples and out on the ferry to Capri just to tell me all is forgiven between us."

His eyes slammed into hers before he looked down at his feet. "*Madre Maria,* the same old Lesley, but maybe everything will change now. Let's sit over here," he urged and tried to steer her toward the patio table.

"Blast it, tell me!" she cried and pulled away from his hand to face him with a defiant toss of her blown hair.

"All right! Uncle Cesare's been arrested by Mussolini's crack personal troops! There, is that what you couldn't wait to hear?"

"Arrested? For what? Mussolini—"

"For something I can't believe, but it's true. He's been arrested as a warning to the aristocrats of Rome, the precious few who still dare to think for themselves, for financing and for actually writing and printing that anti-Fascist broadsheet *Libero* he and I used to argue over—"

Guido's voice broke and he crumpled into a metal chair under the striped canvas umbrella.

"No! Guido, no!" she uttered in a strangled tone before she sank shakily into the chair next to his. She stared aghast at him while he put his elbows on the table and buried his face in his hands. Stunned, so sickened that she almost vomited with fear, she hugged her sides hard while she watched his shoulders heave. They sat unspeaking as her mind attempted to comprehend what had happened. Those secret meetings, the money used for things besides furs and the shop; all the inside information Cesare had tried too hard to glean from their social contacts; his refusal to allow Guido to bring a copy of *Libero* into the house even when Guido flaunted it in his face and called him a hypocrite and a coward.

"Guido, I just can't believe it," she breathed and reached out to touch his hands while he gasped silent tears into them.

He nodded, hit her hand away. "You should have known even if I didn't," he accused bitterly. "I was away. You should have known and stopped him."

"I didn't know. I asked him more than once, and he said there was nothing but some business meetings about money and an occasional donation, nothing else. He became furious if I pressed him. Nothing else—"

"Nothing you wanted to hear, of course!" he exploded, slamming his fists into the table. "You just wanted to live in your own little world, the furs, the twins, Carlo—being Carlo's friend, trying to take our mother's place, just because you look like her, however old you are," he hissed, his face distorted with fury and hatred.

She recoiled into her chair, then scraped it back to jump to her feet. "I've no time to listen to your sick accusations, Guido. I'm going back to Rome, going to Cesare, even Mussolini if I have to! You sit here and hate me if you must, build a greater shrine to the mother you worship and whom you think I mean to replace—"

She started away toward the villa, but he caught up to her, yanked her around by one arm. "You think I loved that slut?" he screamed so loud Stella ran back outside. "You think I didn't know her, know about her affair with Cesare after my father died, then the other lover, the one she met in the afternoons when Carlo and I were supposed to be in school? I saw her with him once, the man she died with after Cesare drove her away somehow. I saw her run toward her lover's auto, a black Lancia, I remember as if it were yesterday. Kissed him right in the street, their mouths open, her all over him, my holy, widowed mother. Got in to kiss him again, half over on the driver's side, the whore, and all I know is you look just like her and you can go to hell just like she did!"

She smacked Guido hard across the mouth with her open palm. The crack and Stella's little shriek silenced his tirade. Lesley seized his wrists and shook them gently as she would a disobedient child's. Her voice came quiet now. "Listen to me, Guido. You've been injured, your body by the war, your heart by your mother. I am not Countess Rissa, and your uncle needs our help and our love. Now!"

"And I suppose he can trust you never, never to run off to someone else you desire, never to betray the Valente name?" he badgered, his tone still caustic.

It was, she thought, as if Cesare spoke to her again with that all too familiar request, or as if her own heartfelt vows from the depth of her soul had stumbled into Guido's words. "Never, never," she promised and nodded fervently. Tears flooded her eyes and tracked down her high cheekbones. They stood together as still as the statues in the gardens below where the twins played.

He shook his head to break the spell, but didn't try to pull away. "They won't let you see him, Lesley. I already tried."

"Then we'll try again. I'm going to motor down to the harbor straightaway to catch the next ferry and ask Stella to stay here to help bring the twins back later." Stella nodded, bleary-eyed. The two women embraced again.

Lesley turned back to Guido. "I need you to come with me if you will help," she implored. "If not, stay here and cry by yourself for the lost days and years when you should have loved your mother and forgiven your uncle."

He dogged her steps as she started toward the villa. "But he drove her to running away, to dying with that man," he protested, his voice a whine. "She never deserted my father for a lover. Somehow, Uncle Cesare could have stopped her!"

She grasped his shoulders and looked into his agonized face. She bit her lower lip. Tears running down her cheeks, she shook her head helplessly. "They were only human, poor Guido. Haven't you learned yet that humans do things sometimes for reasons they can't control in a world they can't control?" Stella and Guido exchanged quick glances, but she had no time for that now. "Listen to me, both of you! As I get older, I'm learning that nothing, not joy and not pain—not love either—lasts forever. I'm going now."

She ran into the house and grabbed her purse from her dressing room. This was all a nightmare. Mussolini had summoned her once; surely he would see her again. Her eyes caught the little Stubbs painting of the lovers, which she had moved here when she could no longer bear to look at it in Rome. Her one little masterpiece among all Cesare Valente's priceless masters. She had lost Paul for good. She couldn't lose Cesare, too. Certainly not to that bastard Mussolini and his insane Fascist cause when Cesare had done something bold and fine and admirable with *Libero*.

She tore down the steps and out into the stony lane behind the villa where they kept the motorcars. In the front seat of her little Alfa Romeo, waiting for her, sat Guido, his shoulders back, his face composed, looking straight ahead. Without another word, she jumped in and they roared off down the dusty, hairpin road to Marina Grande to catch the next ferry to Naples.

The growing panic Lesley had held under fierce control began to strangle her with icy hands in the suffocating heat of the square before Il Duce's Palazzo Venezia in Rome. Last night she could reach no one to help; Cesare's friends had left town or were not available. All morning the guards at the gates of the palazzo had refused to admit her to the grounds or to deliver a message to Il Duce. She waited alone now as Guido had gone back to the Via Tasso prison to try to see Cesare. Her request to see him had been summarily refused when she had gone there both last night and early this morning. Stella had come across the square once from the Valente town house, where she was staying with the twins, to show Lesley the morning paper only to have her read the headline, stomp it underfoot, and send her back. "Traitor to the Empire from Among Those Once Trusted by the Divine Duce" indeed! This lying scandal sheet, like a hundred others she'd seen in her life, could simply go to hell!

"Please," she asked the guard when the next shift came on, "I must get a message to Il Duce!" She and Carlo had driven so easily through that gate over a year ago to show Mussolini those fur stoles.

"No messages from the families of traitors, Countess Valente," the guard replied and motioned to indicate that she should move back. This guard was very young; he dared to look her up and down in the same way as the so-called *pappagalli*, or parrots, who ogled and whistled at women along the Via Veneto, but none of that mattered now. What did matter was that even the new watch on the palace had been told who she was and what she wanted, and her cause here was hopeless.

Tears blurred her sight as she gazed up at the formidable marble and glass palazzo through the iron bars of the fence. She could picture Mussolini playing his role as Italy's leader inside, sitting in splendor in his vast salon at that huge desk, bent over his work, perhaps deciding her husband's fate at this very moment. Her energy and resolve fled for the first time. Her legs nearly buckled beneath her. She had not been able to eat since yesterday; today was as hot as Hades. Yes, that's what this place was. She'd been abandoned at the gates of hell and Satan and his demons would not let her either in or out. She was doomed, Cesare too, the twins everyone thought were his offspring, all she had held dear and hoped for here in Rome.

If the worst should befall Cesare and she was left alone, an enemy Englishwoman without protection here in hostile Italy, with a fur empire and two babies to defend, what would become of them all then? She could think of nothing else to do now that they would not let her see either Cesare or the dictator who held his life in his hands. All the influential people she had tried, including Il Duce's daughter, Edda, and son-in-law, Ciano, were obviously avoiding the Countess Valente at any cost.

She felt faint, wavered on her feet. Then her eyes caught a movement behind the soldiers blocking the gate—an auto caravan that included the big black Asturia with the Fascist flag everyone knew was Il Duce's private vehicle.

She stood back with the few others outside the gates as the soldiers shoved them slowly open, then snapped to smart salutes, their right arms thrust up stiffly. "Duce!" they shouted, though the rest of the small crowd stood silent and unmoving. "Duce!" Trembling, she let the first auto pass, uncertain exactly what to do when Mussolini's went by. Yes, he rode in back on her side, but he was looking straight ahead.

"Duce! Duce!" she screamed as if she meant to join their stupid, patriotic fervor for this horrible man. Then she threw herself at the slow-moving Asturia just as it cleared the gate. She grabbed the silver chrome door handle. In a blur she saw his shocked face pivot to her so close through the glass that also reflected her panicked face. A guard screamed at her; her feet dragged over the pavement as the entourage began to accelerate. Duce shouted to his driver and the auto screeched to a halt, yanking her arm and body against the sleek ebony curves of the auto before she fell off in the street near the curb.

Hands reached for her roughly, but Duce rolled down the window. "Enough! Just help her up!"

She stood, approached him, not taking time to brush herself off or to look to see whether her scrapes and bruises were serious. Tears coursed down her face at the shock and burden of it all. That is, until she saw Il Duce's cruel face had not softened and he actually smiled. She sniffed hard. With two swipes of her hand, she dried her cheeks.

"I told you once to warn your husband, Contessa." The clipped words pierced her.

"Duce, please, as a former newspaperman, as you once told me yourself, surely you cannot hold it against the count to want to be free, have a free press, to write what he believes in. He is still loyal to Italy. If you would but release him, we will pay any fine. We can go away, we can—"

"You can do nothing!" he roared with a jutting thrust of chin. "Traitors, all the rich of Rome who think they can teach their Duce to rule!" His eyes scrutinized her harshly while she stood glaring back, her head held high, despite tousled hair and dirtied face. His brows and forehead lifted, raising the black cap covering his head as if he had ludicrously tipped it to her with no hands. "Here, here, wait," he intoned and bent to scribble something in his lap on a pile of papers. She stared at his profile, hardly daring to hope. He looked pasty-white; he'd lost so much weight since she'd seen him last. But he was writing something—a change of heart, a pardon for Cesare, surely at least permission for her to see him.

He extended the folded square of white paper to her out the window, then in a low voice, "I believe I also told you that one day you would offer me more than a fur coat, Contessa. Every word Il Duce speaks comes true! And now you're all disheveled, so—emotional, and all for a traitor." He clucked his tongue. "If I choose to believe a brazen Englishwoman had nothing to do with this, perhaps that will be pardon enough. But I must be convinced even of that after this betrayal by the Valentes. Perhaps you have learned your lesson at last, yes?" His face became that implacable mask again as he turned away and ordered, "Driver, on!"

She stood shaking, the note pressed unread to her breast as the caravan roared off and the guards returned to their posts at the gates of the palace. Her knees, she noticed now, were bleeding, her hands and arms scraped raw, her black and white flowered silk dress torn and streaked gray with the dust of the pavement stones. Damn Mussolini and this country and its war, Hitler too, all those who only craved power at the expense of other people's lives! She turned away, sucked in a trembling breath, and leaned against the iron fence to open the note. The handwriting was bold, angular, and dark. The message short and simple: "Come alone tonight at eight to the Mussolini Chalet at Castel Porziano outside Rome. Perhaps you can be grateful enough there to convince your Duce to at least consider sparing a life."

To at least spare a life—the words jumped and danced

before her teary gaze. Spare Cesare's life, even hers? So it had come to that—whoring as she had promised Guido she would never do only yesterday. But this would be to save Cesare, not to harm him. Still, she couldn't bear to do it. If she went to see Il Duce, got that close to him, she could argue, plead, maybe convince him and never have to give in at all. Only that horrible look on his face, that smothered, fierce, panicked lust for power, for revenge, for her—

She crumpled the note in her fist and walked dazedly across the sunny square toward the Valente town house.

By seven o'clock that evening she had dressed and redressed three times. She had finally chosen all black, even a French calotte with a wispy black veil to hide her face in case there were guards at the chalet who might tell others who had visited Il Duce privately. She had even gazed long at Cesare's little ivory-handled revolver, put it once in her purse to see if it fit, but then had taken it back out. Even if she shot the dictator, it would probably mean Hitler would step in brutally—as he had when Mussolini had failed in Greece and North Africa. Besides, she had to protect herself for the twins' sakes. If something should happen to both her and Cesare, who would care for Cati and Paolo?

She kissed them both good night, held them to her breast as her heart beat hard against their fragrant softness. And Valente's: she had vowed to Cesare only last week before he sent her to Capri that if he was busy with other responsibilities, she would take good care of Valente's for him. Yet she would give all of Valente's up to have her husband back again away from this danger. He had been so good to her and the twins. She did respect and love him, even need him in a very special way. They had forged something together out of two shattered pasts and a mutual love of creating beautiful things.

"Oh, Cesare!" she whispered as she started downstairs, then clung to the banister in the crunching grasp of terror. "Why couldn't you trust me, tell me?" She sank down on a carpeted step to rest her flushed cheek against her hands, which clasped the carved and gilded spokes supporting the ornate handrail. She waited a moment until the light-headedness passed; it was like being closed in somewhere with no way out, like the dark reaches of claustrophobia, although she was here in the big open space above the downstairs entry hall.

She wished Guido had come back again so she could at least tell him where she was going. He would scream at her perhaps, call her a whore as he did his mother, whom he loved so desperately and whom he had learned to hate. But Lesley Westam Valente and Cesare's eldest nephew had somehow been doomed from the start. There was nothing Guido could do to help her now, except maybe stop her from going at all. If .Cesare went to prison, she would carry on faithfully without him until the war was over and he was released. She would lower herself to beg Il Duce if she must, try to bribe him if she could. If none of that worked and he insisted she "convince him" as he so crassly put it, she would refuse. Perhaps she must go up to get that pistol again— She shuddered and her entire body went cold. She rose and walked in a daze the rest of the way down the stairs. She glanced at the Swiss diamond wristwatch Cesare had given her on her birthday. Nearly seven-thirty. No more delaying. She took her auto keys from her black alligator bag, but as she started down the hall, Cesare's library drew her. She went just inside the doorway, clicked on a lamp.

Here she had first met Cesare Valente, the time when Guido had meant to shock him with how much she looked like her aunt Rissa. But Cesare had seen through that ruse and welcomed her. Now the life-sized portrait over the hearth was of Lesley with the twins on her lap in the peaceful gardens on Capri. The portrait had been painted in softest pastels in an impressionistic style, though the books and dark leathers and deep shadows here still evoked Cesare. She had never seen him write anything for *Libero* here. She had loved two men who were journalists, even though she had once considered journalism a detestable profession. Only now, if she were brave and foolish enough, she knew she would be proud to carry on *Libero* in Cesare's place.

"Lesley? Lesley!"

She nearly jumped out of her skin. Guido! Guido to face, to convince she must go back upstairs for the pistol and go to Mussolini. Perhaps he had some news!

"I'm here!" she called. "Did they ever let you see him?" she asked the moment he looked in.

Her insides pitched as he nodded. He came into the library and she deluged him with questions. His glazed expression didn't change. He closed the door behind him, leaned against it, then turned back to face her in the dim light. "You're in black already," his voice accused.

"Duce said I could have an interview tonight, so I thought— Guido, tell me, tell me what Cesare said! Maybe they will let me see him now, too."

"I'm sure they will. They let me see him briefly today. *Madre Maria*, Lesley," he rushed on, his expression agonized, "Il Duce had him executed a half hour ago!"

She just stared at him. He'd said it all so directly, his eyes unfocused. His words were impossible. Someone had lied to Guido. She had this meeting with Mussolini at eight and that meant at seven— No. No, impossible. Paul had come back from the dead. Cesare would, too. Guido was lying, he hated her. She grabbed the back of a leather chair, pressed it to her stomach and breasts to keep the room from tilting. "Executed?" she heard herself ask sanely before she gave a long, shrill scream and her legs turned to water.

He pulled her onto the couch beside him while she ranted and sobbed, hit out at his hands, then held so hard to them she saw his fingers turn white. She didn't dare look into Guido's face again, hear those words, see his eyes to know it was all true. When she had seen Mussolini this afternoon, he had already condemned Cesare, yet the timing of it would allow her to be with him—oh, dear Jesus in heaven, help me—with him before her husband's body was even cold.

She jerked up stiffly, her hands clasped in her lap now. "I didn't think Mussolini would, because of the Valente name and all," she choked out while Guido bent over his knees, putting his head in his hands. All this time Guido had not really touched her for comfort as she had him, and he refused to look at her now.

"Maybe that's why, as an example to the rest of them to stay in line." His words were thick and slow at first. "He knew the sentence when I saw him, Lesley, and he said that but for leaving his family, it was worth it to him to die for freedom in

Italy. It was—a firing squad. The guards said we can have him—his body—tomorrow for burial." His words came faster, jumbled now. "He said he loved me and we were almost as alike as if I were the son he never had and that's why he expected so much from me. All the things I'd done and said to him and he still loved me and was proud—"

Bitter sobs wracked Guido's body and he turned to her like a child to weep against her shoulder. She held him tightly, yet knew instinctively she could not comfort him, despite how their mutual grief and need changed everything between them for these few minutes. Even in the depths of despair, she was grateful for that. Later, almost embarrassed, Guido pulled away and stood.

"Thank God, you didn't go to Mussolini," he said and wiped his face with his handkerchief. "Not Countess Valente. *Madre Maria*, now we know everything there is to know about that demented son-of-a-bitch tin god!" He blew his nose and shook his head. "Are you willing to give the count—Uncle Cesare—a grand funeral, a martyr's funeral, with me, even if only a few of us have the courage to attend?"

She nodded fiercely and stood, too. "Yes. If it weren't for the twins and Cesare's beloved Valente's I might still keep my appointment with Il Duce—with a gun."

"No, I wouldn't let you, though I thought of that, too. Uncle Cesare wanted me to protect you, and I will if I can. The letter, I almost forgot. I have a letter for you he wrote on the inside of my cheroot pack since they wouldn't let him have paper. I smuggled it out. I'll leave you alone for a little bit while I tell Stella, see if there's any way at all to get Carlo home for this."

"Poor Carlo!" she said and tears crowded her eyes again. But as she reached avidly for the little cheroot pack Guido extended to her, she held his wrist and said, "Poor, dear Guido, too. I've always needed your friendship as much as I've valued Carlo's. Somehow we can make it through this, if we help each other, for Cesare's memory."

He nodded, but seemed afraid to meet her eyes. "He loved you so I will help any way I can, Lesley. The thing is, I'll be sent who knows where now that all this—" A sob wracked him again as he turned away and hurried out.

She sat, hunched over her black-draped knees reading

Cesare's words. Her hand trembled at the tiny, shaky scrawl.
The brave writer of *Libero* writing only to her as his murderer
Il Duce had done earlier today. Cesare's handwriting was not
his own. Surely they had not beaten him. Damn it, this was her
war now! She would do what she could to carry on for Cesare
and the Valentes, for were not her children Valentes in
everyone else's eyes? She blinked back tears and squinted to
decipher the minuscule words:

My countess, my sweet,

So little time to tell you of my love, my joy, my pride in
you. Kiss Cati and Paolo for me, tell them of my duty and
love to them over the years. For the honor of Valente Furs,
I shall trust you always. For the honor of the Valente family,
I must tell you that Paul Kendal is here in Rome as a secret
correspondent using the name Gian Donato—he came to see
me at the *Libero* office shortly before my arrest. Do not seek
him out, only remember if he comes to you that he hated me
and demanded to know more about our twins. Who gave
Duce's men *Libero*'s secret location after all this time?
Never ask Paul Kendal. That warning, and your love, and
your vows I hold you to until we meet again in the arms of
Holy Christ and the blessed Virgin.

Your loving husband, Cesare

Alone, she sat stunned for a very long time, crying,
rereading the note until she had it all by heart, by a heart that
was shattered and lost. Despite the twins sleeping innocently
upstairs, she regretted that now the twins would never remember the man who briefly had been their father and who had
perhaps been betrayed by the man who was their real father.
She felt so alone. As alone as if they would close her in a little
box like Cesare and her mother and her father—Trent, too.
Alone even when Stella sat with her all night and Guido came
back to say Carlo would be sent home for the funeral. From the
grave, from the very arms of Christ as he put it, Cesare told her
that Paul Kendal had actually exposed *Libero* and him, and
warned that Paul was a threat to the twins.

By the first light of morning through the heavy draperies

Stella opened to greet the new day, Lesley had decided the things that she must do. Only then did she wash her face and agree to eat something to regain the strength she already felt coursing through her with her fury.

Saturday, July 26, 1941, the day after Count Cesare Valente's funeral in the church of Trinità dei Monti on the crest of the Spanish Steps, it rained and rained. But still Lesley dressed carefully in her formal black mourning to keep the appointment she had made. Not this time as a young wife desperate to meet Il Duce to plead for a husband's life, but as a young widow to tell Paul Kendal to stay away from her and her children forever.

She had hoped the funeral would flush him out of hiding. When she was leaving the church on Carlo's and Guido's arms, she'd seen him in the last row from behind the netted layers of her black veil. He looked thinner, but weren't they all? A mustache, but she'd recognize him anywhere. She had whispered to Madame Justine to tell the green-eyed man in the dark gray suit and striped tie she must see him today at the Colosseum at four.

She was too physically and emotionally drained to even feel nervous, she told herself, but she was still hurt and angry, and not only at Paul Kendal. Many of Rome's rich and poor had come to swell the congregation at the funeral, some of the same people who had ignored her calls for help only days before. And, miraculously, *Libero* had been printed again after Cesare's death—she assumed it was by another of the underground broadsheets—in a special edition to honor and praise him, to defy and denounce Mussolini for his death. There had been a stack of papers left boldly on the back table by the stall for the altar candles, as if all the guests would want to collect a copy of the newspaper that had killed Cesare.

But she and Guido had decided that they would help whomever had picked up Cesare's fallen mantle. Guido had arranged for the thin girl Carla, who used to give him his copies of the paper, to visit Lesley for funding. Carla, it turned out, belonged to a wealthy old Roman family, the Fraccis. Her banker father had long been a friend of Cesare's and Lesley knew him also. The young woman would come as an occasional customer to Valente's to receive the donations.

Lesley took Cesare's big black umbrella with the carved ivory handle and went down the hall to stick her head in the nursery, where Lilla sat as if guarding the sleeping twins. Lesley tiptoed in and gazed fondly in both their cribs. "I'm going out for a little walk alone, Lilla," Lesley whispered to the girl. Their nursemaid, Eleana, had solved Lesley's dilemma about promoting Lilla by promptly resigning when Cesare was arrested. All Lesley needed was a new upstairs maid now, a position Lilla had promised her younger sister, Anna, could soon fill. Women, at least, were in abundance everywhere here in Rome, so that should make Paul Kendal happy, Lesley thought bitterly and turned away.

"But it is raining so hard, Countess Lesley," Lilla protested quietly as she followed her out into the hall.

"Just a short walk. It will do me good. We English are in love with the rain, you know—we have no choice."

Lilla waved good-bye, her face wan and sad. No wonder any attempt at lightness fell flat now. Carlo and Guido had both gone over to Stella Sollo's, and there was that to fret about, too. If Stella had really decided to tell Carlo she didn't love him, Lesley doubted she'd do it now that both were shattered by their uncle's death, though, amazingly, it was Guido who seemed the most distraught of them all.

The day was muggy, a steam bath outside. Still, she was glad she'd chosen a long-sleeved, full-skirted black cotton dress. Another woman in mourning, though perhaps no one would notice, as half the women in the city wore black now for someone they'd lost in Il Duce's hellish quest to return Italy to the Roman glory of the Caesars. Her reflection strode at her in the water-glazed paving stones of the Via dei Fori as the buff, broken Colosseum, stained to darker shades of saffron and brown by the driving rain, loomed before her at the end of the street.

She would accuse Paul straight out, she had decided, get it over quickly, warn him away for good. Cesare's note had said, "Do not seek him out," but it had to be done this way, threats and all. How far she had come to feel this way, she marveled, her love for Paul Kendal utterly ruined and decayed.

Her bare legs and the hem of her dress were wet and her low-heeled patent-leather toeless shoes squeaked. She entered the portals of the three-story shell of a building where spectators of the ages had gone in to see the games, the spectacles, and the martyrdoms. Stray cats huddled in the shelter of the old vaulted arches. She jerked to a halt. Paul stood just ahead under a wet brown arch, watching her. She had forgotten he was so tall. How strange it seemed to have him here in Rome so close to her other life, she mused, before she reined in her thoughts and put down her dripping umbrella, still open.

"Hello, Lesley."

"Paul." She stared straight at him. His hands were thrust in his gray suit pockets; he dared to look hopeful. "I won't take much of your time."

"I have the time. I wish I could help. I'm sorry about Cesare," he told her fervently. "I met him, Lesley, and admired him."

Liar! she wanted to scream, but his open admission of the fact he'd seen Cesare before she even accused him set her back. "He told me. I only asked you here, you see, to tell you I want you to stay out of my life forever. The twins are totally my responsibility now that their father's gone, and I will kill anyone who threatens their safety if I have to."

"Kill? Is all this pointed at me? Lesley, I wouldn't—"

"I don't believe you! You evidently don't deny you went to see my husband just before he was arrested. Do you deny you asked him about our—his and my—children?" Her voice rose despite all the thinking she had done about how best to handle this. She had decided if he agreed to stay away she would not say these next words, but they spilled from her in a torrent of emotion full of the love and need and desperation she felt for Cesare, who had left her all alone now, too!

"Paul, never mind the glib writer's words," she insisted with a defiant tilt of chin. "I just came to say that if you do anything ever to threaten me or my children, I will tell the authorities about this little newspaper charade you're playing here. Many people can inform on others, these days, you know!" Her voice quavered and broke. She stepped back into a puddle. He strode closer in one giant step, reached his big hands for her shoulders. "No, don't touch me!" she ground out and pressed her back to the dank stone wall.

"Look, you're not implying—he didn't tell you I turned him in, did he?" His green eyes were bright with pain and she was glad. "I didn't think he'd be that desperate. I told him I didn't come to Italy to see you and I meant it, damn it! I went there to help him."

She sidestepped along the wall. "Help him to be caught by Il Duce's secret police? To be shot?" she shrilled. "And of course, in the finest Paul Kendal tradition you wanted something from him too, until he ceased to serve your needs!" Her voice dripped venom. She could not believe these words she had rehearsed now that she heard them. "Just understand, I'm dedicating the rest of my life to honoring Cesare Valente's memory at any cost, that's all!"

He lifted his big hands beseechingly. "I admire that for now, Lesley, but for the rest of your life? You think memories and honor will be enough to keep you the rest of your life?" His deep voice rose in pitch and volume, and he shook his big head in disbelief. "And so, for us, that's all?"

She grabbed her umbrella and started away. She heard his footsteps coming after her; she darted out into the rain and started across the pavement. To her dismay, he followed her into the open. He seized her elbow, spun her back, shoved away the umbrella she tried to lower between them so it rolled over the wet stones and they faced each other in the deluge.

"Always insisting on running through life blindly, madly, aren't you, Lesley? Just get a cause to be obsessed with, just run away—those are responses I thought you'd outgrown!" he roared.

"Take your hands off, I said. You're the last person on earth I want to be seen with!" she cried and struggled to free herself from an iron grip that didn't budge.

"And you believe, really believe—I don't care how shocked and bereaved you are—that I'm the kind of person who'd turn your husband in to the damned, deadly Fascists just to get you back? Your fine career, money, and lofty social position have gone to your head, lady!" he shouted and gave her a tiny shake. "Just go on, then. Run and keep running, and don't worry yourself that you'll ever see me again. Believe me, I have more important things to do here than chase a woman who's lied to me and betrayed me for a title, a stack of lire, and pile of furs!"

When he let her go, she struck out at him. Her hand caught his chin with a harsh rake of long nails. They stood staring at each other, stunned, while little red lines ribboned his face.

She retrieved her umbrella, then hurried away, but not before he saw the rain in her eyes. He stood staring at the moving blur of her white and black and red reflection. Her long legs, the mourning dress, and cognac hair he had so loved. He bent his head into the downpour and stepped back under the shiny arches of the Colosseum to get the umbrella he had left behind. Several cats who had scampered away when they had shouted were back now. He wished he'd brought something along for them as he often did, but he'd hardly thought of that today, only of Lesley, and that was over for good now.

"At least the cats of Rome love me," he said aloud, surprised his voice sounded as if he'd been crying, grimly bemused that his attempt at bravado sounded stupid.

He heaved a deep sigh and felt his lower lip quiver as he leaned against a tattered column and watched and listened to it pour on wartime Rome. The city seemed one vast, shiny mirror reflecting all the other cities under the threat of desolation in this German and Italian war against the world's democracies. Rome, the Eternal City, might not last long if the British had their way and moved farther north from their feeble footholds in the Mediterranean to bomb here, or if something happened to bring the Americans in full force at last. He thought then of a snatch of poem by Byron he'd read ages ago in his halcyon days at peaceful Oxford: "While stands the Colosseum, Rome shall stand; When falls the Colosseum, Rome shall fall; And when Rome falls—the world."

Truly, he and Lesley were only two little people whose lives were all churned up in this great big war, he thought, and cursed himself that this brief meeting with her had pained him so much then. Hell, he might never forget her but he vowed to do everything he could never to see her again, no matter how close her path crossed his or how dear the earlier memories of her were enshrined in his heart and mind. Besides, the initial hurt she'd inflicted by betraying him had helped him to better grasp the individual and collective national pain of fear and loss the British had experienced under the blitz. But for his own agony of mental and emotional suffering, which made his physical injuries pale by comparison, he'd never have found the right voice or sensitivity or depth for *Lions Roar*.

But now that Cesare Valente was dead, Lesley still intended to use him as a barrier, despite that eternal electricity that arced between them whether they fought or loved. Perhaps, just perhaps, whatever he faced in the months ahead in probing the depths of himself and in constructing his new novel could help him gain perspective from this new pain too. For, if not, there was nothing good or fair or sane to come from losing her at all.

Though he was soaked to the skin, he hoisted his umbrella and loped across the pavement toward the tramcar stop in the pounding, pelting rain.

PART III

Only This of Me

If I should die, think only this of me:
That there's some corner of a foreign field
That is forever England.

RUPERT BROOKE
"The Soldier"

❧ ❧ *Chapter Fourteen*

LESLEY STOOD in the center of the upstairs workroom at Valente's in a shaft of warming winter sun from the single skylight. She greeted each worker or saleswoman as she came in, then invited her to the tea table she and her cook from the town house had arranged. December 2, 1942, the beginning of the big Christmas sales season—if there would be any such thing for Italy as the war dragged on in the Mediterranean. Lesley had sensed her women needed a little morale booster at work; she needed it as well, for this would be her second holiday season without Cesare at her side.

Both domestic and foreign business for Valente's had been booming under her iron-lined velvet glove, as Guido called her control of the Valente empire. But who knew how much longer the sales of luxury goods, which were often the last to go in a stricken economy where the rich still were rich, would survive now that one saw almost as many Nazi uniforms on the streets as Italian ones. Unlike many shops in Rome, a city where citizens were known for their tolerance for and fatalistic attitude to change, Countess Valente had refused to place a sign in the window that *Deutsch* was spoken here, even if her year of Swiss boarding school had given her decent enough conversational German to get by.

"Please, everyone, feel free to take another cup of tea and more scones and then find a seat on a bench," she announced as she saw the young Maria, who served as their char, hang back from the elegant table in wide-eyed awe. She made a mental note to ask the girl how her large family was making do. "I realize it's rather a hardship for some of you to come in half an hour early, so I wanted to make it up to you with an English tea to say thanks very much indeed for all you do here.

And I wanted to bring you up to date on the state of Valente's, so to speak."

She mingled with the group for a few minutes, pleased to see how keen they were for the English pastries, touched by how grateful they all seemed for the little repast. Food for some of them was increasingly hard to come by, she knew, and that's why she said nothing when every scrap of the huge buffet lunches she had the Valente cook bring over three times a week for the fifteen of them disappeared into handbags to be taken home to families.

"So thoughtful of you, as always, my Lesley," Madame Justine told her, her long hair fringe nearly obscuring the tops of her tortoise-shell glasses. "And always *c'est magnifique* to enjoy an English tea without Stockman hovering to count how many cress sandwiches I take."

How grateful Lesley had been these past two years since the fur auction in Leningrad that she and Cesare had brought Madame back with them. With Cesare gone and every last man in the shop conscripted into Mussolini's service, Madame's expertise and Lesley's genius had kept Valente di Roma at the top of the design world, even in these horrible times. Like Lesley, Madame was willing to oversee all aspects of the business, even joining in with construction, fitting, selling, and meticulously helping Lesley train the women. Without Stella Sollo's friendship and Madame's support when Cesare had been executed, she wasn't certain she could have managed to handle everything under her care so smoothly: the town house and villa; the vast art collection; the workshop and salon below; the time she donated to the preserving of Roman artworks in case of enemy attack; the welfare of her various staffs; keeping in touch as best she could with Guido and Carlo, who were both serving out of the country again. And most importantly, her beautiful, lively twins.

"It won't be long now before we open our doors for the Christmas buying season, but there are a few things I wanted to share with you," Lesley announced over the chatter, and everyone quieted at once. "I am pleased to report that, as most of you know, Valente's has had a fine year despite the fact we lost the American market I had begun to develop the previous season." The attack on Pearl Harbor had made the United

States Italy's declared enemy as well as Germany's and Japan's. Her thoughts skipped to Paul and she cleared her throat. She had not seen him since that day at the Colosseum when she had accused him of betraying Cesare to Il Duce's police. She had no idea if he even remained in Rome now that his country was sending all those troops and bombers into the Mediterranean to help England against Italy and Germany. In all these months, she had become very adept at thinking of him less and less.

"Thanks to the farsightedness of my late husband, Count Valente, we still have a fine variety of pelts to last us for another year or two. The Countess Valente line, which has done so well here and in other European cities, will be adapting itself to the times by utilizing unusual combinations of furs. This will let us stretch our reserves, hold down the cost of the garments, and yet provide some very exciting designs. In the near future you'll be working on karakul coats with detachable mink capes, astrakhan capes lined and trimmed with sable, and velvet evening coats with kolinsky sleeves and scarves. Yet quality garments will still be the Valente trademark in these difficult times."

Lesley flushed slightly when they applauded almost as if she were Il Duce at one of his rallies. "Of course as the war goes on, more and more people are going to have less and less money to spend even for such things as warm and durable coats. That's why I wanted to explain to you why I have decided to halt our lucrative export trade to Berlin, which my husband began years ago. The Germans love furs, especially Italian-made ones, I give them credit for that," she went on and paused as she saw several of her little army of fifteen women exchange glances or smile grimly at her jab at the Germans, "but, even if it costs us dearly, I do not want furs with the Valente label gracing the backs of people in Berlin. However much they appreciate good furs, Germans seem unable to appreciate the need for peace." She paused as her little audience applauded again.

"Therefore, our policy from now on will be to cease all exports to Germany, even if we are reduced to making dyed-rabbit shawls, although we will not be rude nor endanger ourselves here by refusing to serve customers of any nationality who actually come into our shop. I wish you all a hard-working and rewarding holiday season here at Valente's and with your own families. So, everyone to work now please," she told them with a brisk clap of her hands, a habit she had assimilated from Madame, "as it's nearly time to open up below."

Murmuring, the women scattered to their tasks while Lesley and Madame returned to work on their sketches of next fall's designs in Cesare's office, which Lesley had redecorated last year in subdued peach and beige hues. Her hands and eyes skimmed over her work as always, but today her thoughts darted elsewhere.

The fitted, smooth-shouldered Russian broadtail cape she drew recalled her exciting trip with Cesare to Leningrad, a city now under brutal siege by the Germans despite the huge counter-offensive the Russians had thrown at Hitler and Mussolini forces to protect Moscow. She blinked away tears that blurred her work. Her dear Carlo was still with the four Italian divisions Il Duce had sent to Russia. Before he'd gone, Carlo had told her they had only summer uniforms with them, even though they might have to stay into the winter, and now it was already early December! She was so glad she'd made him take all those extra socks and his skiing underwear. How she wished there were some way to get the truth here in this blasted city about how the troops were doing. It was the only reason she ever, in her wildest dream, sometimes considered trying to find out if Paul Kendal were still in Italy and if he had any way of finding out how things were going for the Italian troops in Russia.

"Lesley, your eyes, they are so much better than mine." Madame interrupted her thoughts and held her sketch out, stiff-armed, to squint at it through her thick glasses. "This flared cape—you think we should sew the pelts on the bias or no?"

As Lesley turned to look at the sketch, she saw Nina, the youngest saleswoman from the salon, in the door wringing her hands, her face very pale. "Nina, what is it?" she asked before the slender girl could speak.

"Countess Valente, three customers downstairs just came in," the words tumbled from her. "One is Bibi Rossi, that

German Eugen Dollman's Italian girlfriend, you know. The other two are men, some kind of high-ranking Germans with black and silver uniforms and even skull and crossbone pins on their caps and lapels with little SS lightning insignias! I thought with what you just said about the Germans—"

"Yes, Nina. Go on back and I will come right down."

"Dollman, that one is trouble, a spy for Hitler, a big spider sitting in Rome spinning his webs," Madame groused while Lesley removed the white smock she sketched in, quickly washed her hands, and donned the jacket of her pearl-gray suede Lanvin suit with velvetlike moleskin lapels.

"You might know the morning I make my statement on these wretches, they drop in," Lesley complained, frowning.

"He's a poison spider," Madame repeated, following her to the door, her hands gesticulating wildly. "A spider like that big black swastika on all their bloodred flags. You be careful, send Nina back for me if you need help."

Finally, Madame's angry voice pierced Lesley's thoughts. "Yes, don't worry. I did say this morning we must be polite to anyone who comes into the salon, so I hardly need you down there to glare and lecture them about France."

Madame dogged her long strides across the workroom floor toward the steps as Lesley nervously smoothed the collar and bow of her ice-blue shantung blouse. "If they want a fur coat, I would like to make them one!" Madame called after her. "One like the grotesque things my countrymen designed for their *fräulein* when told to send their fine Parisian fashions to Berlin for those spiders—all of them!"

Lesley felt angry with herself for her nervousness. They were only Germans, merely two of them that gadabout Rossi mistress of Dollman's had probably dragged in. Nina had panicked at the sight of their uniforms, that's all. Skulls and lightning insignias, indeed! Yet some strange foreboding made her drag her feet on the steps as the workroom sounds receded behind her. Not since she had heard that Il Duce's eldest son, Bruno, had died in a plane crash near Pisa only a month after Cesare's murder by that insane dictator's order had she felt this rippling of fear up her spine. But Mussolini evidently had not seen that loss in his own family as retribution for the loss in hers, and his grief and troubles had so far kept him from bothering her or her family again.

She lifted her chin and forced a set smile as she parted the white brocade draperies and entered the salon. Nina was showing a sable cape to the woman and a short, thin older man with pince-nez glasses perched over a sharp nose and insignificant mustache. A taller, blond man about thirty hovered a few steps back as if to survey both doors and the sweep of room. Bibi Rossi, a buxom bleached blonde, was dressed in a beige wool suit with a fox stole—not from Valente's—that matched the light shades of the salon. The stark black uniforms of the men were reflected in the two opposing looking glasses on the walls, making their images seem to suggest an entire army of SS officers crowded the room.

"Oh, Countess Valente, I told Herr Himmler I hoped you were here to show us things yourself," Bibi Rossi gushed the moment she saw Lesley. Lesley could not even recall at which party she had first met the woman. Cesare had said she was an upstart Italian tart the Roman elite tolerated because she was sleeping with Hitler's envoy Eugen Dollman. The woman had hung all over her when she'd learned who she was, wanted to know all about what fur styles would be fashionable so she could ask her dear Dollman for a mink or ermine cape. At least Valente's had been spared the simpering Dollman's malignant presence today.

"Signorina Rossi, I haven't seen you for a long time," Lesley began with a welcoming nod. She felt both men's eyes assessing her. The one she assumed was Himmler glared with cold curiosity; the gaze of the tall man who approached closer seethed with avid interest. She took the cape from Nina, who stepped gratefully behind her. Bibi Rossi's perfume—was that Lanvin's Arpège?—permeated the room, even her fur, which Lesley fluffed with a slight shake as if to air it. "You wanted to see mink capes today?" she inquired as pleasantly as she could manage.

"Oh, yes, we're all on a little Christmas buying spree, looking for things for friends, you see, especially SS Reichsführer Heinrich Himmler here from Berlin. And this," she said and turned back to bathe the tall man in a beaming smile he did not return, as his gaze still clung to Lesley, "is Hitler's chief liaison between my Dollman and Berlin, SS Lieutenant Colonel Maxmilian Dorff."

The woman sighed breathily to further annoy Lesley. The man was handsome, if one could ignore the Nazi regalia. He wore an ebony visored hat, swastika armband, death-head emblem, iron cross on a ribbon, and razor-sharp creased jodhpurs above tall, polished, tight black boots. One huge hand rested nonchalantly on the Luger at his hip. The hard blue eyes glittered like ice. To her amazement he removed his cap as she politely repeated his title. His sun-browned face was lean, harsh, with high forehead and cheekbones, his hair closely cropped, his shoulders very wide and square.

"Countess Valente," his deep voice intoned, and he offered a hint of bow.

Vexed they had chosen her shop, however many thousands of their bloody reichsmarks they had to spend, she sent Nina for more coats as they requested, then at the suggestion of Lieutenant Colonel Dorff, modeled them herself. Although she knew she could have put them very much at ease by switching to her schoolgirl German, she let Bibi translate for Himmler and Dorff use his slow Italian.

She showed them coats, stoles, and capes, and automatically answered their questions. She tried to recall what she knew about Himmler, but all she could remember was that he was in charge of Hitler's elite guard, the *Schutzstaffel*, or SS. The man looked like a bespectacled schoolmaster but there was something so very cold about him. Dorff's eyes never left her, and she recognized that stare only too well. She had chosen not to reenter Roman society after Cesare's death and had circumspectly refused dinner and party invitations she had received from men. But more and more of them had gone to war or were trying desperately to keep themselves afloat in these rocky economic seas, and they left her alone now. She considered herself still in mourning for Cesare and her heart yet too battered by everything else to even think of responding to a man the way this one's bold eyes demanded. To her chagrin, after Himmler had selected three coats and two stoles, he left Dorff behind to make the arrangements while he and Bibi Rossi sauntered next door to Sollo's leather-goods shop.

Reluctantly, Lesley removed the last of the stoles she wore

and handed it to Nina to be hung and wrapped. Her skin actually crawled at the way his gaze examined her, controlled yet blatant. "As soon as Nina has those ready, you may just give her the delivery address, and she'll make the billing arrangements," she informed Dorff without looking at him again.

"But I was hoping you would do that for me." His voice was intimately low.

She kept her face impassive. "I usually don't."

"Then make an exception, won't you?" His Italian was slightly hesitant, but adequate, his voice rough over the vowels. Hair prickled along the back of her neck under the stray tendrils of her unswept coiffure. She wished she hadn't dressed so carefully for the little tea with her employees.

"Of course, Lieutenant Colonel Dorff, it won't take a moment," she said, capitulating with a defiant tilt of chin.

Get hold of yourself, she scolded silently. Yet she felt frozen by a feeling somewhere between distrust and distaste. She neither wanted to face him nor turn her back to him. She walked away, sat at the small desk, then was miffed when he followed and hovered over her.

"And where are these to be sent?" she inquired matter-of-factly, pen poised on paper.

"I'll take them. Colonel Dollman's Daimler is at the SS Reichsführer's disposal while he's here. I'm here for several months now at least, though I'll be going back and forth to Berlin," he told her while she wrote out the bill. He towered above, casting a shadow across her. No wonder they wore those dreadful midnight-black uniforms with pistols in leather holsters. The uniforms absolutely cowed and threatened one without the wearer having to make a move.

"Here you are then," she said coldly and extended the paper to him, careful their fingers didn't touch. "Made out to Colonel Dollman. Expensive gifts for one who wasn't here to see them selected."

"I agree, Countess, for selecting things oneself heightens the later pleasure of possession."

Her gaze snagged with his as she stood. She remained behind the desk as if it were a barrier. This man was at least six feet four, taller than Paul. Muscular, physically overwhelming, so austere, with a voracious look in his eyes that prophesied something dangerous.

"Countess Valente, Signorina Rossi says you are a widow, but such a young and beautiful one," he offered with a curt nod.

Lesley said nothing.

"I'd like to call on you again if I might."

So terribly polite and yet one got the impression he would be equally pleased to crash and stomp about and take anything he wanted. "I think not," she managed with a little shake of her head for emphasis. "As you noted, I'm a widow and still in mourning."

"After a year and a half? No, Countess Lesley," he told her, pleased she stared at his use of her given name. "I shall be back as I said. Just remember the name Max Dorff and not the long title. And what harm can it do a fine establishment like Valente's to have a good friend in high places in the coming order of things, hm. Ah, the garments, good," he said and replaced his cap to take coats from the saleswoman.

At least she appeared in awe of him, while the beautiful countess looked merely worried and wary. But what a find, in this shop of all the shops Dollman's little Italian whore was dragging Himmler into today, he thought, as he lifted his burden. The devil with the furs, but the flame-haired countess was so exquisite, so beautiful and spirited that he would indeed be back.

He pictured her on his arm in a wonderful, low-cut black satin gown at a huge party he would throw for high-ranking members of the Reichschancellory, maybe with the Führer himself in attendance, certainly Himmler, Goebbels, and Göring. She would decorate his new Berlin mansion set along the park in the Grünwald, he mused. The three-story yellow stone house his loyalty had earned him when Jewish homes were awarded to high-ranking SS men after the Germans finally stood up to the traitorous Berlin Jews in the riots and slaughter of Kristallnacht. He pictured her in his bed in the silk-papered bedroom overlooking his rose gardens in Berlin or even here in his suite in the Excelsior Hotel. As yielding as these plush furs, as soft and elegant. He craved a woman like this one in his life right now, maybe to bear his children, a woman as stunning and aloof as his other countess had been so long ago—

Just before the little Italian salesgirl could open the door for him it swung nearly into his face, and in bounded a slender young woman with a noisy child tugging on each hand. This woman hardly looked grand enough to be shopping at Valente's, he thought, and then turned back for one more look at Lesley. When he saw her face and how the two children ran to her, he knew instantly they were hers and that now he had the key to getting her to see him as often and as intimately as he wished. He hummed his favorite song, *"Unter den Linden,"* to himself while he stepped out on the curb to watch Dollman's chauffeur lock the furs in the huge trunk of the Daimler. Then he went back inside to see his countess trying to shush the children and urge them through the back curtain. Their green eyes and lively cries of "Mama, Mama!" made them double proof she would be the perfect mate for an Aryan hero of the Reich who desperately wanted children for its glory.

"Beautiful children. They're twins?" he called across the wide room and smiled after his countess had nearly pushed the young woman away behind the chattering little boy and girl. She came partway across the room toward him as if to block his view of them. The stiff corners of his mouth lifted. It was the first time of many, he vowed, that she would come to him when he merely spoke.

"Yes. Was there something else?" she insisted, her hands clasped before her, her lovely face so worried.

"I was only thinking how SS Reichsfürher Himmler would have loved to have seen them. He's only recently begun a wonderful program for the fatherland called *Lebensborn,* or 'Spring of Life.' It's an adoption program for Aryan children who lose their parents through unfortunate circumstances, you see, so they are taken to Germany and put into loving homes." The program also forced selected beautiful women to breed lovely children like hers for the Reich with SS men as their sires, but she need not be told of that just yet. "Well, enough small talk," he told her with a taut smile and an exaggerated shrug that made his leather belt creak. "You *will* be in tomorrow if I stop by, so I don't have to look you up at your home, I hope. I know so few people in Rome and would love to have a native's view of it if you'd take me around."

"Didn't Signorina Rossi tell you I'm not a native when she told you everything else?" she dared to say, her voice sharp. "I'm half English." She waited for him to be put off or say something disparaging about her country. Anything if it kept him away!

"Ah, but that pleases me, as I find the Italians lazy and a bit stubborn. I'm afraid Mussolini is right for once when he says his countrymen are a mediocre lot. *Ordnung muss sein*—we must bring law and order here, I think the Italians need it. But a stunning Englishwoman who chooses to, ah, make her bed with the Italians sounds wonderful to me. Perhaps, then, tomorrow evening will be a good time," he concluded, enjoying himself immensely, as if she had said something sweetly conversational to him, as if she had not tried to put him off and the expression on her lovely face had not gone from annoyance and wariness to fear. Good, he thought, a wonderful beginning for them, as a woman was always best in bed and out when she knew who was master.

When he was gone, she paced nervously until Nina came back in, then stepped out the back entrance into the sun a moment before joining Lilla and the twins upstairs. She had not known the children's nanny would bring them around. It was no one's fault, mere chance, as it was that of all the fur shops in Rome, these particular Nazis had ended up in hers. The least she could have done was summon enough courage to ask them how things were on the Russian front; she had a beloved cousin there fighting their filthy war for them while they strolled the Via Condotti Christmas shopping!

She shuddered and hugged herself for warmth although the sun was cheery here in the doorstoop. Max Dorff would be back and what would she do then? He was no potential suitor; he was an adversary. He already knew too much about her, just as Il Duce had. He'd merely seen her precious twins today and immediately voiced subtle threats about that Nazi Aryan program. They probably used it to abduct innocent children from the countries they destroyed.

As so many times before, she wished she could take the

twins and flee to England, especially now that the German fury had temporarily turned elsewhere. Or to Capri, and just live a rural life on the estate like Lucia Belli's parents did, working the land away from all this deceit and treachery. If her children's lives ever became endangered, all of this, including Valente's, might have to be sacrificed. Why was it nothing ever went right for her with men? She lost the ones she loved, and didn't love the ones who pursued her. She nearly jumped out of her skin when the door opened against her.

"Countess Valente, another customer wishes to see you."

She whirled to face Nina. "Not that same man?" she cried.

"No, bless the saints, not that tall blond giant of a guard. It's Carla Fracci, Countess."

Lesley went in to meet the woman who was now her only contact to Cesare's *Libero*. Lesley gave her a donation every month when she came. Sometimes Carla pretended to purchase a garment, other times she went away as if she had not found a thing, but always she carried the little packet of lire Lesley and Guido had vowed would go to *Libero* as long as others were brave enough to continue it in Cesare's memory. His cause had been worth at least that much risk to them.

Lesley and Carla chatted until Nina went out in back, then Lesley slipped the envelope from the bottom desk drawer. How beautiful Carla Fracci had become lately, Lesley noted again as she extended the money to her with a nod and a tense smile. When she'd first seen her years before, she'd looked like a gypsy, lived like a bohemian, and been the dismay of her fine aristocratic banking family. Now she'd blossomed into a lovely woman with huge, flashing brown eyes and sleek ebony hair. She dressed expensively, almost fussily, as if completely repudiating her former life, when she'd rebelled against her parents' commands that she pursue a career and marry the man of their choice. It reminded Lesley of Paul's sister, Kaye, but she thrust that from her mind. Carla Fracci was still unmarried and had a secret career in her dedication to *Libero*. She'd become her own woman, one whom Lesley admired and would have liked to claim as a friend had it not been entirely too dangerous. All she needed was for Carla to run into someone like Max Dorff in Valente's and think she willingly consorted with the Nazis!

"Oh, Countess, I almost forgot," Carla told her and turned back in a flurry to delve into a wrapped package she carried in her arms. Carla never stood still one minute; her hands, even her eyes moved all the time. "Since English is your language and you've helped us so, I wanted to share this book with you. Look, I'm afraid it's smuggled contraband like so much else in the Divine Duce's Italy these days, but it was all the rage in the States and England last year, I heard," she assured her and drummed her fingernails on the crinkly paper of the package.

Lesley gasped. The book Carla Fracci held out to her with a quick glance behind her was *Lions Roar* by Paul Kendal!

"Countess, if you're afraid to have it in your possession, I'll understand and take it back, as there are many others who want to read it," Carla told her, and flipped the book over to study its spine before her eyes lifted to meet Lesley's again. "I just thought since it's all about the British standing up to Hitler—"

"Where did you get it if it's American?"

Carla shook her head as Lesley took the book. "You know what I've learned at *Libero,* what your Cesare taught us," she whispered. "Silence is golden. Look, let's just say I stumbled on the book, that's all. See you next month and I'll take it back then," she called and waggled her fingers in quick farewell.

Lesley wasn't certain how soon she stopped staring down at Paul's name on the dark blue spine of the book. If there had been a dust jacket, it was gone, and it was well worn by those with whom Carla had shared it earlier. His book, that repository of his thoughts and feelings. It felt so solid and heavy as she pressed it to her breast. She tried to keep it out of sight of the others as she hurried upstairs to see Lilla and the twins.

Later that day, twenty-four-year-old Carla Fracci walked in the Borghese Gardens just beyond the yellow brick and tufa wall where her family's grounds and fashionable town house sat along the Via Pinciana. What better place for *Libero* these days than near a public, respectable place, she reasoned. After all, hiding these last few years in back-street, sordid neighborhoods had just gotten them discovered and Cesare Valente killed. The old gardener's house behind her parents' estate, where she pretended to cultivate her zealously guarded orchids, had not been used for years and the single old printing press made very little noise at night. Mussolini's troops, even the clever Germans, would not expect an underground newspaper was being printed once a week under their very noses near the public Borghese gardens where many strolled.

She'd learned a lot these last years about how to get what she desired—although she had so far not succeeded in getting the one man she wanted more and more all the time. Now the last thing in the world she'd allow was for *Libero* and the famous American writer who occasionally supplied her anonymously with articles to be discovered and captured. No, she thought, swinging her alligator shoulder purse from her gloved hand with each quick stride, she had not changed her entire appearance and lifestyle to allow that. She had discovered him and she intended to capture him for herself, however long it took.

She saw him then, coming with that distinctive long stride across the grass among the myrtle and cypress trees. He cut diagonally over gravel paths as if they weren't meant for walking, carrying that briefcase full of books that he sometimes actually sold. Her pulse quickened and she gripped the purse, drumming her nails on the taut leather. He had not yet accepted her invitations to dine at the Fracci villa. Too dangerous, he'd insisted. Yet lately, when she'd not pushed it, when she'd dressed as carefully as she had today, she almost thought she saw those magnificent green eyes waver at times. After all, as far as she could tell, the man lived like an ascetic, celibate monk here in Rome, wherever he kept himself. And a gorgeous male specimen like him, especially in a city of women, as Rome seemed to have become now, was just not the ascetic, celibate type! If it weren't for the fact she'd seen a copy of *Lions Roar* in his briefcase and overheard him tell Cesare he was an American journalist that day before she'd left the *Libero* office, she'd still believe he was just a book salesman from Milan with a flair for writing.

"Gian Donato, it's suddenly a lovely day," she told him, rocking slightly on her high-heeled pumps. She smiled warmly up at him, twisting the strap of her shoulder purse.

He glanced around again before he handed her today's book, an Italian-German dictionary, inside which she knew she would find his neatly folded written contribution at page 100.

"A lovely day," he agreed with a nod, and her heart beat even faster at the mere sound of his voice.

"Stroll into the Fracci gardens behind me and we can have some wine," she suggested, hoping her voice sounded light. "My parents have gone out."

"Then we'd look suspicious, Carla. Some other time, thanks."

"So busy, so businesslike," she began but caught herself. "I do have *something* that might interest you then," she teased, deciding not to pout today as it had gotten her nowhere last time.

"All right."

"We knew some big fish were here to visit Il Duce from Berlin, but I saw Himmler himself on the Via Condotti today. Dollman's big Daimler, which Himmler was using, was parked right outside Valente's before I went in for the money."

She could tell that snagged his attention. He even turned pale. "Himmler shopping for furs?"

"Evidently." She shrugged, then lifted her hand quickly to stroke the arm of his gray suitcoat as if there were a spot there. "We could work together on this, try to find out what's in the wind with Mussolini, why Himmler's here when he's SS. Look, maybe they're checking up on Dollman or Il Duce or both. I hope so—trouble in paradise. Or it might tie in beautifully to our next article on how Il Duce is being made to enforce his lax anti-Semitic laws, since Himmler's rumored to be in charge of Hitler's concentration camps."

"Let some of the others get close to Himmler, Carla, but you stay clear of him. He's too big, too dangerous," he warned, his eyes intense. "He'll have a net of protection around him, and we could blow all we've got at stake here to hell."

"Mmm. I suppose." Reluctantly, she pulled her hand back and shifted the book to her other arm, the purse over her shoulder. "He had some monster blond bodyguard with him today as well as a chauffeur and Dollman's girlfriend. The guard even stayed behind at Valente's for a while," she observed, and twisted a strand of her long hair around a finger. "You know," she said silkily, her voice even lower, "I appreciate it that you're concerned for my well-being."

"What?" His eyes refocused on her. "Yes, yes. I am

concerned. Just steer clear if it's Himmler, that's all. I'll contact you next week. I've got to go," he muttered and turned away toward the Piazza di Spagna.

She was so deflated and angry she couldn't think of a thing to say. Curse the man! Was he going right back where she'd seen those Nazis when he'd just told her they should leave it alone? Next time, she'd convince him she was ill and he'd have to take her back to the *Libero* office. She had to get the man alone! He heated her blood, and she knew he found her attractive, although today he was preoccupied with something else besides his writing. She'd done everything she could to charm him as a fellow resistance worker and now she would do whatever she could as a woman. She heaved a huge sigh and knocked a nervous tattoo on the dictionary as she strode in a roundabout path toward the back gate to the Fracci estate.

Lesley's surprise was superseded only by her panic. She stared aghast as four women and three old men toted tray after laden tray, as well as a café table and two chairs, into the fur salon and stood at attention in a row just as she was preparing to close that night. "Excuse me, but what is all this?" she began with a sweep of her arm. "There must be some mistake—"

"No mistake at all, Countess Lesley," a voice boomed in rough Italian as the last waiter held the door for Lieutenant Colonel Max Dorff, who strode smartly in with four crimson roses in a small crystal bowl. "I simply couldn't wait until tomorrow, and we all have to eat. How wonderful I happened to catch you just now when everyone else is gone. All right, waiters, everything on the table, at once," he clipped out as if he were addressing his troops.

"I'm sorry, but I really must leave," she insisted, hoping her voice sounded calm yet forceful. She met his hard eyes despite the way his right hand dipped commandingly to rest on the holster of his Luger. "I have an appointment for dinner elsewhere."

With a curt nod and sharp-shouldered shrug, he ignored her as if she hadn't spoken and directed traffic as a linen cloth was flapped over the table and china and cutlery clinked. Lids were lifted from delectable-smelling dishes, and her stomach tied itself in even tighter knots. "I cannot stay," she told him, more loudly to be heard over the clatter, her anger and panic rising. "Stop, please," she said, addressing the waiters now. Several rolled their eyes at her; one shrugged and pointed to Dorff, but no one stopped moving until they had deposited their booty and were out the door.

"Now I *do* apologize at the suddenness of all this," Dorff told her and held up his big hands, palms toward her, "but Himmler gave me some time off this evening, and I'm not likely to get any later this week with all that's going on." One stiff corner of his lip curled up in a smile. "I was compelled, that's all."

"Compelled? Not by me!" she insisted, her voice shrill.

"Not by your furs, however lovely they are, I assure you," he said and pulled one of the chairs out for her. "And not by your babies, however lovely they seemed," he went on, nodding to indicate she could sit. "So I conclude it must be by you."

She stood her ground and folded her arms across her chest. "I insist you leave my children out of this."

"I'd be happy to if you will only sit and enjoy the meal. Ah, where are those matches to light the candles? If it's a bit early for the evening meal in Italy, I apologize for that too, but my stomach is still on Berlin time, I'm afraid." He stepped forward to take her elbow, but she stiffened her arm to cast him off. He frowned at that. "Sit, Countess Lesley," his voice ordered, then softened slightly. "We shall just get acquainted without everyone else hanging on, and then I shall escort you home."

"My chauffeur's expecting me to ring him presently, and I really must be off when he arrives."

His big right hand shot out to encircle her slender wrist. His voice crackled now, no longer pleasant or patient. "Not until you and I have spent some time together. We may have only met today, but this is the beginning and not the end. I show tolerance and kindness only to those who earn it. I have invited you to sit down and merely share a meal and some conversation with me. If I have frightened you, I hope the result is not that you will do something foolhardy. There is no man in your

life and you need one." He ended his stern lecture with a
frown.

Not you. Not you ever! she wanted to scream into his face,
but she only tugged her wrist gently back and moved to the
table to perch on the edge of her seat so he could not shove it
closer for her. He sat and poured her wine; her thoughts
searched wildly for a way out, a sane and convincing reason to
be rid of this man. Though she spoke only when spoken to
during the meal, and did little more than push her food around
on her plate, it seemed to satisfy him for now.

The wonderful imperial prawns, stuffed breast of veal with
its mosaic of julienne vegetables and hard-cooked eggs in the
center, Soave wine, and caramel oranges pleased Max Dorff
with their elegance and expense. And Lesley pleased him as
well. She was lovely sitting there all aloof and angry. It made
him want to seize her and make love to her, but he kept up the
flow of conversation to allay her fury, to calm her fears enough
that she would at least let him get closer without protesting so.

He talked about himself so that she would understand his
dedication to and passion for the glories of the Third Reich,
something any woman he committed himself to must share.
Hitler's great genius had brought them back from the economic
Madness of '23, as they called it, when the German middle
classes like his family lost their entire savings. He recounted to
her the horrendous days when inflation drove the price of
postage stamps to ten billion marks and a subway ticket cost a
fortune. But he did not mention how foreigners like the
damned Swiss, Czechs, and detested French bought up the
homes of the German unemployed for a pittance—such as
the two hundred dollars they gave his pitiful father who did not
know how to fight back. Nor did he tell her how he hated his
schoolteacher father for his stupidity of wanting to teach in the
slum of Neukolln in Berlin, where anyone with any foresight
could see the people should be eliminated for their filth and
sloth, not educated and fed precious food the master classes
needed to survive.

He told her about the food the cruel reparations of the First
World War had forced his mother to feed her five children—
turnip coffee, turnip cutlets, moldy bread—comparing it to the

wonderful food he offered her tonight. He omitted how he had detested his four sisters because his parents adored their stupid obedience. They could not accept his need to follow the messiah of his people, Adolf Hitler, because the only way to power was violence, as the Führer explained so brilliantly in *Mein Kampf*. It had served his narrow-minded father right that after becoming chancellor, Hitler sent him away to a rehabilitation camp with other so-called humanitarian intellectuals. He died there, and the SA burned the books his father had loved more than he had his own son!

He told her of his pride and passion the night Hitler became chancellor, when he had joined thrilled crowds marching from the Tiergarten to the Brandenburg Gate while bands played the stirring old Prussian march "We Mean to Defeat France." But he did not tell her of his passions when he was a mere waiter at Kempinski's. There one of the most beautiful of the rich and famous women of Berlin saw him and bought him a tuxedo for his first party with Nazi elite at the famous Bristol Hotel. He had gone in with his knees quaking to find the men in tails and the women all naked. That night Countess Mina Werner-Grunden taught him much in bed, but he hardly shared with Lesley what his passions had driven him to later, either in the service of his Führer or his countess—

"So you are thirty-five and have never been married, just too busy serving Germany?" Lesley Valente asked.

He smiled and relaxed his ramrod-stiff back against the chair at last. He had talked a long time about the grandeur of Germany. It was the first time she'd shown interest beyond asking about the Russian campaign. He'd assured her Operation Barbarossa was going splendidly, although he knew full well the brutal weather as well as the fierce counterattack was killing far too many men. He noted to his surprise he had gripped the handle of his Luger while he spoke and now he nonchalantly put both hands on the tablecloth.

"I am thirty-five, Lesley, but I was married for five years. She gave me no children, you see, and that is inexcusable on her part." One hand moved to grip his goblet very tight. He'd had other affairs, quite a string of them since then, but none of the women had gotten pregnant. Surely he was choosing the wrong women, but then, one who had already born twins to prove her fertility, well . . .

He looked straight into her gray-green eyes as they widened in response to his comments; she was obviously surprised. "I divorced her," he explained with a little shrug. "Regrettable but necessary. She was not the right woman for me. But I do intend to have a marriage and a family when things settle down for me and I find that right woman."

"For the Reich, of course," she interrupted and stood. His last words reminded her of something Paul had said to her in England more than two years ago when he'd been so hurt and angry. She'd sat here listening to this man for over an hour, tried desperately to keep her feelings in check to find a way out, to discover his weakness, and here she ended up thinking of Paul. And all that this man had told her here tonight had convinced her he thought he was completely right, completely invincible. She moved toward the front door before he could stand. Darkness had fallen. She could see her reflection in the glass, like an ebony mirror, as he rose to pursue her, and she saw she hadn't pulled the blackout curtains closed.

"It's only because you don't yet fully understand the German master plan that you use that tone to me," he said brusquely. "Someday I shall take you to Berlin and that will help."

She spun to face him with a bold tilt of chin. "I don't think so. I only know it's been a very long day, and I really must ring my chauffeur. They will all wonder what I'm doing here." But he was too quick for her as she reached for the door. She pressed her back closer to the wall as he set his glass down on the sill of the display window and put one hand to the doorknob over hers.

"What you're doing here is being kissed—just once—before I walk around the corner to have the waiters come back to clean all this up for you," he murmured, his voice an intimate rasp.

"No, I—" she got out before his other hand grasped her shoulder and his mouth dipped to take hers, even though she tried to turn away. His lips seemed both warm and cold, the wine perhaps. His slick tongue darted out as if to taste her. He stepped closer, yet his body did not touch hers as she jerked her head away. "Please don't, Max. I'm not ready for anything like this."

"You will be. Soon," he told her with a curt nod. He opened the door and his black uniform melted instantly into the night as he went out.

From two doorways down the street, Paul Kendal watched the tall, bareheaded SS officer emerge from Valente's and walk the other way; he could even hear him humming. Anger wracked him, a fury that shook him so he could almost have rushed after the bastard to kill him with his bare hands. But then, she'd allowed it. He'd seen that. The cozy candlelight dinner she'd invited him to share, the long conversation in the privacy of Valente's where he'd never yet set foot, that kiss at the door where anyone going by outside could see if they just glanced in. What a fool he'd been to come here to check if she was in any danger after what Carla had inadvertently told him today. And what a fool he'd been to leave someone like Carla to run over here—put Carla off once more.

He ground out his cigarette with his heel, then turned and strode up the street toward the Spanish Steps. Lady Lesley Clarissa Westam, Countess Valente, was welcome to jump into the arms of the Nazis just as she had Cesare Valente's if she thought it was going to help her business. It was obviously all she cared for, that and avoiding scandal. But didn't she know a liaison with a Nazi SS man close to Himmler and Dollman could get her in all sorts of trouble? He cursed under his breath. She was none of his concern, hadn't been for a couple of years and that was just how he wanted things!

His long legs took him up the graceful sweep of steps two at a time past the house where Keats had died, back toward the Borghese Gardens again. For a year and a half a beautiful, brave woman had shown she cared for him and he'd done nothing but bury himself in his columns and his new novel. He admired Carla Fracci; he'd seen her change before his very eyes from the scruffy girl he'd first seen the day he went to meet Cesare Valente to a lovely young woman. Her courage in working clandestinely for her country and for going against her parents' wishes that she marry an old friend of their family had impressed him. Maybe he even continued to contribute pieces for *Libero*, despite the danger, for her sake, and not in honor of Cesare Valente's sacrifice, as he thought, and the idea pleased him. Carla's determination reminded him of his own in convincing his father he wanted to be a writer. In a way, her tenacity reminded him of his sister, Kaye, too—whom he missed so much—even of Lesley as he had once thought her to be. But at least, thank God, he never missed Lesley the way he once had.

Maybe he could find Carla tonight in that old gardener's shed where she'd told him more than once she worked on *Libero*. It really wasn't that late yet. But as he turned into the vast darkened public gardens, the kiss Lesley had shared with that blond son-of-a-bitch Nazi flashed through his brain again and he slammed his leather briefcase hard into the brick wall, once, twice.

He stood for a moment, breathing hard. His body shuddered. Then he seized control of himself. He was done with being a fool! Now he could forget Lesley for good—forever. He welcomed the pitch-dark imposed by the blackout. For a moment, he felt part of it. It soothed him before other thoughts rushed back. He could almost feel Carla's lips under his, yielding, warm, moist, trusting—most of all trusting.

He cut off the gravel path and loped across the broad expanse of grass toward the gate to the Fracci villa set in the dark, distant wall beyond.

❧ ❧ *Chapter Fifteen*

FOR NEARLY SEVEN WEEKS, Lesley played cat and mouse with Max Dorff, hoping he would tire of the chase, praying he would be recalled to Berlin. She told him she was busy—it was true enough. The twins caught measles and that kept her mostly in and him away for almost two weeks. Even though it was winter, she took the twins to Capri when there was no other means of escaping him. But the rumor was that if the tide began to turn against Italy in the Mediterranean, access to Capri might become restricted. He was evidently occupied entertaining visitors from Berlin off and on. But Max Dorff hadn't given up his phone calls and visits to Valente's the last few days, and the fact Guido was home on leave, and she told Max she must spend time with him before he was recalled, seemed to have little effect. But tonight she would not be home if he rang her up, nor would anyone tell him she had gone to a meeting of the Preservation of Roman Art Committee, which she now chaired. A little respite, however brief, from the war of wits and wills she waged with her personal Nazi enemy.

"Guido! Stella! Oh, *here* you are," she joked as she peeked around the door of the sitting room. Paolo and Cati's raucous squeals and shrieks, jumbled with the wild barking of Carlo's dog, Caprice, rent the air. Lesley grinned to see both twins riding Guido's back horsey-style while Stella laughed as loud as they and egged them on. Lilla's fiancé was home on leave too, and Lesley had given her the week off to move home to her Roman neighborhood of San Lorenzo, so everyone had been helping with the twins this week.

"Help, help, Lesley!" Guido gasped in mock terror and stuck out his tongue while Cati yanked his necktie as if it were a horse's reins. "These two attack harder than any B-42's or tank guns I've ever seen. Help me!"

"At least they're not parachuting off the grand piano onto the couch with handkerchiefs held over their heads like last week," Lesley shouted over the din. "All right now, you two," she ordered and lifted Paolo off Guido's back, "settle down or you'll be too excited to go to sleep. You're driving poor Caprice crazy, let alone the rest of us. Caterina Valente, don't pull Guido's hair like that!" Yet all three adults, however much they protested, delighted in the children's antics and innate love of life. The war was only another, greater, more distant game to little people who weren't all weighed down by the threat of death and looming destruction, and some of that spilled off onto the adults.

Lesley kissed the twins good-night and left them finally quiet, while Stella read them a book, a twin sitting on each of their laps just as if they were parents with their children. Lesley blinked tears away as she went down the steps, not only because Cati and Paolo missed having a father of their own, but because she couldn't help the occasional moment of longing, of weakness, when she meant to be so strong for everyone who depended on her—and because she had no man to share things with, to love.

She felt so sorry for Stella, Guido, and Carlo. Stella had told her she had refused to fully surrender herself to her love for Guido until Carlo came home next time and she could tell him in person that she loved his brother. Lesley dashed the tear from her cheek and shook her head grimly. At least Guido had changed for the better since Cesare's death, but what a pity that's what it had taken. Guido had actually admitted he was ready to settle down with one woman, but cursed himself because that woman was Carlo's Stella. The electric tension between Guido and Stella, the desire for each other warring with guilt and pain, reminded her so of the last days she and Paul had spent together in England before they said good-bye and she flew home to Cesare.

She pulled on her black karakul coat over her jade ribbed-wool dress and halted in the big tiled entry hall to fish in her tapestry purse for her key chain. Antonio, the only man still on the staff because he was far beyond the age of conscription, always pulled her Alfa Romeo up in front for her when she was going out. For a moment, she stared down at the little gold lion with diamond eyes that adorned her key chain. How marvelous Paul's novel *Lions Roar* had been, how deeply it had touched her. Besides a spectacular description of brave wartime London, the book had included evocative renderings of her beloved Herefordshire and a marvelous, eccentric old English grande dame who was obviously based on her grandmum. And the Welsh hero and British heroine had shared a poignant love before the war tore it all away from them. She shook her head again to clear those thoughts. No good to think of that now or ever. She'd given Carla Fracci the book back and tried not to make everything worse by recalling the crucible of emotions it had ground together inside her.

She opened the door halfway and looked across the darkening square. Night and wartime blackout were descending, though vehicles spun by still, their slitted headlamps, which did little good when it got quite dark, not yet lit. But tonight, she remembered, there would be a beautiful full moon. The piazza seemed busy, normal enough for a January Friday evening even if auto traffic was down with the petrol rationing. She had her key in the lock of her auto when alarm shot through her like a bullet.

"Since I've been getting no results on the phone lately, I had to come in person," the cold voice clipped out in the crisp, heavily accented English he always spoke to her now.

She whirled about to face Max Dorff all in black, only his hair and face pale in the fading light. He wore no coat. Both gloved hands rested on the handles of his pistols. "I—I didn't see you, Max."

"Obviously, or I doubt you would have come out at all."

"That's not true. I've been busy and I told you I didn't wish to see you."

"But I'm here, *meine Liebe*, and you are seeing me," he stated brusquely and covered her hand with his big one to remove her key from the lock. He tugged the key chain away and jingled it in his big hand while he spoke. "And frankly, since you won't come out with me for dinner or the Opera, it looks as if we're simply going to be spending time at home. I want to talk to you. Let's go inside."

Her mind raced. There would be a scene with Guido and she'd tried to keep this from him. And she'd do anything to keep Max Dorff away from her children.

"I regret to say I have a meeting," she said brazenly, giving a small shrug.

"The meeting is with me, but we'll take my auto and go together then." His hard hands reached for her shoulders and turned her to face him squarely only inches away. "I tire of all this protest, Lesley. If you're not going to see me in public, I assure you, you are going to see me in private. I've reached the end of my tether with you, and I've been in some meetings lately that have not put me in a particularly good mood. If you wish not to be alone with me, we shall simply go back inside and take your children with us, hm?"

There it was again, the knife he always held to her back whenever she managed to outduel him. "I really wouldn't mind if you would just drop me off at the Campidoglio," she told him, conceding defeat for the first time in weeks. "I have a meeting at the Capitoline Museum."

"Fine," he agreed with a glint of white smile as he returned her keys. "Then let's go." But when he drove them away in his sleek, black Lancia Aprilia, he ignored her request and headed immediately out of town, past the Colosseum, out the Via Appia Antica to the south.

"Max, where are you going?" she demanded.

"For a romantic evening ride, as there should be a full moon. A bomber's moon the Luftwaffe call it over England. And if you mean to argue, just sit silently," he ordered, his voice rising. "I'm going back to Berlin in several weeks and you have been wasting my time, our time! And whether you believe me or not, I have an important proposition to make to you."

Her emotions clashed: relief he was leaving, regret they were together for even a few more weeks. And what sort of proposition could this man intend? A few weeks, he said. If she could just slog through for a few weeks until he left! She stared straight ahead as they sped along in the fading light under an ancient arch of tall umbrella pines. It seemed they rushed down a long, dim tunnel past the Chapel of Domine Quo Vadis, past the few other autos and the occasional slow-moving lorry toward the ruins of elaborate Roman tombs that lined the roadway beyond. She fought to kept her voice steady. "What sort of proposition?"

"An official one, not the one I'd like to make you if you'd hold still long enough," he told her and shot her a look she read in the low, full moonlight as something between a leer and a smile. "It has come to the attention of Colonel Dollman and SS Reichsführer Himmler that even in the midst of this vast war, the English Countess Valente has chosen to make her own little protest by refusing to export her beautiful furs to Berlin, when the fatherland would much appreciate a more cooperative effort. But, alas, wouldn't we all?"

She composed a careful answer. "I don't want Valente garments shipped across battle lines, Max."

"Ah, is that all, then?" he crooned, his tone sardonic. "So, if you could be assured the goods would not be in danger, you would allow them to go to Berlin, perhaps accompany the first shipment yourself. And be willing to stage a little showing for some very special guests at a private party being given for the Führer himself?"

"What? No, of course not!" she cracked out just before he veered the little sports car sharply off the road between two mounded ancient tombs like artificial hills, one with the silhouette of a crumbled watchtower on its top. He jerked the Lancia to a stop. He jumped out, came around to her side, yanked opened the door.

"Get out, Lesley!"

Fear slapped her like cold water, but she was angry, too. "I will not!"

"Now, do not try my temper further by arguing or fighting," he told her and half helped, half pulled her out of the Lancia to hustle her quickly around the back of a mound where they could not be seen from the road. "A very private, even desolate place," he observed as she felt her annoyance turn to terror. Her heart beat very fast; her legs went weak. He was dangerous and she had overstepped. The rules were not rational, not sane ones, in the world Max Dorff inhabited and helped to rule. He was furious and his free hand rested easily on the holster with the Luger at his hip.

"Max, I— Don't you think I have a right to try to protect my dead husband's business? It's all I have," she pleaded.

With both hands on her shoulders, he pressed her back against a rough tree trunk while her high heels wobbled in the soft carpet of grass and pine needles. "It's all you have but for your children—and me. And since you happen to be as intelligent and willful as you are beautiful, I am going to explain this to you here where you will give me your undivided attention. You have fought my wishes, but worse, annoyed those above me, Lesley, and I won't allow that, as I intend for us to be seen together often." Moonlight cast cold shadows on his angry face. His blond hair gleamed ghostly white.

"You are half English as you have boasted," his voice rolled on. "Hell, the Reich mistrusts Italians and they are our avowed allies, you little fool, but you're Italian *and* English. You are in a dangerous position, one that will become more so as the Reich comes to control Il Duce's flabby empire. You need to behave, comply, and I'm going to see that you do. You need a strong protector so you don't end up in some prison for dissidents, have your business confiscated, your children—well, who knows what. I hope you understand that you need me in your life, Lesley. If you loved your husband, though I hear he was a great deal older than you, I can honor that. I expect loyalty and fidelity and will have it from you just as I shall have everything else I want from you."

His hard body pinned her against the tree as his big hands lifted to cup her face, to tip her head back and hold her still while his mouth moved hungrily against hers. He crushed the breath from her; her hands, trapped against his hard chest, were helpless as his tongue invaded and plundered her mouth. His pelvis ground her hips back against the soft fur coat and rough, unyielding tree bark. His leather belt with square silver buckle imprinted its shape against her stomach, his holster pressed against her hipbone. He smelled of leather and some faint cologne, and she was so afraid she would have an attack of claustrophobia because he hemmed her in so hard, left her no way to escape. She absolutely froze when his hand intruded between them and harshly molded itself to one breast, then slid lower inside her open coat to follow her heaving rib cage, squeeze her waist, then grasp her right buttock against the tree.

Jumbled fears, thoughts, the desire to grab his gun, made her tremble against him until he was actually holding her up, yet pressing her down, down.

"Oh, Max, oh, please stop—"

He gasped raggedly for breath. "Do we understand each other now? You need me more than I need you, and I need you much more than this, my countess. Do you understand?"

"Yes! Yes, now please, let me go!"

"Yes. I hadn't planned for our first time to be out here like this—" he said almost to himself.

He loosed her almost dazedly, while she wilted against the tree. He tugged down the bottom of his tunic, straightened the ribbon with the iron cross with its oak leaf cluster about his neck. She closed her coat, which he'd pulled awry, smoothed her ruffled hair back. Then he tucked her trembling arm in his, as if they were out for a stroll in the moonlight. The light etched them now in stark silver. Of necessity, she held to him for a moment so she would not fall. "And you will think about my offer to go to Berlin?" His voice broke the strained silence. "I would accompany you, show you all the things I've wanted you to see."

He took her hand, swinging it, and blessedly led her back toward the auto. There he turned her to him, his hands on her shoulders again. "Lesley, Berlin is *wonderful* for lovers! We could go punting through the Spreewald. I know where they make the best gherkins in the world there. Or walk the forest or beaches at Grünwaldsee near my house. It's a completely furnished mansion, perfect for entertaining or a big family." He smoothed his hair back, then replaced his cap before he opened the door to help her in. He walked quickly around to slide in beside her. Even sitting, she could not halt her trembling. His swings in mood amazed her; suddenly it was as though nothing amiss had ever passed between them.

He thrust his avid face close to her carefully composed one. "People take picnics all the time out to the Brandenburg woods along the Müggelsee with kuchen and coffee in hampers, or drink the local Berliner Weisse brew they spike with a shot of raspberry syrup, and the Berliner *Luft*, fresh air, is the finest in the world when the rainbows come out after a short rain, Lesley." His voice plunged passionately on. "I know you'd love it all as I do, and after the war I've been promised a wonderful position there."

She fought to settle her thoughts, control her fears. Go to Berlin into the very heart of the enemy she feared and hated? Leave the twins here to go to Berlin to entertain the Nazi elite with this madman who would not leave her alone, who surely would do more than press her to some tree among ancient tombs and threaten her if she were there with him? Oh, dear God in heaven, she was so alone and afraid, and so many were depending on her to be strong!

"You're so quiet I will assume you are seriously considering all I've said, *meine Liebe*," he told her at last, his voice pure challenge.

"Yes." She looked straight ahead and not at him. "I am."

"Wonderful! Shall I take you home or drop you at your museum meeting, then, as I have another staff briefing to attend?"

He mustn't think he had cowed her or that his fierce touch had done anything but surprise her, she vowed. "Yes, to the Capitoline Museum on the Campidoglio, if you don't mind."

He started the Lancia's powerful engine. "And I will call you at home tomorrow."

"As you wish," she managed. But whatever it took, she had no intention of allowing that.

The art committee meeting droned on in the director's conference chamber of the Capitoline Museum, and Lesley could hardly keep her mind on it despite the fact she had a report to give near the end. No one had asked her why she had come in late nor seemed annoyed that they'd had to start without her; she had repaired her outer disarray if not her inner upheaval. She sat erect at the chairman's place at the head of the long, rectangular marble-topped table, one of two women in the crowded tapestry-hung chamber, and fought to keep her mind on the meeting. Before his death, Cesare had chaired this committee and since then she had taken his place as one of the largest private collectors of Renaissance art in Italy. Reports of the number and locations of bags of sand and pumice dragged by, arguments of whether mosaics would be better protected by foil or sand, reports on key statues and monuments that would be likely targets for the enemy to cart off if they ever got as far as Rome.

"Of course, rumor has it," white-haired Professor Querili put in, punctuating each word with the stem of his unlit pipe, "that it may not only be our so-called enemies we have to fear in this, but our allies, too. I've heard several reports that the Germans have been absconding with art from Paris since the occupation there began. Now granted, the French were hardly German allies, but I believe it could happen here, too. So, I'd like to suggest that the business of this committee be kept secret now that Il Duce seems to have invited more and more of Hitler's top men to town."

Papers shuffled; throats cleared; a pen scratched on paper down the long table from Lesley. Blast it, she thought, they were becoming a nation of cowards when it came to the Nazis! She agreed wholeheartedly and cursed herself for not speaking up to support Professor Querili immediately. Thanks to Max Dorff, she was beginning to live in fear, just like her English countrymen at home did under the onslaught of German bombers. She thought of Paul's book, of the bold pride he'd taken in the English spirit. The Brits had stood up under the blitz, but this last month new low-flying raids by planes *Libero* called Messerschmitts and Focke-Wufs had devastated specific London targets again.

"I agree completely with Professor Querili," Lesley declared loudly and brought her fist down on the table. "Let's face the truth here. Waging war in Italy will be like waging war in a museum every bit as precious as the Capitoline, whoever the enemy is." She leaned forward, her finger jabbing the air. "And I believe we can at least all agree the Germans have a very acquisitive nature."

Murmurs of agreement. Down the shiny tabletop several members turned her way and nodded. Throughout the committee's previous lengthy discussions about preserving Italy's art under attack, she had been for keeping careful records but had stressed that if war came here, any place to shelter any work of art would be acceptable—cellars, even goat sheds or farmhouses away from the city. But her stand had been thought alarmist and had often fallen on deaf ears. Now, she realized, they were listening. Fear of the Germans shone from every face. And fear burned inside her as well after the confrontation with Max Dorff tonight. No, she vowed silently at that moment, she might try to keep private peace with Max Dorff and his cronies for the safety of Valente's and her twins, but it was war here. And she was definitely not going into the heart of Nazi Berlin to put on any fur showings for Hitler's cohorts!

Father Pietro Gracco, the pope's Jesuit representative, had just raised his hand to speak when chaos erupted. A charwoman no less, with two museum officials trailing behind her, rushed into the room. Their faces were distraught, their words mere babble at first. Lesley stood, certain the Germans had somehow overheard them and would storm this meeting. She banged her gavel once for order before she sank back in her chair, only to realize there was no order left in her world at all.

"The German high command, using Mussolini's evening radio broadcast, has just announced a severe defeat—a massacre, it sounds to me—of our four divisions with the Germans in Russia," one intruder to their meeting was shouting while the charwoman moaned and wailed. "The list of dead's been published. I've got one here," he yelled and waved a long white paper, "but the thing is that our few top officers who've been flown back to report to Mussolini say that hundreds of our men died in the snows just because the Germans would not give them transportation for retreat. Frozen stiff and deserted by the fleeing Germans, our men were, and the list is all we'll ever have, no bodies!"

Our men. In Russia. Deserted. By Germans. All we'll have. Lesley knew she screamed. She collapsed against the table, clung to the man next to her, Mauro Fracci, Carla's elderly banker father. He held her while she sobbed soundlessly in the ensuing tumult of cries and protests. People banged on the table with fists, with her gavel. She didn't even need to see the list. She knew Carlo's name would be there, Carlo who was only loving and kind. Carlo was no warrior. He valued art and the villa and wanted a life with Stella and his dear pet, Caprice, who waited so faithfully at home and slept at his bedroom door every night no matter how much she tried to entice the dog to come in out of the drafty winter hall. Carlo who had hugged her good-bye and said she'd been a second mother and good friend to him all in one. He'd teased her about all the pairs of socks she'd made him take so he would not get cold. Carlo, like a loving brother. Carlo, frozen stiff, Carlo.

"Yes, yes, Countess Valente, I am so sorry, Cesare's nephew's name is here in the cavalry listings," someone's voice said in her ear. "Two lost to you in the war, but you still have Guido and the babies. Here, come along, let us drive you home."

Home. Home, where Carlo would not come again and where Stella would never tell him now she loved his brother instead. She prayed he'd never guessed. Mauro Fracci and the kind Father Pietro, who kept up a steady stream of words and prayers in Latin, took her home and volunteered to come inside with her. For the first time since the news had crashed into her, she spoke. Her voice sounded quiet, so broken.

"I'd best tell them alone. Guido, his brother. Thank you both, thank you."

She let herself in, afraid to ring for a servant and have them see her like this before she regained control. Slowly she closed the door on her two escorts' concerned faces and leaned against its hardness. Too much, too much. Guido was the only one left of the three men who had taken her in after Paul had deserted her, and Guido had hated her for so long, partly because she and Carlo were so close. But now— Now, half of Valente's, half of everything, was Guido's, and she was so afraid they would not get along, as she and Trent had not when it mattered so much.

In the center of the entryway she grabbed the statue of Diana, held to her cold marble arm until her feet steadied under her. Diana, always poised and strong, her arm stretched back to prepare to draw her bow at whatever threatened her.

Lesley straightened. Max Dorff had been in meetings all day, and he'd heard some bad news that had put him on edge. When he'd left her, he'd hurried back to another briefing. Max Dorff had known all the time they were together of the massacre and the German desertion of the Italian troops in Russia! Max Dorff knew one of her family was in Russia, probably that he'd been killed, and yet he'd invited her to Berlin to coddle the Nazi hierarchy with furs—furs, while Carlo froze in his summer uniform! Max had probably known it all while he threatened her, kissed her, spoke to her of picnics, and punting, and the pleasures of Berlin!

She tossed her head, lifted her tear-streaked chin. She was done with powerful men like Dorff and Il Duce playing with her like a toy while they took away people she loved! Damn them, all of them, to hell, and somehow she would dedicate her life to doing just that, whatever it took!

She shrugged off her coat and threw it and her purse on a settee. There would be time enough to reason her plans out tomorrow, but first she had to find the strength to tell Stella and Guido, to comfort them all. And then, somehow, she had to find the courage to go with Max Dorff to that spiders' nest in Berlin where the Nazis spawned all this cruel torment, and find some way, any way, to make them pay, to make a difference in this war. London, Trent, Cesare, now Carlo, the most innocent of all—gone, gone away in this war, as if she had not known and loved them almost forever. This was her war too, now as never before. She started up the long flight of stairs to tell Guido and Stella.

Lesley glanced once more behind her across the busy, fashionable Porta Pinciana to make certain no one had followed her, then hit the large, polished knocker at the Palazzo Fracci into its brass base. The impressive umber stone building with carved arches above the marble entryway rose three stories over her head into a clear turquoise February sky. It was a splendid edifice, but then the Fraccis had been a financial power in Rome since the time of the Borgias. She only hoped she could speak with Carla alone without anyone else about. After all her agonizing this long week since Carlo's memorial service and Guido's return to Sicily, Lesley's plans were nearly complete. The cost would be great, very great perhaps, but it had to be paid before the German lust for power took the lives of everyone else she held dear. And she knew no one to turn to to find out what to do with the information she hoped to glean in her spying on Dorff and whoever she met in Berlin but Carla Fracci, who must get her information for *Libero* from somewhere high up in the anti-Axis hierarchy.

A dark-eyed maid in gray uniform with small white apron opened the door. "Yes, signora? Won't you please step in?"

"I'm afraid I didn't ring ahead. Is *la signorina* Carla in? I'm Countess Valente, a friend."

Lesley could tell by the woman's face she recognized her name, maybe knew about her from Carla's father. He had been so kind the night she'd heard Carlo had died, and the Fraccis had attended the service last week. But then Max Dorff and Colonel Eugen Dollman with that Bibi Rossi had dared attend too, and she had taken her first step of her elaborate ruse by pretending she was grateful they attended. Max had been so elated when she had agreed to go to Berlin that she was beginning to believe she could pull the wool over his eyes— and make him agree to behave the gentleman suitor as long as she appeared to be amenable to his long-range plans for her.

"Countess, I'm afraid *la signorina* Carla, she is not in the house, but I saw her go out toward the gate to the Borghese Gardens beyond," the maid told her and gestured toward the back of the long hall. "She grows orchids in the old gardener's house out in back, you see. I'm certain she would not mind a bit if I showed you out to join her."

The maid escorted her through the length of the long Carrara marble hall. Huge Sèvres urns and Etruscan busts on gilded tables topped by polished malachite reflected light from a landscaped patio under tall trees at the back. Beyond, lawns stretched to the Borghese Garden wall screened by bushes. As she stepped back outside, Lesley blinked in the brightness of the sun she had not noticed at all today; she could hardly recall the weather this entire last week. She had agonized so much over how she would be endangering her reputation by consorting with the Nazis. Her plan to learn Nazi secrets was one that would no doubt cause her much grief as she became known as Lieutenant Colonel Dorff's woman in a city that mistrusted the Nazis. Only two months ago she had vowed to her staff at Valente's that none of their furs would go to Berlin, and she knew her family and friends would be shocked. And Guido— she should have told him what she planned and why, but he either would have tried to stop her or would have thought she was just doing it because she loved Carlo much more than she ever had him. Their common grief over Carlo's loss had united them more than ever, and yet she saw a new, tougher,

more bitter Guido emerging, and she feared that as much as
Stella did.

"Countess Valente? Do you wish me to take you out, then?"
the maid said and looked puzzled.

Lesley realized with a start she had simply paused on the
patio steps. Perhaps the woman had even said something else
to her. "I'm certain I can find the gardener's house, and it's a
lovely day for a walk. If you don't mind, I'll simply let you
return to your tasks and go out myself," Lesley told her with
a little smile. "I have no auto today, you see, so that's fine."

The maid went back into the big house while Lesley strode
between newly leafed oleanders toward the back along the
winding gravel path. The grounds looked wilder here, rather
unkempt, and Gram would never have approved. Perhaps the
Fraccis had lost their gardeners to the war effort, too. Hard to
believe that in a few days she would be in Berlin, which was
still mired in winter snows, off without the twins, a situation
she had decided to explain to Guido in a letter she would
entrust to Lilla, to be opened only in case everything went
wrong.

She saw the yellow brick gardener's house back in the
shadow of the Borghese wall and cut off the path toward it.
Cypresses grew tall back here, and aromatic myrtles with their
tiny pinpoints of white blossoms not yet in bloom dotted the
dark shrubbery. Birds sang overhead, a veritable private little
Garden of Eden away from the bustle of street and house or
the public park beyond the wall. She opened her mouth to call
Carla's name so she would not startle her, but then she saw
them and stopped stock-still. A man and woman with their
backs to her—Carla and a big, dark-haired man in a business
suit—sitting on a tartan blanket in a patch of sun. Their
shoulders were pressed together, their heads bent over something they read.

Lesley felt her face flush at her intrusion. Hadn't the maid
known Carla was back here with a man? His long arm lifted to
encircle her waist. She was in the softest mauve and he in
dove-gray with a light blue shirt. How embarrassing this would
be. She should quietly go back to the house and try to see Carla
later, but she had so little time, and she was afraid to use the
phones for something like this. One simply did not ring up

someone in Il Duce's Rome and ask if one's contacts with an underground newspaper could use any information about the Nazis which could be overheard or discovered.

She knew she should retreat, yet stood transfixed as the man turned and tipped his head to kiss Carla and pulled her pliant, slender body closer in his embrace. And the man. He looked so much like Paul Kendal that Lesley stood mesmerized as if the cinema of her mind had filmed his touch, his warmth, his kisses and replayed it all to taunt her. His face was still hidden by Carla's profile, but a young, strong man like that in Rome today, with most of the able-bodied soldiers gone, was most unusual—

She stepped back into a myrtle shrub; under her feet a big twig snapped. She jumped, turned, even as the couple did. Paul! It was *Paul* in Carla Fracci's arms!

"Countess! Oh, you frightened us!" Carla said, then motioned her over. Paul's eyes were dark, his entire face in shadow. He stood, jammed his hands into his trouser pockets, not seeming to notice that Carla had extended her arm to have him give her a hand up until she said, "Gian," and he bent to assist her.

"I'm dreadfully sorry, Carla," Lesley managed, holding her ground, "but the housemaid indicated you were alone. I didn't mean to intrude."

"No, it's all right, Countess. I'm honored, and I'd like to introduce you to my—my dear friend, Gian Donato." Lesley forced her eyes to Carla for the first time. The woman turned to stare at Paul, her face suddenly puzzled.

"Countess Valente."

Lesley's eyes leapt back to Paul. "Signor Donato."

Carla went on about Paul's being an Italian book salesman from Milan. It seemed everything was unreality here, Lesley thought. Surely Carla knew this man was really Paul Kendal, who wrote that novel she'd so venerated. Didn't Carla realize Paul could easily have betrayed *Libero* before and could do so again? But no, she herself had diminished that accusation to mere suspicion in the long months since Cesare's death, after she'd recalled how jealous Cesare had been of other men and her feelings for Paul. But if Carla found out that they had once been lovers, she might be the one to turn her in, despite her passion for *Libero*.

Carla's words and Lesley's thoughts jerked to a halt as Paul spoke. "I know Carla can be trusted, Countess, and I always believe in telling the truth to those I care for. Carla, Countess Valente and I knew each other in England before the war, long before I came to live here and became Gian Donato."

Surprise flashed across Carla's small, fine features as she hurried behind Paul, who was striding toward Lesley. "So, is that right?" Carla cried. "You should have told me when I gave you his novel to read, Countess, but I see now why you looked so shocked when I pulled it out."

"You've read *Lions Roar*? I didn't know," Paul said to Lesley as if Carla were not there. His voice sounded rough.

Lesley looked up into his guarded eyes, which were as green as these alluring gardens. She was aware how Carla watched them now. "Yes. I thought it was marvelous, a real tribute to the England and the people I have known and loved."

"Good. And I was sorry to hear about your nephew's death."

"Thank you."

For a moment there were only birdsongs again and the rustle of the wind through trees before Lesley tore her gaze away and forced herself to speak to Carla. "Really, I do apologize for the intrusion. I only came to tell you I won't be at Valente's next week, so you might as well nip by the week after instead, that's all," she lied, as Paul's accusing words about always telling the truth to those he cared for returned to mock her, however gentle his voice had been just now. He had never understood, never forgiven, blamed her still for everything that went wrong between them when it was he who had deserted her. The pain of losing him stabbed her again and that terrified her.

"Actually, I'm leaving for a few days because I've had a chance to show some Valente furs in Berlin," she blurted out. If Paul Kendal wanted the truth from her, he could bloody well have it!

"In Berlin, but so dangerous!" Carla said, swishing her skirt impatiently with one hand.

"I'm certain I'll be quite safe. I'll talk to you about it when I return, Carla."

"But safe from what in the arms of the Nazi top brass I believe I heard has been courting you lately?" Paul demanded.

"I certainly hope, as a famous and no doubt well-paid journalist, you don't just go by rumors," she shot back. Her pain crashed to anger in such a rush that her hands gripped her shoulder bag so tightly the strap bit into the padded shoulder of her teal-blue wool suit jacket.

"I believe I've learned the hard way to see people for what they are and judge accordingly," he accused with a scowl.

"Now, look you two—" Carla began, but Lesley cut her off even as she started away toward the gate to the gardens. She wanted to get out of here, to get away from them, from this man who had lied to her, seduced her, deserted her and her twins. But when she recalled his cruel parting words to her last time about her always solving things by running, she turned back.

"As you can perhaps guess, Carla, your friend Gian Donato and I are not friends. I haven't seen him for months and quite regret I did today. And best watch your business interests around him, as I've always found certain journalists have a wretched tendency to switch sides when it suits them."

"Someone literally making her bed with the Nazis should know, Countess!" Paul clipped out, then bit his lip, annoyed he had told Carla anything of Lesley when he should have just let her back out of this chance encounter. Now he'd have to explain more than he wanted to Carla, and that would only churn up all those feelings toward Lesley he'd hoped were buried forever. No one who'd felt the thrill he had today when he looked up and saw her there, even when he was kissing someone else, could lie to himself that he no longer cared. And he'd have to make this up to Carla. He did care for her, did need her in his life. He turned back and took her hands in his just when he heard the wooden door to the public gardens bang back against its frame as Lesley walked out.

❈ ❈ *Chapter Sixteen*

THE VIBRATING SWAY of Adolf Hitler's personal train was familiar to Lesley now as the powerful steam engine pulled them through the snowy Austrian Alps and northward toward Berlin. Despite two glasses of wine with her meal and high-heeled alligator pumps, she followed Max on fairly steady feet through the plush dining car with its white linen tablecloths and arrangements of white calla lilies and red roses under black curtains with red satin sashes. They had just dined with Colonel Dollman, who at least had not brought Bibi Rossi to gush over all the luxuries of the Führer's private train. Nazi decor was a mixture, Lesley had decided, of Victorian clutter, Gothic grandeur gone awry, and rococo excess with its fringed silks, tufted velvets, garish Nazi flags, and gold-plated eagles. And there were the ubiquitous gilt-framed photographs of Hitler in the First World War, Hitler in Bavarian attire, Hitler reviewing his troops, Hitler with his dogs—Hitler, Hitler, Hitler like a demigod in a bizarre shrine! How strange that anything in these surroundings seemed civilized, but the six-course dinner had proceeded calmly from cream of wild mushroom soup to apricot and raspberry parfait while she had listened avidly to everything Max and Eugen Dollman said.

"Still with me, *meine Liebe*?" Max turned back to ask as they traversed the noisy, swaying accordion connection between the dining carriage and the Führer's favorite teak-paneled observation car. For once Max wore an expensively tailored black pinstripe suit—with no Lugers—but the effect hardly calmed her.

"Right behind," she assured him and forced a smile. Pretending to be interested in Max, yet keeping him at arm's length, was wearing on her already. Her sleeping compartment was next to his, yet she'd convinced him to settle only for kisses last night. He'd agreed over protests to allow her to stay at the Adlon Hotel in Berlin instead of his Grünwald mansion, but she knew he would expect some sort of further compliance for that favor. It was, she mused, as if she herself swayed along the thin threads of railway track, fearful of being crushed by the encroaching iron wheels of a steam engine as it rushed and shrieked its way deeper into Germany.

This carriage too was lighted by small brass lamps with fringed shades attached to the rich marquetry of the walls. It offered two groupings of comfortable maroon moquette high-backed seats with embroidered antimacassars. Glass-fronted shelves displayed numerous morocco-bound copies of *Mein Kampf*, maps, hanging pairs of binoculars, collections of engraved vellum notepaper embossed with the swastika and eagle, more photographs, and a huge collection of Hitler's favorite Wagnerian recordings for the gramophone in the corner. Max soon pulled her away from her scrutiny of the carriage and its contents, and seated her. He leaned over her, one hand on each arm of her chair.

"More Rhine wine, Lesley?"

"No, thanks awfully. I've had quite enough." And enough of all this already, she thought, but she steadied herself, tried to appear calm.

"I'll never get enough of you," Max murmured. He bent down for a kiss. She obliged for a moment, then sat quickly back in her seat to gaze out the window as he plopped down beside her with a deep sigh.

"My wonderful countess, don't look away, and no more moodiness about the twins you left behind, all right?" he cajoled.

"All right, I won't." It had torn her apart to say good-bye, so afraid something could go wrong here, so that she would never see them again. For those she loved, for her home and her two homelands, which the Nazis seemed hell-bent on destroying, she had decided to do this no matter what befell her.

"Lesley, I would like you to tell me truthfully what made you change your mind about me," Max inquired and pressed toward her with a big hand on her knee. He turned her head toward him with one finger. "I'm hoping, you see, it wasn't only fear for your future safety. I was upset that night I took you out the Appian Way, and I didn't mean to issue ultimatums to the woman I love. I have wonderful, long-reaching plans for us, so it wasn't only that, was it?"

Her eyes met his reluctantly. "No, not only that. But I was afraid of you at first, at least of the way you were so insistent."

"But that's the way we Germans approach something we want very much," he declared, his voice and face now hard and proud again.

"So I've seen. Blitzkrieg." She pulled away to peer out toward the back of their train. The sharp ridges of the distant Alps cut into a night sky that held light like an inverted cup of fine bone china. She watched as the eight carriages snaked around a curve of white, fir-covered foothills and plunged into yet another tunnel. In the dark, the windows were ebony mirrors that enabled her to look directly into his eyes even when turned away like this. "As I said, Max, I prefer to be courted and trusted to make up my own mind in time, not just swept away, even by a very powerful, attractive man."

She saw his taut features relax at another of the compliments she forced herself to offer him from time to time. His arms were warm around her waist. "But power is the ultimate aphrodisiac, they say, *meine Liebe.*"

She stiffened in his loose embrace. "Do they? Well, not for me." She let him hold her while the train exploded from the tunnel and her mind skipped back to Mussolini's apparent assumption of the same thing that day in his huge salon when she and Carlo had taken him the furs. Even Paul had accused her of marrying Cesare for his power. She admitted she wanted power to create her furs, protect her family, and control her own life, but she would rather earn it herself and not merely borrow it from the men around her.

"And why me, Max?" she asked, daring to put him off when he nuzzled her neck. "Of all the German or Italian women you've met and who wouldn't have struggled in the beginning, why me?"

"But can you look at yourself in a mirror and ask that, my countess with the two beautiful children?" he rasped, his breath hot against her skin. "I would love to have children like that someday, perhaps four or five." He lifted her hand to kiss it in a way he assured himself was a gallant gesture that this unfathomable woman would appreciate.

She seemed more assured all the time, Max told himself, but her aloofness and that self-contained strength she emanated lured him to conquer and possess her as he had Countess Mina Werner-Grunden when he was only nineteen and she taught him so much about her elite world and exotic sex. But when she'd married again and told him he must stay away for a while, he'd been even more desperate to get back into her life and her bed. Only when he'd sent her old bridegroom of six months, a retired Prussian admiral, an anonymous note telling him where he might find his bride in a compromising situation with another man at the Bristol Hotel did she eventually take him back. Even then, she had other lovers and screamed at him that he was an inept, selfish lover despite his godlike body. He had grown up in that moment when he realized she had never loved him. It was almost the same tearing pain he'd felt when he knew his parents loved his sisters and not him, their heir, the son who would carry on their Aryan name. He'd lost control of his temper with his countess, of his sanity, of his hands around her slender neck, as he'd forced himself between those writhing legs again, and then—

"Max, I'm a bit sleepy if you wouldn't mind my going to bed," Lesley said. "Tomorrow with Berlin— Well, I'm rather done in, that's all."

Her voice had actually startled him. He still gripped her hand tightly until she tried to tug it back. "Of course, *meine Liebe*, for I have wonderful plans for just the two of us in Berlin before I let anyone else meet you at that party at Göring's Karinhall. You'll need your rest. Come along, then."

She was relieved she managed to be rid of him after several of his hot, wet kisses in the narrow hall. He seemed suddenly preoccupied. She simply had to learn to read his thoughts better, she realized as she closed and locked the door to her elegant if tiny sleeping compartment. At least it helped that he and Dollman had no idea she could grasp most of what they said when they spoke German between them, and she hoped that would be useful to her in discovering Nazi secrets, however much it placed her at a social disadvantage in Berlin.

She surveyed her compartment to be certain nothing was amiss. Her Vuitton wedding trousseau luggage lined the brass racks overhead. From the plush, high-backed sofa along one wall her bed had been made up with snowy sheets and big, plump pillows. She sighed and opened the rosewood marquetried panel to the hidden porcelain washbasin and towels and poured herself a tumbler of mineral water from the cache of necessities there. She turned off the small brass lamp with its red silk shade attached to her tiny table by the window and pulled open the brocade curtains. Despite her fitted royal-blue jersey floor-length gown with its mink epaulets and the radiator nearly at her feet, the chill of the mid-February night outside pierced her. She sat staring at the blur of passing silhouettes of bare-boned alpine forests, steep chalet roofs, gentler hills, her mind wandering, for how long she wasn't certain until she jolted back to earth as they pulled into a small, plain, wooden station with lights. She closed the draperies partway so the crowd on the platform would not stare.

Then it hit her: this was late at night in a small rural village, and the large crowd consisted of men, women, and children bent against the wind as they were evidently being herded from one end of the platform to the other. The Führer's train ground to a slow halt. She pressed her face to the cold crack of window. Women lugging ill-looking children who were too big to be carried, some men with pitifully wrapped bundles, a few carrying elderly people, and all seemed to be actually marching off into the cold night. Fear on their faces, their wild eyes darting as guards with bayoneted rifles or machine guns shoved them along like cattle. Their sounds came to her in the silence that seemed strange after she'd been listening to the steam engine and iron wheels for hours. Their voices, cries, a shout of encouragement to someone back in the line. The barked orders in German she wished she could decipher through the glass. And sewn on every chest of the wanderers was a yellow star like she'd seen in graffiti on some buildings in Rome. "*Juden*," the accusing word had said.

"Jews! Those are Jews!"

She rushed out into the hall, rapped sharply on Max's door. He opened it almost immediately, bleary-eyed. He'd thrown a robe over his pajamas; he held his Luger down at his side.

"Lesley, *Liebe*, what is it?"

"Outside in this little station wherever we are. Soldiers are pushing a huge crowd of Jewish people out into nowhere off some train down the tracks!"

His concern crashed to annoyance. "Damn, Lesley, it's late. You said you were tired and you're not even undressed."

She hadn't thought of that. She hadn't been careful enough.

"I just thought you could do something," she insisted.

"The war makes many refugees, Lesley," he explained, his voice taut. "Because supplies must move during the day, refugees are often relocated at night. They're only being taken somewhere out of harm's way, I assure you."

"Then the rumors about the Third Reich's treatment of the Jews are untrue?" she demanded.

"What rumors? Whose propaganda have you been reading?" he exploded. "As Goebbels has said, '*Die Juden sind unser Unglück*,' 'the Jews are our misfortune,' but I told you that you are to trust me, not come with all these questions, and I meant it! Come in with me then, and I'll be certain you get into bed if you insist on discussing this further!"

He pulled her hard against him, with his arms around her neck where the cold Luger rested along her cheek. He spoke low in her ear now, and his hot breath ruffled the hair against her temple. "My countess, you are being honored by being invited into the very heart of the Reich to show your lovely furs, and you have been invited into my heart because I love and wish to protect you. But if you do not stay in line, do not please me on this trip, I have the power to take you into *Schutzhaft*, protective custody."

She shuddered. She'd tipped him off to her true feelings again when she meant to make him trust her. She would never even remain free to carry off her plans if she persisted in railing about things that she had no concrete knowledge of.

"I'm sorry, Max. It's just I was so sleepy I lay down on the bed this way and then was wakened by the noise out there." She lifted her head to stare him down. She forced the corner of her mouth up in a shaky smile. "Now I'm going to kiss you, and then we'll both get a good night's sleep without any more fuss. And I'm looking forward to Berlin." For the first time between them, she initiated a kiss, then extricated herself from his arms, relieved he looked surprised and pleased. Before he could react further, she quickly slipped back into her compartment and locked the door.

She was learning to play by their rules of deceit and lies, she assured herself, but it made her feel so dirty, so lost. And those people out there, those mothers so frightened and so cold! When the train jerked and started to roll away from all the grief and terror she'd witnessed, she lost her fine dinner prepared by Hitler's personal chef into the pretty painted porcelain bowl.

"Countess, your furs were lovely, just lovely," boomed Hermann Göring, the portly host of the party at the opulent, sybaritic mansion Karinhall, forty-five miles northeast of Berlin.

She thanked him as her eyes scanned the salon and his chatter rolled over her. Under vast gilt-framed oil paintings extolling the glories of the Aryan master race and the Third Reich, the glitterati of Nazi Berlin mingled, drank, and buzzed their gossip in each other's ears. Lesley sensed the energized electricity in the air was only dulled by the thin veneer of distrust Hitler's cadre felt for each other, let alone the rest of the world. The tuxedoed men reeked power as their women reeked French perfume amid the glint of jewels, the sheen of satins and poshness of velvets or furs, some of them newly purchased Valentes. She had vowed to herself and her staff that Valente furs would never grace the backs of the German enemy, yet here she was with them, displaying and offering the very gems of her line and all to allow her to spy. A tremor of foreboding wracked her again as she forced herself to focus on Göring's words.

"What a perfect gesture by our Italian allies to send you here to us, though I'm afraid one unfortunate part of your narration tonight sent a few ripples through the crowd," Göring said with a shake of his big head.

Lesley knew exactly what he meant, but she pretended to misunderstand. "But furs imported from Valente's to Germany must be quite expensive, especially in wartime, Herr Reichsmarschall Göring." Tonight, at the very outset of her narration, she had not been able to stem her bitterness and anger as she'd gazed out over the sea of these smug, self-righteous Nazi faces, despite her desire to make them trust her enough so she might overhear important inside information. After the applause had died down from Göring's grandiose introduction of her, she had begun, "Despite the terrible times in which we all live, I am proud to serve my Italian countrymen and the other once-independent nations in Europe in a career that can do so much to promote warmth and beauty. Fur garments can make people out in the cold feel warmer. Fur garments can allow people to show love, kindness, and respect to each other. And fur garments can give those who appreciate and cherish God's beauty in the midst of a sometimes ugly world a way to do so.

"After all," she'd gone on, her voice becoming even bolder under their puzzled, hostile stares, "the tradition of being a furrier could come from no more hallowed beginning. I understand Bibles were included among the books the Third Reich has seen fit to burn. However, I recall that early in the Bible—in Genesis, the Lord God himself"—she knew her voice had faltered here as the words came to her—"the Lord God of Israel, showed his continued love for Adam and Eve after they sinned by making them 'coats of skins' before He sent them out of the Garden of Eden into the cold, cruel world. Surely, no matter what sins all of us have committed, we must keep in mind such love and forgiveness when we wear coats of skins today."

Yes, those accusing words had been a risk, but then coming here to Germany had been, too. She'd stared defiantly out over their stunned, angry faces as she hurried on to describe the fur coat on the first German model. She knew Max was smoldering silently over her insult to the Third Reich, but it had not put Göring off from hanging on as her escort. Though he was plump and jolly, she'd learned not to trust appearances in any of the high-ranking Germans she'd met these last two days. Men who looked the part of kindly grandfathers spouted "*Seig heils!*" as easily as they downed Göring's torrent of French wines and champagne, and the limping, spindly Dr. Goebbels had declared to her entire table in bombastic German he would make a "shortest war is total war" speech tomorrow. At least Göring spoke English with her so she didn't have to pretend to grasp so little. She'd found few Germans spoke Italian and chose not to use English, the enemy's language, though they obviously understood it well enough.

"You must admit Valente furs looked splendid modeled on our lovely young women of the Führer's Faith and Beauty Corps here tonight with their torches and the flags," Göring said, breaking into her thoughts. "Did I tell you I intend to have Valente's make me a second sable coat for myself to wear over my new sky-blue Luftwaffe uniform? A bit of extra room needed in the armholes and shoulders for the newest medals and more ribbons, you know. And"—he lowered his voice to a mere shout—"I want to pick out one of those silver fox stoles for my Emmy, too."

Lesley's eyes darted across the room again as Göring gestured toward his wife, the actress Emmy Sonnemann, whose wedding extravaganza Max had told her he'd attended and admired as much as he did the grandeur of Karinhall, which she found tacky and tasteless with its palatial pomposity. Frau Göring waved back from her little coterie of friends, which included the woman film director Leni Reifenstahl, whom Lesley had met earlier. The woman, she took it, had directed many recent Nazi films on the Reich's glories. The brunette singer Marika Rokh waved back, too. The talented Marika had moved the Germans to tears before their eight-course dinner tonight with her rendition of what Max had said was his favorite song: "Under the linden, on the heath, where my sweetheart waits for me." This party, which was purported to be both a late birthday celebration for Göring and an early one for Hitler, had already gone on for hours, and although she'd learned so many things, she wasn't certain any of it would be useful to help bring the Nazis down.

"So you liked Berlin?" Göring was asking for at least the third time. Perhaps as host he spoke to so many he forgot to whom he'd said what, but who else was here who had not seen Berlin before? Previously the huge man had worked the room the way she'd seen Leonard Stockman work a Sackville's society showing in the old days in London, only Göring was soothing his guests while they waited for Adolf Hitler, who had supposedly been here for hours and was working or resting upstairs. The Führer had a deathly fear of getting fat, she'd overheard, and often ate alone when the banquet was decidedly

Lucullan. After all, someone had said, when the American
Duchess of Windsor and the abdicated King Edward VIII of
England had been the guest of Göring and Hitler here at
Karinhall before the war, the duchess had snidely remarked,
"One never could be too rich or too thin," and everyone had
thought her not only charming but terribly clever, too. But
what good was any of that sort of personal gossip or this
Göring-type chitchat to her when she needed to learn secret
plans, strategies, weaknesses to take back to Rome with her,
Lesley fumed silently.

Göring steered her across the room, bragging about his
artworks here at Karinhall again. Numerous people she'd
already met stopped them to compliment her furs, though some
looked at her askance. They passed Dr. Goebbels; fish-eyed
Himmler; von Ribbentrop; actresses; designers; handsome
Speer, Hitler's personal architect. Many of the women were
expensively coiffed and gowned, with jewels on their bosoms,
while those poor women Lesley had seen from the train wore
only their mocking yellow stars. She began to feel ill again: it
was worse to see the polished patina of these people than their
ugly cores.

Finally Max materialized at her side again with another glass
of blond bubbles from the golden-eagle fountain. When he
wasn't looking, she'd poured her last glass into one of the
numerous massive vases of red roses he'd explained adorned
every party the Führer attended because they were his favorite
flowers.

"Here you are, *meine Liebe*. Shall I retrieve her now, *Herr
Reichsmarschall*?"

"No, no, Dorff. You just keep an eye out for the Führer's
entrance, as I intend to speak to your countess about a fur for
my Emmy like the one the Führer bought Eva Braun, and
maybe give her a little tour of the art hall, too," Göring insisted
with a vague sweep of fat arm to dismiss Max.

Despite the way Max had been flaunting her with Hitler's
higher-ups tonight, she could tell Göring's attachment to her
was wearing thin. "But she's seen the theatre, the pool, your
pet lions, the tapestry collection, your new patent massage
machine, and the wonderful model trains in the basement."
Max's voice rose precipitously as the full orchestra began to

play again in the ballroom through the flag-bedecked portal. She'd never before had dinner or been expected to converse over the rolling, crashing strains of Strauss and Wagner.

"Now, Dorff," Goring chided and shook his head so his double chin wobbled. "She hasn't seen my finest Dutch masters, and you yourself said the lady is an art connoisseur, eh. Just come find us if the Führer appears, and keep the other ladies happy, hm?"

Göring swept Lesley away, though she threw Max a quick smile and wave. At least if she had Göring alone, she might get something out of him she couldn't from Max, she thought. Göring threw open the door to a small dining room off the front oak-paneled hall. A fire burned merrily on yet another marble hearth of the three-story, sixty-five-room mansion. "I adore Dutch masters," Göring admitted with a wink, "though I store a good number of them upstairs in unused bed chambers when the Führer's coming. He likes to see that production-line Nazi art he commissions, you see. Now, wait, there's a parlor full of art over here I think you should take a look at first," he insisted and indicated she should precede him.

She hesitated a moment despite the annoying press of his plump hand in the small of her back. Even the strains of a full orchestra were somewhat distant here, so how would Max find them if Hitler did make his entrance from upstairs or wherever he was? She thought again of her wildest fantasy: she would come upon Hitler alone; she would shoot him with one of their damned Luger pistols and flee into the dark Schorfheide forest surrounding Karinhall and then somehow get back to Berlin, or better yet to Rome, before they discovered the madman was even dead. But she knew she was mad to even imagine something like that, especially that they would ever let her escape.

She moved forward slowly to the open door Göring indicated, her pearl-gray satin evening gown with the silver lamé panels rustling around her silk-stockinged legs. She gasped and hesitated at the door. This room was all papered in red brocade, its walls dominated by four massive paintings of blowsy nudes in provocative poses.

"Really, Reichsmarschall, this sort of thing is not to my

taste," she protested, hoping he took her double meaning without having to actually insult him.

"Nor mine!" came a sharp voice in German from near the fireplace. Both Lesley and Göring jumped and stepped back as, from the tall wing chair facing the hearth, Adolf Hitler rose to face them.

Göring snapped to a stiff-armed salute. Lesley just stared, her heart pounding, her fantasy of shooting him leaping through her mind again. "We were awaiting your presence in the great hall, *mein Führer*," Göring clipped out, speaking now in guttural German.

"So I understand, *mein* Göring." The voice was decidedly mocking. Unlike the men in tuxedos tonight, Hitler wore a black uniform with silver trim similar to Max's usual garb. "And this must be Countess Valente since you two have been chatting and not in German," he said, his tone sincere now. "I heard about your furs earlier, Countess, and if the Reich did not take all my waking hours, I would have seen them." He offered a nod that bounced his slick black hair over his pasty white forehead.

"*Herr* Hitler," was all she could manage, hoping Göring would not wonder at her apparent understanding of Hitler's German when all evening she had pretended not to grasp more than a few conversational phrases. Hitler's black eyes snapped. She knew she should have said in any language that it would have been a great honor if he had seen her furs, but the cajoling words she was learning to use with Max would not come.

Göring cleared his throat. "We did not startle you, I hope. Perhaps you heard us coming, Führer."

Hitler's fists jerked up and down as he spoke. "Perhaps I did, or perhaps that was someone else who spoke of your Führer's poor artistic taste, his preference for the grandeur of our Nazi artists!"

Göring's fat face paled. "No, you misinterpret, Führer. I—"

"I do not misinterpret, nor do I need my closest, trusted council members speaking English so I even need to interpret!" Hitler roared. "Everything I do, everything I say is history, so I never misinterpret, Reichsmarschall Göring!" The tirade built to a crescendo with wild, quick gestures. "I swear, even my German shepherd Blondie is more loyal than my closest advisors at times! Dogs—dogs at least are to be trusted!" he concluded and spun away and turned his furious profile to them.

Lesley held her ground. She'd heard that strident staccato delivery in newsreels both in England and Italy, but it still awed her. Hitler spun back. His rectangle of mustache bobbed, the ebony slash of straight hair across the forehead bounced again as he inclined his head in a slight bow. "I apologize to our guest as you have not the courtesy to do, Göring, but I would speak with you for a few moments here, now, before we go in. About the art, and I do not mean these fat nude women on your walls. The imported art for my Führer Museum in Linz. If the countess would just wait for us back with the others—" His voice left the thought unfinished.

Lesley could not pretend to misunderstand. "Of course, I don't mind," she said, stubbornly clinging to her English. Blast them, she *was* English, and not any more cowed than her fellow countrymen had been by the bombers these two devils had sent! "I understand how busy you all are planning the welfare of those who have fallen under your care, Herr Hitler," she said, pretending acquiescence, but unable to keep the tone of bitter contempt from her voice. She immediately stepped out the way she had come and closed the door rather loudly.

She couldn't help being angry, she thought as she started back toward the party, then jerked to a halt so fast her skirt swayed into her legs. She needed to take any opportunity to overhear information, and this was not only the head of the demonic Luftwaffe but Satan himself she had a chance to eavesdrop on.

She sidled back to the door and pressed her ear to it though their voices carried clearly. They spoke so fast she wished again she'd paid better attention to her schoolgirl German. They were arguing about—yes, about French artworks they were having sent to them from Paris by Hitler's man, Alfred Rosenberg, at the Jeu de Paume Museum. Hitler had evidently just discovered that Göring had been keeping back some of the best works for himself for a museum to be dedicated here at Karinhall. He was furious the Führer Museum he intended to leave the Reich at his birthplace in Linz was being slighted, a museum to be filled with artworks from all the conquered lands, and which would surpass the Louvre and the National Gallery.

"Only last week I told Speer the drawings for Linz were not grand enough, and then I find you have been rigging or selecting the photographs of art Rosenberg sends me, me, your Führer!" Hitler screamed so loud she actually stepped back from the door.

"But you purged all those lascivious paintings, like the works of Gauguin, from German museums, *mein Führer*. I am only saving you the trouble of that here," Göring protested and his voice actually squeeked.

"Lascivious paintings like the ones in this room that you bring a beautiful woman to see? You want someone who knows Il Duce, as the Countess Valente no doubt does, to tell him the Führer's men have great mansions full of fat, nude women, do you? I hate fat people and here you stuff yourself at these banquets, Göring! From now on, I see *all* the photographs of *all* the art before it leaves Paris, Rome, anyplace, for Berlin!" Hitler shouted. Lesley gasped. Rome! They were planning on stripping Rome of more than its human resources then, and that meant they must be planning to control Mussolini more than they already did somehow!

"All right, all right, *mein Führer*, I was only trying to relieve you of some of the more plebeian duties, which your hands and genius should not have to touch," Göring said placatingly. "The other paintings, perhaps one hundred million reichsmarks' worth, are being stored for you in the caves and salt mines near Salzburg where we had planned to hide our gold and other things—"

Suddenly, she was seized from behind, one iron arm locking about her arms and waist and one hand clamping over her mouth. Lifted bodily, her feet off the floor, she was hauled two doors away into a sort of sitting lounge. Her captor yanked her around and shoved her back against the wall, a hand pressed hard against her mouth while her heart nearly pounded out of her chest.

Max! Max, looking furious and yet triumphant!

"Do you know what could happen to you now, you little fool? Do you? I've taken an oath, 'My Duty is My Honor,' and I find you like this," he hissed, his face distorted with rage, spittle flecking his lips. "And you obviously understand German well enough and lied to me about that, too!"

He held her so she couldn't move, couldn't speak. Her entire body trembled with fear and fury as she fought to calm herself.

"I believe, at least, I can dispense with the gentlemanly role you duped me into playing!" he raved on. "I shall do things my own way from here on out! And I swear that you will cooperate and convince me you enjoy every minute of it, or I'd just as soon turn you over to the Gestapo as a spy. My own little Mati Hari," he gloated, his face an obscene leer.

When she struggled to speak, he uncovered her mouth slightly. "I wasn't spying," she gasped, shaking her head defiantly though it bumped the wall. "They were just talking about art, that's all, and I was fascinated by their opinions. My German's very poor. I was ashamed of it until I learned it better to please you. Besides, how would it look for you to turn in the woman you brought here to display furs?" She sucked in another deep breath. "Turn me in for what? Listening to a chat about a few paintings—" She got out before his body and harsh embrace crushed her back against the wall.

But he was suddenly aware he crushed her gown and coiffure, too. He controlled himself enough to let her go, and stood back, wiping her smeared lipstick from the palm of his hand with his monogrammed linen handkerchief as though her mouth had cut him. She still breathed hard, warily watched him as he concentrated on his task. He'd seemed ready to explode a moment ago, but now he had bottled it all up somehow.

"We must return to the salon after you repair your face," he said in a low voice, "quickly, before they come out. And then we will be leaving shortly as we have a long drive back to Berlin. I can apparently trust you here no longer with your clever comments at public gatherings and your eavesdropping at private doors."

She said nothing else. She was glad she'd stood up to him and even took his arm in silent defiance as he escorted her to the powder room and waited for her outside. He did not let her out of his sight for the next hour as Hitler joined the party. Then Max stepped briefly outside to tell the doormen to pull up his Mercedes Benz and to be certain to deliver the fur coats from the showing to the Tempelhof Airport in Berlin by four the next afternoon. Had Max even bade farewell to Hitler and Göring? she wondered, but she had no desire to see any of them again. She steeled herself for a tense hour's ride back to Berlin through the dark forests of February Germany, but she was convinced the worst was past.

"Max, this isn't the way to my hotel. Max!" she protested, trying to stem the panic in her voice.

He'd said little on the drive back into Berlin. Now, he only swung the Mercedes down another dark, quiet residential street lined with snow-burdened mansions and tall, bare trees.

"Max, please take me back to my hotel."

"In the morning to pack. If you've convinced me by then," he clipped out—in German.

"If you're still angry about my having had some German and not telling you," she answered in English, "I explained that."

"But you have explained everything, *meine Liebe*," he said in a mocking voice. "I want no more talk tonight—only very fervent, very passionate convincing that I should trust you and believe you because you care so desperately for me. Then the fact that I have the grounds and the duty to have you questioned by the Gestapo, at the very least, will slip my mind as we make our plans to remain together permanently."

He wheeled sharply into the long, curved driveway to his mansion in the exclusive section of Grünwald where he had proudly showed her about her first afternoon in Berlin. Her stomach knotted even tighter. Though he had not said so, she sensed the mansion was ill-gotten booty from some unfortunate family that had fallen afoul of the Reich. He jerked the Mercedes to a stop under the wide porte cochère and turned to face her at last.

"I will tell you this carefully in English so there will be no more misunderstanding between us, Lesley. I want you to be my lover, my woman, my wife, bear my children, but I will not protect a spy I might have brought here into the Reich's bosom. Either you convince me with your actions tonight—all night—that you came to Germany only because you desire me as a lover and future husband, or you are not going back to

Italy with me tomorrow, and perhaps not at all." His sharp eyes raked her; his face was a stiff mask of barely leashed fury. "And I will see to your Roman shop, your home and people—and I will have your twins if you will not give me my own children from your body, as I would prefer!" he concluded as his voice rose.

She listened to the tirade wide-eyed and aghast. The worst had happened. She should never have attempted such a thing, never have thought she could beat them this way, playing the game by their rules. He was obsessed with her, with control and power over her, with having children, the Reich. He threatened everything she held dear. She felt so cold inside. He gave her no alternative; she had no choice but to believe his fanatical threats were true in this fanatical world she had observed in Hitler's Germany.

She didn't mean for her voice to catch and tremble so. "You know I care for you, Max. I'm not some sort of spy. I did come to Berlin for you, but you said—that you'd give me time."

"Time is up. Either I take you by force before I give you to the Gestapo, or you will seduce me to show your love and will promise to marry me, and I will take you back to Rome tomorrow."

Suddenly it all smacked into her as hard as the icy air when he came around and pulled her out. His hand hard on her elbow, he hustled her into the quiet house, down the mutely lighted hall. They climbed the curve of carpeted staircase with busts of lovely classical women in niches, as nameless and dead as she would be if she failed. She heard no servants, though his butler was no doubt here. It would do no good to scream for help. Stunned with fear, her mind searched desperately for a way to escape his plans for her—abduction, rape, torture, death, marriage. And which of those would really be the worst he could do to her then?

In his sitting room off his big bedroom, she stood as if dazed while he removed her fur coat, but she became alert as he flung it across the chamber onto the Napoleonic divan along the wall. It was as if he'd hit her. Fury flooded her, more fury than she'd ever felt, at his assumption that his power over her could excuse these brutal acts. She pulled away from his touch, whirled about to face him. His eyes pierced her; they looked crystal-blue, as if lighted from within. Damn him, he thrived on her fear!

"We'll begin here with you on one of your fabled Valente furs and move to the bed later—the way I always see you in my dreams," he threatened, his voice a lewd whisper.

"No, Max," she insisted and stood her ground, feet slightly apart despite trembling legs, arms crossed firmly over her breasts. She lifted her chin and met his gaze. Her voice rang out so clear and strong it surprised her, urged her to deeper anger. "You swore to me you would wait if I vowed to wed you." She nearly choked on those last words, but plunged on. "I agree to your proposal of marriage as I agreed to come here to Berlin, in order to help you and your career, enhance your reputation, to please you." Still he looked at her steadily until she took one step back and her knees hit the divan.

"Max, if you do this tonight to me—force me—it will be breaking your vow, and how can I ever believe in anything you represent or want me to share then? Besides, what would the Führer's Gestapo say of your good judgment when they hear you suspected your fiancée of being some sort of professional spy?" She clasped her hands imploringly, then let them drop to her sides. She was lost if she began to plead. "It's only your actions here tonight that can ruin everything for us, Max."

Her tactic of facing him down had obviously surprised him. He stood stock-still. His facial muscles tightened; his voice came softer now; he pointed at her as he said, "Convince me, *meine Liebe.* Convince me all your words were true tonight when I found you eavesdropping on my Führer. I love you, desire you, but I will give you to them unless you become mine now and always! Show me!"

"I said I will marry you, bear your children after this war ends," she lied, "and that's how I show you. If you can't trust my vows and insist on breaking yours, then we're doomed and you might as well hand me over to your Gestapo, as their methods would no doubt be kinder than yours."

Blinking back burning tears at her growing fear that his temper would flare again, she pressed her clasped hands against her clenched stomach muscles, then, when she sensed he hesitated, she lifted her fists to her hips. Control and power, that was it. She had faced him with what he, perhaps all men, understood best. She forced herself to stare straight into those eyes that seemed so like a serpent's until, at last, he blinked.

Yet in that moment it was not Max Dorff she saw in her mind's eyes. Memory tantalized her, baited her with a tiny escape. It was love and sharing she craved, not control and power over a man. In her imagination she no longer stood in this chilly, shadowy mansion in Berlin with all its hovering ghosts and Max Dorff's gleaming eyes on her, but with Paul in that sunny, warm French garret chamber, with its bright splashes of color, where they'd shared their love.

"You will marry me, give me children, be true to me, no one else?" His impassioned question shredded her reveries. "You swear it?"

"True to me"—Cesare's words. She had barely forced herself to nod when he lunged at her. His arms crushed her to him. When his eager lips ravished hers, and he mumbled, almost incoherent in his fervor, that she and the twins were now his forever, she sensed he still expected her to prove her promise by submitting to him. But she would not, could not do that, not when she'd felt real love once. She struggled to pull away from his iron embrace, and then, as if she'd prayed or willed it, someone pounded on the door. A man's voice in the hall! She blinked away tears of gratitude for this moment free of his touch.

Max stepped back, loosed her. He raked a hand through his hair, cursed, then strode away to yank the door open. Limp with relief, she crumpled onto the divan. Even when she sat, her knees trembled and her teeth actually chattered as she heard his butler tell him Göring was on the phone from Karinhall, shouting that they should not have left so early, insisting he return immediately for a meeting. The Führer, it seemed, Lesley grasped in the guttural gush of German, was still furious at something, at Göring, at someone, ranting and raving. A tiny smile touched her bruised lips. Imagine, she thought, saved for once in these hellish times by Satan's very summons.

Max pulled her to her feet, kissed her, grappled her to him a moment, but all that hardly registered on her now. Frenzied in his hurry, he rushed off telling her to use his suite and get a good night's sleep, and that he'd be back in time to make their plane tomorrow, and couldn't wait to formally announce their engagement—

After his footsteps faded, and his muffled auto roared off into the night, she could not stomach even being in his bedroom. Tears tracked jagged paths down her cheeks as the treasured visions of her lost love for Paul, her memories of their passionate engagement to be married, shattered and fled, and she could not get them back.

And all night in Max Dorff's sitting room, she sat bolt upright on a chair by the window watching the blowing, bonelike trees of Berlin hunched over the back gardens. She understood at last the terrible bleak blackness of a single, frightened soldier at his duty, bombarded in his little trench amid a world at war.

❄ ❄ *Chapter Seventeen*

LESLEY WIPED smeared marzipan from the wedding cake off Paolo's mouth while Stella tended to Cati. From the ceiling of the little Roman working-class restaurant, swags of flowers and ribbons over their heads swayed slightly as the lively music, chatter, and revelry swirled around them. Guido had wangled a two-day leave from beleaguered Sicily, and they were celebrating that as well as the wedding reception for the twins' nanny, Lilla Menozzi, who had just married her Italian Air Force sweetheart, Lieutenant Giovanni Batisto.

The Menozzi and Batisto families lifted toasts not only to the bridal pair but to their honored guests, the Valentes, whom they insisted take a special table next to the bridal one. The bridal table stood in the center, with tables arranged around it like spokes in a wheel. Guests stopped repeatedly at the Valente table to say hello; many stared. Yet the family gathering made Lesley so happy she didn't mind. The Valentes and Stella lifted a toast of Chianti to Guido's temporary return after each bridal toast. The day was beastly hot even for the middle of July, at eighty-six degrees with high humidity, but everyone's spirits were high. The twins cavorted, Guido smiled, and Stella was ecstatic. Joy in these terrible times— any celebration—was precious and contagious. And Lesley's mood was buoyed by a private joy: she had not seen Max Dorff for almost a month now, since Berlin had temporarily recalled him.

The Allied forces in the Mediterranean were giving the Axis powers "a real run for their money," as *Libero*'s latest issue had put it. Lesley recognized Paul's brash Yank wording there. She wished Paul and Carla only the best. After all, Paul Kendal had not married the long-suffering Melissa Pearson any more

299

than he had Lesley Westam. Carla Fracci was welcome to him, Lesley had assured herself more than once as the mutual admiration between her and Carla grew. Since she never intended to see him again, she'd decided to trust Carla, who had given her a contact for passing on information she gleaned from the Nazis.

"It's hotter than the hinges of Hades, or at least the Pope's idea of purgatory, in this place," Guido observed and wiped his brow vigorously as Stella tended to Cati's messy face.

"Too hot for a decent honeymoon, too," Stella put in and rolled her eyes at Guido sitting next to her.

He laughed and reached out to tweak a stray tendril of her hair. "I didn't know there was any such thing as a decent honeymoon, Stellina *mia*," he teased, "and I don't intend for mine to be if I ever make it through this hellish war." He stubbed out his cheroot in the ashtray and got to his feet. "I'm going out for a quick breath of air. I'll be back with a whole tray of that good Valente wine and maybe we'll bathe in it instead of drink it."

"And more orangeade for the twins, Guido!" Lesley called after him as she fanned her face with her napkin.

It really was a lovely wedding despite the heat, she told herself. It certainly didn't stop most people from dancing to the music of a little group of mandolin and accordion players who glistened with sweat right along with the revelers. Lilla looked radiant in her traditional white lace gown with scalloped layers that Lesley had had her seamstress make for the girl when she heard Lilla had so little money she intended to wear her only suit. Nor had Lesley realized how poor this neighborhood of San Lorenzo was until she'd seen it today with its nearby freight yards, which, with the Tiburtina Station practically next door, served as the major marshaling area for the southern wartime effort.

With potatoes up to the ridiculous price of ten lire a kilogram and the cost of pasta double, she wished she could help the Menozzis and their neighbors more in the future, but these people had their pride. The family had refused her offer of money for the reception but had allowed her to donate the wine. And as a special surprise, she'd hired the old-fashioned coach and horses for the bride and groom to ride in from the Basilica of San Lorenzo to this *ristorante* and then off into the sunset later for their two-day honeymoon. Lilla had confided to her that she'd seen an old photograph of her parents taking a coach on their wedding day and admitted that it had been her childhood dream. Childhood dreams, Lesley mused, how wonderful!

Her eyes followed the twins, who looked so smashing in their matching navy blue and white pinafore and sailor suit, as they darted off again across the room to play with the other children. She spoke with Stella about the poignancy of wartime weddings, but her mind drifted. Childhood dreams. That lilting little poem her father had taught her as a child bounced through her mind in time with the mandolin music: "Be good, sweet maid, and let who will be clever. Do noble things, not dream them, all day long, and so make Life, and Death, and that For Ever one grand sweet song."

But what had she made of her life now? Granted, the fur empire had survived till now, and she'd managed so far to delay sending any of the garments ordered from Berlin. She had her twins, and Guido was supportive of how she ran things in his absence. But he had been furious she had endangered herself to go to Berlin, until she'd explained she had little choice after Himmler and Dorff had discovered that Valentes had a policy not to export to Germany. And up to now, she'd kept both him and Stella from realizing the extent of her involvement with Max.

But then there were dark blots on her life, hardly the noble things of her father's poem. Trent and Cesare and Carlo were gone forever, and she missed her elderly grandmum terribly. She wondered how that other war, the one for control of her parents' Westam empire, was faring. She lived in constant danger when she passed on anything she overheard from Max to her contact at the laundry two blocks away from Valente's. The twins were without their father and would never know who he really was, although he still lived in the same city. And then she'd vowed to wed Max that terrible night in Berlin when he'd kissed her again and again, and she could hardly stem her revulsion for him or his beloved Reich—

"I said, it's kissing time again, Lesley." Stella's voice and the racket grabbed her back. "See?" She laughed and pointed.

"Lilla and Giovanni were razzing everyone by not kissing right away."

The crowded room rang with the dings of spoons against wine glasses and the cries of *"Bacio! Bacio!"* for the traditional bridal kiss. When the newlyweds at last dramatically complied, everyone whooped and applauded.

Immediately, to tease the couple for their delay, the clatter began again with the cries of *"Bacio! Bacio!"* But in the midst of it all, Lesley froze and strained her ears to listen. There was a whine, a drone outside, a shrill echo of some terrible buried memory she tried to shake off. An instinctive chill raced up her spine. "Stella, do you hear that high-pitched sound?" she shouted to her over the din as Guido raced back toward their table through the crowd, his arms waving, his mouth moving, though they could not catch his words yet.

She grabbed Stella's arm and dragged her to her feet, her eyes searching for the twins in the cluster of young children across the room. She had known what Guido would say before she heard him shouting through the applause after the kiss. Then it was deathly silent in the hot *ristorante* but for Guido's frenzied words. "Planes! Planes, bombers! The sky's full of them! Get down! Everybody down!"

Through the chaos of scrambling, shrieking people, Lesley fought her way across the room and scooped up the twins as they heard the first whistling, splitting cracks nearby. It was so heavy to lift them both together, but she had hold of them as others dove for their children and a woman screamed. Guido was behind her with Stella. He grabbed Cati from her, shoved them all under a table in the corner of the room.

- They huddled there together while the world outside exploded. Germans, she thought, the Germans have turned their Luftwaffe against Italy as they did England, and I have to be strong to survive this again. With one hand grasping little Cati's shoulder, Lesley hunched over her screaming, terrified son to press him to the thin carpet while Guido and Stella arched over Cati, who only whimpered. Guido's arm was around Stella's shaking shoulders, binding her to him. How Lesley wished Paul were here this time with his strong arms to save her from destruction, but that thought was foolish and irrational, as insane as a world gone mad with bombs. But if she died like this, or the children—if she could have told him the twins were his—

The very earth shook her thoughts away, but except for shattering windows their building stood.

"Out, out into the streets in case this place can't withstand another pass!" Guido yelled. He dragged the four of them out from under their table and hurried them into the milling, shouting crowd. Across drifting smoke and plaster dust, Lilla knelt, on the glass-littered floor, her pristine gown smeared red as she cradled Giovanni against her breasts.

"Damned, bloody Germans!" Lesley clipped out and handed Paolo to Stella. "Go on out, and I'll be right there. I've got to help Lilla!"

"Germans?" she heard Guido shout behind her as she pushed her way toward Lilla. "*Madre Maria*, I saw them coming from outside, Lesley—American B-24's. Lines and lines of them—"

Pandemonium writhed around the bride and groom. They clung together. Lilla rocked Giovanni like a child while his cut forehead and chin wept crimson against her gown. Lesley removed the linen waist sash of her pale yellow dress and tied it around Giovanni's head while Lilla crooned to him as if he were a child. Giovanni looked stunned, his eyes blank. Together, she and Lilla helped him to his feet, and Lesley guided them outside to join the others. But at the door Lilla screamed and pulled back.

Outside, chaos reigned. Warehouses just across the line of trees belched a monster fist of black smoke into the sky. Entire buildings looked chewed in half. Pieces of railroad ties littered the street like tossed toothpicks. People ran about screaming. The bridal carriage and horses had been exploded to nothingness just down the way, and whirling spirals of swallows, pigeons, and sparrows wheeled noisily overhead in search of roosts that were no more.

"Come on, Lilla, help Giovanni. We have to go out, come on!" Lesley shouted desperately.

Her eyes searched for her family, then Guido motioned her over into the square. She hurried Lilla and Giovanni toward them. "They're going to make another pass, damn them!" Guido shouted. "This wall's as good as any—" He got out before everything shuddered, shrieked, and vaulted skyward around them again.

It went on incessantly for nearly two hours, row after row of planes spitting their bombs like golden candy drops while the sun was soon blotted out by debris and drifting smoke. An air-raid siren screeched needlessly through churning clouds of dust and the stench of incinerated goods nearby. Bombs on Rome, Lesley kept telling herself as she cuddled first one child and then the other, talking to them even though they could hear nothing over the crashing inferno. She must do what she could to get the children away to Capri where they would be safe from Max, from the war, even if she had to return without them. Bombs on Rome, bombs from Paul's America because they were enemies, all of them—

"That's the all-clear siren!" Guido's voice pierced her thoughts after an eternity of deafening noise. "Lesley, I'm going to see who's hurt and try to help."

She grabbed his arm. "Guido, wait. Let's see if the Bugatti's all right and send Stella home with the twins, and I'll help, too."

They found Cesare's jade and cream Bugatti Royale down the street crushed under the wall of a collapsed building, but there was no time to mourn an auto, however many memories it evoked. While Guido stayed behind in San Lorenzo, Lesley and Stella took the twins and started walking out of the devastation. They had only gone two blocks when a bright red sports car honked and squealed over to the curb. Carla Fracci was waving wildly.

"Countess Valente! Lesley!" She stuck her wind-tousled head out the window. "I've come to help, and it looks as if this is as close as I'm getting unless I walk. Whatever were you doing in this end of town? Are you all right?"

"We were at a wedding, but there are many who need help," Lesley bent down to tell her. "Could my friend borrow your auto to take my twins home and then return for us later? I want to go back to help, too."

They loaded the terrified children in with Stella, waved them off, and started back into the stench of chaos together. Suddenly, the sight reminded Lesley of the scene from that new American film *Gone With the Wind* Gram had wanted her to see at the Alexandra Cinema in Hereford when she was last home in England. Now this Italian war had become America's too, and ahead of her and Carla lay another Atlanta burned, rows of the injured and dead laid out for blocks—but no Rhett Butler to love Scarlett O'Hara anymore. And she remembered what he had said to Scarlett at the end of the film when he was deserting her, something Paul might have said to her when she married Cesare, might even say to her if he were here now and she asked him to forgive her—"Frankly, my dear, I don't give a damn!"

"I thought Gian might come down here too, but I couldn't wait for him," Carla confided as if she'd overheard Lesley's tangled thoughts. She glanced at Lesley and swung her purse while they walked. "He's always looking for stories."

"Perhaps he could write a charming, cheeky article about how jolly well the American bombers did all this—" Lesley's bitter voice caught in her throat as her arm swept the scene.

"I know," Carla said and knitted her fingers together as if she were praying. "But it's Mussolini who's to blame for putting us between the Germans and the Allies. Poor Mother Italy can only hope the Americans and your countrymen will be the heroes in the end. Gian heard something like this might happen here soon. He has his sources, I guess. Evidently some frequent the best hotel bars in town, but he won't take me," she admitted and shook her head as they walked on.

She hadn't meant to tell Lesley that Paul Kendal, even as Gian Donato, wouldn't take her out in public anywhere. She didn't mean to sound as if she and Gian ever disagreed, but it was so hard for her to convince herself sometimes that her handsome, moody American would ever belong totally to her. In the five months since he'd first kissed her, he still insisted on seeing her seldom and erratically for security's sake. It absolutely wore her out sometimes to try to adapt herself to his every mood, especially when he seemed so preoccupied. She always felt it was she who chased and seduced him, though that was well worth any risk.

So she never mentioned her desperate love for him and tried to keep it all calm and light. No, she would say nothing to him about that any more than she would tell him that his old flame, Lesley Valente, really didn't love her Nazi SS man at all but only used him to get information for the Italian partisan underground. She'd vowed secrecy to Lesley and she meant to keep that pact. No need to have Gian admiring Lesley any more than she was afraid he already did—even though he never asked about her or spoke her name unless Carla brought her up first.

But there was one other thing that seeing Lesley's children for the first time today had made her think of as she geared up for the personal battle she intended to wage for Gian Donato. She flexed her fingers open, then nervously drummed them on her purse.

"Lesley, your twins are so darling," Carla told her and darted her a quick sidelong glance. "Such green, green eyes, a miracle really, since Cesare's were so very dark."

At the edge of the bombed area, Lesley turned to face the slender woman. "But my eyes are green," she protested, her voice quiet when Carla's question made her want to wail and cry like the wounded up ahead.

"But grayish, too," Carla said with a shrug. "I mean, didn't you ever study Mendel's laws and all that about genetics at university? Green's very recessive if one parent is brown-eyed, you know," she blurted out.

Lesley's stomach knotted tighter, but she stared down Carla with a defiant thrust of chin. "We've a lot to do here, Carla. Come on," was all she said and hurried away.

"Look, they're lovely twins, that's all I meant," Carla called and ran to keep up with Lesley's long strides.

Rescue and medical work went on for hours. Lesley and Carla almost never looked up or talked to each other all that time. Hospital aid, such as it was with the war usually elsewhere, rushed to San Lorenzo to be both helped and impeded by volunteers and those from other parts of the city searching for family or friends. Lesley saw Guido once with a team of men digging through debris for survivors. Comforting the injured and covering the dead, she and Carla worked side by side despite the new unspoken tension between them.

Pope Pius XII, a native Roman, arrived amid the rubble in his black Mercedes with its yellow and white Vatican flag and walked among the dying, offering a general extreme unction to anyone in the area. The next time Lesley looked up from cradling a cut child still screaming for her missing mother, the old, wrinkled, white-mustachioed King Victor Emmanuel stood down the way. Shouts both loving and hostile greeted him as people recognized the man Il Duce had virtually deposed. Lesley had never seen him before as he now lived a reclusive life in a country villa, but with Mussolini out of town to meet with Hitler at Feltre, he dared return to comfort his people. "Look! Look, little one, your pope and your king have come to see you," she told the dark-eyed child she cuddled, and then turned away to tend yet another.

The next time she looked up from the line of tattered, moaning bodies, Carla stood over her with four buckets. "It's taking the doctors so long to work their way over here. Look, the water lines are broken, but a woman told me there's an old fountain on the next street we could walk to. I've got these buckets."

"All right." Lesley rose stiff-legged to wipe her hands on her skirt. "Some are calling for water. It won't take us long," she agreed and they started off with two buckets each.

"Our friend Gian told me you two were caught in the blitz in London once," Carla said as they turned down a narrow street with debris spilled out into it like crumbled children's sand castles.

Lesley sighed inwardly. Why did Carla, whom she so admired despite everything, insist on speaking of Paul today. It was the one thing that could surely ruin their friendship as well as endanger their truce, Lesley thought.

"Did he?"

"You don't mind I know?" Carla swung her buckets as she walked. "I was curious to know how close you were once, that's all. Look, I love him, Lesley, and I wanted to clear the air between us since we have so much in common and need to work together—since we both admired Cesare even," she implored as they reached the old well.

Jumbled emotions, a deep pain she could not name, kept Lesley from answering as she lifted the first bucket to be filled under the frustratingly slow spigot of the old mottled fountain. What did this woman want from her? How much had Paul told her and why? And those implications about the color of the twins' green eyes earlier. She needed Carla Fracci to be her friend and confidante and not to betray what she knew about Lesley's dealings with Max and his Nazi friends. And yet the words the woman evidently wanted to hear—that she never had or no longer loved Paul Kendal—would not come to her lips even when she willed them to. How much easier it would be in all this chaos of her life if there were no Carla Fracci to love Paul and probe for the truth and want some sort of assurances she was not capable of giving.

Lesley set the first heavy bucket down and bent to lift another to the slow trickle of water before she turned to see that Carla had crossed the street to a building and stood in the skeleton of the blown-out first floor.

"Lesley," Carla called, not turning back, "I'd swear I heard a baby cry somewhere here, but maybe it's a dog or cat. Do you hear it?"

Lesley put the half-filled bucket down. "That building looks shaky, Carla. You know," she observed as she hurried toward her, "I actually think those are railway ties blown out of Tiburtina Station that are caught right above you— Car-laaaa!"

Her own scream reverberated in her ears as the building shuddered, settled, then rumbled apart. The upper floor with the heavy beams cascaded down around Carla, and the patch of floor where she stood tilted and split to suck her into the rubble. Carla's scream joined Lesley's as Lesley dashed forward.

Below what had once been the doorstep or entryway, lying facedown half in, half out of rubble, under a sifting scrim of sawdust and plaster, Carla Fracci was very still. No! Lesley's stunned mind screamed at her. It was as if—right after she had half wished Carla were not in her life or Paul's this happened. No!

"Carla! Carla!" Lesley called down to her, then squinted up at the corner section of the roof, which still held. Through the settling dust of debris, it seemed to teeter against the moving, puffy smoke and clouds in the blue sky. She tore her eyes away. "Carla!"

Before she could think, before anything else could fall, she half scrambled, half slid down beside Carla, while the broken pile rumbled in a miniature avalanche after her. One of Carla's legs and one arm were buried. Lesley felt for a pulse at her neck. Still alive!

She dug with both hands like a madwoman to free her, resting only when she dislodged stones to start a new, threatening cascade. "Carla! Carla, please, we've got to get out of here now. Now! Carla!"

She dragged Carla out, scraped, bruised. She was desperate to keep her own footing on the ramp of rubble and not to slide lower into what had been the cellar. She pulled her to her knees, tugged one inert arm around her neck. "My leg, my leg," Carla moaned.

"Sorry, but you must help me get us up, out of here, Carla," Lesley gasped. "Everything's shifting. You must help!"

"I can't. My leg! You wouldn't leave me because of what I said about Paul—" She mumbled and fainted.

"Help! Can anyone hear me?" Lesley screamed. "Down here! Help us!" Blast it, had everyone run over to the next street to see the doctors and the pope and king?

Dragging Carla, trying to steady them both to avoid rock-slides, she inched them up the rubble slope until she could grasp the concrete pavement at street level. But when she reached for it, Carla slid away and she had to scramble for her in the tumble of pieces of sharp brick, timber, and stone. Part of a telephone, a scrap of ruffled curtain, geranium leaves, a child's top rattled by in the pile. If Carla had heard a child or dog here, it cried no more. Foothold by tenuous foothold, she lugged Carla and herself up high enough in the shifting pile that she could roll them out onto the battered pavement. Then trembling, gasping, she dragged her out into the middle of the 'street and scrambled for a bucket of water to wash the ghostly white dust and red blood from Carla's pale face. Finally, her legs steadied under her enough that she could run for help. She turned back only once to watch in horror as the rest of the building where they could have been entombed together crashed inward, until there was nothing left but a mounded pile of broken stone topped by blasted railroad ties the bombs had blown a block away.

The statistics of the July 19, 1943, Allied daylight raid on San Lorenzo were appalling: five hundred bombers, one thousand tons of bombs, thousands of civilians killed or injured, despite the fact they had nearly obliterated their target of the Italian marshaling yards. Yet barely one week later, the Italians put those griefs behind them to celebrate their greatest joy since before the war. Mussolini had been toppled by the voice of his Fascist Grand Council, including his own son-in-law Ciano!

Wildly, that moonlit Sunday night Italians took to the streets with shouts of *"Viva la pace!"* Dancelines snaked their way through the squares, and torches and fireworks lit up the night despite blackout restrictions. Screaming crowds tore their wartime ration books to fluttering confetti. What did it matter if the new government was led by old General Badoglio at the weak king's request, with promises of help from the Allies? What difference that Badoglio and the king soon fled south to the protection of those Allies who had only last week bombed Rome? Surely, this meant the end of the war for the Italians now that Rome was declared an open city!

Lesley rejoiced too in her own heart, glad Il Duce, who worshiped and misused his power, had lost it at last. It was some compensation for Cesare's death and Mussolini's callous treatment of her and the Valentes. But to Lesley, who watched the antics of frenetic Romans in the square below her town house windows, the scene reminded her of Il Duce's gatherings in the old days. Only now, the masses threw paint on his palace and tossed weeks' worth of rations of tomatoes against his pictures before burning them in a blazing bonfire while others chipped the hated fasces carvings off official buildings. As of yet, she thought, no one else stood across the way in the balcony of the Palazzo Venezia to tell the people what they must do.

But she knew the Germans, indeed, knew them rather too well. It would not be long before the beguiled crowds and their rapturous joy would be crushed to silence and submission once more by the roar of Nazi war machinery and the tread of jackboots she had heard in Berlin. And she, who had vowed to Max to share his future, must find some way to ruin his future. For herself and her beloved, adopted Eternal City of Rome, she knew that the worst was yet to come.

* * *

Stella Sollo dashed next door to Valente's, yelling for Lesley all the way up the steps to the work area. Sewing machines halted, eyes looked up, quick hands paused. Only the fur tumbler thumped on as Stella darted into Lesley's office and slammed the door behind her.

"Lesley. Madame Justine." Stella halted breathless and shook her head in disbelief as she spoke. "Mother just heard on the wireless and phoned me. The Germans are not only occupying the city today but Dollman and Kesslering have allowed a twenty-four-hour sack to soften everyone up and gather weapons and supplies."

Lesley's shoulders slumped as she stood bent over her drawing board. The Germans here permanently and who knew for how long, she thought. But at least she'd already hidden the Valente art collection in the wine cellar and garage of the town house. The very worst had happened, Max would be here perhaps full-time, and she had not yet found a way to get the twins to Capri. The Allies were in Sicily now and the Italian troops had been forced to draw back so far that the Americans held the approaches to Capri. Lately, Max had been here so erratically she was never certain when she could grab a day or two to get away to take the twins, and she had no idea what he would do to her when he found out they were gone. She'd been managing to hold off Max while he came and went, ever since she'd promised to marry him after the war. Still, she prayed for all this to end. She would find a way to deal with Max Dorff when the time came.

Her voice was very calm. "All right, Stella, I think we can agree these shops on the Via Condotti will be targeted, at least by Hitler's blasted storm troopers, who'll be wanting gifts for their mothers and sweethearts." Her mind and words raced. "Nip back over and put out only goods you think you can spare—you can't have too many empty shelves if the soldiers come crashing in on you. Who knows what the barbarians will do if they find nothing. Don't be over there when they come, a young girl shouldn't face them alone!" she warned as Madame nodded her agreement. "You come back over here or hide somewhere."

"But I'll have to protect the store!" Stella protested, fists clenched in her skirt. "What if they burn it?"

Lesley put her hands on the girl's shoulders reassuringly. "The Nazis don't intend to rule over seven hills of blackened rubble. Go on, hurry, and then get out!" she urged and gently pushed Stella toward the door.

Madame hovered at her elbow as Lesley followed Stella out. In the workroom the others waited, their faces stiff with fear. "Now listen, all of you," Lesley announced. "Word is that in the next few hours the Nazis are going to run amok through Rome. I'm asking each of you to go home straightaway and take with you and hide one Valente garment. We'll wrap them in muslin so it looks as if you're carrying soiled laundry. If you do not wish to do this, of course I'll understand. Do not come into work tomorrow unless you are certain things have returned somewhat to normal." She held up her hands to quiet the buzz of apprehension. "I assure you, ladies, the Germans need Rome more or less in one piece to fight off the Allies' encroachment from the south. I'm sorry the furs are so bulky. Only take what you believe you can manage."

"But what of all the rest of the coats and pelts, Countess?" Anna Paro, a seamstress, called out from behind her sewing machine. "What will you do with all those?"

"I'll have to put out a few for the bloody beasts, and the rest—I'll manage," she told them. Despite the fact she knew many of her workers had been puzzled and ashamed because she'd gone to Berlin to show Valente furs, she was touched to see how each willingly crammed what she could into parcels or made up a laundry sack and hurried out.

"Yes, and what will we do later?" Madame scolded from one step behind as Lesley dashed back into her office.

"I need your help now, not later! Come on!" Lesley urged, as she felt Madame's sharp eyes on her back.

It was only Madame, as far as she knew, who so far had actually seen her with Max. Lesley longed to tell her and the others the truth of her apparent relationship with him, since it was threatening her reputation, but she couldn't take that risk. Only Carla Fracci, recovering from her broken leg, arm, and ribs, knew. Lesley's saving her life had brought them closer, but there was still tension between them over Paul.

"You think your friendship with that blond spider will save all the rest of the furs we have here?" Madame's shrill voice ranted at her as Lesley desperately stripped half-finished coats from the mannequins.

"No, Madame, I expect no favors from the Germans. I am going to put the pelts we haven't worked yet, in case they find our storage area, into what's left of our muslin and get them to a laundry two blocks away from here on the *vicolo* behind the Via della Croce. Then, if the bloody Nazis insist on going through sacks of dirty clothes, I guess we'll lose them and have no Countess Valente line next year. Now, will you help me or not?"

The renewed admiration in Madame's magnified eyes warmed her as they quickly bundled up the pelts in rolls of muslin and carted them in four fast, exhausting runs down the back alley to the laundry, where Lesley knew her underground contact would also spread the word. Storm troopers walked with astonishment through the wide-open doors of Sollo's Fine Leather Goods and Valente di Roma that afternoon, when most barred shop doors had to be battered down. When they delightedly carted off a small number of items for loved ones back in Berlin, Lesley only added it silently to the list of wrongs for which, one day soon, she would help to make them all pay.

It was almost eight and nearly dark when Lesley closed up the shop, dropped Madame and Stella at their doors in her little auto, and started home. German trucks and tanks blocked many streets. Already soldiers cluttered the curbs while military police every block or so stopped the little teal-blue Alfa Romeo convertible Cesare had bought for her the day she had given birth to the twins. Despite the clinging heat of the day, she had the canvas top up and all the windows, too. Only about a mile from the town house, a burly soldier stepped directly in front of her and motioned her to halt. Immediately, three others surrounded her. She was so exhausted, frustrated, and on edge she was tempted to bump them right out of her way, but she dared not.

"Yes, what is it?" she asked in German, hoping that would make them pass her on. Grudgingly, when the burly soldier motioned her to do so, she rolled her window down partway.

"Orders to requisition all civilian vehicles," the gruff voice under the helmet answered with barely a nod to acknowledge that she spoke his language.

"This is my private motorcar and I haven't broken any laws."

The man actually snickered; she could smell alcohol on his breath. "The Reich makes all the law here now, *Fräulein*. But we will be happy to drop you at your home, the four of us," he said and shot his big arm in her window to grab at her door handle to unlock the auto. He yanked the door open even as she snatched her purse and the bundle of sables on the seat beside her, darted over to the other side, and got out away from them. Blast him, but she had the boot of the auto full of fur garments they would find! She thought of using Dollman's name or even Max's, but she was afraid they might deliver her to them. Relieved all they wanted was the auto, she cursed them under her breath anyway and stood with tears in her eyes as they piled in and roared off down the Via del Corso.

With the bundle of two nearly finished golden sable coats in her arms, she started her long trudge toward home, stepping into doorstoops or darting around corners if she saw another noisy group of soldiers approaching. Finally, limping from blisters, furious at today's events, she used her key and entered the town house. She breathed a sigh when everything looked untouched inside—only to see Max Dorff appear at the door of Cesare's study.

"*Meine Liebe*, I've been so worried! Are you all right?" he demanded and rushed toward her.

She knew she should look happy to see him after nearly five weeks apart. His usually stern face lit up like a candle, but she couldn't stem her anger. "I'm fine, jolly fine," she muttered, and shook his hands off her shoulders. "No matter that the soldiers of your illustrious Third Reich have looted half my stock and just stolen my auto." Her voice turned mocking. "Are they coming soon for the brandy and books in my husband's library? Perhaps you've been packing them up already?"

His face fell. "I'm sorry, my Lesley, really. Of course you're upset, but they have orders only to arrest political dissidents, so you're quite safe. I stopped by the shop just now and you had gone. These city-wide maneuvers are only for one day and are intended to settle everyone in for the duration." He took the bundles from her tired arms and put them on the end of the closest settee. "*Liebe*, aren't you glad to see me?" He lifted her chin with one finger. "Despite your little maid Lilla's protests, I helped tuck the twins in, and they're as beautiful and wonderful as ever."

Her gaze collided with his. So they were still at that impasse, unspoken, but just as understood as the fact that the Germans could abscond with anything here in Rome that took their fancy today. "I—yes. Of course I'm glad to see you, Max, but I'm so exhausted and upset with everything. I just can't tell you how it's been—" she began and crumpled onto the settee to hide her face in her hands.

Tears wracked her at the injustice and the cruelty of it all. She felt so alone, so on the edge of disaster. She had to get the twins to Capri, to Lucia Belli's family, who farmed the land above the villa. She only hoped they would take them in. Attempts to get a travel pass out of the city and to Capri might be futile. As of tonight, she had no transportation but two old sports autos and no petrol-rationing coupons for them. Somehow she must find a way not only to evacuate the twins but try to escape any sort of a private reunion with Max tonight. Tucked them in! Max Dorff, with his hands sticky with the blood of so many, had tucked her children in bed!

"Lesley, *Liebe*," he whispered and sat beside her to hold her as she knew he would. She cried against his tunic, darkening its ebony to sleek sable, her cheek pressed to his cold medals to stall for time. But as he shifted closer to her, the leather holster with his Luger pressed into her hip and she pulled away.

Sniffing, she accepted the handkerchief he extended. "I love to comfort you, Lesley. You need me very much, you know, and it angers me when you struggle so against the inevitable between us. You and I are fated. After all this is over, when the Reich rules Europe, everything will be perfect for us, you'll see," he vowed, his face so earnest.

"I'm just—I'm tired, Max." Under his steady gaze, she dabbed at her slick cheeks. "It's only that losing the furs and

the auto today reminded me of when I came to Rome and some
Fascists on the train beat me and took a sable coat, my money,
my ring, luggage."

He pulled her into his arms again to kiss her slowly, then
released her. "I'll try to trace your blue Alfa when I can, the
furs too if you'll just trust me. And who was this who took
your sable and the rest?" Just to talk, to keep him from kissing
her again, she told him the whole story of Lidia Comi and her
daughter Daniela luring her off the train and the beating by the
two men.

"So perhaps that little family of thieves came to Rome, eh?"
he asked as if to comfort a child. "My poor *Liebe*, just leave
everything to me—everything. Come in now and we'll talk,
get caught up on all this time apart, hm?"

She stood with him, nodded. But at the door to Cesare's
study, she hesitated. Max looked all wrong here. He had no
more right to be in her house than the German brigands had to
be in Rome. He darkened the room, closed her in as if she were
in a black box from which there was no escape.

But she steadied her shoulders and lifted her chin. After all,
what should one expect but fear and hardships and losses in a
full-scale war against one's enemies?

"You have taken down most of your wonderful artwork in
the town house," he observed as he indicated they should sit on
the couch. "Such a clever lady, considering everything that's
happening."

She looked straight into his eyes. He still had never realized
everything she'd overheard Hitler and Göring discuss about the
intended rape of Italy's art that night at Karinhall, nor that
she'd passed that knowledge on to the Italian underground as
she had other things since. She forced herself to sit casually,
one arm slung along the back of the deep leather couch, one
tired leg curled under her before she answered. "With the
wretched American bombings, I could hardly risk leaving them
on the walls, Max."

His gaze narrowed almost imperceptibly and the skin
tightened around his mouth as he looked away. "But at least
you left my favorite here over the hearth. You know, *Liebe*,"
he told her as he leaned forward and she noted he had indeed
helped himself to Cesare's brandy, "the Valente collection

you're saving for us will be perfect in our Grünwald mansion someday soon. But I hope you wouldn't mind if I take this portrait of you and our twins back with me next time I go and hang it over our bed until we are all together as a family at last." He turned to her, his slitted eyes a challenge, waiting, just waiting for what she would say in this perpetual battle they waged between them.

She fought back her impulse to burst into tears again. She nodded and set her lips in a little smile. "A lovely idea. I should have thought of it. Pour me a brandy too, won't you, and then tell me everything you've been doing and how soon I'm going to have to do without you here again."

❧ ❧ *Chapter Eighteen*

LESLEY HAD NEVER been so hurried or desperate. She glanced behind her every half block and walked so fast when she was certain no one was looking that she soon had a stitch in her side. Nervously, she stroked loose tendrils of her hair upward under the oversized beret of Guido's she wore. No need to have her distinctive hair draw attention or be remembered in the places she was going today. She knew it was not wise to be out here on the streets of Rome alone like this, since the Germans were forever trying to pick up women and careening along in pilfered autos or armored trucks with mounted machine guns, but she had absolutely no choice. Max was gone for four days. In that time, she had to save the twins, and the only way left to do that was to find Paul Kendal.

Looking both ways as she crossed the street, she pulled the navy jacket of her old Chanel suit closer. The mid-September breeze blew the pleated skirt about her legs as she mounted the steps of the elegant *fin de siècle* Eden Hotel near the entrance to the Borghese Gardens. With a quick glance around the sparsely peopled lobby, she strode directly for the lift. "Penthouse Restaurant and Bar," she told the hollow-eyed young woman who worked the mechanism, and their little cage rose slowly above the lobby. She tried to breathe more quietly, relieved the woman did not stare or make conversation.

She'd already been to the Hassler Hotel Restaurant and Bar. She had recalled Carla telling her that Paul got his information frequenting the best hotel bars. If she didn't locate him today without arousing suspicion, there were only three days left to save the twins. Max had become adamant that Cati and Paolo be sent to Berlin, away from American bombing, to await the end of the war when he and Lesley could join them there.

Hidden on Capri, they would be safe. The Americans controlled the island and evidently used it for a rest and relaxation retreat. But she was terrified because she had no way to get them there but to ask Paul.

Her eyes searched the bar as she chatted with the barkeep, but he did not know a Gian Donato. Soon, she was on the street again heading for the Quirinale, the next hotel bar on her list. She perused its quiet reach of lobby and side salons, silently cursing the Nazis for their theft of her little auto, their brutal petrol rationing, their ban on taxis and bicycles, after Italians had fired on the Germans and then sped away. Even streetcars were halted at times when electricity was sporadically cut off, and riding them, one too often had to hand over the mass of new identity cards for inspection. In her purse clamped under her arm she carried her residency permit, ration card, ID card with photo, business card, and Rome travel permit. Without these, arrest would be certain if she were stopped.

Disappointed again at this barkeep's not knowing Gian Donato even when she described him, she went out the back door next to the Teatro dell' Opera where Cesare had brought her so often when Rome had belonged to Romans. In front of the impressive building she saw two Nazi soldiers, their faces split by grins, both so boyish and awed they reminded her of Carlo when she had first known him. They stood taking pictures of each other with a camera, the very thing, along with wireless radios, the Germans had forbidden the Italians to possess. When one of the young men saw her, he motioned to her either to take their picture or get in the photo with them, but she dared to shake her head and hurry on.

If she didn't find Paul by this evening when she'd have to be in by nine o'clock curfew, she would have no choice but to go to Carla Fracci first thing tomorrow morning and explain to her why she needed him. Surely Carla would understand and help. Yet she wanted to avoid anyone else knowing, especially Carla if she could. Despite Lesley's exhaustion and the return of the stitch in her side, she quickened her pace toward the one restaurant she had on her list, the luxurious Osteria dell' Orso. Paul Kendal had always liked the best. Hadn't he gravitated to the Savoy and Ritz in London, the George V in Paris, and the Gritti in Venice? And would this Gian Donato persona she did not know at all be of such a very different stripe, however much Paul tried to hide behind him?

By now it was getting late enough that the places she visited were full of patrons eager for a drink or dinner before curfew, both rich Italians and the Germans, though in their separate clusters. Rationing and hard times in Rome hardly stopped the bar and restaurant businesses, which got their liquor and food who knew where. It reminded her she had meant to ask Max if he knew any outlets for food besides the black markets or rationing suppliers. Lilla's family and neighbors in bombed-out San Lorenzo were desperate for food, and she thought if she could only get some, they would accept that from her even though they would not take her money.

In the Osteria Blue Bar where she and Cesare had enjoyed many cocktails before many meals, the jovial barkeep, Felix, still hummed while he polished his tumblers and goblets. He recognized her instantly—and he knew Gian Donato, and to keep his voice down, too. "Sure, sure, drinks Scotch and soda, rare for a Milanese," Felix told her quietly with a hint of an inscrutable smile, like a shadow of his exuberant personality she recalled from the old days. "But he hasn't been in for a week or so. Shopping for some books in person, Countess Valente?"

Lesley was so intent, she didn't even return his smile. "No—he's a friend of my nephew's, that's all."

"So, I could keep a message in my head for his ears only."

"No, it's not that important, though if he comes in today or tomorrow, you might mention Guido Valente would like to see him." She wondered for a moment if Paul even knew where they lived in Rome, but she dared not go into that. "You don't by chance know anyplace else *il signor* Donato gets his Scotch and sodas, do you?" she asked as she turned to go, ignoring the offer of a drink from the well-attired man sitting in the corner seat at the bar.

"Try my friend Pietro's place at the Grand, you know, down the steps with the piano player," he whispered and, for some reason, even winked.

It was nearly eight-thirty, a half hour before she should be off the streets, when she arrived, panting and perspiring, at the Grand Hotel just off the Piazza della Republica. The muscles in her legs ached badly. She scolded herself for not coming here earlier. The Grand with its Renaissance-palace façade was one of the great hotels of Europe along with Rome's Excelsior. The Germans had recognized that and had taken the Excelsior over months ago as their headquarters. It was where Max always stayed. She smoothed her hair up under her beret again, wishing she had not chosen this old suit. She went in under the impressive arched entrance with its carved loggias and cornices and traversed the thick Oriental carpets laid across veined marble floors. Piano music drifted to her as she strode across the expanse of lobby with its brocade couches and ottomans, malachite tables and fringed lampshades, with just a few guests waiting or chatting. She hurried down the few steps to the piano bar Felix had mentioned. Pietro, he had said: the name of the barkeep here was Pietro.

Slowly her eyes adjusted to take in the low cedar ceiling, the profusion of potted palms, the round, marble-topped tables and maroon velvet banquettes surrounding the grand piano. Mostly men here, none in uniform, a few women. The brass rail on the polished mahogany bar and the suspended glassware like a second crystal ceiling gleamed at her through drifting cigarette smoke.

And then she saw him.

Her insides tilted. She grasped her purse so tightly to her she felt it bend. Tears burned her eyes. He was here and he would help her. He would understand. He looked so solid, so—real. He was speaking to the barkeep and smiling, but then, through the smoke, his green eyes lifted.

His big head jerked up. He frowned, throwing his eyes in shadow. He'd let his hair grow a bit longer; his mustache was shaggier to give him a bit of a roué look, but very Italian. Even in the dim light, she could see the outline of his beard. He looked thinner too, his high cheekbones slightly more pronounced, the cleft in his chin more visible. So much change in the eight months since she'd last seen him in Carla's garden. Before she even moved closer, he stood, put some money on the bar, and came toward her, holding his drink and cigarette. He wore dark brown slacks and jacket over a stark white shirt with no tie but a brown smoker's sweater. Quickly, she composed what she'd meant to say, opened her mouth to speak. The pianist began another slow, moody piece as Paul went right by her without a look, out and up the steps.

She gasped and darted after him. She hadn't expected this. Yes, that he'd be surprised, even angry—she was prepared to handle that. But not that he would just ignore her. "Gian. Gian, please!" she whispered as she chased him up the steps.

He turned back, towering above her with the brighter lights of the lobby entrance gilding his large silhouette. "Sh!" he said. "Up here, not there."

Breathing easier, she followed him at a distance to the corner of the lobby with its now barren reading racks and spindles empty of newspapers. So far, the Nazis had done a thorough job of purging all the news, and most papers had not yet started up again. It almost made her long for the days when there were journals on every corner in London, whatever tripe they printed. He seated himself in an empty alcove and stared at her as she approached on trembling legs, then sat, of necessity, to keep their voices quiet, on the very next cushion of the deep umber leather couch.

"I know this is a surprise, Gian." How strange to use that name, she thought, the name Carla called him all the time. "I need help desperately so I've been looking in all the hotels today and—"

"Then why didn't you just go to the Excelsior where your friends hang out?" he cut in harshly.

Tears stung her eyes but she blinked them back. He knew about her and Max, knew the latest about the Germans, probably so he could write about it for the Americans, who were somehow both the enemy and the best friend Italy could now hope for. She gripped her purse tighter in her lap. "I wouldn't ask for myself, you must know that. Gian—Paul," she pleaded, "I need help to get my children away to Capri where we have a villa and friends. The Americans hold the island now. It's not just the bombs here, though that's bad enough. Please. They—they've been threatened."

He sat forward now, his drink untouched, the ash on his unsmoked cigarette dangling to a silver snake that fell unnoticed to the carpet. "How? By whom?"

She told him about Himmler's *Lebensborn*, told him she'd exhausted other means to get them safely away after some high-up Germans suggested the twins be sent to Berlin for safekeeping. She explained about the Belli family with whom she could hide them on Capri. If she absolutely had to, if he refused, she was prepared to tell him the twins were his, but she couldn't bear to face all that except as a last resort. She did not tell him she had agreed to marry Max Dorff, nor about her spying, nor how very, very much she wanted to just fall into his arms and cry out the truth of everything to him and have him take these terrible burdens from her shoulders.

His body and face tensed even more as she spoke. "For two innocent children, I'll see if there's anything I can do," he said at last and lit another cigarette.

She heaved a sigh of relief. "It has to be as soon as possible."

"You never ask much, do you, Countess?" His voice cracked like a whip. "The Allies are hunkered down just south of Naples and hold Capri while the Germans are busy fortifying the road we'd have to take between here and there, and they're both lobbing mortars and bombs at each other when the mood hits them."

Tears trembled on her lashes again. "I heard. I can't help it."

"Can you get money? Bribes still go a long way, and I don't mean for me."

"Yes. Anything for the twins."

"Lucky twins. I'm pleased to assume they come before the fur empire, then," he said, giving her another hard look.

Her temper flared at the cruel remark, but he had said he'd help. "Of course they do—my Valente family," she finished lamely and looked away for the first time.

"I'll try, I said." He glanced at his watch. "And now, I want you to hurry home, take the smaller streets, and don't look back. I'll be just behind to make sure you get there even though you won't see me. Go on. It's nearly nine."

So that was it between them. He'd said he would help and she believed him. She hurried out, feeling his angry eyes still on her. But she was so grateful already, felt so safe for once on Rome's occupied streets. And she didn't see him, not even when she peered back before she ducked into the town house through the servants' entrance. She only hoped she'd see him soon.

* * *

Paul came at seven the next morning, then returned at ten in a Nazi private's uniform, which startled her at first, to collect them. In a rusted, ramshackle old Fiat, they headed south out of Rome along the Appian Way. She was relieved he'd barely looked at Cati and Paolo as she'd hurriedly piled them into the tiny backseat with a few favorite toys and a change of warm, informal clothes he'd insisted on for all of them. At least she'd evidently been right to assume Carla would never say a thing to him of her obvious suspicions about the twins' paternity. Besides, they said parents were often the last to be able to recognize their offsprings' resemblance to them; she hoped so.

"Wherever did you get that horrible German uniform?" she inquired as they left the city behind.

"I thought it would make you feel right at home," he said.

"Please, Paul," she whispered. "The children take everything in."

"Do they?" He shot her a quick look, then snapped his head back to face straight ahead. "Better than adults, then. Let's just say the less you know about what I've had to do to get us to Capri, the better off you are."

"Mama, you said his name is Gian. Is it Gian Paul?" Cati's voice surprised them from the backseat. They exchanged a guilty glance. Lesley realized Paul was surprised the twins spoke English as well as Italian.

"It's just like my name, too," Paolo piped up.

"Now listen," Lesley remonstrated and craned her neck back to look at the two of them. "I told you Gian is our friend and he's taking us to Capri and we might have to play some pretend games along the way. But you are going to have to be very quiet and do exactly what Mama says, remember? Oh no, there's a checkpoint up ahead already," she moaned when she turned back around. "Now, remember, you two, you're not to say one word."

As they had hastily planned for this first leg of their flight, Paul would be a German chauffeur driving a requisitioned Italian auto to take a visiting German baroness and her children to a villa outside Rome. Since his German was miserable, he would get a coughing jag when questioned and Lesley would do the fast talking. Soon, their ploy and the forged passes Paul brought had worked twice, getting them as far as Cisterna, but each time they were stopped, Lesley's heart nearly stopped until they were passed on.

"I like those guns back there. Bang! Bang!" Paolo exploded from the backseat after over an hour of enforced silence.

"Those are called ack-ack guns, Paolo," Paul told him before Lesley could shush her son. "But they hurt people and they're not toys."

Lesley shifted in her seat. How desperately Paolo, Cati too, needed a father. Guido had made an effort since Cesare's death, but he was gone so much, and then Guido was always Guido, sharp-tongued and too subtle for children to understand half the time. What a mess she'd made of things. How she detested herself sometimes for not telling Paul they were his. She glanced back at the two of them trying to be so good and brave, not quite believing this was all the great game their mum had made it out to be. Carla had been so right, and she'd always known it: they had Paul's eyes. Besides, Cati had a softer, more feminine version of his chin. Blast it, but all this was so unreal! Danger lurked on each kilometer of this journey and yet she was somehow happy. But for her lie to Paul she felt almost at peace inside for the first time in months, years. She mustn't ever let him know his presence did this to her. She mustn't ever let him know so many things.

Paul tried to keep his eyes only on the road, but they kept straying to the rearview and side mirrors where he could glimpse the children. Alert, healthy, wide-eyed, beautiful. He was pleased she was teaching them English as well as Italian. He'd meant for this to be all business to him, just another humanitarian mission like the other things he was willing to risk his life for in this war. Just like getting his news reports out of enemy Rome and hoping they served to inform the American military what was going on as well as the other readers of his newspaper columns. Doing this for two children who needed help because their selfish, spoiled, strong-willed mother had gotten herself in over her head with the Nazis in order to protect and promote her damned Valente fur empire, he told himself, was just like his donating all his proceeds from *Lions Roar* to the American War Bond fund. It was the same thing as taking a chance with his life to gather information for his war novel on Italy, *To Have and Hold*, which had been smuggled out to the U.S. over a month ago. He wasn't, he assured himself again fiercely, even doing this for Lesley for old time's sake, or for Lady Sarah, whom he still respected. It was only for the children, maybe even, now that he'd seen them, because they reminded him so much of the way he and his sister, Kaye, looked as kids.

Damn, but there was another big checkpoint up ahead and he knew they had been pushing their luck to get even this far. At the next little crossroads with the sign to Sperlonga, he veered sharply off the Appian Way.

"Whatever are you doing?" Lesley demanded and grabbed for the dashboard to keep from flying into him.

"Hold tight, everybody!" he ordered. "Countess, it's just my instincts tell me we'd better catch our slow boat to China earlier than I thought. I'd hoped to get us clear to Formia or Mondragone before we left the Appia to find a boat to rent, but that's a fortress they're building up there. And no German baroness, however beautifully she smiles at these Huns, is going to charm her way through it."

They jolted along hairpin roads until they came to the sea, got through one more German roadblock, and pulled up near the fishing docks of sleepy Sperlonga by the Tyrrhenian shore exactly at noon. Paul took the money she'd brought and went shopping for a boat while she fed the children and waited. The sea looked rough to her today for mid-September but, as often happened at Capri too, the storm clouds seemed to cluster only on the distant horizon. Some thirty miles by sea to Capri from here, Paul had said. Open, choppy sea with Germans along the shore and the occasional American or Luftwaffe planes in the air.

He was back in twenty minutes. "All right, let's go, guys. We're going for a ride in a real fishing boat!" He took Paolo's hand and both small canvas suitcases under his other arm while she gathered her things and led Cati. "The old woman in that corner house is going to hide the Fiat until we return, Lesley. Bring the food, but nobody eats until we see how rough it is out there."

"But we already did!" Cati told him, bug-eyed, and Paul's gaze met Lesley's guilty stare.

"Well, that's all right," he assured them with a cryptic look at Lesley over their heads. "Mama always knows best."

The sea troughs churned deep green to black, and the spray soon soaked them all in the little boat piloted by a one-legged skipper, but no one got sick. Still, after they had all taken turns changing to warmer clothes, it was rough enough that Paul insisted the twins stay inside the little cabin with Lesley. He stood at the prow, his legs spread, his big hands on the wooden rail, looking straight ahead, his wet hair glistening in the spray. Perhaps he thrived on danger, she thought as she watched him through the foam- and salt-sprayed window. Paul Kendal always loved the challenge of getting off the routine paths of life. She stood there a long time, until the twins dozed under a blanket on the single wooden pallet, but when she heard strange sounds, she hurried outside.

"Is that shooting?" she asked as she walked rubber-legged toward him on the small spray-slick deck.

"Mortar fire or smoke shells to cover whatever they're doing, I suppose," he told her and let go of her arm as soon as she had hold of the rail beside him. "Fortunately, it's not aimed at us. It will probably get worse the closer we get to Naples, but I'm just hoping the Stukas that have been going over could care less about a little fishing vessel."

"Stukas?" she gasped, squinting skyward. "Where?"

He scanned the sky even as the *crump, crump* of mortars sounded from the shoreline again, and she watched little cauliflowers of smoke rise, one for each sound. "There, see?" he said and turned her away from the shore with one hand on her shoulder and pointed up at the planes that flew high overhead. "Charming little things with red and white mouths that grin like sharks when you see them close up, but you'd just think they were out for a little pleasure spin at this distance," he observed.

"Where have you seen one close up?" she asked and tasted salt on her lips already.

"One crashed in Berkeley Square in London." He let go of her shoulder and turned back to the mesmerizing frothing roll of foam below their bow as he remembered the scene with the dead Luftwaffe pilot still strapped in his seat. Hell, you couldn't tell what most things in life were really like until you were staring down their throat, just hoping they didn't spit flak or that the bomb bay door wouldn't open to explode you to smithereens. Lesley had done that once to him, and he wasn't going to allow it ever again. Yet his hand tingled where he'd just touched her. His eyes darted to her again while she stared raptly over the waves. He loved to look at her, to be with her still, though they always argued. Today, despite that same oversized beret she'd worn yesterday, the sun gilded her tumbled cognac tresses golden and blushed her cheeks to a rose-petal hue.

He tried to picture Carla, but the impact was never the same, however lovely and appealing she was, however much she tried to please him. She tried too hard to please him, to match his moods, agree with all his ideas, so that he wasn't sure when she was herself. Sometimes it was like gazing in a mirror of his own thoughts and desires. It was impossible to tell what the other person was really like then. He'd once thought Carla had the same strength as his sister, Kaye, as even Lesley, but— Damn, maybe he was just too much of a perfectionist, expected too much of women. If only he could blend some of Lesley's independence and bullheadedness with Carla's jumpy desire to please, he would have what he wanted. The Americans might have demanded and got unconditional surrender terms from the new Italian government, but he would never demand the same thing in a woman. Still, he loved the way Carla Fracci obviously needed and wanted him. After the war, he might even consider marrying her—and having kids as terrific as little Caterina and Paolo.

"Way out here on God's green sea, it's difficult to believe— Stukas and mortar fire or not—that there's really a war going on." Lesley's words broke the long silence between them.

"True. But Churchill's said, 'Whoever holds Rome holds the title deed to Italy,' so it's going to get worse before it gets any better," he warned with another long glance at her. "And I meant to tell you, *Il Messaggero* hit the streets again today, though I recall you detest journals and journalists."

She stared down into the waves sliced by the prow to avoid his hard, assessing stare, but the sea-flash of tumbling wet gems in changing light below them only reminded her more of his eyes. "I don't detest journals and journalists anymore, even after everything," she told him, "though maybe I still distrust them. So what did Rome's biggest daily paper have to say even if it's all filtered through Berlin's black-tinted glasses now?"

"That Hitler's crack parachute troops rescued the illustrious Benito Mussolini from where he was being kept prisoner at a ski resort, and the Germans have named him head of the new Italian Socialist Republic in direct opposition to Badoglio, whom the Allies are propping up."

"What a blasted mess! All of it!"

"Listen, Lesley, I just wanted to mention something else," he said and his big hand touched hers on the rail before he pulled it back. "I know you give Carla money for *Libero* in Cesare's memory, but be careful not to pass on anything else that could ever be linked back to you if it were printed. People who fence-sit in this blasted mess, as you put it, may not survive when the next enemy troops take Rome."

"Meaning that just because I've been seen with a few Germans, your Americans would lock me up or whatever?" she challenged, her voice much too shrill.

He looked away and shrugged exaggeratedly. "Whatever."

"I happen to trust Carla, and I'm surprised you don't," she said. "After all, she's the one who finally convinced me it never could have been you who informed on Cesare and *Libero*, because the office had just been moved again after you visited him. I was very upset then, Paul, and I am sorry for what I thought and said to you about that."

He turned back to her. She was surprised he looked so angry when she'd just apologized. "I know you saved Carla's life and she's grateful, as I am, Lesley, but did you ever stop to think that Carla may not always be in a position to be a good friend to you, especially since she gets so nervous about the past we've shared?"

"That was over long ago, though I can see why you'd want me to stay away from her, so I wouldn't tell her a few things—"

His voice and raised hands cut her off. "That's all on this topic, Lesley, period, or we'll end up shouting and stomping off and there's nowhere to go out here. For a while we need each other for the children's sakes, at least. So you won't lecture me on Carla Fracci, whom I care for deeply, and I won't mention your playing footsies with that blond SS King Kong, all right?"

Shocked he'd obviously seen Max, sputtering with fury, she stalked back inside to sit with the twins until they put into Capri. Two hours later they arrived at Marina Piccolo on the southern shore.

Even on its less populated side, Capri was ringed by American Marine Corps guards who took Paul, Lesley, and the twins into custody the minute they disembarked. Lesley waited with the children in a one-room whitewashed dirt-floor house by the beach that was evidently their command post, while Paul walked outside to talk to the soldiers. It was nearly six and the children were tired, cranky, and didn't understand why they couldn't just go to their big house on the cliff. Eventually, Paul came back in with the Marine corporal right behind him.

"Lesley, only Americans and permanent residents are allowed into Capri for the duration of the conflict, but I convinced the corporal here that wives and children of Americans ought to be included." He lifted his dark brows, then lowered them in some sort of silent message. "I've explained to him what I've been doing in Rome and he's even read *Lions Roar*. So if you'll just sign this release he has here," he went on, and indicated a white sheet of paper in the Marine's hand, "stating that you're Mrs. Kendal and the children are mine, he'll even call for a jeep to drive us up to the villa."

She nearly fell to the swept dirt floor. She felt her face freeze and she feared that words might not come. It had actually come to this, but perhaps Paul thought nothing of it and that was all that truly mattered. If the Marine did not ask the twins if he was indeed their father, it might work. Anything to have them safely on Capri and out of Max Dorff's reaches.

She nodded. She smiled at the soldier and brushed her salt-glazed, wind-ripped hair from her eyes. "I'm not one to want to keep our marriage a secret from anyone but the Nazis, Paul, but you've seen the children so infrequently, just don't ask them to sign any such thing," she said and forced a shaky little laugh. Paul looked relieved. He nodded, his eyes both surprised and proud. But she bit her lower lip hard to stop the tired, foolish tears as she signed on the permit paper that she was Paul Kendal's English wife and that he was the father of her two children who were, therefore, half American.

The next day on Capri was stunningly beautiful, as if to taunt her, for she knew now there would never again be anyplace left on earth she loved which Paul Kendal would not haunt. Westam, London, France, Venice, Rome, now Capri—there would be no refuge, for his presence and her memories of it touched them all.

Lucia Belli's parents had been pleased and honored to be asked to care for the Valente twins during the war, and though Lesley kept dreading the hour of final separation from them tonight, she had left them at the Bellis' sturdy five-room farmhouse above the villa until lunch to get acquainted, while she and Paul crated and hid the villa's paintings in various stone goatsheds above the property. The villa's large household staff, but for Lucia and an old gardener, had already been dispersed, and the twins would be much safer at the Bellis' small farm. Besides, the fewer people who knew where the Titians and Tiepolos were being secreted, the better.

"I saw that little George Stubbs painting you carted clear from England in a room upstairs next to where we took the last one down, Lesley," Paul mumbled through the nails he held in his mouth as he hammered yet another board across the door to a shed on the windy cliff above the sea. "Do you want to store that one somewhere?"

Her eyes instantly misted, but she'd been on the verge of crying all day. She looked away, pretending the wind stung her eyes. "It's survived so much, but I think I'll take it back to Rome with me. It's already come so far," she added half to herself, but he caught her words as he stopped pounding.

"Haven't we all, maybe not always for the best."

She turned back to him. "I can't thank you enough for everything, Paul."

He jammed the nails and hammer into the leather pockets of his work apron. "That's about the same thing you told me the first night we met, Lesley, and where did it get us? And I think I told you someday we'd find a way."

"And now everything's too late." Her voice broke. "Nothing lasts forever."

He pulled her back with a quick hand on her elbow as she walked away. "Maybe not here on earth, but human beings can try for almost forever. If it's the best we have, I say we've got no choice but to pursue that."

She almost swayed against him, pushed by the wind, pulled by the sun on his face. But there was Cesare's ghost still in this place, and her promise to him and the Valentes. There was Guido, the fur empire, all those people depending on her. The children too—and Carla. Max, and this war she had vowed to fight any way she could. She thought, she actually hoped—terribly weak thing that she was whenever he looked at her or touched her like this—that he would kiss her.

But he did not. He only said, "Hell, that's the writer in me coming out again, I guess, the lover of words instead of reality." He shook his wind-mussed head. "Let's go back up to the Bellis' to 'collect' your twins for that little picnic we promised them."

The four of them sat on a huge blanket together on the shelf of tall grass near the ancient, lofty ruins of the Emperor Tiberius's Villa Jovis, where the slant of land and gnarled kabob trees broke the wind enough to warm the autumn sun. As if they were, Paul thought, on a peacetime picnic at Coney Island, safe in the heart of America, he and Lesley laughed as they listened to the children and stuffed themselves with food and lemonade. But the delicious tiny dark oval sea-date clams from the shore below and the leaf-thin layers of *sfogliatelle* filled with custard were hardly the hot dogs and ice cream he longed for, nor were the children his own, the ones he hoped to have someday. And when Lesley finally got to what she'd been dreading—trying to explain to the twins why they were going to have to stay here with the Bellis while she went back to Rome—it tore his heart. The twins clung to her and cried, and he feared the joy of their little imaginary family picnic was ended.

"Now, I told you," Lesley murmured to them after they were quiet again, "that there are some quite wretched things in this war and we will all have to be very brave, indeed. At the

Bellis' you two will have each other to play with and love. And Mama expects you to take very good care of each other and help each other to keep happy."

Her teary eyes met Paul's where he sat with his chin in his hands, and he looked away. "Mama isn't happy when you are in Rome because one of those bombs could hurt you, so it will help me to know you're safe here," she told them more quietly.

"It isn't because of that man, is it, Mama?" Cati asked with a swipe of fist across her wet cheeks.

"Because of Gian?" she said. "No, of course not."

"No, that other one who shows us his ribbons and medals, but I didn't want to say they're pretty. The one who put us in bed that time when Lilla said he shouldn't," Cati blurted out.

Lesley's face went scarlet despite the cool air. "No. No. Now Gian said he was going to tell you a wonderful story all about baseball in America, wasn't that it?" she asked quickly to avoid any discussion of Max. She had actually been thinking, pretending, that they were all here so happily together and that the past, beginning from her and Paul's separation in Venice, had never happened at all. Silly, stupid, so wrong of her to dream like that, she scolded herself as she shot Paul an imploring look, hoping he would tell the twins the story he'd promised them.

"Well, I thought I'd tell one about baseball, cowboys, and Indians all in one," he told them. Paolo's head lifted from Lesley's shoulder, though Cati still clung hard.

"About guns and planes, too?" Paolo asked.

"Sure, why not?" Paul said and stared hard at Lesley as Paolo deserted her to sit close to his side. "But I was just wondering what your sister would like to hear about. Do you think girls like all those things, Paolo?"

"Cati does. She likes the same I do. But furs and dolls, she likes them, too," Paolo informed him with a serious face.

"Furs at her age!" Paul pretended to be impressed. "You know, the Indians had furs to keep them warm in the winter." He began to tell his elaborate tale as Lesley cuddled Cati and they all listened. The story he made up as he went along, Lesley marveled, turned out to be about two Indian children who had to be very brave to live away from their mother when there was an Indian war. Cati's head lifted at last. She listened intently, though not with the open adoration in little Paolo's eyes. He watched Paul intently as he did all the voices of the characters and even the sounds in the story. When Paul and Paolo went off a little ways to toss a ball, Cati sat away from Lesley's side for the first time in an hour and looked straight up at her mother with a set face, her eyes older than her years.

"You told the soldier on the beach Gian is our father," her clear child's voice accused.

"But I explained, my love, we had to pretend that so they would let us stay on Capri." She reached for Cati's hands. "I know it's hard to understand."

"I don't want to stay here without you."

"Please, my sweet, sweet girl, don't make Mama cry again. I don't want to leave you, but I have to and that's that."

"But if he really was our father, could we all stay here?"

"Cati, no!"

"But you won't let that other man be our new father?"

"You're not going to have a new father!" Lesley cried, then lowered her voice with a glance at Paolo and Paul. "At least not for years and years, maybe never. After this war ends, we will all be together, you and Paolo and me, maybe Guido and Stella, too. I promise, my darling girl," she vowed with a nod. She hugged Cati, pulling the slender body into the circle of her arms to rock them both. "Please, please, don't you worry. Everything will be just fine!"

But later that day, after hide-and-seek games on the heights and another of Paul's stories, when Lesley had to finally leave them with the Bellis and go back to face Nazi Rome again, she felt her resolve shatter. On her knees beside the Bellis' hillside vegetable garden, she clung to the twins with silent tears streaming from her eyes. If only this day could be real and there was no war, no Max, God forgive her, no Valente fur and art empire to worry about and protect! It staggered her to think something could happen to her and she would never see Cati and Paolo again, but they were safer here. This had to be done. If only it could be Paul and her and their twins, a family, with a little plot of ground here, anywhere, together, almost forever, as he had said.

But she found the strength to walk away, to only turn back once to wave and head down to the waiting fishing boat in Marina Piccolo. She stared at the shrinking whitewashed waterfall town of Capri and the stone terraces like giant steps leading up to the Villa Valente and the Belli farm beyond as they set out to sea at sunset.

Paul stood beside her at the stern rail, unspeaking. At least, she thought, their countries were really on the same side now, despite the fact the bloody Germans held so much of Italy and might cause Rome's destruction when the Romans only really wanted to capitulate to the Allies.

"Thank God for your Americans," she said, her voice sounding strangled in her throat. "At least if anything happens to me, the Germans won't be able to get to the twins here."

"If anything happens to you, you've signed a paper that makes my Americans believe the twins here are mine," he said, and looked at her at last.

Her head jerked around. She gasped. Her insides cartwheeled. Their eyes, even in the dusk on the rolling sea, met and locked. "But it was the only way! You wouldn't use that—"

"I would use it only to return them to your nephew or wherever they should go," he interrupted. "Calm down, Lesley! You haven't trusted me in the past, but you have no choice but to trust me now."

She breathed a huge sigh of relief, but guilt leaned hard on her heart again. She turned away as the tears she'd fought all day blurred her vision, made the line of gray sky pressing black sea bend and jump. Legally, even morally, the twins should go to Paul if anything happened to her; she knew that in her heart of hearts. But it was too many years and too many heartaches too late for that. He had deserted her, deserted them! They were Valentes now, and he had Carla Fracci, with whom he might have other children someday. She had to go inside now, get away before they said something else that would change this tenuous truce between them that protected the twins, protected them all.

But when Paul's arm crept around her trembling shoulders she collapsed against the strength and warmth he momentarily offered. And in a fragmented second of utter, bereft weakness before she pulled away and ran back into the little cabin, she sobbed bitterly for all the things she wanted and would never have.

❦ ❦ Chapter Nineteen

LESLEY LOCKED HERSELF in her bedroom to read the day's copy of *Libero*, dated Sunday, October 19, 1943. It reported that Il Duce's ugly anti-Semitic policies, which he'd imported years ago from Hitler, had at last borne their hideous fruit: three days ago before dawn, Nazi troops had rounded up as many of the Jews of Rome as they could find and shipped them away by train to Germany. And the Germans were cordoning off streets daily to search for those who had escaped, as well as gathering any able-bodied labor conscripts they could send north to do the dirty work of the Third Reich.

She read the paper carefully, wondering if Paul had written any of the articles. Then she burned it in the grate of the fireplace that she feared would be her only means of heating as winter approached. Already it was cold for October, and the Germans had depleted the coal supply for the city. No fuel was available at any price to anyone but German hotels, and even gas for cooking had been cut to ninety minutes at midday and half an hour each evening. This had been an endless first month away from Cati and Paolo, but she was grateful they were not here to suffer through it all. Having the twins out of Max's reach made her so much bolder. She felt almost drunk with rage as she stood up to him sometimes, and if he tired of her and his obsessive idea that she must marry him and bear his children, so much the better!

Despite the dearth of food and the exorbitant prices for what could be found, she had finally discovered a way to help others. Max had promised to obtain a permit for her to get surplus German food, which she fully intended to donate to the refugees of San Lorenzo, some of whom, Lilla had told her, were hiding escapèd Jews because the Germans would never

337

suspect people without homes themselves could hide anyone.
She smiled a rare smile as she scuffed the ashes of *Libero* into
the hearthstones.

She'd just removed the suit she'd worn to church and pulled
on warm wool slacks and a white cashmere sweater when she
heard the commotion below, a pounding on the door. Were
those footsteps? Max? But he always came alone. She ran
down the hall, down the staircase as voices rose. Women's
voices. Lilla shouting. Men's voices, not Italian.

Across the black and white marble tiles in the downstairs
entry hall, two German soldiers dragged old Antonio, Cesare's
seventy-two-year-old chauffeur, toward the front door. Lesley
rushed down the stairs, pushed the screaming cook, maid, and
Lilla aside. She chased after them into the street where other
old or quite young men were being pulled from houses around
the square and tossed like sacks of cabbages into a waiting
truck with a huge swastika on the side.

"Wait! Stop!" Lesley shouted in German, and, startled, the
two helmeted Nazi guards halted before they could heave the
old man up.

"That man is my concern. He works for me. He has done
nothing!" she told them, her voice crisp, forceful. The Nazis
always spoke to others like that.

Her German and her bravado confused the two burly
soldiers. A crowd of her neighbors had gathered, mostly
women, many screaming protests and curses as servants or
relatives were hauled to the truck. "Work camp, working for
the Reich!" one guard insisted to Lesley, and they yanked the
dignified, terrified old man farther away.

Her eyes snagged with Antonio's helpless gaze. He clasped
the crucifix he wore around his neck in both gnarled hands,
and a huge tear rolled down one sunken cheek. They'd dragged
him out here without a sweater or coat. He was trembling with
fear and the chill. He'd been loyal to Cesare for years, driven
the big Bugatti for her aunt Rissa, worked for the Valentes
before Carlo and Guido were even born. Lesley had seen the
quiet, dear man mourn when Cesare and Carlo died—and
again when she'd told him the Bugatti that had so long been his
pride had been crushed in the raid on San Lorenzo. Since there
was no need for chauffeuring lately, he'd willingly helped with

the balcony garden and in the kitchen. He'd always been so kind to her children, even at times filling in as a grandfatherly figure for them.

"No!" she insisted to the guards, fighting to keep calm, to keep from crying. She clamped a restraining hand on the gray arm of one soldier's thick winter coat. "You've made a mistake. SS Lieutenant Colonel Dorff needs that man here!"

She hadn't meant to use Max's name in public, especially not with all her furious neighbors listening, but she had to save Antonio. Work camp, death camp—it was all the same to these fiends! Instantly, she saw Max's name had an effect on the two, and they hesitated while another man went to get their commanding officer. It was then, as if heaven had sent him for once, that Max in his official Daimler pulled up with another Nazi vehicle close behind. Lesley stepped forward to take Antonio's arm despite the other guard's gun and bayonet so close to her face. And then, in the truck, peering out amid the helpless, lost faces, she saw Mario, the man who had been her contact at the laundry, for passing on information about the Nazis.

He saw her, too. Quickly, he held his finger to his lips and shook his head as if to warn her not to let on that she recognized him. For the first time, she realized she was very, very afraid.

"Countess Valente," Max clipped out as he strode quickly to where she stood in the ring of angry soldiers and protesting neighbors, "you will come inside with me."

"I'm only out here because these men are trying to abduct my servant Antonio," she insisted, and stared up unmoving into his icy blue eyes.

"His work permit has lapsed as have all the others. They are needed elsewhere," he ordered, his high forehead crushed in a frown.

"He is seventy-two years old, and I will be very, very angry with the German effort if he goes, Lieutenant Colonel Dorff."

She had never defied Max in front of others before. His mouth set in a hard line and the little pulse at the base of his throat jumped rhythmically. Even when he put his gloved hand to Lesley's wrist to pull her away, she held stubbornly to Antonio's arm. "Leave the old man here," he said to the guards through gritted teeth. "And disperse this rabble at once."

He escorted her back inside, propelled her immediately into the library. He slammed the door behind them. She stood her ground, glaring with arms crossed over her chest, as he removed his coat and adjusted his holsters.

"You know, *meine Liebe*, you do nothing but arouse my passions lately, and I do not mean with desire for you!" he exploded. "With all my new duties and responsibilities, I did not need this display of defiance from you today!"

She thrust her chin up, didn't budge. "But you told me you admire my loyalty. That old man has served the Valentes for decades, and he'd die if they took him," she shot back.

"So might you all, if you do not learn to behave! I do so much for you, woman, come to see you with gifts to please you and you embarrass me before a crowd of Roman rabble by arguing with the Reich's soldiers indirectly carrying out my orders!"

He actually trembled with rage. His hands gripped the handles of his Lugers so hard they vibrated in their leather sheaths. She backed slightly away as he stalked her until her legs hit the couch. "Max, I didn't mean to embarrass you, but I needed your strength and that's why I used your name. I told you once power didn't attract me, but along with so much else about you, I must admit," she said, deliberately softening her voice, "it does matter to me."

He grabbed for her, pulled her down on the couch. "I wish I could believe that, but you continually defy me. And I haven't forgiven you for allowing the twins to go off to stay with your sister-in-law in Milan when I wasn't here to consult!"

"But I knew Milan would be on our way north when we finally leave for Berlin, and I won't have those damned Americans drop a bomb on them!" She'd convinced him she'd let Cesare's sister, Baronessa Consuelo, take the children with her on the spur of the moment, and she only prayed he would not have someone check her story.

"I must admit that it will allow us more privacy when I am in town," he murmured, his voice normal for the first time. She forced herself to respond warmly when he kissed her, even stroking the short hair at the nape of his neck because she knew it calmed him. But she always felt so dirty when she let him touch her. She'd managed to get him to promise they would not sleep together until they wed in Berlin, but still, her skin crawled.

"And now, the surprises for my *Liebe*," he announced proudly and released her at last. "New reasons among the many others why she will try much harder to please me in the future. Ah, my beautiful, willful countess, how many favors you owe me and how soon I may insist you repay," he boasted.

She sucked in a breath. "What do you mean?"

"If—just if—the Germans should ever have to pull back from Rome, you will be going with me, but enough of that now. Your Max does not bring you candy and flowers and jewels as any mortal suitor might," he said and grinned as if he'd made a clever joke. "Your little Alfa Romeo has been retrieved—it's parked out in back." He grinned as he dropped the keys in her lap.

"Oh, Max, I'm so glad to have it returned."

He absolutely beamed, then sobered and shook his head. "The fur garments were gone from the back of the auto but I'm working on that. And here's the food-supply permit you wanted to be sure your families at the fur salon don't starve. After all, we may want to take some of the workers with us to Berlin when you open a shop there. And now the biggest surprise of all. Klaus!" he bellowed at the door, which opened immediately. His aide, square-faced, stolid Klaus Schultz, whom she had met once before, stepped in with a stiff salute, then pulled a woman in after him. Her hands were tied behind her back, her bent head spilled greasy salt and pepper hair that hid her face. She wore a dirty, torn black dress. Klaus dragged her across the floor to stand before the couch and Lesley jumped to her feet. Klaus shoved the woman to her knees.

"Recognize her after all this time, *Liebe*?" Max inquired with a smug smile while Lesley stared aghast. "Woman, lift your head."

Klaus stepped forward to yank the woman's head up by her lank hair. Lesley stared down shocked and horrified into a tearful and frightened face that was black and blue with bruises. The woman's lips were puffed, split; the nose broken and so swollen she breathed through her mouth. It took Lesley a moment to realize she stared at the woman who had lured her off the train in Orvieto and whose family had beaten and robbed her. Lidia Comi.

"Max, how—what happened?"

"What happened? Nazi justice, for you, my countess. It took me a while, but the criminal has been found, a whore, a thief. Her daughter still steals for her evidently, though the husband and son who have shirked their Fascist military duty were sent to an Austrian work camp last month. And she's admitted everything, haven't you, thief? Well?"

"*Si, si,*" she murmured and nodded, though it was obvious the woman would have agreed to anything at this point.

"Countess Valente, I place the prisoner's fate in your hands," Max declared. "She's admitted to robbing you and many others. You can have her shot, sent to German or Polish work camps with her daughter—"

"Shot? Work camp with— But her daughter must be only ten!" Lesley protested, horrified.

The woman's eyes met hers at last. "*Si,* my Daniela. Have pity, I beg you, *contessa!*"

"Max, she's obviously been punished enough," Lesley argued with a jerky sweep of her hand toward the woman. "Besides, you surely can't send a ten-year-old girl to some awful prison camp. Just let the woman work here in Rome somewhere and have her take better care of her daughter."

"How soft you are, countess." His voice became suddenly husky instead of triumphant. "But then, I could learn to appreciate that." He jerked his thumb toward the door. "Get her out, Klaus, put her on a work detail in the kitchens of the hotel, something. Out."

Lesley shuddered. Gooseflesh prickled her skin. How often at first she'd wished for revenge against the Comis, then hated them in more distant, muted terms for what they did. And yet, now that she'd seen war and death and suffered so much through her own losses, she couldn't bear to see anyone hurt—anyone but the Nazis. Klaus slammed the door behind them to punctuate her thoughts.

"Oh, yes, there is something else, *Liebe,*" Max told her and fumbled in his tunic pocket. "Would you believe we actually retrieved something the woman stole from you after all this time? She'd sold everything else, but kept this for her daughter's wedding someday, she told Klaus. No one denies Klaus anything when he questions them. Here."

Afraid to look, Lesley stared down at the ruby ring with antique gold roses that Paul had given her for their engagement that last night in Venice. Tears blurred her gaze; the ring and his hand jumped, doubled. "And since I retrieved it, and it's so obviously precious to you, let's just call it an engagement gift from me to you, hm?" Max's voice slid over her, chilling her.

Weak-kneed, she sank to the couch as he slipped it on the same finger she'd worn it on before. Until recently she'd worn her wide gold wedding band from Cesare on that finger, but it was hidden away with her other jewelry. "And, Lesley, with this ring, I vow to be loyal to you and you will vow the same to me. Women of questionable loyalty end up in the San Gregorio Prison here in Rome or the Ravensbrück north of Berlin until men like me decide what will be done with them. Be certain you understand that, *Liebe*, and that you have my utmost devotion."

She gazed up into his narrowed blue eyes. Sometimes she was certain he was insane to mix love with control and hatred so completely. She looked down again at the ring on her hand, Paul's ring. "Yes, I do understand you now, I'm very certain I do," she said, her voice quavering.

He pulled her back down on the couch and began to kiss her, deeply, fervently. He pulled her sweater up, her brassiere awry, bent his mouth to ravage her soft flesh. The door shot open and they both looked up. Stella Sollo stood there horrified as deep regret and agony churned in Lesley. Then Stella slammed the door and fled.

As the months of German occupation ground by and Christmas approached, Lesley felt more and more isolated from all she loved. It would be her first Christmas without the children, and she had no way of even knowing how they were. How she wished she'd thought far enough ahead to leave something with the Bellis for Yuletide or Boxing Day gifts. As for the rest of her diminished Valente family, Guido had evidently gone over to the Allies or into hiding to escape the

Germans after the fall of Naples. She had no idea where he was or if he was safe, and she was afraid to ask Max after what had happened to Lidia Comi. Besides, rumor said the Germans had massacred over eight thousand Italian soldiers at Cefalonia for not remaining loyal to the Reich, and Lesley was terrified she might lose Guido as she had Carlo. She had no illusions about the Nazis anymore.

As for her friends, Stella had been avoiding her since she'd come upon her and Max in the library two months ago, and her neighbors in the square had spread word all over town about her and Max. Her work staff treated her with deferential but sullen politeness now, while Madame berated her regularly and threatened to resign from Valente's. Lesley felt like "Scandal's Child" once again as people whispered and pointed behind her back over something they did not truly understand, something for which she was not to blame. Only her relationship with Lilla, to whose family and neighbors she delivered food today, and with Carla Fracci sustained her at all. She still had a tenuous truce with Carla, since Paul had evidently never told her they had gone to Capri together. And then she had the unswerving devotion of old Antonio, whose life she had saved.

Lesley glanced at Lilla as the auto entered bombed-out San Lorenzo, then turned back to her driving. The girl was sulky and fidgety today, not herself at all despite the dangers they faced in taking this illegal food to her neighbors and the Jews they were hiding. "We'll just unload the boxes in the church as usual, but we can't stay long, Lilla. No good for my auto to be seen by the wrong people."

"I know," Lilla agreed without looking at her. "Just think, only four boxes of goods, but they're probably worth a fortune with eggs so high and a sack of rice at thousands of lire. My father had even taken to collecting cigarette butts off the street and trading them for food before you got this permit from your Nazi friend."

"Nothing these days gives me more pleasure than helping those the Nazis would like to do in!" Lesley declared vehemently in the tiny, packed auto.

Lilla squirmed in her seat and looked at her at last. "I just hope it's worth it to you, Countess Valente—what everyone says and all, even a few who know you're on the Italian side, too."

Lesley expelled a breath through parted lips and gripped the steering wheel tighter. How she wished she could share with Lilla, with everyone, the truth of her relationship with Max Dorff. But she'd seen what the Germans could do to make people talk. She had to do this alone and not endanger any of those she'd once called her friends.

After parking in the alley behind the partially ruined Basilica of San Lorenzo, Lesley and Lilla lugged in boxes of eggs, rice, bread, and flour. Then, as always, they knelt briefly to light a candle and pray. They knew as soon as they left the sanctuary the food would disappear for the needy.

Her gloved hands clasped together so tightly they trembled, Lesley prayed for the twins' and Guido's safety. And, as she had every night since her trip to Capri, she gave thanks that Paul had helped her to rescue their twins. And she asked forgiveness for lying to him about who had fathered them. She stared so hard at the large gold Christ on the cross in the wavering candlelight that she imagined for a moment His fluted ribs moved. She gripped the prayer rail. He suffered and yet He forgave. His friends deserted Him and yet He loved them still.

Outside, they blinked in the December sun. And then, at the same time, they saw what someone had done to her little teal-blue Alfa Romeo. Huge, deep swastikas were scraped in its shiny paint, and the black leather convertible top had been slashed repeatedly. The crude accusation *"Prostituta Nazista!"* was splashed in red paint across the front and back windscreens.

While Lilla just stood like a statue with her hands pressed to her mouth and stared, Lesley leaned back against the cold stone of the basilica and shuddered. Here, even here in San Lorenzo where she'd tried to do some good, they wouldn't let her without turning against her. No one understood; everyone hated.

"Countess Valente? Countess, I'm so sorry," Lilla told her hoarsely, "but I can understand their resentment. You know they dislike taking things, even indirectly, from the Germans." She backed away from Lesley as she spoke. "I don't think I'd better go home with you. I'll just stay around here and see you later."

"Lilla." The girl stopped to face her in the alley, her face wet with tears. Lesley's voice was bitter, hard. "Tell your neighbors to enjoy their food, but since I no longer have a usable auto, I don't know if I can bring them any more. And tell them even our Lord forgave others at the very last minute."

Lilla shook her head and shrugged helplessly. "I'm sorry, Countess Valente. Really. If you still had the twins to care for, I'd come back with you."

"But I don't have them or anyone else to care for. Go on, but tell them, whoever the hypocrites are who did this," she said, her voice rising, "the auto's theirs too, because it obviously doesn't belong to me!" She spun to the car and smeared the words "Nazi prostitute!" to oblivion across the window with quick swipes of her gloved hand. "Tell them that!" she shouted at the stunned girl.

With a sob, Lilla hurried away. Lesley ripped off her ruined glove, then dug in her purse for her auto key, which she yanked off her lion key chain. She threw the key and the glove into the defaced little auto she had once treasured for the freedom it gave her. No one had freedom anymore. She was past running away. Paul was right that it had been her weakness once, but there was no place for any sort of weakness in this war. It was only an auto, and those, unlike the lives and art and entire cultures she wanted to help salvage, could be replaced someday. She sniffed back her tears, squared her shoulders, and began the long walk home.

By the time spring came, Lesley felt she lived in the big, echoing Valente town house like a hermit. She still went into the shop some days, but her creative powers were drained. She worried her presence kept some customers away, so she turned the shop management over to Madame four days a week and worked at home. It was better for her, better for Madame, better for Valente's. She had finally told her workers and her German customers, whom she despaired putting off any longer, that she had run out of pelts. It was not quite true, but the supply was low and she couldn't bear for her things to go to Berlin or be purchased by anyone who would have money

for furs in such perilous times. Now even the Roman middle
classes were in the soup kitchens to survive. Instead, she'd
given entire coats to her workers to take home to wrap their
children in to survive the cruel winter.

Romans shivered with no coal in their high-ceilinged,
big-windowed houses with marble floors and sills where
everything—china, furniture, one's own skin—always felt
cold to the touch. Everyone lost weight; everyone suffered
from chilblains. And what chilled her most was that, since her
auto had been ruined and the town house defaced with graffiti
more than once, Max had put guards on her front and back
doors and she was to always tell them where she was going
when she went out.

She spent long hours keeping a diary for the twins, recol-
lections about her childhood, her parents and grandparents,
Westam, things she wanted them to know, places she hoped
they'd visit someday. And it helped her to write them daily
letters she might never send, they might never see. She
realized now during all these lonely hours of introspection why
she had instinctively loved furs from the beginning and wanted
to dedicate her life to sharing them with others. Stripped now
of nearly everything she'd ever loved, she realized she'd
always longed to help others experience the beauty of the
world, to lift their spirits, to make them feel warmed, loved,
free, individual and special—and furs did that for people. Furs
were a form of art, and art was the very special essence of
mankind's potential and individuality, which the Nazis were
trying to destroy by ruining civilization itself. And how very
desperately, at any cost, she longed to do something—
anything—to stop them!

But for now, she only catalogued all Cesare's art both from
the town house and the villa for Guido, or for Paolo who, when
he was old enough, could claim the title Count Valente. She
carefully noted where each painting was hidden in case
something happened to them—or her. Then she wrapped both
diary and catalogue in canvas and, with Antonio's help, hid
them under the corner flagstone in the balcony floor of the
town house.

When Max was in town, she spent time with him off and on,
though he was forever busier the closer the Allies slogged their

way through winter mud and sleet toward Rome. Each morning they shelled the city, and spring bombing raids were common. In April, rumor had it that President Roosevelt had asked King Victor Emmanuel to abdicate in favor of his royal son, and the Germans became increasingly desperate and clamped a tighter lid on Rome. Talk in town now often centered on whether the Germans, if they withdrew, would destroy the city and its population when they left. She had passed on everything she could glean to a new contact Carla had recommended, but Lesley considered the contact unreliable, and had long ago decided that if she came across anything really worth knowing, she would go to Carla straightaway and demand another person to tell.

And then, out of the blue, on Wednesday, May 24, when Max arrived for a sudden visit, she got her chance. She had just served him tea on the balcony after Antonio had carried the serving tray up from the kitchen, when Max's driver came rushing into the house to hiss something in his ear. Max's face stiffened; he excused himself immediately to make a call at the hall phone just inside. Her pulse pounded and she stood slowly. He never made or took calls at the house. Everyone knew the lines were often cut by partisans to discourage the Germans, and many tried to spy by using Il Duce's antiquated phone system. So, she thought and her heart leapt, this must be desperately important for him to take the risk.

Pretending to rearrange teacups and spoons, she inched closer and strained to listen. He spoke in German. "What? Damn it all to hell! Well, Dollman and Kesselring too know there are only two possible roads the Allies can take from there the way things are. Yes. Let us only hope the American bastards do not find out that defenses are that light on the road to Valmontone! That would trap us, I'm afraid. Yes, I'll be right there."

She began to clatter the china. The road to Valmontone was the Via Casilina, Highway 6, and it led directly into Rome! Her hands shook. She rattled Max's cup in his saucer so hard she had to put it down.

"Just going to freshen your tea, Max," she told him with a forced smile when he strode back out. She noted from the corner of her eye that his hands gripped the handles of his Lugers so hard his fingers went white.

"I've got to leave, *Liebe*," he told her curtly and bent to sweep his hat from the chair.

"But you've only just got here," she told him, secure in protesting after what she'd just heard.

"I'm afraid I will be busy. Don't leave the house, eh?" he said and darted a hard kiss on her mouth. "It would be foolish anyway, as I'm going to tell the guards you're to stay in right now. Things might get out of hand."

She saw him out. The moment the door closed on his back, she locked it and darted for the kitchen. Guards on the doors or not, she had to get out of here and get to Carla. The entire Allied approach to Rome could hinge on this! She didn't have a bit of time to lose, had to think of something.

She found Antonio polishing an old dueling pistol that had belonged to his father. He kept it always nearby now in case the Nazi soldiers returned for him, and she did not blame him. She kept Cesare's pistol, which she'd once wanted to use to shoot Il Duce, under the other pillow on her bed. He moved to stand when he saw her but she motioned for him to stay seated.

"Is he gone?" he inquired as he placed the elaborately filagreed pistol into a tailored black mink pouch Cesare had given him years ago. "I have Cook tell me every five minutes if he's behaving when he's with you."

She sat at the big wooden table across from him staring at how cleverly the gun fit inside its fur cover. The idea sprang to her full-blown then, although she shuddered at what she would have to do to carry it off. Still, with one of Max's Nazi guards at the front door and one at the back and no autos that ran, what choice did she have? It could mean everything. She had to conquer her fear for this.

"Countess, are you all right?" His old wrinkled face looked so worried. "You do not mind the pistol?"

"No. Not at all, Antonio." She lowered her voice. "It's only that I need your help to do something against the Germans that may be very dangerous."

"For you, anything!" he declared soundly, and a thrill shot up her spine that someone who was obviously afraid would still help her.

* * *

Within an hour, trembling but determined, Antonio fought to conquer his fear of the Nazi soldier who stopped him immediately outside the house to question him. Lesley, curled up within the crate of furs Antonio rolled in the wheelbarrow, fought to keep from screaming out her secret presence, all closed in within the black box of furs.

Together she and the old man had carried the crate up from the wine cellar. She'd lined it with mink and fox coats, the finest home delivery Carla Fracci would ever receive—if someone did not stop them first. She'd begun to quake and perspire the moment Antonio had hammered the slatted lid onto the crate. But she'd held her silence and her breath as he finally convinced the soldier that Lieutenant Colonel Dorff's countess was only sending furs to a friend. The wheelbarrow rumbled off down the pavement. It was a long way to Carla Fracci's house and Antonio was not strong. It was eternity for a claustrophobic to be encased in a box lined with furs.

Lesley tried to listen to street sounds and pretend she was outside walking along with Antonio, but that didn't help. She pictured herself on the high, free, sunlit cliffs of Capri with the children, but Paul kept appearing there too, watching her, smiling at the children. She thought of standing with him at the prow of their dipping boat far out in the green sea, thought of the gardens of Westam her grandmum tended with such love, but every time the street jolted her, she felt things pressing in.

Paul. She hadn't seen him since last September when he'd let her off in the *vicolo* behind the town house after they came back from Capri; he'd pulled away almost immediately in that ramshackle Fiat. He saw Carla, she knew he did. He would probably marry Carla, but the thought made her breathe so very fast and hard that she was terrified someone would hear her panting or that she might forget herself and scream. She twisted the ruby ring on her finger; Max always insisted she wear it. Her beautiful gift from Paul once, but now it was like a bloodred chain linking her to Max Dorff.

She could hear the old man wheezing and was glad when he finally stopped a moment to rest as she'd told him to. It seemed

they had gone on forever already, far on, far back, rolling
endlessly to some destruction. She remembered when her
mother died in the iron lung at the clinic and how she wished
she had been able to hold her. She wished she had the twins to
hold now, and not just the sleeve of the mink bolero she
gripped so hard. She remembered the night she'd hidden from
Trent and Constance in the closet of her mother's dressing
room at Westam and how she'd escaped them with Paul's help.
Paul's help. Come on, Antonio, start moving again, she
prayed.

But she heard footsteps scraping closer. No, no! Men,
several. Raucous voices, harsh, speaking guttural German.
"You, old man," they called. Inside the dark pelts, Lesley held
her breath as she heard Antonio's shaky plea to let him go on.
She smelled tobacco clear in here, penetrating the furs,
pressing in on her as the voices, the Germans did. They were
strangling this whole city, Europe, her world. And now one
dared to put his boot on the wheelbarrow; she heard it, felt it
tip. They would challenge Antonio, find her, drag them off.

"You know any bars here sell schnapps, old man?" one
asked in halting Italian.

"Just two blocks over, someone said," Antonio answered
shakily. Probably a lie and Lesley blessed him for it. The
wheelbarrow nearly tilted again. Someone laughed, and then
the steps faded and the wheelbarrow jerked on its eternal slow
way again while tears of gratitude squeezed through Lesley's
tight lashes and she breathed deep, warm, fur-scented breaths.
It seemed hours, eons, before she at last heard Antonio whisper
over the pounding of her heart, "Almost there, Countess. I
know you said not to talk unless I had to, but we're almost
there."

Instantly, her spirits buoyed her up. She had almost conquered the fear she had carried with her like a great, pressing
burden for so long. She felt the wheelbarrow stop, felt it being
lowered. She heard Antonio shuffle on without her. They must
be here! She heard him knock. It took every ounce of
self-restraint not to yell at him to get her out of here. "Furs
delivered for *la signorina* Fracci only. From the Countess
Valente," Lesley heard the old man say.

* * *

Carla thought Lesley's message so important she insisted they both go to different contacts with the news. Then, after they were certain someone could pass it on to the Allied forces, they would meet back here and prepare a box of orchid plants with a false bottom that Lesley could use to get back into her town house. Carla had already gone out ahead because the one contact was available earlier but at a farther distance. She told Lesley to delay a half hour before she went out and she'd be back here waiting for her by the time she returned.

Lesley paced the gold, white, and yellow sunroom of the Fracci mansion, her thoughts as quick and nervous as her steps. If the Allies could get in fast and rout the Germans, they would have less time to destroy things when they left. Then, of course, when Max insisted she go with him, she would have to find a way to escape. If it would only be very soon, perhaps she would be best off to just never go back until he was gone, but she could not endanger Carla by hiding here, and there was nowhere else she knew to go. Here she was risking her life to defeat the Germans, and she could think of no one in the entire city who would hide her from them. If Max had time to vent his anger at her desertion before he left, he could destroy the town house, and the shop too, where Madame had taken up residence since Nazi soldiers were billeted in her *pensione*.

She glanced at her watch again. Carla had said not to leave early, so she would have to wait when she felt so keen to get this over. Imagine, looking for a contact who was an old woman with balloons during rationing and wartime. The twins had always loved balloons.

She heard quick footsteps in the hall and spun to the door just as it opened. "Honey, I know you didn't expect me, but—" Paul Kendal began as he jerked to a halt.

Stunned, they stared at each other for a moment before Lesley managed, "She's gone out for a while, I don't know how long."

To her dismay, he came in, closed the door behind him and leaned against it. "Then you're up to something with her, and I believe I warned you about that."

"Look, Gian," she said with bitter emphasis on his pseudonym, "we're all up to something or other these days, you included, so don't lecture me." It made her angry he had just breezed in like that, called Carla honey. How dare he treat her like some child he had to scold, especially when she'd come up with the news that could help his Americans. She almost told him what she'd discovered, but only spun away so he wouldn't read her thoughts, as he seemed to do far too often.

"Hell, you're no more touchy than anyone else lately!" he shot back and walked closer.

She shrugged her shoulders exaggeratedly. "It's just I only see you every eight months or so, and I don't need your dramatic warnings."

"Don't you?" his deep voice challenged. He'd come far too close to her, she thought. "What do you need, then?"

She whirled back to face him. That blasted cheeky American tone she loved. This was going all wrong. She didn't answer, couldn't wait to get rid of him.

"I don't suppose you've heard some way how the twins are?" he asked in the awkward silence between them, his eyes so intent.

"No. And it's been an eternity."

"I know."

She moved a few steps away. Perhaps they could at least be pleasant. "How are things going for you then, Paul?" she asked but did not meet his eyes again.

"All right. Actually," he told her, "I just heard through a rather elaborate grapevine that my second novel's being published, the one I wrote here, *To Have and Hold*."

"Congratulations."

"Actually, Lesley, and I mean this as a compliment, the heroine in it is very special. And she's based on you."

She met that riveting green gaze fully now. "On me?" That was all she needed with everyone else whispering about her lately and shunning her! He'd always been a journalist at heart, just out to use people, find out their inner lives, and take anything he could for his own profit!

"I don't appreciate that, Paul," she clipped out, with an angry thrust of chin. "I resent it, as a matter of fact, and if we lived in civilized times, I swear I'd sue you!"

"The real Lesley." He nodded. "Yes, that's in the book, too."

Everything she had been bottling up inside for weeks roiled through her. The book probably claimed she married Cesare for his wealth and power, as he'd accused her of so often. It probably said she was a traitor to consort with Max Dorff, even that she slept with him! Everyone who ever pretended to be close had betrayed her!

"I only wish you could have mentioned that I'm engaged!" she shouted before she could stop herself.

His eyes narrowed and shot to the left hand she gestured with before she remembered she wore the ruby ring and jerked her hand down for her purse on the glass-topped table. Before she could edge around him, he lunged at her and grabbed her wrist.

"The ring! My ring! You told me it was stolen!" he roared.

"It was. Let me go!"

He yanked her hard toward him, his hands pinning her upper arms to her sides. "Engaged to whom, that SS bastard? Is that it?"

"Yes, that's it! Take your hands off me!"

"Oh, I will. I've no desire to touch used, spoiled Nazi goods." He thrust her back hard onto the gold and white striped silk sofa. She bounced; her skirt flew up above her knees. She scrambled away from him, stood, backed in the direction of the door, afraid to break the linking of their fierce gazes. She knew then, more surely than ever before, that she'd always loved Paul Kendal, and yet it was all ruined, too late for them.

He stood as if frozen where he was, breathing raggedly, his face livid, his fists at his sides. "Despite all the lies you've told me, Lesley," he ground out, "I'm sorry to say, I believe you're telling the truth about the Nazi. If so, you deserve him, but you'd better leave your twins permanently on Capri to be raised by those poor, honest, loving farmers there."

She opened the door and stood stiffly beside it to indicate he should leave. Carla had told her not to go out yet, and for once, her pride, which was all she had left, would not let her run from him. "Good-bye, Paul. Forever now, not almost."

He moved slowly to the door, his glare brutal. She stepped

back, but she needn't have. Without another word, he stalked straight out and down the hall toward the back of the house. Even when there was silence again, except for her own sobbing breaths and the thumping of her heart, she still imagined she could hear his footsteps inside her, fading, fading away.

❦ ❦ Chapter Twenty

MORE THAN a week later, still unaware Lesley had passed on information that had allowed the Allies to push nearly to the outskirts of Rome, Max commanded she dress as elegantly as possible that night to accompany him and other members of the Nazi hierarchy left in Rome to the opera. She'd just walked him to the front door of the town house after one of his brief visits. He looked distracted—almost frenzied. But she'd been on edge, too.

"Max, tonight? The opera?" she'd blurted out in disgust and defiance, her chin outthrust, fists on her hips. "The Reich's enemies are pounding on the door of Rome and we're dressing to the nines to go to the opera?"

He'd slammed her against the inside of the front town house door and grasped a breast to knead it the way he knew she hated. "I'm wearying of your sharp little tongue, *Liebe,* as much as I'm looking forward to possessing the rest of you! Yes, Kesslering's requested Verdi's *Masked Ball* especially for Eugen Dollman," he said through gritted teeth, "and don't be a bit surprised if everyone there is wearing masks of one sort or another. That includes us too, doesn't it, my countess?" he'd insinuated, his voice thick with lust. He'd ground her hips against the door while his Lugers rubbed almost obscenely against her soft belly. "You're going to look very happy, very calm, and very much in love with me tonight, Countess Valente. You see, I still intend to take you with me if the Führer allows us to retreat, and I don't want Kesslering or Dollman wondering why."

At the opera, she soon learned the reason the Nazis wore masks of pretense, as she overheard snatches of terse conversation among them. The German powers-that-be were putting on a show of confidence and solidarity for the benefit of Rome. But at this close range, she could tell they were all nervous, even afraid their Führer would order them to hold the city at any cost, including their lives.

"We've done what we can, but a retreat is still going to be one hell of a mess because it will all be at the last minute," German Field Marshal Kesslering hissed at Dollman within Lesley's earshot while she took her time searching in her gold and tortoise-shell minaudière for her lace handkerchief. Kesslering's bald head glinted under the crystal chandeliers as did the horsey smile he'd plastered on his face whenever he turned so the audience could see him. This could almost be comedy, Lesley thought desperately, if everything the Nazis touched didn't turn to tragedy.

"We've hidden two hundred pounds of nitroglycerin in the telephone exchange to knock out communications and cause chaos if worst comes to worst," Dollman whispered back. "And if the order to evacuate comes, we'll have to send our wounded soldiers from the hospitals immediately and that will clog the roads."

Lesley intercepted murmurs, observed exchanged looks when she could, but it was obvious she would never get away from Max long enough to tell anyone, maybe never get away from him ever again the way he was watching her. Her stomach knotted; her knees began to tremble as they stood to applaud Renato's aria *Alla vita che t'arride* about the rebellion brewing. Lesley just shook her head at the irony of the Germans applauding this opera, which she knew ended not in celebration of the masked ball but in violent overthrow and murder.

"You look absolutely stunning tonight, Countess Valente, stunning," said the effeminate Eugen Dollman at intermission, ignoring a pouting Bibi Rossi draped on his arm.

"How terribly kind of you," Lesley managed, her voice brittle despite the stiff smile she managed. "There's been so little opportunity to celebrate these last few years," she dared, pleased he looked confounded at her daring retort. Luckily Max had evidently not overheard it.

Lesley had done as Max asked when she'd gowned and coiffed and jeweled herself tonight, not to please him as he supposed, but rather to throw him off any suspicion she might disobey him at the last minute. She felt as much in costume as the singers on the stage, dressed for fantasy and escape in these harsh times. Under a stole of white fox she wore a white and shimmering jade satin Patou gown with softly draped bosom and gold metallic belt to match her minaudière and gold lamé heels. Antonio had dug up her cache of jewels to retrieve her emerald and pavé diamond choker, bracelet, and earrings, and she had pulled her hair up in sculpted rolls pierced by a single hairpin of a diamond butterfly Cesare had given her on their first anniversary.

How long ago it seemed when she and Cesare, Carlo and Stella, Guido and one of his women whose name she could not even recall were all together here at Rome's ornate and gilded Teatro dell' Opera. Her eyes scanned its familiar four levels of curved, carved, and columned loggias and cherub-topped boxes lined with red velvet as if she were looking at it for the last time.

"Max, if you don't mind, I'm going to nip round to the powder room," she said with a calculated glance up at him through lowered lashes. "I'll be back directly."

"Quite a crowd tonight to get lost in. Let me walk you," he insisted politely, though his cold gaze raked her.

In the richly carpeted and papered suite of ladies' rooms, so few women rested, checked their faces or hair, gossiped or chatted compared to the old days. Yet, because the Germans were rabid opera patrons, two gray-garbed maids with frilly white aprons hovered in the outer room, and inside, tiny fragrant bonbons of colored soap filled crystal dishes next to a lavender-scented basket of small linen towels. Lesley breathed in more easily just to be out of Max's brooding presence. If there had been another door out of here besides the one where he waited, she would have taken the risk of her life and run out somewhere to hide.

To stall for time, Lesley sat at the gilt-framed mirror and pretended to fuss with her hair. "Oh, Countess, isn't all this so exciting?" Bibi Rossi gushed close behind her as the woman made her way out. Bibi wore flaming red and, with her black elbow gloves, looked almost as if she were wrapped in one of those vile, garish Nazi flags, Lesley thought to herself. And that pilfered Lanvin Arpège perfume she always wore over-whelmed the atmosphere as if she'd actually bathed in it.

"The opera? It's very good." Lesley pretended to misunder-stand and continued to powder her nose, hoping Bibi would go out without waiting for her.

"No, no!" Bibi hissed and leaned so close over Lesley that the slap of perfume nearly suffocated her. "I mean, the excitement of us all being in Berlin soon where we'll be safer! I heard there's bombing there, but my Dollman says Berlin weather's simply *wunderbar* this time of year. I only hope he marries me, as I know your Max will you. If you get a chance, I'd ever so much appreciate a little word to him. They all admire you after that triumph of yours in Berlin."

Lesley's face felt fragile, as if it would shatter like the glass into which she stared at this horrible, stupid woman. Lesley lifted the corners of her mouth and nodded. "Yes. I can't wait. As for a word to Dollman, I can't promise, Bibi, but of course I'll try."

To escape further conversation, Lesley excused herself and went directly into the long, narrow tiled room with the loos in separate cubicles. On the other side of the door, she ran directly into Carla Fracci. "Oh, Carla, I had no idea you were here!"

They steadied each other for a moment from the slight collison, then stepped back to assess each other. Carla's low-cut, ruffled pale blue gown was lovely if rather fussy. Her face looked absolutely radiant. "I'm sitting way at the back. But I assure you, everyone's seen you," Carla noted and twisted her small white beaded purse on its delicate gold chain.

"I can imagine." Lesley lowered her voice, glanced around. "They're putting on a show, Carla, insisting that everything look normal tonight."

Carla's big eyes widened further. "They're running? Soon?"

"As soon as Hitler gives the word. They've put explosives in the telephone exchange somewhere and who knows what else."

"All right," Carla whispered. "I can tell Gian. He can't wait to help the Americans. He's going out to their lines tonight after we leave here, so he can pass that on and—"

Lesley felt doused with cold water. She grabbed Carla's wrist. "He's here. With you?"

"We figured they have to worry about—how is it my Gian put it?—their own hides now, so it's the first time we've been out in public together, but not the last, I assure you!" Carla told her with a flip of her head. She gently disengaged her arm from Lesley's hand, then picked at the flounces on her skirt. "After Gian comes back with the Allies, we can be much more open about our love!"

It was over then, Lesley thought, that dream she'd held to stubbornly through it all. So foolish, so wrong of her. She couldn't stem her emotion as tears filled her eyes and her lower lip trembled. She turned quickly away to the partially open window to lean on its wide marble sill, but not before Carla had seen.

"You still love him, want him," Carla hissed, half in awe, half in horror, her voice bitterly accusing.

Lesley shook her head, lifted her chin, looked away. "No. Of course not."

"You always have. I knew it, know the twins are his, too!"

"Please, Carla, not now with everything else."

"Oh, don't worry," she said through gritted teeth. "I won't tell him any of it, if that's what you're afraid of, and I'm hardly going out to chat with your Nazi friends. Thank God this war's almost over for us all, one way or the other, depending on how many of us the Germans slaughter on their way out the back door, because I'm just afraid you and I have lost our ability to really work together. I'll tell my fiancé, Gian, what you said about the phone exchange and their imminent retreat, but that's all, so just keep away from both of us!"

"Carla! Carla, please—" Lesley called out to her but Carla, in a flourish of icy blue chiffon and silk, was gone. Fiancé! She'd actually said fiancé. She hit her fist onto the marble ledge. It was absolutely none of her business anymore.

Lesley leaned both elbows on the sill, wiping carefully under her eyes with her handkerchief, breathing in the June night air to calm herself to face Max. She'd been in here too long and he would become even more suspicious. Surely Act II was about to begin; he'd be sending storm troopers in for her if she didn't go out. But she could no longer bear to sit with him in the reserved German seats right behind the orchestra where everyone—Carla and Paul especially—could see her.

Still, she forced her feet away from the window when another woman came in. And then she thought of it and turned back. The ledge of this tall window was as wide over the street as it was inside. She poked her head way out. A decorative stone shelf about a foot wide ran around the entire building with access to many other open windows, although it was three stories off the ground.

"A lovely night out there," the woman who had come in said. "Hard to believe it when the air's usually filled with mortar smoke and the stench of Germans lately."

"How true," Lesley replied, half listening. There was no more time now. She had to go back out to Max, but during the next intermission, she would risk it!

"Are you quite all right, *Liebe*?" Max asked her when she rejoined him, his face, which always looked stern these days, obviously relaxing to see her. He did love her in his sick, convoluted way, she supposed, and she did hold a certain power over him. But none of that mattered. It might be the only chance she would have to get away, and if she fell to the street below or were captured, imprisoned, beaten, killed even, how could that be worse than having to go with Max Dorff to wartime Berlin to be his bride?

He had almost not let her go this intermission, she thought as she strode directly into the back room of the ladies' suite without looking right or left, relieved that clinging Bibi Rossi had not accompanied her. Anxiously she sat, fully dressed, on the mahogany seat of the loo in one of the compartments, pulling up her full hem to catch it in her belt, putting the long gold chain of her minaudière around the back of her neck, waiting for two other women to leave. If they kept coming in like this, she'd never get a head start on the time Max might give her in here.

She closed her eyes to try to calm herself, but she kept seeing Max's taut expression as he'd leaned close to kiss her in the hall outside. Her stomach was queasy, she'd told him. It was probably the excitement of trying to decide what to take in just a few suitcases until she could send for the rest later, the thrill of reuniting with the twins as they headed north to Milan and then Berlin. Evidently, he'd believed her.

The tiny lull in the room when the last woman went out screamed at her. Now. Now! She dashed out, had her shoes off and stuck in her belt in a trice. She'd left her stole behind her on her seat, anything to make him believe she had every intention of coming back. She hoisted herself up to a sitting position on the inside ledge, grabbed the open casement to steady herself. Women's voices coming. They would see her, perhaps think she meant to throw herself out. And rather than ever let Max Dorff touch her again, perhaps she would! Barefooted, she stood, wavered, then simply bent over to step through the tall, narrow window onto the ledge, shuffled a bit sideways, and leaned against the cool façade of the back of the building.

A nearly full moon silvered the rooftops that seemed stacked far into the vast, velvet black. She stood only a few seconds to gain her balance before she began to inch her way along, still pressed to the façade. She came to the next open window and heard a male singer's voice gliding up and down his scales. Dressing rooms along here perhaps. Soon, surely everyone would have to be back on stage and she could get inside somewhere. The breeze caressed her perspiring face, lifted the draped swags of satin over her bosom. At least she had no fear of heights; she preferred them to any enclosed room anyplace. When she shuffled her way around the corner, she even smiled and bit her lip with joy as the first sense of freedom in weeks, in years, assailed her. Now even if Max crashed into the women's room as she pictured him doing, even when he looked out the window, he would see only the dark rooftops of the city he wanted to destroy and the vast, free sky he could never touch.

Afraid to come out, afraid the Germans would find her, Lesley hid for that night and the next day and night in a small, cramped dusty attic storeroom of the Opera. She'd heard German voices once in the hall; someone had opened the door, shone a light in, but gone right back out. She huddled there in the dark behind crates of French champagne no doubt meant to tingle the throats of the Germans.

When she dared to crack the door into the hall once, she saw the cases and bottles of her hiding place read Moët and Chandon and Veuve Cliquot. Those were two of the vineyards, she recalled painfully, she and Paul had visited near Châtillon in France, the champagne they'd brought back to share with the Guyon family at their beautiful little inn. This chamber might be tiny and dark, the stacked cases hemming her in, yet she felt so safe and free here from everything but her memories, while she waited to be certain the Germans had fled.

She'd lost so much in these war years—worst of all, Paul was Carla's now. But she knew, at least, the salvation of Rome had come when she peered out a narrow window across the hall the morning of June 6 and recognized British and American uniforms in the streets below. Delivered from everything now but her eternally haunting love for Paul Kendal. Even if she'd drunk all these hundreds of bottles of champagne instead of merely sipping from one to allay her thirst, she could never become intoxicated enough to forget him. With tears streaming down her face in tempered joy and relief as the crowds of Romans celebrating below increased, she gathered her arms full of champagne and went down into the wild, raucous streets.

Rome, all of Rome had gone crazy! She offered the bottles to the first American servicemen she saw and accepted their frenzied hugs and kisses in return. Dazed, she walked on through the burgeoning, screaming masses toward home. Red, white, and green partisan armbands and Italian and American flags sprouted everywhere. On the Via Cavour a shouting crowd rocked, then toppled to its side a German flakwaggon antiaircraft gun mounted on a half-track that had somehow been left behind in the scramble to retreat. The Americans were not conquerors; they were deliverers, saviors, and the Romans were rejoicing to help them as never before.

People threw violets, poured wine down the parched throats of dirty, sweating soldiers, hugging them, asking them their names and hometowns. Women kissed men they had never seen and walked with them carrying their backpacks. Italian children rode the shoulders of the foreign troops as if they'd known them all their young lives, when in truth they'd known little but war and lack of fathers and elder brothers. People joined in twisting, jumping snake dances down the streets screaming, *"Viva la pace! Viva Americani!"* until it became a tribal chant. Despite the din, some soldiers marched only so far and then fell asleep on the sidewalks or in door stoops. Soon exhausted GI's littered the steps of churches and curled up against carved stone deities in fountains long gone dry from bombs hitting the aqueducts.

As she got closer to home the narrow streets smelled not only of fish and garlic but of the pungent aroma of Lucky Strikes, Philip Morris, and Chesterfield cigarettes, and made her long desperately for Paul again. Had he gotten through to the Allies? Had he returned safely to join in this wild fray? She walked slowly on, drinking in the joyous scenes of reunions, the antic craziness, the freedom. Tears of mingled joy and relief ran down her dirty face. Soon, soon, perhaps the twins could come home and life begin again. Soon, she would have to put her career back together and pray that Guido came home, that Stella and Madame and Lilla and her staff at Valente's would forgive her when she explained. And pray that she could really forget Paul as she had so miserably failed to do each time before.

Ludicrous to be standing here on her own doorstoop in this evening gown and the jewels she'd left the house in nearly two days ago with Max, she thought, as she fumbled for her key in her tiny purse. She'd know as soon as she swung the door inward if this house were free of Max Dorff for good. She closed the door on the bacchanalian celebration behind her in the square. The tiled floor, the sweep of staircase, the whole place seemed deathly silent, a tiny oasis of expectation amid the raucous world outside. She made it as far as the calm, pristine statue of Diana in the center of the entry hall and stopped to cling to her arm. "Antonio? Cook? I'm home!"

Footsteps sounded from upstairs. Heavy. A man. For one instant she feared Max might have actually stayed to settle everything with her. Her yearning, foolish, exhausted heart dared to hope perhaps Paul had heard she was missing and had come to look for her. Or Guido, perhaps Guido was home!

The feet came to the first landing. The man bent to peer down. "Oh, Antonio!" she cried. "I'm home! Is he gone?"

"Gone, Countess, gone with all of them!" he told her in a voice rough with emotion as he hurried down the stairs toward her as fast as his old legs would take him. "Gone, didn't even have time to leave a note when Hitler told them they could finally retreat, but he ransacked the house looking for you like a madman in case you'd returned. He said he'd be back and took the portrait of you and the little ones from Count Cesare's library, he did."

She started toward him, then just fell into the old man's outstretched arms. "He'll never be back, Antonio. Surely they're beaten now." And in the midst of rapture in eternal Rome, the arms of Cesare's old chauffeur, Antonio, had to do as she sobbed out her joy and bitter agony at last.

Early the next morning Lesley began to put back in order the rooms an enraged Max Dorff had randomly ravaged when he'd returned to look for her. But everything seemed so much brighter already. The sun shone, and she'd explained it all to Stella, who'd been so relieved, so happy it was all over, at least for Rome. Guido would have a chance to come home. Stella had even insisted on helping her with the house. And, as soon as possible, when everyone decided who was really in charge in the continuing chaos outside, Lesley intended to get permission to go to Capri for the twins. Other than the ruin of a few lamps, mirrors, and porcelain pieces Max had upturned or shattered, the house stood and the shop did, too. Finally, after years of pressure from the Fascists and the Germans and nine brutal months of occupation, Lesley felt almost in control again. If she could only find out that Paul was safe—but then, he was obviously no concern of hers anymore.

"Every lamp broken in here," Stella remarked in the library with a helpless roll of her eyes.

"A small price to pay," Lesley assured her. "We'll just make do with some from upstairs."

"He must have been insane with anger," Stella said in awe. "You obviously weren't hiding behind a lamp or anywhere in this room. It gives me the shudders to think he's got that painting of you and the twins. Sorry, Lesley. Didn't mean to go on like that," she apologized and touched Lesley's shoulder. "I hear someone at the door. I'll get it."

"It's all right, Stella. I'll go," Lesley said, and hurried out.

Carla Fracci stood there, red-eyed, hitting her purse rhythmically into the stone wall. She shouldered her way in before Lesley could even react.

"Carla, didn't he come back?" Lesley demanded.

"You mean you haven't seen him?" Carla's fist smacked her palm as she spoke. "He came back but I won't let him leave!" she blurted out defiantly.

"What? He's all right? He's safe?" Lesley cried and grasped Carla's hands to still them.

Carla yanked free. She looked as if she were no longer listening. "Then there's only one other place to look," she mumbled and turned to go back outside.

"Carla, what's happened? Please wait. Tell me!"

Carla turned her head back, still not looking at Lesley, not breaking her quick stride as Lesley dashed after her. "He explained it all very carefully to me just an hour or so ago, Countess Valente! Look, I admit I lied the other night when I said he was my fiancé, but I still can't believe it." She halted at the corner of the house, leaned her head momentarily against the wall. Lesley bent close in the noise of the celebrating crowd to hear her words. "He had it all figured out! I've got to find him, tell him he's at least right about that." She whirled to face Lesley. "But he's mine! He has to be! I've changed everything for him. Sometimes I don't even know who I am anymore! I have to tell him." She ended on a sob and tore away as Lesley chased her.

Carla had lied about being engaged to Paul! She had to know how he was, what had happened. Carla ran like a woman possessed, but Lesley caught up with her, grabbed her arm just as she heard someone else shout her name.

"There's Countess Valente! She's one of them! Whored for that high-up Dorff, had fancy Nazi guards at her house even."

Still holding Carla's arm, Lesley swung around. A small crowd of women—no, there were a few men too—carried placards with slogans like "Shame to Them That Shamed Us!" and "Down with Nazi Collaborators!" and "Punish Nazi Whores!" Before she could react, they grabbed her away from Carla and shoved her toward the big square.

"Carla!" She looked back at Carla standing there as shocked as she. "Carla!"

Carla caught up to them, yelled at the crowd that Lesley was only spying for the Italian underground against the Nazis, that she had helped to support underground papers against the Germans. Harsh hands dragged Lesley along despite the fact she too argued with the women who held her arms.

"Get lost!" a man in the crowd finally shouted at Carla and shoved her back. "That's what they all say when justice finally catches up with them. We're only gonna strip her down, shave her head, and brand her with her favorite German swastika," he yelled. His eyes were fixed now on Lesley's shocked face as she'd begun to struggle in earnest. "The countess here's been tight with the Nazis and used to get special food from them for her friends. We know all about her, so get lost or come watch justice in the square!" the rabble's spokesman roared at Carla as the little vigilante group started off again.

Lesley craned her neck to shout at Carla again. "Please get help!" she managed before she lost sight of her in the churning crowd. "Find Paul, someone!" she yelled. But what she'd just asked terrified Lesley as much as did these shoving, poking people and their threats. Carla had only been her friend when it did not concern Paul and obviously Paul had upset her terribly. She could not depend on Carla to find Paul or to tell him about this until it was much, much too late.

When the crowd delivered her to the corner of the Piazza Venezia under Il Duce's old balcony, both Stella and old Antonio had found her and were screaming at the crowd. Antonio waved his pistol until someone hit him from behind, seized the pistol, discharged both its shots into the air, then pushed him down on the pavement near the small wooden platform.

Lesley almost vomited in fear as they shoved her into the line of women being stripped to their underclothes. They tore at her blouse until she stood in her slacks and brassiere. Ahead of her, Bibi Rossi screamed and kicked, held down on a wooden chair while they ripped her outer garments away. Her slip rode so far up her flailing thighs pink underpants showed. Two men held her while another hacked her blond hair raggedly short. Then another shaved her completely bald with

a large stropped razor that cut her scalp each time she jerked.
Wild with fright, her streaming eyes rolled, darted.

Lesley's mind went absolutely blank for one instant. Her
legs nearly buckled; she locked her knees to stand. Other
women, standing along the back of the platform, had already
been shaved and bore crude black swastikas from some hot
tarlike substance on their foreheads, chests, and upper arms.
Someone in the crowd threw orange peels and an occasional
tomato at the terrified group of prisoners while the crowd's
chants finally pierced her terror. Where were the authorities?
These people had no right to judge or to harm others. But they
ignored the fierce, furious words that poured from her as they
merely shoved her along in the line.

Two men dragged Bibi away still screaming, "He left me,
left me, don't you see? He didn't want me, didn't want me
ever—"

Lesley ached for Bibi, but the words might have done for her
and Paul, too. She felt as if she were in line for execution; at
least they would kill the last shred of her pride.

Suddenly, her whole life flashed before her. Is this how it
felt to face death in war, when there was no escape? Trent.
Cesare. Carlo. At least Paul had survived, Paul and the twins,
her family. And dear old Gram tending her precious flowers at
beloved Westam, no matter how brutally Constance tried to
slice it all up, tear it all apart. Her parents had loved each
other, and her, no matter how the crowds stared, pointing like
this. Somewhere, distantly, she heard Stella's frenzied voice
screaming her name, screaming at the crowd to stop. Didn't
Stella know that at the last minute there came a strange inner
calm when you knew that at least you had once been truly
loved? Her parents were gone now and Paul had deserted her,
but he had given her the twins, had helped her save them, had
sat with her on the heavenly cliffs of golden Capri and smiled
at her over their wind-tousled heads of hair—

Hard hands seized her to loosen her hair, to yank her
forward to the chair. She saw their scissors, the razor poised.
Someone bent her hands behind the chair and held them
brutally. One of her captors grabbed a handful of her curls gone
russet in the sun. "You're just like the Nazis, lowering yourself

to their level, judging others, punishing like this when you have no right!" she shouted at them all, but no one listened. She was certain she kept talking, pleading, insisting. Then a burst of shots, men's shouts, crowd screams drowned her thoughts.

Paul! Paul and two American officers with pistols on the platform! Paul in a uniform, Paul without his mustache, but Paul alive was all that mattered. They untied her hands. He covered her with his jacket, lifted her in his arms and started away down the steps while she heard one of the officers say in very bad Italian, "This crowd is gathered illegally! Go home or be arrested! No more of this! No more!" Then Carla Fracci's voice over the noise made Paul turn back around.

"These Americans are right, they are right!" Carla screeched to silence the seething crowd. "Countess Valente is a patriot! She spied against the Nazis, risked her safety to feed starving Italians in San Lorenzo." Lesley and Paul lifted their eyes to see Carla stride the platform back and forth as she spoke, gesturing to emphasize each word.

"Look, I'm telling you the countess even helped the Americans come here by finding out what road was least fortified! I know! I carried that same message! I am the one who put out *Libero* these last years after Il Duce killed her husband, Count Valente, for it! Countess Valente risked her life to save mine once. I'm telling you the truth, and even now I ask you to help and forgive these poor women you have hurt today!" She shouted and stalked the perimeter of the scaffold as if she were leading one of Mussolini's old political rallies.

Lesley nestled closer in Paul's arms as Carla's voice got stronger, fiercer. In her dreams over the years he had rescued her like this from pain and fear and loneliness, and now, in this tiny moment, it was true. It was true, and Carla was up there assured and forceful, as if she had found a new self all over again.

"She's wonderful, your Carla," Lesley murmured against his shoulder.

"Your friend Carla, my friend too, but I told her a few hours ago she could never be more to me in the long run, Lesley. She told me what was going on when these officers dropped me off in front of your house. Otherwise, I never would have found you in time. She only needed a new cause to replace me. I told her earlier she should turn *Libero* into the greatest newspaper Rome had ever known, but perhaps politics will be her passion now. But my passion's elsewhere, Lesley, always has been. It's here," he murmured and squeezed her hard as he began to walk again.

He had come for her. He held her so close and walked along as if there were only the two of them now in all of war-torn Rome, the whole world. Holding her even tighter against his chest, he turned directly into the front door of the town house Stella and Antonio joyfully held open for them.

The hours flowed by so quickly, like the tumbling crescent of water from the dolphin-boy fountain on the roof balcony where they sat and talked over lunch, over late-afternoon wine, over dinner. Paul had been captured by German troops as he returned from telling the Allies the Nazis were fleeing. It was only just before the retreating Germans nearly shot him at the city's edge he'd realized Carla must have gotten what she had told him from Lesley at the opera.

"But even if I hadn't figured out how you were using that SS bastard when it was almost too late, when they put me up against a stone wall and lifted their rifles," he told her, leaning across the table to take her hand again, "I would have still known at the end how much I loved you. All I could think of before my last-minute rescue by one of General Clark's advance divisions was that I still loved you and always would no matter what you'd done or I'd done—and that I'd never get the chance to tell you."

Tears filled her eyes. "I too, escaping at the last minute—I knew it was always you I'd loved," she told him, her voice silky and shaky.

"It tore me up that you were with him—that you were his," he admitted and his green eyes glittered with unshed tears. "It was actually worse than when you married Cesare. Ever since that night over a year and a half ago when I saw Max Dorff kiss you good-night in the fur salon doorway, I could have killed him with my bare hands."

"You were there outside? Oh, Paul, Paul. But I didn't sleep with him. That was my part of the bargain from him if I promised to marry him, but *I* would have killed him with my bare hands before I'd ever have gone through with that, at least after we got the twins out of his reach."

"You kept him out of your bed?" he asked, his face incredulous. "Hell, that's the Lesley I knew at first, but—you did?"

She bit her lower lip and nodded as dreadful memories of that night in Max's mansion in Grünwald crept back again. He'd almost raped her but she had stood up to him, defied him. She wanted so to tell Paul all about that, about everything, during these precious hours of sharing when he took so much of her burden on himself by just being here, by listening to her, smiling at her. Still, he was leaving in the morning with General Mark Clark's troops to chase the Germans north, to cover the war openly at last. General Clark had made him a special army news attaché and his duty would take him where the action was. He was leaving her again like before for his duty, so the truth about the twins would wait until she was certain they could all be together for good.

"Lesley, I love you. If it's painful, I don't meant to pry. It's been so long for us, and I don't want to shatter all this—" He pulled her into his lap, encircling her with his arms. They'd both been through hell, he thought. She'd told him she'd been caught spying on Hitler himself and his Luftwaffe chief, Göring, and she had survived. So far, they and their love had survived.

"Let's not mention all that again, nothing sad between us tonight," he murmured fervently as he tipped her chin up to gaze deeply into her eyes. "Listen, sweetheart, I've something to apologize for—one thing among the many I'm going to be working on for years if you'll let me."

Her eyes narrowed almost imperceptibly. "Such as, Gian Paul Kendal?" she challenged with a tremulous smile.

He grinned. He felt relieved he'd mentioned the years they had before them. Funny, how she'd evidently sensed his need to lighten this conversation, to lift them back into the realm of happiness they'd shared years ago. "I'm just damned sorry I accused you of always running away from problems, because it's the best thing you ever did to go out that window at the Opera. Someday you can tell the twins, 'Yes, your old mum spent the end of the German occupation in Rome going out bathroom windows and drinking French champagne while those bloody awful Nazis hightailed it out of town.' "

" 'Hightailed it?' Is that how you crude Yanks talk about one of the most glorious retreats of this whole damned war?"

Their eyes held. They would have laughed, but they were too spellbound in the rush of love that encompassed them. Their first kiss since bombs had blazed about them in burning London years ago made explosions all of its own.

Night crept upon them, and diamond pinpoint stars leapt out in the sable sky above their heads. He would write to her. If she wanted anything, she need only ask the American commander left behind in Rome. She would rebuild her life and Valente's here. After the war, she would get the American market back, bring the twins to New York to him if he could not return right away. They would marry, they would really become a family at last after this was all over. And then, she vowed to herself, she would tell him he had fathered Cati and Paolo. They talked and dreamed and held and kissed. As if they'd never been apart, as if the night were new and this were Venice and he had just given her the ring and the promise of a future together, they went in to bed.

Nothing cruel or terrifying mattered at this moment. There was no destruction, no danger, no harsh separate pasts. Staggered by the impact of their love, she felt again every nuance of touch and beauty she had forgotten. She sensed all the possibilities of heart and mind and body she had put away forever without him. And when they joined, they had never been apart.

"My sweetheart, my sweetheart," he whispered, his voice suddenly so desperate, "all the time we've wasted. We were both wrong, so wrong to struggle and deceive like we did, to put anything else first—"

"Sh. I love you, always have, Paul. Always."

They moved in perfect unison like the cresting, rolling green sea. They set forth together on the deep, whatever might befall. She lost herself in waves of desire—no, shared herself with him—and for this little time, the war was over almost forever and they were together that long, too. If morning ever came on the dancing horizon, they would go on, merged in spirit if not in flesh, and no one, not even this whole vast hovering war, could ever threaten them again.

PART IV

Forever and a Day

Now tell me how long you would have her
                    after you possessed her.
Forever and a day . . .

SHAKESPEARE
As You Like It

✿ ✿ *Chapter Twenty-one*

IN LESLEY'S OFFICE at Valente's, Lesley, Madame Justine, and Stella bent their heads together over sketches of the new 1944 Countess Valente line of furs they intended to hurry into production this month. They had decided to merge their leather and fur concerns, at least for the next season, since Stella's mother had died last month and Stella had moved temporarily into the townhouse with Lesley and the twins. They gestured, pointed, talked all at once to share ideas. Yet every so often in a lull their gazes would link before someone looked away with a hint of frown and lips compressed. Though they leaned over the worktable shoulder to shoulder, each woman's thoughts drifted into their own private worlds.

Madame was longing to see Paris again, newly liberated last month by the Allied forces chasing the Germans through France. Stella's moods swung precipitously between certainty that Guido was dead and the firm belief he would return any moment now, unharmed, in love, still Guido—and ask her to marry him. How much easier everything would be now that Lesley had made her feel a part of the Valente empire and family already.

Lesley—no matter how hard she worked, how happy she was to have the twins back—missed Paul terribly and thought of him all the time. It was as though only half of her walked and talked. She was designing a new line to take advantage of the meager resources both Valente's and Sollo's leather goods had salvaged after the ruinous German occupation. It was sometimes as though only Paul's last fierce caress and impassioned words as he'd left her that morning after their only night together in five years propelled her on without him: "The war isn't over yet, sweetheart, and we both have jobs to do, but the war between us is over. Swear it, Lesley, swear it!" he'd insisted desperately, and she had.

"I swear," Madame was saying with a flourish of both quick hands, "this line is brilliant, *magnifique*! So innovative, even if it is partly forced on you by lack of materials and the fact it will be a while before anyone will have money for large pieces again. Unless, of course, you can get that rich American market back, no?"

Lesley could see Stella struggle to refocus her attention on the sketches Madame indicated: three-piece ensembles that could be purchased in separate pieces or complete; an extensive line of gloves in cedar, rose, and ecru suede that would be cuffed with skillfully cut scraps of karakul and mink pelts; sable and mink and fox peplums to wear over skirts and suits; wraps of lamé edged in sable; reefer coats of leather and beaver inspired by the Allied military look; and an entire, fashion-setting line of women's sporty bowlers, berets, and fedoras with fur trim.

When Madame went back next door to Sollo's for more swatches of leather, Stella sank into a chair and stared down at the drawings of the hats again while Lesley took the sketch of the reefer coat over to the window to refine the lines. Whatever would Cesare have said if he had been here to see her producing an entire collection of fur mixed with other materials? But he would simply have had to understand. So long ago, Cesare. Even memories and nightmares of Max were starting to fade now, thank goodness, as he'd been gone three months. But Paul had been gone that long too, and yet she thought about him more and more.

She sighed and leaned forward on her elbows to look out over the busy Via Condotti. Not many fashionable shoppers these days, although even women without money still strolled along and gazed in the windows as though they had something to spend. Several of those open autos the Americans called jeeps buzzed by. How welcome they were compared to the too familiar Nazi Daimlers, Mercedes, and tanks. As difficult as things still were, at least no one stole autos or paintings or food from the Italians anymore.

On the narrow pavement below, she saw Madame leave the shop and hurry into Sollo's. Poor Madame, yearning for Paris

as she was yearning for Paul. And he'd written of terrible
recent destruction in France, much worse than when the Nazis
had originally taken the country. He'd been with Patton's Third
Army in Alsace-Lorraine while the Allies pursued the Nazis
toward Germany, close to the same area where they'd toured so
happily in his big yellow Buick before the war. She could
almost hear Paul's voice now in the four precious letters he'd
written her that came through the Allied Commander here in
Rome, letters of which she'd memorized every word.

"My Sweetheart," he'd written in the one where he'd been
to Châtillon. "Sweethearts," and "my loves" were sprinkled
through the letters. She smiled. His voice, concerned, strong,
capable of dipping to an unsuspected tease, warmed her even
now. "I'm as safe as possible, but I have some bad news I
know will grieve you, and yet I want to share it. We have to
share everything from here on out, the good and the bad. The
second day after I transferred from General Clark's Fifth Army
to be here with Patton's Third, I had a chance to visit the little
inn where we stayed a week with the Guyons in '39. It seems
almost forever ago. Sadly, the exterior of the place is pock-
marked with artillery-shell holes and tumbled down back by
the kitchen by some bigger blast. Our little garret room has no
roof to speak of and the Germans or someone have thoroughly
looted the place. And in the cellar, with two geese her only
companions and a half sack of grain I think she'd been eating
too, I actually found the girl Anne-Marie hiding, the one you
felt so sorry for. She was terrified of me at first, men in
general—I shudder to think what must have happened to her
when the Germans came through. Later she thought I was
someone else. A man named Claude, her brother perhaps?
Anyway, she was filthy and starving and we took her to a
neighbor to care for and gave her some food and money—"

Lesley's eyes misted and the scene below her on the street
blurred. Poor, innocent Anne-Marie and all the other Anne-
Maries the war had abused who would never have their
Claudes come home to them. Thank God, she had Paul. If only
he would not be angry with her when she eventually told him
the twins were his. "We have to share everything from here on
out, the good and the bad," he'd written.

Then, on the pavement below, she noticed a rumbling,

swaying cabbage cart pulled by a skinny mule. It reminded her of the way she'd first come into Rome to join the Valentes, to seek her future as a furrier, so nervous with only one set of clothes to her name. Now here she stood in charge. But it was not just the cabbage cart that drew her gaze and made her hold her breath.

It was the thin chap who clambered down from the cart beside the driver as she had once done. His hair was just like Guido's, but she dared not arouse Stella's hopes only to dash them. No, he was much too thin, dressed like a field hand, and he limped. But when he looked straight up at the façade of Valente's and she saw his face, she jumped back in shock. Her sketch and pen tumbled to her feet. She pressed clasped hands to her breasts.

"What is it?" Stella said without looking up. "I thought that drawing was quite good and—"

Lesley darted at her, grabbed her wrist, pulled her toward the door. "Guido. I saw him. It's Guido!" was all she could say before she burst into tears as they both tore through the surprised group of women assembling garments.

They thundered down the stairs like children, Stella in the lead screaming, crying. "Guido! Guido! Guido!"

He was just inside the front door when they exploded from behind the brocade curtain into the salon. He gave a whoop as Stella threw herself into his arms and he spun her just once around before he stumbled and stopped. Tears glazed his face. He kissed Stella once hard, his hands cradling her head. Then he turned to Lesley, his face ravaged with emotion, so unlike himself. He held out his hands to her. "I didn't worry about anything here, not even Stella," he said and his voice broke. "I knew my favorite countess would take care of everything—"

He hugged her hard, repeating her name as a child might—as Carlo might have if he had ever come home. "Guido, thank God. Thank God!" she murmured and kissed his wet cheek.

The three of them sat all afternoon in a café on the pavement of the Piazza di Spagna and, like the old Guido, he regaled them with his stories of hiding from the Germans to avoid either being made to fight the Americans or executed, of his four-month deathly bout with typhus fever, and of the old woman in Acerra who had nursed him back to health.

"I promised her a mink coat when I left, and you know what she said, my lovelies?" he asked as he took another swig of his Frascati and a long drag on one of the cheroots he had somehow come up with on the way into Rome in a cabbage cart.

"That she'd consider it payment for putting up with you all that time as long as it was a Countess Valente mink!" Stella put in. She was so excited, flying so high Lesley knew the girl didn't realize what she was doing half the time, holding Guido's hand, kissing it, kissing him, alternating between tears and smiles.

"That too, Stellina *mia*," he said and brushed a stray lock back from his forehead. "No, she said she'd heard minks were something like rats and her house had enough of those, but she would like to have new white curtains for her windows someday. It seems the Americans had to use them for bandages when they first came through, though some GI had paid her in packages of gum. *Madre Maria*, packages of gum! They may be heroes, but they're as crazy and uncouth as they are clever, Lesley," he teased. "And you're quite sure you're in love with an American?" he demanded, the old glint back in his eyes.

She and Stella had told him the entire story of the German occupation and her rescue by Paul from those bent on revenge against collaborators. Lesley had told them she'd known Paul before the war but, luckily, they were so intent on each other they never thought of all the other questions to ask about Paul Kendal. Lesley was so happy for them she insisted they stay here as long as they wanted. She kissed them both again, waved good-bye, and walked back alone the short distance to Valente's.

She returned people's frequent greetings with a smile or wave, stopping to chat with neighboring shopkeepers when they insisted she step in. How different it was for her now that Carla Fracci's new "Liberated *Libero*," as she jokingly called it, had told the whole story. Lesley now owned one-third of the newspaper—imagine, Lesley Westam Valente owning part of a newspaper! And yet, just as everything else, even people's kindness and friendliness made her long so for Paul. If only the

Allies could chase the Nazis clear to Berlin and make certain
all of them who had fled there like rats would never harm
anyone anymore. And if only it didn't take too long!

"Health and wealth to the newlyweds! Much love and many
happy years together," old Antonio proclaimed proudly when
Lesley asked him to give a toast for Guido and Stella at the
Christmas Eve gathering at the Valente town house. Glasses of
hot spiced wine punch were lifted in unison toward the
beaming Stella and serious Guido, including the two cups of
orange punch the twins held. Cati and Paolo, just four months
short of turning five, were so excited to be up late and have a
decorated tree in the second-floor sitting room. It wasn't a fir
tree or very tall, but it would have to do until this war was
really over everywhere, Lesley thought. The ribbon, pieces of
broken stained-glass decorations, and the strips of silver lamé
she'd cut from an old gown for makeshift tinsel were a far cry
from what she recalled from her childhood days at Westam, but
during these times, one must make do with what one had.

"Married nearly three months and it still seems like yesterday!" Guido said, accepting their good wishes and lifting his
glass dramatically for another toast. "The prodigal son hath
returneth and this lovely little soiree certainly beats the hell out
of a fatted calf or the places I've been the last few holiday
seasons. And I'm so pleased and honored to be partners in
business with my best friend, Countess Lesley Valente. A toast
to her and holiday cheers to all of us here together." He kissed
Lesley on the cheek and hugged a blushing Stella to his side.

Bravos warmed Lesley as she smiled at the little gathering.
It was originally just intended to be family and servants in the
Westam tradition—Antonio, Cook, the maids, Lilla with
whom she had reconciled and who had brought her husband,
Giovanni. Poor man, he'd never quite recovered from shell
shock and always bore a skittish look of perpetual surprise.
And of course Madame Justine, but Lesley had also invited
Carla, who had showed up with quite an entourage to swell the
little group: her elderly parents; two journalists she'd recently
hired to write for *Libero;* and a British Army sergeant from
Edinburgh, Scotland, who had actually played his bagpipes for
them earlier.

Carla had become a new Carla now in the second metamorphosis Lesley had seen in the few years she'd known her. A new, wild exuberance, and new, wild hairstyle with frizzed locks rampant around her petite, elfin face with the huge eyes. Her clothes were tasteful but severely tailored, neither the Bohemian nor excessively feminine look of the two earlier Carlas. The fervent dedication to a cause had remained, even grown, as had the single-minded passion for a man. Only the man was now a red-haired Scotsman, and who knew what would come of that?

Lesley was relieved to see Carla so busy and happy, and grateful their friendship had survived their subtle battle over Paul, whom they never mentioned once after Carla had inquired each time if he was safe. They had not even discussed Paul's new novel, *To Have and Hold*. He'd sent Lesley a copy from Paris where he'd been assigned to spend the winter and she knew Carla had read it because of a review of it in *Libero* last month. The review had called the book, and justly so, "incisive, heartwarming, and inspiring." At least, Lesley thought, Carla had not called it true, as indeed she must know a great deal of it was. In a way, it was one long love letter to the heroine of the novel, the heroine Paul had told her once she had inspired.

"If everyone will excuse me for a moment, Miss Caterina and Master Paolo Valente are off to bed as it's nearly eleven," Lesley announced. It was past their bedtime, and she needed a moment alone from all the rush as she did sometimes lately.

"Oh, Mama!" Cati protested. "We're not a bit sleepy!" And Paolo nodded so vigorously in agreement he spilled his punch.

"Come on now, this isn't Capri where we run about till all hours," she teased and took their hands to lead them away.

"But we didn't!" Paolo bemoaned. "When it got dark there we had to go to bed."

"So, you see you're lucky to have modern lighting here or you'd have been in bed hours ago. Say good night now," she urged them with a decisive nod.

When she and Lilla had them tucked in and Lilla went back downstairs, Cati, the master of nighttime delays, said, "Could you read us just one little part of Paul's book again, Mama? Any part would do."

"We'd be ever so sleepy then," Paolo piped up, wide-eyed, from his bed next to Cati's. Since coming back from Capri where they'd slept in one room, they'd been afraid to be apart at night, and so far, with the war still going on, she hadn't pressed it. Sometimes she felt afraid at night too, and still kept the pistol under the other pillow of her bed. But this was a little game the twins had played ever since she'd told them Paul had written the big book and explained his name was not really Gian at all. They took turns fetching her copy of *To Have and Hold* from her room and turning randomly to a section which she would read. Somehow, it was a game that intrigued her almost as much as it did them.

"All right, but hurry, whoever's turn it is," she said, capitulating and sitting on the edge of Cati's bed. "Mama has to get back down to her guests."

Paolo ran for the book and Cati flipped to a section and pointed her finger. Lesley had told herself that if they ever happened to choose one of the several fervent love scenes in the novel, she would just have to think of something to recite. Quickly, they cuddled into their beds while she sat on the edge of Cati's bed and skimmed the section Cati had chosen. Then she began.

" ' "Dreadful how the war makes everyone age before their time, especially the children growing up too fast," Clair told him. "My son's childhood was every bit as much a victim as my stepson who died—in the Russian campaign." ' " Lesley's voice faltered at the end of the paragraph.

"Just like Uncle Carlo died in Russia," Cati put in solemnly with a roll of her green eyes.

This had been a bad idea tonight, Lesley thought. Bad timing. This was a section Paul had obviously based on her—and it voiced things that had worried her throughout the war. The next time she saw him in person, she had to tell him the twins were his. And then, someday, somehow, she had to tell Cati and Paolo.

"Isn't there more?" Paolo prompted, bouncing the bed.

" 'It just makes you realize childhood, like life itself, is a gift to all of us. Pretending, playing, all those carefree days when everything is so secure because Mother and Father are there to—tuck you in at night,' " she read, and her voice caught before she went on as if she had to finish. " 'A real childhood's a far cry from a kid wondering if he'll ever see his father again or diving under the kitchen table every time a plane flies over.' "

She closed the book, pressed it into her lap. Here it was Christmas Eve and everything was getting to her, touching her, shaking her. She jumped as Cati's small hand reached out and covered hers over the book. "Don't be sad, Mama. Paolo and I aren't afraid of planes flying over anymore, are we?"

"No. I never was," Paolo boasted. "I want one of my own to fly someday, just like the one you told us our uncle Trent had."

Fighting tears, she kissed them both good night and left the door to the hall slightly ajar in case they wakened and called out to her as they had when they'd first come home. She stood quietly a moment, hearing the distant voices of the party below, wishing desperately she didn't feel so alone without Paul even in the midst of friends and family. Soon. This war and his assignments with the American army had to be over very soon, and next year they would all be together at Christmas. At her dressing table she quickly repaired her streaked mascara, dabbed powder on her nose, and went back down to her guests.

But it was another year apart for them as Paul was sent to Berlin from Paris and then to Washington, D.C., until the Japanese finally surrendered as Germany had before them. She had worried terribly while he was in Berlin, imagined him stumbling across Max there somehow as she remembered how he'd said he could have killed him with his bare hands. "All those deaths of all those key figures in the war so close together," Paul had told her during a scratchy trunk call from Paris, "as though God had decided it was over all of a sudden and was wiping the slate clean. President Roosevelt's death on April twelfth, Mussolini shot on April twenty-eighth, Hitler's suicide two days later." That had been the last call she'd had with him before his orders took him back to the States.

She recalled *Libero*'s accounting of Mussolini's brutal end and shuddered. The "Divine Duce" was fleeing north to Germany when he was captured by partisans and shot with his faithful mistress, Claretta Petacci, at his side. Both bodies had been displayed on meat hooks in a garage in Milan while crowds hurled abuse and spit on their bloody corpses. It was justice again, and yet so cruel, so inhumane, as if the war had ruined civilized justice forever. Of the Nazis, Göring was being tried with other high-ranking officers at the Nuremburg Trials and Himmler had committed suicide with cyanide when the Allies captured him.

She felt, in a way, as if she had helped ruin Göring and Hitler's grandiose plans in the end. From overhearing their argument so long ago in Berlin, she had been able to tell the Allies where to look for the looted artworks of France and Italy, and eight months ago in caves near Salzburg and Salzkammergut, American soldiers had found two hundred million dollars worth of stolen Nazi goods. Now if only she could hear something definite about Maxmilian Dorff, then that part of the nightmare could really be ended, too.

She still dreamed about Max some nights and woke sweat-drenched. It was always the same in the dream: she was trapped in his big dark mansion in Grünwald while he pursued her from room to room until there was only his bedroom with the big, black bed hung with swastikas and flapping golden eagles, where he pressed her down into deep sable coats until the plush pelts turned to rolling waves and she sank from sight, unable to breathe.

"Blast it, it's finally getting to me!" she scolded herself aloud and snapped back to the present. She had to forget about the past and go on. This was mid-February 1946 and the war was over. She had to finish her packing for she was finally going to see Paul. It had been a year and half of separation— the war, and then his father's sudden death just when Paul was planning to fly here for Christmas this year. How she'd sympathized and grieved with him for the loss of his father, every bit as sudden as it had been when her father had fallen over that day out on the gallops at Westam.

But now, she was going to join him in New York for two weeks to work everything out between them while Stella and Lilla cared for the twins here. She knew Paul would be so pleased she was putting their love before family business by sending Madame and Guido to the first Leningrad fur auction since the war without her when she should really go herself. Yet now, settling his family business had to take precedence in their lives. They both would have to accept that it would sometimes be that way for them, so he would never accuse her again, as he had in the past, of putting her ambitions before their love.

Despite how well Kaye Kendal had carried on at Kendal and Son during the war, their father's will had still bestowed the family business on Paul. He was arranging everything so his sister could take over with the help of Barry Pearson, father of Paul's one-time fiancée, Melissa. He was, at least, preparing to turn everything over so that he could move permanently back to Europe to write. Still, Lesley felt strangely afraid, not of the flight to London where she would at last see her grandmum, who had been ill and was confined to a wheelchair, nor of personally facing the struggle for Westam again now that the British courts were back in full swing after the war, nor of the ocean voyage alone to America where she'd never been. What frightened her was the feeling it all seemed too easy, too perfect now after all the terrible times she and Paul had been through to survive the World War and that other war they had waged between them. And the fact she had yet to tell him about the twins and that she'd lied to him over the years about that grieved her. She'd had no other choice, and he simply must understand!

"*Liebe*," a voice whispered somewhere near, and she thought at first it was a trick of her guilty, distraught mind. "*Liebe*."

She gasped and whirled to face a man who'd come in the bedroom door, open so she could hear the children if they called. He quietly closed it behind him. He wore a heavy tweed coat against the February chill. His soft felt hat was pulled down to hide his face. But he was tall and broad-shouldered and no figment of her imagination with that gun held in his gloved hand.

"Appalled instead of happy to see me, *meine Liebe*?"

"Max! But how—" Her own instantly pounding heartbeat terrified her. He took off his hat and sailed it onto the bed beside her half-packed suitcases and shifted the Luger from one hand to the other while he pulled off his gloves and stuffed them in his pockets.

"How? It's not important, but I'll tell you. The *Romische Weg*, 'the Roman way.' Many of us who have money flee on from Innsbruck. We are smuggled through the Brenner Pass and then, luckily for you, my countess, on to Rome. Forged International Red Cross passports, entry visas to South American countries. Quite easy, you see, for the price and the danger." He shrugged and the corners of his mouth lifted in a taut smile. "Actually, I'm one of the last of the Führer's elite to avail myself of it for reasons I won't go into here. But I came back for my love, my countess. You and I are off to Paraguay on a ship late tonight for a new life together."

She stared aghast. "Max, I couldn't. The children!"

"They look wonderful, sleeping like innocent lambs before the slaughter. I peeked in."

That old threat, the only one he knew would work. Her skin crawled; her stomach churned. He was really here, had gotten in past Antonio somehow, maybe had a key made from before, she didn't know. But she couldn't depend on Antonio for help and Guido and Stella had gone to a party. Lilla and Cook were out. All her fears had come true. It was not over for her, the terror. Max held a Luger that glinted as coldly as his eyes.

"Not running to throw your arms around your Max, *Liebe*? Not wild with joy to see him after you were so unfortunately separated from him that last night when the Führer ordered us to flee?" he mocked and took a step toward her. "Convince me that is what happened, *Liebe*, convince me with your body this time and not your words as you refused to do in my mansion in Grünwald." A step closer. A wolflike grin of anticipation as his hard eyes raked her. "Then maybe I really will let you go with me to Paraguay, open your own furrier shop there someday. Convince me now, *Liebe*, and maybe I will let you take the twins with us and not kill them first."

She ran at him then, knowing she should use the pretense of welcoming him, unable to dissemble in her fury. "You won't hurt them! You wouldn't—"

He grabbed her by one arm and twisted her away from him, then yanked her backward into his iron embrace with his arms crushing her belly and arms. While she struggled, he dragged her back to put the gun down on the bureau, then dragged her to the bed. "Packing suitcases, *Liebe*?" he hissed at her. "Good, I'll let you take some things with you after you've convinced me you want to accompany me—want to be my loving, dutiful wife."

The suitcases bounced and one lid slammed shut as he pushed her on the bed and lay hard across her, pinning her down, pressing her into a fur coat laid out just as in the nightmare. She had to think, get control of her wheeling, crashing thoughts and fears. He had the strength of a madman as he tore her velvet robe open, clawed at her silk nightgown. His face, despite the thin, blond beard he'd grown to disguise himself, was the same, the ice-blue eyes so hard, lit within by demons, by his insane rage.

"Max, please. Please, not like this . . ."

"All the times, all the months you put me off, my countess, promising to be my wife. More deceitful than I ever was, lying to me, leading me on! Convince me now with your lies and your body, or I swear you will never even live to see Paraguay!"

"Yes, I want to. Please, I just can't breathe like this!"

He loosed her slightly, breathing hard, staring down at her, then let her sit while she slowly removed her robe. Anything for a moment of time to think, to delay his touch. Tiny flames flickered deep in his eyes. He threw his heavy coat to the floor; his gaze was riveted on her as he fumbled with his belt. Then, she knew what to do.

Cesare's old pistol lay under the pillow next to hers. She would have to let him begin to—to touch her and she could slide her hand for it, hold it on him, make him get off, get up. He'd never reach his Luger in time. Her entire body quivered as his hands spread her ankles wide and slid heavily up her thighs, ruffling her silk nightgown around his wrists like huge cuffs. He pulled her down under him and straddled her. She fought the urge to burst into frenzied tears. Instead, she stretched her arms out as if to welcome him into them. His words, "more deceitful than I ever was, lying to me, leading me on," swirled through her mind as if she'd said them, as if she feared Paul would say them. The gun. If he would just lower his head to kiss her, she could seize the gun.

But her right arm pushed, then shoved her robe to the floor, and he looked away for one moment. He jerked, then gasped. Her eyes followed his as he grabbed for the photo on the bedside table of her and Paul, which Antonio had taken that last morning just before Paul had set out with Clark's army. They were standing on the town house balcony with the roofs of Rome in the background, Paul in his American uniform, their arms around each other, smiling into each other's eyes after their secret shared night of passion and love. Max stared a moment. He asked nothing, said nothing. He simply smashed the framed photo to the floor and seemed to explode. His voice so different, not his own controlled, menacing one now—loud, wild, berserk.

"Traitor, traitor, just like her," he roared directly into her face. His features looked blurred, distorted. Spittle flecked his lips and her face. "Said she loved me, threw me out for someone else. You, too! Admit it! Laughed at me, my lovemaking, so I showed her then and there in the Bristol, in her bed, who was master, showed her for all she'd done—"

"Max, please, I don't know who you're speaking of. Max, Max don't!" she managed as he slapped her once then pressed her down again. His hands moved to her throat, grasped her there. He was repeating some other woman's name, someone named Mina as he crushed her. His knees jammed her legs farther apart. She kicked, flailed at his face. She couldn't breathe! Vibrant, brilliant colors flashed through her brain. Instinctively, she tried to shove him off, then reached desperately for the pistol, not caring if he would see it or not. Shoot him in the arm, the hands choking her. Shoot him somehow, his horrible face, make him stop. Couldn't breathe—couldn't stop him . . .

He saw the gun, tried to grab it. His hand over hers on the gun! He would kill her now, shoot her. The twins, too! Paul, they're yours, always were and I too—

The crack of sound boomed in her ear, bounced in her head. He jolted upright, his eyes wide with shock. She tried to twist out from under him, shove him off, away. She grabbed great gulps of air into her lungs. No searing pain anywhere but in her chest. Had he shot her? She turned back to push him away again, but he toppled to the floor, rolled over once, facedown, lay still. But he'd had the gun in his hand, hadn't he? She didn't see it anywhere as she hunched there at the edge of the bed, terrified he would move, get up again more ravenous than ever. She continued to gasp in long, jagged, sobbing breaths. She glistened with sweat, yet the chill of the room slapped her, made her shake until her teeth rattled. At last, she scrambled off the end of the bed and backed away.

Was he really dead? Had no one heard the shot? Was no one coming to help her? From a few yards away she said in a low voice, "Max?"

He lay so quiet and still next to the bed with its silk spread pulled awry. There was a crimson puddle on her velvet robe and broken glass from the picture frame of her and Paul beneath his outstretched hand. The twins, at least the twins were safe now. But even as she thought of them, she heard Cati's voice outside the door, then a quiet knocking.

"Mama! I heard a sound. I had a bad dream. Mama, the door's locked!"

She looked down at herself. No, like the bed itself and the fur on which they had lain, there was no blood on her, so had he somehow shot himself? She couldn't remember. Surely she had done it. She'd wanted to do it! And the dark, wet stain was spreading from him now, creeping everywhere.

"Mama!" Cati's voice jolted her back. She rushed to the door. Max must have locked it. She touched his Luger on the bureau, its metal ice-cold. She put it in the drawer, opened the door, then closed it after her and, kneeling in the hall, took Cati into her arms.

Tears streaked the frightened little face. "Did you have a nightmare too, Mama?"

They clung hard to each other. "Yes, my love. Yes, I did. Everything's fine. Won't you go on back to bed now?"

Cati pulled back, wiping her cheeks with her fist. "But didn't you hear that bang? There was yelling, too. Is Guido angry with Stella, do you think? Mama, I'm so glad you're not gone to New York yet to see Paul," she cried and threw herself against Lesley again.

New York. Paul. Impossible. She'd just killed Max Dorff, who had tried to kill her, and now all the scandal would begin again. "Nazi Lover Returns to Claim Countess" . . . "Lovers' Tryst Turns to Murder" . . . " 'Scandal's Child' Charged." People would find out. She would have to stay here to protect her children.

"My child, my darling Cati, please go back to bed," she murmured, her face pressed to the little girl's fragrant hair. "Everything's fine now. Mama's decided she can't go to New York right now, so don't you worry." She knew it was true the moment she said it. Not with this, not go to Paul after this defilement and all the deceit over the years about the twins. "We have to share everything from here on out, the good and the bad," he'd insisted, but how could she after this? If he didn't forgive her—and who could blame him?—it would be as if she'd killed their love, just as she'd killed Max Dorff. If he was indeed as dead as he looked back there—but she couldn't bear to touch him, to roll him over. Damn, where was Antonio and why didn't Guido come home!

She got Cati back in bed and sat, Luger in hand as if guarding a sleeping man who could leap up and attack her again, order women beaten, order men dragged away to brutal labor camps, threaten her twins, Rome, the Jews, the world. She stared down at his tousled blond head and the black stain under him for a very long time, waiting for Guido and Stella to come home. His limp, bloody hand stretched out over the shattered photograph of her and Paul seemed some sort of terrible sign. It made her so afraid and so certain that everything beautiful between her and Paul was never meant to be. In the morning she'd cable him to say she could not come. She could hardly tell him all this in an overseas trunk call. Threat of Communist riots in Rome, she'd tell him; that was true. And the absolute necessity of accompanying Madame Justine to Leningrad for the first fur auction since the war ended. She'd insist Guido go to the three American openings in her place in April, when she'd told Paul she'd be coming back again. But the real reasons she could not go to Paul were the man who lay here dead on the floor and the two children who lay asleep in the next room—

She sat very stiff, very still. She only realized she was shaking from the cold and had not yet put on another robe when she heard Stella's and Guido's voices at last. She pulled one from her closet and tugged it on. She put the Luger down and ran to meet them in the hall.

❧ ❧ Chapter Twenty-two

It was a lovely April day in New York City, warm and sunny with the slightest breeze, and the walk from Kendal and Son to the seven hundred block of Fifth Avenue was not far. There was absolutely no reason for him not to go. Actually, Paul thought as his long strides took him by the glossy windows of luxury jewelry shops, leather stores, and French fashion house branches, there was no way he could not have gone. The opening of Valente di Roma's New York store was today, and though he knew she wouldn't be there, he had to go. He could have brought Kaye and Melissa along too, as the three of them often went to lunch together at their favorite Manhattan spots in this interim period while they were all at Kendal's. The women would have loved to see the furs, but not today.

There it was, between two jewelers, with its taupe scalloped awning edged with white and the name Valente di Roma over the entryway. He stared in the gleaming showcase window at his reflection superimposed over the stunning sable coat displayed against eggshell-draped velvet. Only that single garment in the entire window with the gilded words in metal script next to it: "Russian Crown Sable, Countess Valente Collection." Memories and longing made his legs nearly buckle, but he locked his knees and straightened his tie. Granted, that sable looked a great deal like the one she'd fled Westam with the night he'd first met her, the one she'd had stolen on the train into Rome, but no doubt she'd spent her time and energies and her passions on that coat instead of on him, as she'd promised.

He turned toward the glass and brass door, then hesitated. Just when he'd begun to believe that he could be an integral part of her life, she'd done it again to him like before. She'd as good as run out on him. She'd put her love for her dead husband's Valente empire ahead of her promise to come to him in New York two months ago after his father died. He was done with her, knew he should settle down with Melissa. She'd waited so faithfully while Lesley had let him down so many times. It was the last straw that Lesley had suddenly gone back on her word and traveled to the fur auction instead of coming here when she knew he needed her. Then to top that off, she'd claimed she couldn't risk leaving Rome because of the political climate. She didn't even take this chance to come to New York and, the papers reported, had sent her nephew instead. Hell, he was done with her—and yet he'd had to come today.

He stepped inside the busy room onto plush beige carpet and looked around. Muted striped wallpaper embraced the tasteful room. White furniture and potted plants had been pushed to the side for the chairs they'd brought in for the audience. The showing was still in progress, with the parade of models on the elevated, draped runway. He noticed right away all of them wore sharp fur-trimmed hats and suede gloves in muted shades. Always something new for Lesley Westam Valente; never a dull moment. He recalled the time he'd gone looking for her in London at Sackville's and come in on a show like this, only then she'd been there just for the watching, the very moment he'd first known he wanted and loved her.

But this was today, he reminded himself and looked around more objectively as he stood in the small crowd behind the larger seated audience at the back of the room. The man narrating the show from the platform had a strong Italian accent. He was quite thin, long-faced, with a somewhat beguiling yet acerbic edge to his voice these buyers and journalists probably adored. Perhaps that was Guido Valente. He'd stay just a few minutes, maybe even meet him, though he wasn't sure why.

"These designs are exquisite, but daring," one woman whispered to the other right ahead of him. "They'll set the American fur fashion world on its ear! You know, rumor is, except for the striking accessories and hats they've been showing, everything you see here will have to be ordered. The war supposedly wiped out their supplies but for odds and ends."

"Some odds and ends, but what a gambler Countess Valente must be, then. These coats are worth waiting for, I'd say. Imagine, the Italians were our mortal enemies two years ago and now the Valentes conquer us this way!"

They nodded and smiled, put their heads together to chatter on. Paul shuffled closer to the back row of chairs. Then, off to the side by the table with champagne glasses and sweating sterling buckets of bottles in crushed ice, he saw a huge portrait of Lesley on an easel. He went over, studied it. It was a black and white photo that had been enhanced with tint in what was being touted as new color photography, but it muted everything, never quite captured the subject, he thought, especially her. Her hair here was not the vibrant, dancing cognac hue he knew so well, her eyes too pale a green. But her lips looked blushed and lovely as when she wore no lipstick, like that day they'd sailed to Capri to deliver the twins to safety and she had signed the paper declaring they were his.

He sighed and his big shoulders heaved. Dreams and fantasy, fiction as surely as his novels, and yet even those were based on truth. And her cheeks in the photo glowed with rose-petal hue, the way they tended to whenever he teased or surprised her with some suggestive comment. Hell, why had he come to torment himself like this? He should just leave now before he got a chance to talk to Guido Valente, but he hadn't written Lesley in weeks nor placed any of those shaky overseas calls to Rome, and her letters had stopped too after this last betrayal. But damn, damn it! He had to know how she was.

"She looks quite young to be so talented," a short, plump peroxided blonde who'd sidled up next to him observed. "Oh," she gushed when she turned to face him, "aren't you that author? My husband reads your books. I've seen your photo on the book jackets, haven't I? Paul, ah Kent?"

"Kendal."

"Oh my, that's it. Wait till I tell him. I'll have to read them too now, but my motto's always been just to forget that horrible war since it's over, you know what I mean."

"Yes, I know. Excuse me," he mumbled and moved away. After the show ended, he edged nearer to the man he assumed was Guido Valente while people gravitated to the champagne and canapés. He didn't really see a family resemblance to Cesare but then he'd seen family members—even parents and children—both resemble and not resemble each other, so that didn't mean a thing. He started when the man's eyes caught his and he stepped directly toward him.

"You are Paul Kendal, yes? I was wondering if you would come, hoping. I was planning to contact you if you didn't, you see."

Guido escorted him a few steps away, then, when they were pursued, let him into a back salon. When Paul spoke Italian to him, Guido seemed grateful to converse in his native tongue.

"You wanted to see me?" Paul prodded, hoping his voice sounded calm.

"Yes, very much. I recognized you today from copies of a photograph Lesley used to keep here and there," Guido said, pushing his hair off his forehead with a quick hand.

"Used to. Yes, I can believe that."

He hadn't intended to start like this, Guido thought, to make the man uncomfortable. "I really didn't mean that like it sounded, Signor Kendal."

"Please call me Paul, Guido."

He offered Paul a cheroot, which he took, and Guido lit both of them with his silver lighter. He'd bought it at Tiffany's yesterday along with a bracelet for Stella and earrings for Lesley. Crazy how he instinctively liked this tall, tense American when the part of him that still honored his uncle's memory wanted not to. He understood now how wrongly possessive the count had been of Lesley because of losing his mother's love that way. Finally, he'd grown up enough to accept that. He ached for Lesley to be happy now, as happy as he and Stella were, because if anyone ever deserved that, it was Lesley. She'd been through so much, including the accidental murder of that bastard, son-of-a-bitch Nazi who deserved to die!

She'd been so stoic after that awful night, but so depressed. Then she'd thrown herself into her work with a vengeance, created the finished coats they showed here today. They would have to be shipped to Boston and then Chicago until the coats from the pelts she and Madame bought in Leningrad were completed and shipped over. It was a tremendous financial risk to seize the American market before any other European fur house could recover enough to get a hold here, but he trusted Lesley's judgment implicitly. The Americans were going wild for her designs, with orders pouring in already, although all the buyers could actually take away until autumn were the hats and gloves and smaller pieces Valente's had been surviving on at home.

"So, why did you want to meet me then, Guido?" prompted Lesley's American, so rugged-looking despite his elegant pin-striped suit, when he hesitated on how to proceed.

"I just thought I would pass on the word about Lesley's family estate in England—I believe she said you'd been there, knew her grandmother even," Guido said, wishing he had the nerve to just blurt out the truth about how he wished Lesley and Paul could bury their problems and reunite.

"I get *The Times of London* here and haven't seen a ruling on the legal battle for the estate," Paul said, his voice even more wary. "But how is the indomitable Lady Sarah?"

"Weaker all the time, yet she insists on giving commands from her wheelchair about how she wants the gardens planted, I take it. Anyway, just before I left Rome, Lesley found out that she may not be able to keep the estate after all, even if she wins everything from Constance in the lawsuit. Or if Lesley only inherits the money part of her father's estate, she still can't afford to buy Westam from Lady Malvern. But it's the house and grounds Lesley wants, not the money."

"The court's not going to rule against her!" Paul exploded.

Guido shrugged, folded his arms across his chest. "We still don't know. Times are dreadful in London, worse than during the war financially, so Lady Malvern's demanded Lesley make an offer on her half of the estate to buy her out. But we've got so much tied up in these new American ventures, besides recovering at home, that Lesley can't buy Lady Malvern out and the place is up for sale. My hope is that may force the court to rule more quickly. Still," he said, studying the American's eyes as they narrowed in thought, "it's breaking Lesley's heart to put it on the market."

Guido continued to study Paul Kendal as they went on to discuss the latest political unrest and the inflation in Rome,

Libero's status as a legitimate newspaper under Fracci-Valente financing, Churchill's defeat at the polls in London. He listened to Paul describe in the most clear and evocative terms the beauty of Lesley's childhood home, as though he cherished it, too. Guido was certain of what he wanted to know now. The man loved her still, though he was hurt and angry she had gone back on her word to visit him. But neither he nor Stella, he recalled bitterly, could get her to budge from her decision on that, almost as if she were afraid of more than merely trusting someone who had evidently hurt her years ago.

Unfortunately, he'd convinced Lesley that if she let him take care of everything concerning Max's death, he would tell no one what he had seen that night in her bedroom: the dead man covered with blood from a single shot to his chest; Lesley in a state of shock that had sent her to bed for days. She'd insisted on moving to her old bedroom where she'd first stayed at the town house, refusing to sleep in her and Cesare's old room. That night Guido had wrapped the dead Nazi in a rug, taken him out the old Appian Way and buried him among the ancient tombs there. One more body recovered by archaeologists in an archaic cemetery one day far in the future when a brutal modern war would mean nothing. He longed to tell Paul all about it but it had been his idea to keep everything secret when Lesley had told him she was going to go to the authorities about Max's death. Maybe, in a way, he bore part of the fault for Lesley and Paul being doomed to be apart like this when they obviously loved each other.

"I didn't mean to go on about Westam like that; it's the writer in me, I guess," Paul remarked at last and looked away. "I've always had a soft spot in my heart for that part of England. Tell her I hope she can hold on to it." Paul realized it had helped him to talk about Westam; it was something she loved. And, obviously, she did not love him. Guido looked very distracted, aggrieved all of a sudden. "Is there something else?" he asked him.

"I wanted to meet you, thank you in person for saving Lesley from the vigilante crowd looking for collaborators in Rome," Guido told Paul and expelled a rush of smoke.

"No thanks needed," Paul assured him and edged toward the door with Guido right beside him. He noticed the man limped as he turned back to shake his hand. "I met your uncle once briefly and admired him, Guido."

The dark, sad eyes met his again. "I thank you for those words. It took me a long time to realize it, but I admired him greatly, too. He was a most difficult man sometimes, but we all make mistakes and need to be humble enough to admit it, yes?"

"Yes." The words poured from him now as if to keep from asking Guido a hundred other questions he was afraid to know the answers to. "I really have to go. Look, Guido, I'm not sure why I wanted to stop by. Mostly to wish good luck to an—an old friend on a new endeavor. Please convey to Lesley that I wish her the best of everything. Tell her I'm glad she'll have her career and her family over the years ahead."

Guido frowned, put his hand on his arm to stay him. "The war changed us all, my friend. I know it did me, took the harsh edges off, made me understand and appreciate people better, especially Lesley. Listen, she's going home to England soon, to Westam to settle things, and that's a good deal closer to you than Rome if you're still busy here with family matters—"

His voice sharpened, grew slightly desperate, Paul thought.

"*Madre Maria*, of course you'll be busy with your career and your family too over the years, but will it be enough?" Guido Valente demanded, his eyes glossy with emotion.

Paul felt tears prickle behind his eyes, and gently disengaged his arm from Guido's hand. In answer at first he only shrugged and looked away. He was done with these wrenching feelings. He was stupid to come here today to hear all this. Lesley was fine, loved her Valente empire and family, took risks as she always had, but she'd survived in style, and that was that. He had to forget her and build a life for himself.

"I've really got to go, Guido," he repeated, afraid he'd blurt out something he'd regret. "I'm glad to meet you. As I said, I wish Countess Valente all the best."

He strode through the buzzing, crowded Valente salon and out onto Fifth Avenue, purposefully, quickly. And, damn it, he was going out of Countess Valente's life for good that same way.

* * *

"You can tell, I'm afraid, I didn't put each plant in the soil myself, but they're quite lovely considering the sort of help for hire from town these days," Lady Sarah's voice rose lilting and strong as Lesley wheeled her chair down the gravel paths. All around them, the rainbow riot of early pink and white roses edged by royal-blue lobelia and snowy alyssum in the gardens surrounded Westam House.

"They're beautiful and wonderful, Gram, just like you," Lesley told her, and stopped the chair to come around to smile down at her.

"Rubbish, my dearest, but then flattery will get you a lovely cream tea in an hour or so and some frightfully yummy Frears Almond Biscuits." Lady Sarah smiled smugly up at her beloved granddaughter with a pert tilt of sleek coiffed head before she shook her head and frowned at her next thought. "Imagine that woman daring to come back here to stay after all this time, as if she'd never left, and actually try to throw out my favorite biscuits just as she used to and substitute her wretched French macaroons and bonbons! I'm the one who stood guard at Westam these war years up in that chauffeur's flat, not her!" The old voice cracked in fury. "Oh, how I wish we could buy the place from the wretch and have the pleasure of tossing her off the grounds for good!"

Lesley didn't answer or she knew she would cry. Except for one thing in life, she wanted most to be able to save Westam from having to be sold, especially when Gram was alive to see it go. But she'd sworn years ago to Cesare—and owed it to Guido and Stella—not to sell off any of the Valente art or properties to pay her own family debts, and she could hardly take back the money she'd invested in Carla Fracci's newspaper. She'd already committed millions of lire to opening the three American branches of Valente's when her solicitors told her Constance, First Lady Malvern, insisted on selling any claim to the estate.

It was almost as if Constance had known it would be the last way to hurt her. Economic times were so ruinous in England after the war that Lesley was forced to agree to sell. The Labour government, which had displaced Churchill, had imposed new, higher taxes. Everything was being nationalized, and the punitive death taxes for Father and Trent had been devastating. Back in Rome, inflation and political instability were rampant. The most she could ever hope to salvage of her beloved heritage at Westam was perhaps some land down along the river Wye where she could build a holiday cottage for herself and the twins someday.

"Lesley," Gram said, interrupting her silent agonizing. "I certainly didn't mean to blame you. I've never been prouder of you, my dearest." Lesley knelt on the grass by the sundial and embraced the old woman, who felt as delicate now in her arms as blown glass. "I have always known how loyal you are to people and places you love, Lesley," the voice went on, undaunted. "That's always been your long suit, that and your strength. Your receiving the George Cross from the king proved that to everyone at last, but I'd always known it to be true."

The scene in the throne room of Buckingham Palace last week darted through Lesley's mind again. The nation's greatest civilian honor, the George Cross, dangling from its royal-blue ribbon around her neck with its silver Saint George and the Dragon . . . The king's ringing words about her passing on German information to the Italian underground and the Allied forces in Italy regarding the easiest access to Rome, and where to find the artwork the Germans had looted . . . The phrase, "For acts of the greatest heroism and the most conspicuous courage in circumstances of extreme danger." Later, the applause of the crowd on the lawn; Churchill's handshake and hug in that cloud of cigar smoke. Then the articles in the London journals extolling her war adventures, as they called them, praising her courage—and not a mention of the old Scandal's Child shame. At last, she'd given interviews with no rancor or dismay, no regret or anger. At last, in the land of her childhood she was as welcome and honored as she was in Italy, where she and Carla together had been awarded the Order of Merit of the Italian Republic, though her speech that day had made clear she accepted that honor in her brave deceased husband's name.

"Sometimes I don't feel either loyal or strong, Gram," she managed at last and stood to wipe her tears.

"You've been going it alone too long. And you've let that woman's presence do you in. Reminds you of when she crashed in here when your father died and took over your mother's rooms, doesn't it? I tell you, Lesley," Lady Sarah declared, jabbing one crooked finger to emphasize each word, "she hasn't won yet!"

"It's hard to believe anymore she'll get her comeuppance someday," Lesley admitted and sighed. It was tearing her apart to have Westam on the market, but it was really her love for Paul wearing her down, not her dislike of Constance. She had to go to him, tell him the truth about the twins. Whatever became of them, she owed him that, owed it to the twins to at least know their father was the kind, brave man they'd taken to so well those days on Capri. And so, as soon as she knew the estate was sold to someone she had met—she drove Westam's London real estate managers batty insisting she meet each potential buyer as if it were an interview—she intended to go to New York to tell him.

Lesley saw Melly Mott across the tops of nodding pink hollyhocks and waved to him, grateful for a diversion. "Melly! The buyer's not here yet?" she called.

He loped toward them with that gangly, awkward stride. "Haven't seen hide nor hair of him. Is he late, then?" he asked.

"Not yet."

He rested his big hands on the handles of Gram's wheelchair, where Lesley had seen him so often since she'd been back. "All the blokes with enough bob for this place seem to be foreigners, but then who else could buy Westam in these blimey times if the Westams can't keep it, eh?" Melly said. He squinted down at Lady Sarah's sharp, upturned look. "Mum sent me to fetch Lady Sarah in for her rest before tea, she did."

"Rubbish!" Lady Sarah snapped with a bang of fist on the padded arm of her chair. "I've told Samantha once if I've told her a hundred times, I can quite do away with my little lie-downs while Lesley's home. I'd like to get a look at this latest buyer, too."

"Then you can peek at him from your window while I show him about the grounds, Gram," Lesley cajoled. "I just hope Constance doesn't materialize and hang on trying to argue prices up again. It quite scares them off."

Melly began to wheel the disgruntled Lady Sarah away. "Where's this one from this time, Countess Lesley?" he turned back to ask, his long face serious. He knew she'd promised she would never sell to anyone who wouldn't keep the Motts on the estate in their current capacities; no one in Herefordshire liked change.

"Another American," Lesley told him with a tilt of chin.

He nodded matter-of-factly and started off again, but not before Lady Sarah called back over her shoulder, "Just be sure we don't sell to a flaming Frenchman! Never trusted a one of them, not since that other war that took my boy, your uncle Andrew—"

"No, no Frenchmen, Gram. Don't worry and get some rest now." She would have to honor that wish of Gram's, that and the other requirement besides the Motts staying on. Gram had cancer and was dying, though her doctors had not been supposed to tell Lesley, and Gram didn't realize she knew. Any potential buyer had to agree that Lady Sarah Westam could be buried on the grounds in the gardens surrounded by the yew hedge out past the gallops. No cold marble mausoleum for Lady Sarah. Lesley turned away from the house and quickened her pace. It made her feel so desperate as well as sad. She could not bear the idea of losing the old woman after everything else. She wanted Lady Sarah and the twins to know each other before it was too late for them all.

Too late—almost—the story of her life, she thought grimly, as her steps slowed on the gravel lane that led toward the main road. The wealth, the honors, the admiration others heaped on her—even the fulfillment of her dream to design furs and own a furrier empire—all paled in comparison to what she'd lost. At times she thought the twins would be everything to fill her heart over the years, but as they turned six this month, she knew it was not true. Even Carla Fracci, as much as she had changed, had married her Scotsman last month. It both warmed and pained Lesley to see Stella and Guido so very much in love.

She arched her back against a tall, venerable lime tree near the road into Fownhope and sighed. Its solid strength felt comforting against her. Through it all, this line of trees, these arches of yew hedge beyond had been here guarding Westam, growing but basically unchanged, and it would be so when the Westams were long gone. If only she had it to do all over again: try harder to be friends with Trent; even, God forgive her, to get along better with the vicious Constance. If she could just meet Paul over again under better circumstances, better times, and unravel all the pain and agony there'd been between them.

She realized she might be soiling her pale yellow silk dress and straightened to brush off her shoulder. The slight breeze tugged at her straw hat and tickled its ribbon against her face. Her eyes lifted to the road as she saw a large auto the very color of her dress, her ribbon, the hundreds of Gram's daffodils that had always blanketed Westam's lawns in early spring.

Her heart pounded to drown out bird song and the rest of the world. The auto turned into the lane. She took two steps and froze. The driver in the big car—the Buick. Yes. Yes! Her hat flew off as she began to run.

The auto jerked to a stop as she did. Its big wheels skidded on the gravel. Paul. Paul! He got out. Always taller than she remembered, his face so serious. She fought back tears and the urge to hurl herself into his arms. They stopped five feet apart.

"Welcome to Westam, Paul. What a lovely surprise," she managed and brushed back blowing hair from her eyes.

He jammed both hands in the pockets of his tweed jacket. "I'm glad to hear that." He cleared his throat and squinted into a shaft of sun through the trees. "I thought if you knew it was me, I might be told not to come."

"If what was you? You mean," she gasped, "you've come to buy it?"

"It depends on whether the price is right. I guess I'm a little early for the appointment," he went on and pulled one hand from his pocket to sweep the area. "Or do you always hang around on the rural lanes of England just waiting to be collected for a ride?" he suddenly challenged and a little smile softened his rugged face.

Her heart soared at the brash way his eyes went over her. "Yes, that's it. I'm mad keen for fancy American autos. To be 'picked up,' as you Yanks put it." She clasped her trembling hands before her and lifted her chin as he came two steps closer.

"I'm serious about buying Westam, Lesley. But the asking price your real estate managers quoted me in London is about twice what I can get my hands on right now. I thought maybe, if we could come to terms, you'd have enough for the other half and we could own it together."

Her mouth dropped open. Was he teasing or crazy or did he mean something more wonderful? She tried to reason it out even as he took the last step and pulled her hard into his arms. She clung to him, her arms tight around his neck, her feet off the ground, as he swung her around under the trees and then stopped to kiss her. How simple this was, how perfect. And yet there were still things to ruin everything, and she couldn't think when he touched her like this!

They stood a tiny distance apart at last, breathing hard, eyes locked, his hands still on her waist. "I've come farther than just New York to tell you I've always loved you, Lesley. I've been to hell and back, and I think you have, too."

"Yes. But this is heaven. I love you too and—"

"Then marry me."

"Yes. Oh, yes, Paul, I want to—I was coming to see you to tell you that and—"

He exploded with a whoop and spun her again, then lifted her to carry her to the Buick. The motor hummed steadily. It still smelled so rich inside. The Buick had come through the war unchanged, although nothing else had. He was in beside her instantly. "We've got to tell Lady Sarah," he was babbling, "got to get the Motts and have a party. We'll call Guido in Rome. I have to thank him for what he said in New York. I know somehow we can swing bailing you out here together until that damned court ruling comes through, then send for the twins and our families as soon as we pick a date so we can be married here."

Her hand stopped his as he reached to engage the clutch. "Paul, I have to tell you something first before we tell anyone else. This is all so wonderful, so fast. I have to tell you something."

His thick brows crashed down to obscure his eyes. The tiny scar that remained from the *Athenia* disaster whitened against his brown forehead, but she went right on. "Paul, I lied to you about something, but I didn't know what else to do. I was so devastated the day of my wedding when you suddenly sent that cable saying that you wanted no part of me."

His hands grasped her upper arms and slid her to him on the seat. "I was willing to bury all that, but you want to talk about it, fine," he said, his voice cracking. "How about the first cable I sent, which you answered by telling me you were planning to marry Cesare Valente while I lay there in that Canadian hospital? I'm telling you, it was easier to recover from being torpedoed, in a coma, and nearly bleeding to death than it was from that!"

She shook her head in fierce denial. "Paul, I swear to you, I saw no other cable, nor did I send one."

His angry face went very still while she held her breath. Cesare, protective, jealous Cesare, she thought, and felt as if a fist had punched her in her midriff. Then, as quickly, part of her great burden lifted. Paul had not deserted her, and that deceit had been Cesare's true legacy to her. But no, he'd been the sort of man he was for reasons beyond his control, just as things had kept her and Paul apart all these years. And it was never going to happen again.

"Cesare," she whispered.

He nodded. "I don't doubt it. He went berserk that day in the *Libero* office, accused me of being in Rome only to see you. God forgive me, whatever other reasons I thought I'd come for, maybe that was the truth. But that's past for us now, Lesley. Let's bury it and the fact"—his voice came at her edged with bitterness again—"you went to a fur auction in February instead of coming to New York to me."

She told him then about Max's return the night she was packing, the gun, her agony. Paul held her to him while the motor ran and she talked and talked and the spring day went blithely on around them and another burden lifted from her shoulders. And then, when he had reassured her and put his hands to the wheel and clutch again, she said, "There's one more thing, the most important."

He turned back to her, his eyes the greenest green, just like Cati and Paolo's eyes. "Paul, I never would have married Cesare when I thought at first you were dead, even when I believed you had deserted me for someone else, if I hadn't found out I was pregnant."

His eyes glittered with an unreadable emotion. "And not

from sleeping with Cesare Valente the first month you were in Rome?" he asked, his voice shaky.

She shook her head. "Not from Cesare at all. I never slept with him until the night of our wedding. Cati and Paolo are yours. I was terrified of scandal, you know that," she rushed on, "afraid my child would have to go through the shame I did for a parent's mistakes, and when I thought you were dead and Cesare offered—"

He put his fingers gently over her lips, and they looked deep into each other's eyes. Then he nodded. She kissed his fingers. He didn't look a bit surprised, only very serious. "Our love was never a mistake, Lesley. And as for the twins being mine, I had suspected and hoped and finally just despaired it could ever be true. On Capri, I almost willed it to be true. I couldn't bear it when you had to say good-bye to them that day, because I couldn't bear deep down to say good-bye to any of what could have been. Let's send for them and tell them together. It's more than I could have ever dreamed. Forgive me for not marrying you the moment I knew I loved you, for leaving you in Venice and going back home. Those were the mistakes, ones we've both paid dearly for!"

They clung together again. When she next looked into his passionate face, he was smiling, but tears were running down his cheeks clear into the cleft on his chin. The cleft Cati had so clearly inherited that would have told anyone they had to be Paul Kendal's green-eyed twins.

They told Melly and Samantha Mott first because they were setting up for tea in the sunroom, and they could not contain their joy. Melly loped down to the cellar for champagne while Samantha scurried into the drawing room, which had been converted to Lady Sarah's bedroom, to wake her. In each other's arms on the couch, whispering plans already, they did not see Constance come in to glare at them in blatant hatred.

"*Sordid Sex in the Afternoon* or *Hollow Happiness Amid the Ruins,* we'll call your next novel, Mr. Kendal," she said, her acidic accusations interrupting them.

They looked up, but pulled apart slowly, still holding hands. "What a great honor to have you remember me after all these years, Lady Malvern," Paul said, his tone mocking.

"Who else would still be tagging about the countryside after the illustrious Italian Countess Lesley," she said with a grand sweep of her hand that floated her long butterfly sleeve of French printed satin and cigarette smoke after her. A satin hostess gown and ruby necklace and drop earrings in the middle of the afternoon for tea, Lesley thought and glared at Constance while the woman inhaled deeply through her diamond-studded cigarette holder and blew out a perfect blue smoke ring.

"Besides," Constance went on, her voice knifelike, "I keep abreast of what parties are interested in buying my estate and just called the realty office in London. I told them 'the mystery buyer' had already arrived and I just wanted to check his credit rating, so your covert little plot was easily discovered," she crowed and laughed throatily. "My, my, my, just like the little secret shenanigans during the big, bad war again. But then it's always been rather evident to me what you were sniffing around here for. By the way"—she cut off Paul's protest with a flourish as she draped herself across the arm and back of a chair across the tea table—"your credit rating and reputation are quite healthy, I might add." One clawlike hand fingered the ruby necklace against her throat as if it were some evil talisman and her sardonic smile crushed to a frown. "But if you seriously intend to buy Westam, I withdraw my offer to sell until someone with better judgment comes along."

"I hope I'm allowed to engrave all this sweetness and light on my memory, Lady Malvern," Paul clipped out and started to rise before Lesley put a restraining hand on his arm. "Inspiration for depraved villainesses in my books are at times a little hard to come by."

Lady Constance sat forward now, jabbing the air with her cigarette holder. "Just let me make myself clearer then. Never is my son's birthright and my rightful estate going to any friend—and dare I say, long-time stud, just like the stallions about this wretched place—of an infamous Italian countess. One countess ruining my and my son's lives was quite enough over the years!" she shrieked.

"Can't you ever let go of your hatred?" Lesley cut in before Paul could try to battle this woman on her own terms again. She jumped to her feet and stalked around the table to tower over Constance. "My father's dead, Trent's dead. The war's changed the country unalterably but nothing changes you. You just plan to charge merrily ahead as greedy as ever, as unkind to my grandmother as possible, doing anything to hurt me. Blast it, you can't anymore. Paul and I are going to be married, and we'll find some way to own Westam together—"

The woman's face went livid. She leapt to her feet to shake a fist at Lesley as raw contempt spewed from her crimson mouth: "You'll never stop me! What will you do, sue me on top of the lawsuit we've had between us for years? That's what's kept my money and this house from me! You think I'll keep this boring barn of horrible memories when it's finally mine?" she shrilled and swept her arm in a dramatic arc as if to encompass all Westam. "I'll sell it to the highest bidder as long as it's not you or your American gigolo here! I'll drag you again through the press, tell them the truth of your sexual favors to bidders here, tell them how you tried all those years to turn Trent against me. You poisoned him, you and your grandmother who al—"

"Constance!" a clear voice behind them commanded. Paul, who had risen to put himself between the two women, turned toward the door. Lesley jerked around. Constance stopped in mid-word. Lady Sarah in her wheelchair had shouted the name that still hovered in the moment's silence. "Constance, I insist you shut your trap and pack your bags and get out of here for good," Lady Sarah announced with a triumphant smile. "You're a sick, deranged, spiteful woman and we're all dreadfully full up of you. Besides," she went on with a wag of her head, "Lesley's barrister from London just rang up with the news. Lesley's won the Westam court case, and it's all over the London papers, something like 'War Heroine Wins Another Battle.' You've lost, Constance!" Lady Sarah shouted as Lesley and Paul cheered and threw themselves in each other's arms. "It turns out you have won a small monetary settlement through Trent's will, but not enough to keep or run this house and estate. The mansion, land, and funds to run it all have gone to the living heir and that's Lesley. And I want you out of my granddaughter's house immediately," the old woman yelled over the noise, "because she would probably be too kind and loving to throw you out herself! Out!"

For once, Constance gaped speechless. They didn't even notice when she fled the room because they all talked at once and hugged and toasted one other with the champagne Melly Mott suddenly appeared with while Lesley's barrister rang back and could barely make himself heard in the din. Soon word spread to neighbors and even the local newspapers from Hereford. Lady Sarah invited everyone in to share in the celebration, which turned out also to be the announcement of Lady Lesley Westam, Countess Valente's engagement to be married to the famous American novelist Paul Kendal. What a story! the rural journalists congratulated themselves as they scribbled it all down dizzily between swallows of the cool bubbly.

Then, just before the sun set, when the Fleet Street reporters were rolling in from London, Lesley and Paul posed for photos in Lady Sarah's vibrant gardens with the spring sun and their future bright and warm in their smiling faces.

✿ ✿ *Afterword*

LESLEY HERSELF went to the door of the house on Capri when the bell rang. The servants were preparing the noon meal while Paul had taken the twins, Vanessa, Charles, and Guido's eldest two for a hike up on the grassy terraces above Villa Valente. She'd been expecting a man from the States to interview Paul on his being chosen *American Publisher* magazine's "Author of the Year" for 1956. Again the date struck her: how quickly these ten years as Mrs. Paul Kendal had flown by. Two children in addition to the twins and another on the way, although she'd be forty when it was born and had never meant to have a fifth. Still, how exciting it was. How happy she and Paul had both been when they heard. It did boggle the mind to look back sometimes. Yet, when things were quiet and she closed her eyes or was alone with Paul, the garden wedding at Westam seemed only yesterday.

She opened the heavy door and smiled at the man standing there. "Hello. Mr. March, isn't it? I'm Lesley Kendal," she said and shook his hand. "Won't you come in? My husband's out with some children in tow like the proverbial Pied Piper, but he'll be back soon. He's expecting you."

The man was nice-looking, she noted, as he followed her in. He seemed somehow shy for a writer, but then she knew better than to judge everyone by Paul and select journalists she'd known. Mr. March seemed quite serious even when he smiled, but his blue eyes twinkled pleasantly. He was dressed almost as if he were off for a round of golf. Then too, perhaps the distinguished silver hair around the temples made him seem more scholarly than he really was.

"Alex March, Mrs. Kendal. Please call me Alex. My, what a stunning home," he told her as his eyes swept the spacious

413

inner reaches of the living room, which spilled into other rooms and merged into the sunstruck patio. "And such a view. I must admit I usually get sent to do interviews in Brooklyn or Connecticut, but for author of the year, this lovely Italian sky and sea's the limit."

So he did have a writer's cleverness. She smiled at him again. "I'm glad you like Capri. We've always loved it here and have a sort of extended family reunion each April while the children are on spring recess from school in England—which reminds me, you'll have to mind your step through here. Seven children about with toys and games, you know," she warned with a helpless shrug and little laugh that enchanted him.

"Seven!" he breathed as he pulled his notes from his folder and narrowly missed stepping on a cricket bat next to a baseball glove Lesley bent over to retrieve.

"Not all ours, I assure you. We have sixteen-year-old twins and a daughter Vanessa who's eight, and a son Charles five and I'm obviously growing another, as they say. The other three belong to my nephew who lives in Rome and is here with his wife this week. I do hope you have a brood at home too, so the noise today won't do you in. Really," she assured him with a nod, "they're very good children but they live it up, as you Americans say, when they get to Capri together every spring."

"I understand, really. No, I have no children. I'm a widower of several years."

Her ears pricked up at that. Paul's sister, Kaye, was here with Paul's mother this week, and Kaye was still quite unattached, as if wedded to her antique-furniture empire. This visit from a man who was about her age, unmarried, and lived in New York as she did might just be good for more than honoring Paul's writing.

They sat on the patio on metal cushioned chairs in the shade of a striped canvas umbrella while the bustle of laying the meal and Stella and Guido's splashing in the pool with their youngest, Rissa, went on around them. Lesley poured Alex March a glass of cool Frascati while Carlo's old dog, Caprice, came over to curl up under her feet as she did whenever Lesley alighted long enough.

"You wouldn't mind a few questions before your husband comes back?" he asked her. "It's a real coup to be able to speak to the wife, famous in her own right, to get a different slant on things."

"If I can help," she told him, but her eyes skimmed the grounds for Kaye. She simply had to introduce Alex March to Kaye before the meal so neither would balk if she just suddenly seated them together.

"I must have my facts wrong, I'm afraid," he was saying. "You mentioned your twins were sixteen, but I had from my notes you and Paul Kendal were married in England ten years ago."

She looked straight at him. How a question like that from a writer with pencil poised would once have sent her into a spin, made her feel everything was closing in. But no longer. "Both those facts are correct," she told him. "You see, Paul and I were separated for a long time by the war."

She watched him while he crossed out two lines in his notes, then looked up at her in the shade of their umbrella. "I don't intend to confuse the readers with a bunch of dates anyway. I know, Mrs. Kendal, you were a war heroine."

She looked away now, out over the row of cypress and terraced olive trees and then beyond to where sky met sea, as distant, yet as distinct as her memories of those times and the loved ones who were gone. "I believe that any woman who survived those terrible war years was a heroine, Alex." She looked back into his eyes. She was surprised he seemed so spellbound. "As another writer said once, 'It was the best of times; it was the worst of times,' and mostly the worst, I'm afraid. But ever since Paul and I married, times have been the best."

He nodded silently. His blue eyes actually shimmered with unshed tears. Then, Paul and the children exploded from around the side of the house where the path led up to the cliffs toward the Belli farm and the ruins of Tiberius's villa. Lesley excused herself to hurry over to greet them. A kiss from Paul, quick words to the twins and Vanessa and Charles to go wash up for the meal while Stella herded her three into the house. When they were finally all assembled and she had managed to put Alex March between Paul and Kaye and whispered to Paul not to monopolize the man too much, grace was said and the meal began. She wondered more than once if Alex March didn't long for such an exuberant scene and someone to love despite all the noise and private family joking.

"I see your children definitely resemble one of you or the other," he observed at one point as if determined to remember why he'd come to Villa Valente. "Do any of you Kendal children want to pursue a career as a writer or furrier someday?"

Lesley and Paul exchanged knowing glances. Indeed, the man had no children if he thought youngsters this age had a definite notion of that. "Cati?" Paul prompted.

"I want to be either a lawyer, because everyone says I'm good at arguing," the irrepressible, lovely girl began with a toss of her sable ponytail, "or work at Aunt Kaye's in New York, or be a landscaper—"

"Cati's inherited her great-grandmother Westam's gardening talents," Lesley put in, "and even helps to oversee the grounds of our home in England."

"Or I might want to breed Persian cats or design furs or clothes or be a model," Cati finished.

Alex March, Lesley noted, got the point, but Paolo wasn't about to let his twin sister have center stage. "I'd like to play professional tennis or be a pilot," he announced and delved immediately back into his ice cream.

Vanessa sat shy and wide-eyed, but their youngest, Charles, was not about to be left out. Charles was the only one of the four with pure Westam looks, and Lesley cherished him for the memories of her father, and, yes, even Trent, he evoked. "Well, when I get older, I'm not going to be anything, especially not go to school anymore, just stay on Capri and hike and swim forever."

Guido's nine-year-old snickered with Vanessa, but it was the sixteen-year-old man of the world who piped up, "Come on, goofy. When you grow up you can't stay here forever, can't do anything forever. You'll have to get a job, travel like Dad and Mama sometimes, have a lot of adventures—maybe even find a girl and fall in love," he finished with a devilish roll of his green eyes, as if to disprove he was in the throes of his first crush at school and very self-conscious about it.

More teasing snickers. Lesley could tell Paul was going to reprimand Paolo, so she covered her hand with his. She knew sibling bitterness when she saw it and this was not. Charles remembered his manners to put down his spoon at least, then gestured boldly when he answered his older brother with that brash American tone he, more than any of the others, had absorbed from Paul. "Oh, yeah? Well, maybe I can't do what I want forever, but I'll do it almost forever, just wait and see!"

Everyone laughed, everyone smiled, and chattered on as if the boy had spoken the merest childish nonsense. Even Alex March leaned closer to Kaye to whisper something while she smiled and nodded. But Paul and Lesley joined hands under the table and, for one moment, looked only at each other, silent amid the familiar hubbub. For they had found together there was at last, at least, an almost forever.